THE
MATING SEASON

Werewolves of Montana Book 6

BONNIE VANAK

THE MATING SEASON

WEREWOLVES OF MONTANA

www.Bonnievanak.com

CHAPTER 1

None of her fantasies had ever made her feel this alive, nor this free.

A handsome man carried her in his strong arms, his sensual nature swirling about him like the most intoxicating aroma. He planned to remove her clothing, tumble her onto his soft, wide bed and ravish her. Her lover intended to keep her trapped in his bed, giving her such pleasure that she would cry out his name over and over as she clung to him and he made her his own.

And when he was finished, she would be carrying his child, for his true purpose was to impregnate her with his much-desired heir.

"You are mine, Nikita. I will never let you go. I will make love to you until you scream with pleasure and your belly grows big with my child," he whispered.

Nikita Blakemore opened her eyes on a dreamy sigh. And then she looked up to see her lover's smoldering gaze.

He had not whispered those words in her imagination. He had spoken them aloud and this was reality. She was his captive and could not escape.

Her trembling arms hooked around the neck of

Tristan, the powerful Silver Wizard, she closed her eyes again, wishing she were back inside her lonely basement apartment, with only girlish fantasies for company. Too weak and sick to escape his implacable grip, she could only hold on and plan a later escape.

Her captor barely spoke since spiriting her away from the only home she had ever known. He watched her, quiet, assessing, as if she were prey and he was a wolf about to devour her whole.

Nikita had feared him ever since he'd laid claim to her. He'd done so after her twin Nia won the heart and the hand of Aiden, the Mitchell pack alpha, back in Montana.

She was now the property of the wizard who had saved her from the parvolupus virus.

With his dark, silver-tipped hair and his burning black eyes, the wizard looked dangerous. Nikita hid her emotions. They would not serve her well. She'd been dying until Tristan had poured a magick potion down her throat. Then he'd spirited her away. And she had feared the immortal wizard virtually since birth.

All her twenty-five years of life, she'd been safeguarded and protected to keep Tristan from taking her.

And despite all the safeguards, the secrets and her twin's determination that no one should know of her existence, here she was, captured in his secure embrace.

Her head ached, her throat hurt and weakness gripped her limbs. She could not fight him. Not yet. First, she must regain her strength. How could she fight a wizard who could flick a finger and turn a werewolf into ash with a bolt of energy? An immortal wizard who was the guardian of shapeshifters and ruled over them?

They said he could kill with one look, and slay a woman with pleasure with another.

Deep inside, another fear tugged at her, a fear she did not understand. She could not trust this wizard or lose herself in his kisses and caresses because he had done something to her in the past.

Something terrible.

Tristan shifted her weight in his arms as they stood outside the entrance of the Sandy Dreams Grand Hotel on a Florida beach. All he had done was blink and they'd materialized here. The method of travel was efficient, but dizzying.

Moonlight dappled the wet pavement and stars glittered overhead like a fistful of diamonds against velvet. To pass the time while she was secluded in her apartment, she had surfed the internet and seen this hotel, fantasizing about staying here with a handsome lover who longed to become her mate.

And now here she was, with a handsome wizard carrying her as if it were their wedding day. It was a dream hotel, but the man holding her was her worst nightmare.

Tristan glanced down at her, his expression inscrutable. "We're spending the night here. You're too weak. You need rest."

An ancient prophecy foretold that Tristan would take her away and then she would die. Lately, she'd experienced dreams that warned her they'd had a past life together. But in her dreams, the wizard didn't kill her. He made love to her with such passion that it left her limbs weak and her sex pulsing when she awoke. And she wept, not from passion, but from grief because the lover in her dreams always died a painful death.

Prophecy or not, she was still ill. Tristan wasn't going to ravish her tonight. Or, it seemed, kill her. She didn't know which fate she feared more. He held her tightly, as if never wanting to release her.

Tristan nodded and a uniformed man opened the door for them. Niki blinked at the brilliance. The hotel's Renaissance décor had appealed to her as she'd surfed the internet. Vaulted ceilings with elegant, gold-leaf trim edged reliefs that she knew were painstakingly hand-carved by artisans. Figures from Greek and Roman mythology pranced through the murals. Niki spotted an impish Cupid aiming his bow downward, as if to shoot at incoming guests.

Cupid, stay your arrow. I have no need of love. I would appreciate a way to get out of this, so if you could loan me your wings and I can fly home, I'd be much obliged.

She tried to avoid looking at her captor.

But she could not avoid the stunned gaze of guests as Tristan carried her through the lobby, over the thick wool carpet with its intricate design, beneath the glow of elegant chandeliers designed to mimic 18th century lighting. He walked with her past the tastefully arranged groups of chairs and sofas, banked by polished wood tables adorned by sprays of white orchids. At last they arrived at the check-in desk. Lamps glowed softly upon the wood counter, giving the impression of an elegant living room in someone's grand private mansion.

The starched uniformed clerk behind the counter looked no less shocked at their appearance than the guests.

It must be the dress.

Gone were the jeans and shirt she'd worn at the ranch when the Silver Wizard abducted her. Instead, with a wave of his hand, Tristan had covered her in a violet and silver velvet gown, with flowing sleeves adorned with silver embroidery, her long blond hair caught up in a silver snood. Niki caught sight of herself in a nearby mirror: it wasn't an average, every-day outfit.

Loneliness gripped her. It was bad enough, being hidden away inside her basement apartment for more than two decades like a fungus, never venturing out unless she'd imitated Nia, her identical twin. And now, on her first appearance in society, she looked like an escapee from a medieval movie set.

The mirror rippled, like a pebble tossed into a still pond. Suddenly she no longer saw the glittering hotel, the lights, and Tristan holding her in his secure, unyielding grip.

She saw a blonde woman, dressed in a long amethyst gown with silver thread embroidered on the bodice and sleeves, standing in a room facing a table. No longer did her body bear the ugly dark streaks caused by the parvolupus virus.

A man in black, his long-legged stride filled with purpose, approached her from behind. The dark-haired man caught the woman in his arms and tore her gown off, leaving her nude. He bent the woman face-down upon the table, spread her long legs open. Nikita caught a glimpse of the female's wet, pink sex.

The man loosened his breeches. Nikita saw his thick, long phallus and her own sex pulsed.

Fisting a hand in her long hair, he drove into the woman with a harsh growl, and the woman shrieked, whether from pleasure or pain, Nikita could not tell.

Over and over he plunged into the woman as she moaned, then he licked her spine and growled. Seizing the woman's plump hips, he threw back his head and howled, jerking and convulsing as the woman screamed, this time the cry one of undeniable pleasure.

Nikita blinked and the mirror became an ordinary mirror once more. But the vision had been so incongruous with the elegant opulence of the hotel that a deep flush ignited her body. She felt wanton and shamed, as if the Skins, the word Others used to describe humans, had caught her viewing a porno flick.

Sensual excitement twined with fear and dread. The man in the mirror had been fierce, nearly driven to a mating fever, the blood frenzy of Lupine males denied the touch of their mates for too long. More brutal than a mating rite, the fever was all consuming, and could last for days until both lay panting with exhaustion, and the female carried his young in her belly.

She shivered, the sensual excitement fading. Was she destined to become nothing more than a brood mare to suit the wizard's purpose?

The Silver Wizard glanced down at her, his full mouth curved in a knowing smile. She looked away. Was this a vision of the future? What did Tristan plan to do with her?

The night clerk looked over Tristan's black velvet tunic, his leather pants and doeskin boots. "May I help you?"

"I need to book your penthouse oceanfront suite for two nights. We just got married."

The clerk relaxed a little. "Oh, so that's why you're dressed that way."

"It was a Medieval wedding." Tristan gave the

woman an intense smile, and she melted like hot wax.

"I'm a history buff. I adore the Dark Ages!" the clerk gushed.

"They were quite dark," he murmured.

The clerk looked at Nikita, who felt another flush rise to her cheeks. "And this is the fair maiden you rescued, Sir Knight?"

"My wife." He winked at the desk clerk. "I promised to carry her over the threshold, but our home is some distance from here."

Some distance. Try a million light years. Tristan, the Silver Wizard, lived in Tir Na-nog, the afterworld. Niki wanted to laugh, but her stomach hurt too badly.

The young clerk blushed, obviously smitten. Fingers poised on the keyboard, she clicked and clacked over the keys, then nodded. "You are in luck, sir. We have the penthouse available. A beautiful view of the Atlantic, wet bar, king-sized bed…"

As she prattled off details, Niki closed her eyes. Her stomach tightened again. *Goddess, I hope you have a bathroom because I feel sick all over again.*

"I need a major credit card, Mr…?"

"Tristan," the rogue said. "Mr. Tristan Kearney. With a 'K.' And this is my wife, Nikita."

Tristan reached into his pocket and pulled out a black card, handing it over to the clerk.

As the clerk ran the card, the wizard looked down at her. "That is my true name."

Niki looked away. She did not care.

He must be quite strong to hold her weight with only one arm. Most female Lupines were big and had plenty of curves, and she was no exception. She looked down and saw his arms relaxed at his side.

Oh dear goddess. He wasn't holding her. She was floating in mid-air. The desk clerk was totally clueless. Nikita closed her eyes and tried to control her increasing nausea.

"You are all set, sir. May I get a bellhop for your luggage?"

Nikita opened her eyes.

"Not necessary. It will be arriving later. Please do not disturb us. We plan to be busy." Tristan looked down at her again, his expression inscrutable, though she felt the incandescence of his brute sensuality heat her body like a fire. "Quite busy. Thank you and good night."

She watched Tristan pocket the card, and then his arms slid around her once more—muscled, strong as steel and equally unrelenting. Through the heavy velvet she could feel the warmth of his skin.

"And you, Mrs. Kearney. Best wishes. Is there anything you require?"

Niki looked at the woman, who appeared to be about her age. She wanted to say "a one-way ticket home," but courage failed her. She remained silent.

Seeing more strangers stare in their direction, Niki closed her eyes again as Tristan strode with her toward the elevator.

When they reached the room, he carried her inside and snapped on the lights. Niki opened her eyes. Her dreams paled in comparison to the reality. Gold and white silk paper lined the walls. An elegant white and gold sofa with matching armchairs, whitewashed furniture and an elegant marble coffee table overlooked a wall of sliding glass doors. These opened to a long balcony overlooking the ocean. There was an eight-seat dining table with cushioned chairs, a sideboard holding a spray of fresh lilies and a small chandelier made from seashells.

A small kitchenette opened to the living space, and next to it was a mirrored wall. She caught her reflection and shivered. No vision now, this was the ugly reality. The black streaks still marked her neck and her face looked pale and smudged with purple shadows.

Tristan gazed down at her. "I created an illusion for all the Skins that you do not look ill. The marks will fade when you rest. You will return to normal, I promise."

She didn't know what normal was anymore.

Tristan walked across the carpet into an adjoining bedroom with more elegant white furniture and a lounge chair by the sliding glass doors opening to the balcony. Waving a hand, he turned the covers down. Blue and white decorative pillows floated from the bed to pile neatly upon the lounge chair. He set her gently upon the king-sized bed. She curled into a ball, too miserable to appreciate the soft mattress beneath her, the fine Egyptian cotton sheets.

Tristan pressed his mouth to his forefinger, a whisper of a kiss, then reached out to touch her. Niki jerked away.

He sighed as he shook his head. "I see it will take you some time for you to become accustomed to my touch. I've waited more than eight centuries to have you in my arms again, my sweet. I am patient."

Can you wait another full century?

Her stomach pitched and rolled as if she lay upon the deck of a ship in the midst of a churning ocean. Niki bit her lip.

Tristan waved a hand and suddenly she was clad in flannel pajamas with little hearts and flowers, her long hair done in her favorite French braid.

Niki looked down in stunned amazement. No silk nightgown or worse, bare skin.

"The pajamas are your favorites. I thought you'd like something familiar."

It was sweet, but she was far too miserable to appreciate the gesture. Her bones ached and her stomach felt full of ground glass. Then he went into the bathroom and returned, carrying a gold waste bucket. Tristan set it on the floor next to the bed.

He sat on the bed. Niki turned, staring at the moon that glinted on the ocean through the partly-drawn drapes. It was lovely. Soothing, much more so than the intimidating man whose thigh was intimately pressed against hers.

He reached for her, but she shrank back, fearing the prophecy. A flicker of vulnerability crossed his expression. Tristan sighed. He waved a hand and the drapes opened to display the stunning vista. She glanced at him.

"I'm afraid you will not enjoy the view, no matter where you are. You are in for a rough night, my sweet. The potion I gave you has saved you, but it's changing your cell structure. Your body is changing and the process can be…"

Nausea churned in her stomach and her throat tightened. She reached over the bed and retched into the gold bucket he held out.

"Brutal," he finished. He stroked her hair as she continued vomiting. "I'm sorry, Nikita. I never intended to make you sick on our first date."

She raised her head, taking the wet, warm washcloth he offered. Niki wiped her mouth.

She had not spoken much to him since bidding good-bye to her twin back at the ranch before Tristan whisked her away.

"Usually women don't get sick of you until the second date?" she croaked.

His dark gaze twinkled. And then she flung herself over the bed and vomited again.

He sighed. "It's going to be a long night."

Eventually, she slept, a deep dreamless sleep. When she awoke, the sky outside was leaden, the sun peeking over the horizon of the ocean. Hugging her pillow, Niki rolled over. The most delicious smells pierced her senses. Sharp, pungent cedar, the salty tang of the ocean, and the sweetness of orange peels.

"I can vary my scent according to my mood. Or yours, and what pleases you the most, my sweet," a deep voice murmured.

Clad in the same black tunic, black leather pants and soft doeskin boots, Tristan sat in the chair by the sliding glass door, looking at the view. The slider was open, allowing in a gentle ocean breeze that lifted the edges of his silver-tipped hair.

He glanced at her and his gaze softened. "Good morning, Nikita. How do you feel?"

"A little better." She reached for the water glass he had refilled and drank. "I slept through the night."

"You slept for a full day. You needed the rest after your ordeal."

An entire day! No wonder she felt like Sleeping Beauty. Daring to sneak a peek in the dresser mirror, she was relieved to see her complexion back to its normal color, and the horrid black streaks gone from her neck.

"It's the first time I didn't dream in weeks."

"I know. I gave you a little mental push so you could rest."

Niki set down the glass with a steady hand. "You're the one who sent me those dreams I've been having for the past month."

"They were not dreams, but memories. I merely triggered your dormant memories of our life together." He stretched out his long legs. "A life we shared as Lupines back in 1085 A.D. before I died and the goddess Danu made me into the Silver Wizard, guardian and judge of all shifters."

All shifters. Not just Lupines like her. Nikita felt a chill rush down her spine at the idea of such power. Tristan was an immortal, powerful being.

Sensual awareness sparked his gaze. "It was a most pleasant time when you and I were mates. We had a very active love life. I seldom left you alone, but for when I had to travel."

In those dreams, Tristan had made love to her and made her scream with pleasure.

A heated flush tinted her cheeks, and she knew it wasn't from the fever, but her thoughts. "That was more than nine hundred years ago. I have a long-term memory problem."

He flashed a roguish grin, reminding her of a pirate from her favorite romance novels. The kind who tore off the clothing of fair maidens and ravished them and kept ravishing them.

12

Niki smoothed down the flannel of her pajama top. Hearts and flowers. Hardly the type of seductive nightwear meant for bedding by lusty pirates. She had no clothing, no provisions. But she was at the beach at last, and even if she had no control over her fate at the present, she was going to enjoy herself before Tristan ravished her.

Or killed her.

After spending her entire life hidden away like a dark secret, she craved freedom and sunshine. Her natural sense of adventure surfaced. Maybe there was a really nice beach where she could walk and pick up shells. She craned her neck to study the cool blue sweep of ocean showing outside the sliding glass doors. And she could swim as well. All those movies she'd watched in her basement apartment had made her yearn to see the ocean.

She looked at Tristan. "Can you find me some jeans and a shirt? I'd like to shower and then walk on the beach."

"Clothing, yes. Walk on the beach, no. You're still weak and recovering." He frowned. "You should not leave the room today."

"Is that an order?"

Tristan raised a dark brow. "It is for your safety."

Safety? Suddenly her fears began to fade, replaced with resentment. How many times had she heard that before? From her father when he was alive, and her brothers, and later her identical twin? *Don't you dare leave this basement, Niki, it's not safe. We can't risk anyone seeing you. If Tristan finds out you're alive, he'll abduct you and you'll die.*

And now her family's worst nightmare had

happened. And the wizard she'd been taught to fear was going to imprison her like she'd been imprisoned for twenty-five years.

"I've remained cooped up my entire life on my father's ranch to protect me from you. And now that you have me, you're going to keep me locked up like a jewel?"

He set down the pen upon the table next to the chair. "You are a jewel, my sweet. I am thinking of your safety. My intention is not to incarcerate you. Does this look like a prison?"

Since strength had returned to her limbs and her stomach was more settled, Niki felt her courage rise more. "A prison, no matter how luxurious, is still a prison if one cannot leave it. The basement apartment Nia created to keep me hidden from you was filled with everything I needed, except I could not leave it."

Tristan drummed his fingers on the armrest "Now that we are together, you are vulnerable to my enemies. Trust me, Nikita, I am more than fourteen hundred years old and I know much of the world. There are dangers here in the mortal world and you cannot remain here long. We must journey to Tir Na-nog. Only there can you be fully safe, and your spirit and body healed."

"Terrific," she murmured. "Of all the gin joints in all the towns in all the world, you had to walk into mine."

The wizard knit his brows.

She sighed. "It's a line from *Casablanca*. I watched a lot of movies. It was my only real entertainment."

Tristan kept his expression blank, as if hiding his opinion of her movie watching.

"What kind of dangers are you talking about? If

you're a powerful wizard, why should you worry?" She swung her legs over the bed's side, feeling more rested, but still fragile.

"Mara." Tristan took the hotel pen and twirled it between his fingers. He had long, elegant fingers. She wondered how it would feel to have those fingers stroking over her bare flesh...

Niki glanced up and saw his lips curl in a knowing smile. She sniffed and hugged herself.

"What's a Mara? It sounds ugly."

"In spirit, yes, but outwardly, Mara is breathtakingly beautiful. She's a powerful Fae who has lived more than two thousand years." He lifted the pen by the tip of one finger and began spinning it in the air like a top. "I always did attract older women."

Niki rolled her eyes.

"She cannot kill me, for I am immortal. But she can hurt you, badly, while you remain here on Earth. She is lethal and knows how much you mean to me and that makes her jealous of you." Tristan's piercing gaze settled on her, and Niki shivered.

It was unsettling, knowing she was the one this powerful being wanted above all others, wanted her because once, long ago, she had been his love.

And she remembered nothing of it.

Pressing her fingers against her forehead, she studied the soothing vista of the blue ocean. "Is this Mara someone from your, our, past?"

"Back in our day, she was a force of reckoning. I enlisted her help to find dragon eggs, the eggs that contain the most powerful magick from dragons. The eggs were pivotal to winning the Drakon War. She did, but the gold I offered wasn't enough."

The pen fell to the floor as he studied her. "She wanted to become my lover."

Her throat tight, Niki looked away. "And you lay with her."

Tristan left his seat and knelt before her. He put a finger on her chin, turning her face to meet him. "You were my mate. I was Lupine and we mate for life. I would not violate my vows and dishonor you."

But I have no real memory of our time together. It means nothing to me. "And what did she do?"

"Mara said she understood, but she is manipulative. She lies in wait for what she desires, like a fat spider spinning a sticky web." Tristan dropped his hand and his expression grew hard. "She told me she would become my lover, when I lost the 'impediments' barricading our time together. Meaning, you and the child you carried in your belly."

Niki's nausea returned. She pressed her hands against her churning stomach, wondering why the idea of being pregnant made her want to weep.

Rubbing her aching temples, she shook her head. "Let me get the details straight, Tristan, and why you want me. You and I were mated, in the 11th century, oh, about 1085 AD. And then you died and became the Silver Wizard, the immortal judge and guardian of all shifters. And I died?"

"You died and the babe you carried in your belly died as well."

Her lips parted. "I have no memory of this." *I wouldn't want it back, either.*

Tristan's gaze grew stormy. "I have enough for both of us. I carried it through the years, the decades, the centuries, waiting for you to become reincarnated and return to me."

Fisting his hands, he stared at the silk-patterned walls. "After I died and went to Tir Na-nog, the heavenly afterworld, the goddess Danu asked me to become the Silver Wizard, the guardian and judge of all shifters. I did so on one condition. I told her I would protect, guard and judge shifters if you would eventually return to me and give me what I had been denied when I was mortal."

She feared to ask. "And what do you want?"

His dark gaze gleamed. "A child."

CHAPTER 2

His beautiful, brave Nikita stared at him, her lower lip trembling. She drew back as if he were a monster who wanted to rape her.

Tristan knew it was a lot to digest. Hell, how could he ask her to just blithely accept their past life together? He had hoped the memories he'd triggered over the past few weeks would help, but clearly, she still feared him.

Twenty-five years of her family teaching her to be terrified of him would do that, he thought ruefully. Damn the prophecy that foretold he would abduct her and kill her. That was the trouble with ancient prophecies. The words became twisted over the centuries and the truth warped. But still, her family had believed every word.

How could he create a baby with her in loving passion when his past/future mate looked at him as if he wanted to slay her?

Slay her with pleasure, yes. Even now he trembled with the terrible want of her, the need to tear off her clothing and plunge his sex deep inside her, bonding them together in the flesh at last. The vision she had

18

obviously seen in the mirror had been a manifestation of his darkest, deepest desires.

Kill her? Of course not. But her family had drilled it into Nikita's head that he was a monster, who was foretold to destroy her. Nine hundred years ago, Nikita had captured his heart with her beauty and her gentle spirit and courage. He had never forgotten her, had never ceased desiring her all these centuries.

He had made a promise to her that would not be broken.

Patience, he reminded himself. You've waited hundreds of years for this moment. Don't screw it up.

Blue eyes wide, she blinked hard. "Inconceivable."

Tristan rocked back on his booted heels. What?

"I do not think it means what you think it means." Nikita licked her mouth. "Princess Bride."

"A good movie." He had watched this one. Tristan waited.

"A child." She gnawed on her lush lower lip and he nearly groaned, for he badly wanted to touch her, taste her. "You want to make a baby with me."

"Yes," he said quietly, watching her face.

Niki hugged herself. "Mind if I have a shower first and a walk on the beach?"

Tristan stared, and then laughed. After all these centuries, his Nikita was still…Nikita. Ah, that pragmatic streak that kept him grounded, and laughing.

A vision flickered from his past. The hook the executioner lifted, sunlight glinting on the cruel metal…Nikita's terrified screams for them to stop…

Tristan ceased laughing.

"It's far too dangerous. We'll dine here, in the room, while you gather your strength."

She lifted her chin. "I'm strong enough now. And it's only a walk on the beach. Maybe collect a few seashells. How dangerous is that?"

Nikita knew nothing of the dangers of this world or the Others who possessed such powers and wouldn't hesitate to use them against her. He had many enemies. Shifters whose loved ones he had been forced to exterminate when they turned to darkness. Shifters, more than any Others, had long memories and were loyal to family.

Taking a deep breath, he sat beside her again, fighting the temptation to kiss her senseless, keeping her distracted from the beach in a much more pleasant way.

"Seashells can be whittled to sharp edges that can cut your skin to ribbons. The ocean tides can rise up and drown you. Or a sinkhole can appear beneath your bare feet and the sands can swallow you forever. Those are but a few tricks Mara can pull, not to mention the harm ordinary shifters can cause you." And there are a few shifters here in this hotel.

"They hate me that much?" Nikita's pulse raced.

"They hate me that much."

Tristan rose and began to pace the room. He wanted to win her heart again, but after all this time, he grew impatient. The Nikita of his mortal life had been mostly docile and sweet, but she had possessed a hidden stubborn streak.

That hadn't changed much, he thought ruefully.

"The potion I gave you has transformed your body. You now possess some of my powers, and my ability to journey from this world to Tir Na-nog without dying. However, the potion doesn't make you invincible, like me. Nor immortal. You're still vulnerable. And the effects are temporary. They will wear off in five more days. Unless I get you to my home in Tir Na-nog before those five days are up, the process will reverse and it will be…most unpleasant." He sat and picked up her hand, marveling at the velvet softness of her skin.

"More unpleasant than dying from the parvolupus?"

He thought of the possibility of the potion wearing off and his chest tightened. "I will not allow that to happen. I will guard your time and keep watch."

Tristan rubbed his cheek against her hand. "Your mortal body is susceptible here on Earth, much as it was before you drank the potion. You can still die."

And that I will not allow to happen. And when you finally surrender in passion to me, and learn to trust me, there is a way to make you immortal so we can be together forever. Because otherwise, I will have to let you go in the end, for I have my duties as the Silver Wizard and I cannot live on Earth, nor can you live permanently in Tir Na-nog, unless you are as immortal as I am.

The thought grieved him, but he set it aside. He must focus on her needs.

Seeing her unhappiness, he added, "Perhaps after we have breakfast, we can go to the beach, if you remain at my side."

Niki smiled and the joy in that facial gesture made his own heart thump. Gods, he had loved her so much during their brief time as mates.

Could she learn to love him again?

Love isn't necessary for what I was promised. Passion, yes. I will teach her passion, and let her own natural desire arise. Danu promised me an heir to continue my name so I will not be forgotten when the ages have passed and I have become naught but a memory. My son will be my legacy.

Desire rose as he studied his past/future mate.

The son I will plant in her belly.

He nodded at the bathroom. "Go shower. I will order breakfast."

"Bacon," she said, her eyes bright. "Lots of bacon. I'm starved. And a cheese omelet, and an English muffin, buttered, and oh, honey, not jelly."

He grinned. "You enjoy eating honey?"

"Definitely."

Tristan thought of all the tantalizing ways he could use the honey. Smeared all over her body while he licked it off, very slowly…

Not now. Later.

But he would taste her. One small kiss as a reward for his patience. Staring at her mouth, he leaned forward. Niki shrank back. Biting back a frustrated sigh, he merely brushed his lips across her forehead, then went into the living room to give her privacy.

Breakfast. He could conjure food, but perhaps she would enjoy room service. Decisions, decisions. Tristan phoned room service and placed an order for a plate of bacon, a cheese omelet with a buttered English muffin and honey, adding coffee, orange juice and for himself, Brie and toast.

He sat at the armchair by the sliding glass door to wait. Sounds of the shower began, and Tristan closed his eyes, imagining his Nikita beneath the spray, droplets of water gleaming as they slid down her nude body, imagining her taking the soap into that sweet, honeyed warmth between her legs…

He'd love to join her, wash her back and many other

22

places. His body tightened and he reluctantly leashed his desire.

A soft tap came at the door and suddenly a man materialized in the room. He glanced up. "Don't you knock?"

"I just did." Xavier, the Crystal Wizard, strolled over to the sofa.

The Crystal Wizard was one of the three other members of the Brehon, the judges and guardians of Others. Xavier ruled over trolls, ogres, nymphs and goblins. But while Tristan was busy with Nikita, Xavier promised to take over his duties temporarily, sharing the responsibility with Gideon, the Crimson Wizard and ruler of Fae.

His brother wizard had long, dark curls tipped at the edges with white crystals, a bearded face and a tall, muscular frame. Known for his flamboyant dress, he had dressed in clothing outrageous even for him; a neon green sweater and tight white pants.

"What are you wearing?" he asked.

X looked down. "The latest fashion. I have heard of these trousers with sayings embroidered on the back."

The Crystal Wizard turned around. On the back of his pants was embroidered the phrase "Sexy Thing."

Tristan rolled his eyes. "Those sayings are for sixteen-year-old girls. Not seven-hundred-year-old wizards, my friend. Did you visit the Mitchell Ranch?"

"Yes. I did as Aiden asked."

"How are Aiden and Nia?" He was especially concerned about Nia, since she had been upset about being parted from her twin.

"Very, very busy. Especially in the bedroom." His blue gaze twinkled. "Nia is quite happy, and she can once more shapeshift into her wolf, but she and Aiden keep working the magick."

Good. Aiden would keep his mate distracted, and keep her from worrying about Nikita.

"Do you have the report on Alexander for me?"

Xavier handed him a roll of parchment. Tristan unfurled it and read the ancient, cramped script. The heir of the Drakon clan, Drust's clan, Crown Prince Alex was headstrong, had a temper and was fiercely loyal. It seemed the one-hundred-fifty-year-old crown prince, who was only thirty-five in human years, was missing.

Tristan knew exactly where the very important dragon shifter hid—with Drust, his dead great-grandfather in the afterworld of the Shadow Lands. And the prince refused to return home.

Perfect.

Now that he finally had his Nikita back, he would exact his revenge. Drust, the dragon shifter who had caused his capture nine centuries ago and caused his agonizing execution, would finally suffer for betraying Tristan.

"What are you going to do to Drust? I thought you were only venturing to the Shadow Lands to take Nikita to Tir Na-nog."

Absorbed in the report, Tristan did not answer. The only way he could take Nikita to his home in Tir Na-nog was through the Shadow Lands, the purgatory for OtherWorlders who died and had to make amends in order to ascend to the heavenly afterworld. He rolled the parchment and handed it back to Xavier.

"What are you planning to do to Drust?" Xavier repeated.

"I'd kill him, but he's already dead. I plan to take

away the one thing he wants above all else. Drust cherishes his descendants."

And I have none. Not even the babe Nikita carried in her belly when I died.

Xavier's gaze narrowed. "You can't kill the crown prince of Clan Drakon. Tristan, has the Florida sun overheated your brain?"

"I have no desire to harm Alexander. But I will remove something that Drust cherishes."

"His balls?"

"No. I would never do that to anyone, and inflict that agony on a man. Except perhaps Drust. It is not...a terrific feeling."

Blood drained from Xavier's face. "That's what they did when they killed you all those centuries ago?"

"One of the things they did," he said softly. "The others were brutal as well."

Tristan's chest tightened as he remembered the agony of seeing Nikita's tormented face watching his torture, hearing her screams echo his own. Though he tried hard to keep silent, the pain had grown intolerable and he screamed and screamed.

Not the confession the Fae executioner wanted, but he cried his mate's name over and over.

Nikita!

"Though I must admit feeling quite different after losing my balls. I suddenly had the urge to shop, sing soprano, wear my hair up in a snood and start asking, 'Does this outfit make my ass look fat?'" He fingered his shoulder-length locks with a rueful smile.

"Stop joking. This is serious."

Tristan blinked. "I am serious. Does this tunic make me look fat?"

Xavier growled and flicked a finger at him. A crystalline bolt of energy sailed into the air and hit Tristan in the mouth. It bounced off his face and hit the wall instead, denting it. None of the four wizards of the Brehon had the ability to hurt the others. The rules Danu set up long ago were firm. They couldn't fully share powers either or the punishment would be most grim, she'd warned them.

"I am not going to hurt one hair on Crown Prince Alexander's head. Trust me." Tristan locked his gaze on his fellow wizard. "Are you willing to do what I asked you before?"

Xavier waved a hand and conjured a pair of silver scissors. "Be quick about it. I am fond of my hair."

Drawing in a deep breath, he handed Tristan the scissors. Tristan took one of Xavier's long, dark curls and snipped, cutting off the end where the crystals grew. Immediately another crystal appeared in its place.

Palming the glittering lock, he studied it and then set down the scissors.

"I am most curious. Why do you need one of my crystals?"

"I will tell you everything later. Thank you for this." He tucked the crystal into the pocket of his tunic as Nikita emerged from the bedroom, a hotel robe wrapped around her body.

Both he and Xavier stood. Blood drained from her face as her gaze whipped back and forth between them. Tristan felt her agitation. Two powerful wizards, both over six feet tall, and quite intimidating.

He hated seeing her fear. Tristan's gaze dropped to her bare legs. She had very nice legs, but they were on display for Xavier's admiring gaze.

Xavier gave a small bow. "My lady Nikita. It is a pleasure to meet you. I am Xavier, the Crystal Wizard."

Niki gave him a dubious look. "You're one of the Brehon?"

"He is leaving to attend to his duties, right now," Tristan cut in.

X's blue gaze shot from Nikita to Tristan. "I can stay," he offered.

"No," Tristan snapped.

"So if you're one of those other powerful wizards, maybe you can teach Tristan how to conjure proper clothing for a lady after she showers so she has no need of a hotel bathrobe," Nikita said, her gaze alert as a frightened deer's.

Xavier laughed, but Tristan felt a stab of guilt. He had forgotten her most basic need. She must think him totally lame for neglecting her.

Shivering, Niki wrapped her arms around herself. He felt her fear, smelled it as clearly as he scented the briny ocean breeze drifting from the open sliding glass doors. Two powerful wizards here with her, the Lupine who had remained locked away. Tristan sent a tendril of calming magick into the air and felt Niki's pulse return to normal.

Waving a hand, he clothed her in baggy sweatpants and an oversized sweatshirt that displayed nothing. Niki blinked and looked down.

She was still tempting and lovely. Perhaps sackcloth and ashes…

Her huge blue gaze went from Tristan to Xavier.

"Why are you here?" she asked Xavier. "Does it have to do with Mara?"

Tristan stiffened. "He is here to do me a favor. It has nothing to do with Mara…"

"Who is this Mara?" Niki asked. "If she is such a threat, why can't you do something with her?"

They exchanged glances. "It's not that simple," Xavier began.

Enough. Nikita deserved the truth. "Mara is Gideon's sister," Tristan said. "Gideon, the Crimson Wizard."

Niki frowned and sat on the chair furthest from both of them. "And she is the one who tried to seduce you?"

A note of faint jealousy rippled through her voice. Tristan wondered if she were even aware of it.

"Mara assisted me during the Drakon War, after Gideon asked her to help us. And yes, she tried to seduce me, which is why I have avoided her all these centuries. She is the only living family Gideon has left, and it's a quite delicate situation."

"Delicate?" Xavier snorted. "It makes politics in the United States Congress look like a day at the beach."

Niki yawned and stretched. "I'm so thirsty. It must be the effects of that potion you gave me."

Before he could even blink, she flicked a finger and a glass of water appeared in her hand. Xavier stared.

"Whoa," he said quietly.

Whoa was right. Niki didn't even seem to be aware of the enormity of what she'd done as she drank the water and then set down the glass on the table beside the chair. A chill raced down his spine. With these powers, could Nikita find a way to break free from him?

It must not happen.

He and X traded glances. Does she know? Xavier asked, using the Brehon's special form of telepathy.

No. I shall tell her.

Dude, she has your powers.

All of our powers, he told his friend. For the potion contained your blood as well as Cadeyrn's and Gideon's. But only droplets.

A droplet of our power is more powerful than gallons of the most potent shifter's magick. Then telepathy is next. Be careful, Tristan. If one of your shifters discovers she is endowed with the Brehon's magick, they could use her against you.

He knew this and flashed Xavier a warning with his eyes, letting them surge to bright blue, signaling the rise of his powers.

"Fine," X said aloud. "Just a friendly warning."

As the Crystal Wizard stood and went to the door to look at the ocean view, he displayed the back of his trousers.

Niki stared at Xavier's buttocks. "Nice pants."

Tristan growled deep in his throat. Turning, X looked delighted. "Why Tristan, are you snarling at me? I have never heard you growl."

"I can do more than growl." He went to Nikita, sat on the chair's armrest and slid an arm around her shoulders, unable to prevent his protective streak. "Take those trousers off."

X began to laugh. "Truly?"

"And put on normal clothing," he snapped.

Still chuckling, the Crystal Wizard waved a hand and covered himself in nothing but a lime green Speedo bathing suit, displaying his long legs and other assets. "Better? We are in Florida."

Nikita's eyes widened. "Oh…my."

Tristan covered her eyes with his palm. "Get out of here, X."

The wizard waved a hand and dressed himself in blue jeans and a football jersey. "You don't like my style? The ladies say I look good in green."

He removed his palm. "Honestly, Xavier, with your manner of dress, how you can attract a date is beyond me."

Even as the words slipped out of his mouth, Tristan remembered Ciara, the nymph Xavier had loved.

Xavier's smile dropped. He looked distant and sorrowful. Remembering the reason for his friend's emotions, Tristan felt a pinch of guilt.

"I am sorry," he said, meaning it. "I forgot."

His friend shrugged. "I cannot have a relationship with Ciara. She was not promised to me, and I will not neglect my duties to form attachments. Cadeyrn told me I will see her again, and she will play a role in my recovery."

Tristan's curiosity rose. Cadeyrn was the most powerful of the four wizards and more than any of them, he had the ability to foresee the future. "From what?"

Xavier frowned. "He was very vague."

Xavier was expert at hiding his feelings, but Tristan knew how much the nymph had meant to his friend. He went to the dining table and traced a few runes on the surface, bringing up a window to the future. Each wizard could see vague glimpses into the future of each other's lives, but not their own.

Mist shrouded the vision, but he saw enough to make his blood run cold.

Ciara would play a role in Xavier's recovery, but what the Crystal Wizard would suffer was a direct effect of something having to do with Nikita. A chill raced down Tristan's spine.

He waved a hand and the window vanished. No use upsetting Xavier or Nikita.

"Ciara will indeed be part of your future, my friend. She will be very important to you, and you will see her again, soon."

The Crystal Wizard blinked, and his mouth curled into a smile. Then he shuttered his expression. "Thanks, but I refuse to live in the past, or wait for the future any longer. However, I am most pleased that Tristan has found you at last, my lady Nikita. He has waited long enough."

Xavier gave her a gentle smile. "If you need me, call upon me. I am here for both of you."

With a meaningful look at Tristan, he waved a hand and vanished.

Niki's blue gaze was huge as she stared at the place Xavier had occupied. "I don't know if I shall ever get used to that. Who is Ciara? Her name made him sad."

Tristan felt another ominous shiver race down his spine. "Ciara is a nymph who made Xavier love-struck. He is the guardian and judge of nymphs. But we of the Brehon are not to form attachments with our charges, so he let her go."

"And I'm a Lupine, yet here you are, with me." She gave him a pointed look.

"What we have is different. You were promised to me ages ago when I became the Silver Wizard."

Nikita knit her dark gold brows. "Why was he here? Are you expecting others?"

He gently tweaked her nose. "No others. I plan to keep you alone, for myself."

"So you can seduce me?"

Tristan's mouth thinned. No, I am saving that

31

moment for my home, when I can relax at last and don't have to worry about protecting you from a fire, flood, landslide or a mad Fae turning you into a toadstool. Even with your powers, which will not last, you do not know how to protect yourself from these dangers, my sweet. You have been sheltered too long by Lupines.

He was saved from answering by a knock at the door. The waiter wheeled in a cart filled with covered dishes and set up breakfast at the dining table. Tristan signed the bill, adding a healthy tip. When the waiter left, he studied the food and added a slice of raw liver to Niki's plate.

As she sat, he told her, "Eat the liver first. Your wolf needs the fresh meat after your illness."

He cut a slice of the liver, forked it and held it to her mouth. She parted her lips and he slid the food inside, hiding a smile.

Did Niki realize that taking food from his hand was an indication of acceptance of becoming his mate? Traditional Lupine ceremonies had the male feeding the female as a symbol that he would provide for her.

Tristan handed her the fork. Provide for her in many ways, both in feeding her and taking care of her sexual needs as well.

Careful. He needed to leash his rising desire, lest he fall into a mating frenzy. Mating frenzies affected male Lupines who had been denied their mates' touch for too long.

I'd say that nine hundred years is far too long to be denied her touch...

As she began to eat, she made little sounds of pleasure that heated his blood. Ah, he would enjoy hearing those sounds when he had her in bed at last...

"Aren't you eating?" she asked.

"I don't require food. I enjoy the taste from time to time, but I have no need of it."

She picked up a slice of bacon. "Why?"

"I renew my energy differently than from caloric intake."

"How?"

He reached over and took a slice of bacon, feeding it to her. She opened her mouth and he popped the morsel inside, relishing how she enjoyed the treat.

"It is a secret, my sweet."

"A big secret?" Her gaze darkened. "Tell me. I hate secrets. I've lived my whole life as a secret."

"There are some questions I cannot answer right now. That knowledge lies within certain parameters of the forbidden."

Niki finished the bacon and dug into her omelet. "I can see this will be a one-sided relationship. You hold all the power, all the knowledge. And I'm a cute little accessory for you, like a scarf."

Tristan's temper began to rise. "Hardly. As you can see from my manner of dress, I am not prone to accessorizing."

She sipped her orange juice. "I know. You wore the same thing the day the Fae King executed you."

His cold heart raced as she stared at him and set down the glass with a shaky hand. "Dear goddess, why did I remember that? It just came to my mind…that image. It was horrid."

Niki's chest rose and fell with the rapid increase of her breath. She hugged herself again, moisture gathering in her eyes.

Tristan slipped into the past.

He could feel the hard wood beneath his bare feet, hear the angry, derisive shouts of the Fae crowd, the agony of the lacerations that had abraded his flesh…and see Nikita screaming as she stood nearby and they forced her to watch, her hand reached out toward him as King Emer's chief executioner picked up the gleaming hook to tear into his skin…

He took a deep breath, regained his composure and sat beside her. Picking up her hand, he squeezed it. "Breathe. Deep breaths. You'll get through this."

Two fat tears slipped down her cheeks. Gently, he traced one with his thumb and then brought it to his mouth. It tasted bitter, like vinegar, laced with a touch of honey. How he had longed to do that the day they brought him in chains to be tortured before the crowd for starting the rebellion to gain freedom from the Fae for shifters. How he'd wanted to comfort her, assure her she would be fine and he would always be there for her in spirit, for neither heaven nor hell would keep him from her side…

Tristan picked up her hand and rubbed it against his cheek, deeply shaken, but knowing he must hold together emotionally. She walked unknown territory in the memory of his death, while this was a familiar path upon which he had paced back and forth for more centuries. And despite the time that passed, his death still haunted Tristan, for he always saw her screaming and crying, reaching out to him as his spirit fled his body…

"I don't remember anything else, except that. If you and I were mates in a past life, why do I recall your death? I don't want to remember that!" She wiped her eyes with the linen napkin.

How he wished he could purge that terrible time from her memory. He could not protect her from remembering the horror and terror. "The most powerful and emotional memories are returning to you first." He stroked her shaking hand as she rested it on the table. "It is a nasty side effect of the potion. I had hoped for something much more enjoyable, such as the time we got naked and played chess in bed. I recall that I took your bishop that day, but you did the most amazing things with my king."

At last, he thought with relief as she smiled. "I dare not ask exactly what I did, but I suspect when you say 'king' you don't mean the chess piece."

Tristan kissed the back of her hand. "Let us forget the past for a while. Finish eating, to regain your energy, and we'll walk on the beach so you may find seashells."

As she began to eat again, he went over to the sliding glass doors. Waving a hand, he changed his clothing to a gray T-shirt, black cotton cargo shorts and black flip-flops.

His hand trembled as he traced a rune on the clear glass for protection. He wanted her to remember the love they had shared, and the passion, and learn to trust him again.

But how could she recall those emotions when all she could recall was the horrid way the Fae King killed him? Soon, she would soon remember the terrible words he had told her shortly before he died.

Tristan's chest tightened. I'll deal with that when it comes. And hopefully in nine hundred years, she has learned to forgive me…

CHAPTER 3

After breakfast, she brushed her teeth using the hotel supplies, and then asked Tristan to provide her with shorts and a T-shirt. The baggy sweatpants and sweatshirt were too ugly and warm.

He waved a hand and clad her in a shapeless gray dress that draped down to her ankles.

Hands on hips, Niki gave him a pointed look. "Sackcloth would do better."

With a sigh, he waved another hand.

"I left clothing on the bed for you, so you may choose to dress yourself as you wish."

Delighted, she went into the bedroom. There were piles of clothing, neatly stacked upon the bed. Underwear first.

She picked up a pair of white granny panties and sighed. "Oh Tristan. Seriously?"

Bras, none with the lace and colors she liked. But at least he'd conjured clothing that was suitable. She chose a pretty pair of white shorts that came to mid-thigh, and a blue scooped-neck pullover shirt with lace scalloped sleeves. Niki slid her feet into a pair of white sandals with little blue gemstones and gave a happy sigh.

Life had changed drastically in the past day, but she would live in the moment, not fret about the future. After spending twenty-five years never leaving her father's ranch, she was going to enjoy her first walk on the beach. Freedom at last!

But freedom always came with a price, and Tristan's price was steep. Nikita, to become his mate and bear his child.

He saved your life and did not destroy it as the prophecy foretold. But don't trust him. There's something there he's not sharing, something that you know from the past...

But what?

Her body tightened as she thought of the quiet way he'd stated she was to bear his child, how he'd looked at her with such heat in his gaze, but a fiery coldness as well. As if she served no more than his purpose—a vessel for his pleasure and not a person with her own will.

She unbound her hair, brushed it and secured it back with a butterfly clip she found in the bathroom. When she emerged from the bedroom, Tristan's gaze traveled from the top of her head to her toes. Shivering with pleasure from the heated intensity of that look, she tried to control her galloping pulse.

But seeing him like this, so handsome in the shorts and the T-shirt that displayed the curve of his biceps, was far better than the horrid vision of him being executed...

Her gaze traveled up and down the length of his legs. He had very nice limbs. Long, trim with muscle and dusted with dark hair. Athletic legs that could probably run for miles, or support him as he lifted a woman against the wall and thrust deep inside her...

Heat suffused her face. Not going there.

"You could have zapped up some nicer underwear for me," she told him. "Some silk lingerie would have been nice. Peach or emerald green."

He arched an eyebrow. "Why, when you will not be wearing it for long when we reach my home?"

Niki felt her blush deepen.

He held open the door for her as they left the room. Silence draped between them as they rode down in the elevator. Standing in the opposite corner, Niki smoothed down her shorts, too nervous to speak. He stood there, tall and impervious, this powerful wizard who had been her mate in a past life.

She, who barely even dated in this life.

The elevator pinged softly at the tenth floor and slid open. A couple in shorts and polo shirts entered, saw Tristan. Their eyes widened as the doors slid shut. Catching their scent, Niki realized they were like her. Lupine.

Lupines were ruled by Tristan. The couple suddenly bowed before him and she smelled their anxiety, as sharp as cleaning fluid. Tristan sighed. She wondered if he found this tedious, always having Lupines in awe of him, worried about encountering him because they feared he'd punish them for some minor infraction they didn't realize they had committed.

A tendril of thought curled around her, and she startled, realizing it came from Tristan. No clear words, but a sudden, resigned loneliness, as if he stood alone atop a tall mountain, and down in the valley below were people who lived, laughed, loved and never wanted to see him.

Feeling a surge of empathy, she stepped closer to Tristan and slid her hand into his. He looked startled, and then pleased.

"Good day," he told the couple as they straightened.

"Are you here for one of us?" the man asked.

"No." Tristan gave a gentle smile. "I am here, like you, enjoying the seashore."

The couple exchanged glances. Then the woman spoke in a shy voice. "May I ask you a question about our future?"

Tristan blinked and his smile widened. "Yes. It will happen."

The couple beamed at each other.

"Congratulations," he told them.

The elevator doors slid open. "Thank you," the woman told him and they walked away, arms around each other, laughing like the young lovers they were.

Niki threw him a questioning look.

"She wanted to know if they would get pregnant on this trip. It is the reason why they are here, to escape from the pressures of their pack and their duties, so she can conceive."

"And she dared to ask you, as if you are a crystal ball?"

He shrugged those broad shoulders. "Lupines like to ask questions about the future, particularly concerning their families. I am accustomed to it. And what is the harm in telling them the eventuality, when they will spend the week doing what will result in the desired outcome?"

A twinkle sparked his dark gaze. He gripped her hand as they strolled into the lobby, and then walked outside to the pool deck. Niki sighed happily. The sun burned brightly in the azure sky and a cooling breeze blew off the turquoise ocean waters.

Tall palm trees and colorful fuchsia flowers ringed

the Olympic-sized pool. A few sunbathers lounged in deck chairs by the pool. Tristan walked past them, his gaze whipping back and forth. Tension radiated from him, changing his scent from ocean brine and delicious orange to bitter almonds and sharp steel, laced with a scent her wolf instantly recognized.

The scent of a male alert for trouble, and in protective mode.

She had smelled this before, when her father and brothers were alive. Niki gently disentangled herself from his grip. When he shot her a questioning look, she touched his arm.

"Relax. I'm not going to run away and there are no dangerous monsters lurking here."

A reluctant smile touched his mouth. "I shall try, for your sake."

When they finally reached the sandy beach, she raced down to the water's edge. Tristan was at her side in an instant. Niki kicked off the sandals. The tangy smell of briny, fresh air invigorated her senses.

Dangling the sandals by one finger, she ran to meet the water, loving the way the wet sand squished between her toes. She laughed as the slightly cool surf washed over her bare feet. It felt delicious, better than in her imagination, which had conveyed nothing more than the sandpaper roughness of a wolf's tongue lapping at her feet.

Warmth filled her and she laughed, throwing out her hands. "It tickles!"

Tristan's mouth curled into a smile, and he shoved his hands into the pockets of his shorts.

"Come on," she called, crooking a finger at him. "Tristan, this is fun! Take off your shoes."

Kicking off his flip-flops he joined her, then he grinned. The boyishness of it was such a drastic contrast to the mien of the severe, powerful wizard that she melted inside.

He gave a furtive look around. "No Skins nearby. Watch this."

Tristan made a circular gesture with his index finger and the waves curled around his feet, swirling in playful loops. Niki giggled.

"The waves are doing that because they're reluctant to touch your big, ugly toes," she teased.

"I have not big, ugly toes." Grinning, he pointed a foot at the surf. "I have nice feet, though not as nice as yours."

He actually did have nice feet. Long, square and tipped with perfect toes.

"Big hands, big feet, big paws," she told him.

His grin turned wicked. "Big something else too."

Flushing, she darted away, kicking at the surf. His words made her belly curl with anticipation and she needed space. Everything was moving far too fast.

"Don't go far." Worry sharpened his voice.

"Don't be such an old man," she called back.

"Old man?" he sputtered.

"You are more than fourteen hundred years old."

Niki placed her sandals out of reach of the tide, and squatted down by the water's edge. After all these years she was finally at the beach, and determined to make the most of it. She began to scoop out handfuls of sand, shaping them into walls and turrets.

Tristan joined her, giving her a dubious look. "What is that?"

"A castle, silly."

Kneeling in the sand, he frowned. "It looks like a lopsided house."

Niki flung seawater at him and he ducked.

A dim memory tugged at her. Castles. Turrets and opened doorways, and magick, shapeshifting silver dragons who soared into the air, then slept in the courtyard by the gatehouse. Her mind slipped into shadow and she found herself staring at the sand, willing it to take shape...

"Whoa," Tristan murmured.

The lopsided structure she'd made from sand had vanished, replaced with a tall, foreboding castle that looked as if a master artisan had crafted it with intricate tools and brushes.

She touched the castle with a shaky finger. "Tristan, you did this?"

"I did nothing."

Niki stared at the tall castle, with its majestic turrets, moat, bridge, the keep, and the replica of a sleeping dragon lying in the courtyard by the gatehouse.

"I did this?"

"You recreated it. Castle Baldwin. Our home," he said softly. "You lived there with me."

A sense of unreality washed over her. "But...I cannot."

Tristan took her hand, gently stroking her fingers with his thumb. It felt soothing, but inside, she shook badly. What was happening to her that she could imagine a castle and conjure it out of thin air?

"I need to tell you, Nikita. In order to claim you as my bride and save your life from the virus, I obtained permission from the goddess Danu to make a potion. The potion you ingested contained droplets of my blood which contains my magick. It also contained a droplet of blood of the three other members of the Brehon. Part of our magick now resides inside you."

As she stared at him, he added, "Not a significant portion, but enough to endow you with magick that enables you to conjure more than mere clothing out of thin air, as you do when you shift back from your wolf form."

She felt as if her world suddenly tilted on its axis. "If this is so, why are you so worried about me being vulnerable?" There was much she didn't understand.

"Because you do not know nor understand how to harness that power. It takes time to learn, and you need a safe place for me to teach you." His voice deepened. "If they knew of your abilities, there are Others who would harm you, and drain your powers to use them for evil."

Niki glanced up and saw the Lupine couple from the elevator strolling along the shoreline. Suddenly their carefree innocence no longer seemed innocent. They took on a new meaning and threat. Was this what power meant? Always seeing threats everywhere? Freedom suddenly took on a new meaning.

"Is there no place that is safe here, on Earth?"

He shook his head. "I must take you with me to Tir Na-nog. When you enter my home world, you will be safe from all harm," he said softly. "You will be stronger, and healed from the injuries your earthly body has suffered, and better prepared to carry my child."

Heart pounding, she stared at his fingers laced through hers. Sex. He talked about when he would bed her, and impregnate her, for that was his ultimate goal. Suddenly faced with this prospect, her childish whim to play and walk in the surf in her bare feet seemed ridiculous.

She had been building castles made from sand, while his goal was to build a legacy, with her as the vessel for carrying his son.

And I will be a prisoner once more, only this time it will be a prisoner to his lust and his desires. Her life would be all about him and what he wanted…when she hadn't even had an opportunity to figure out what she herself wanted.

Niki shivered, not because of the sudden gust of wind blowing over the ocean, but because of the ruthless intent shadowing his expression. No romance existed between them, only Tristan's grim purpose. In her dreams, they had shared a life, shared a bed, shared their bodies and had come together in love and passion. But when she awoke she remembered little of that past, a past he was determined to recreate, eventually impregnating her with the child he'd longed to have.

"How can you ask this of me?" Niki yanked her hand away. "You want me to become your lover…"

"My mate," he corrected.

"Lover, mate, does it matter? You want me to become the mother of your baby, and I haven't even really lived my life. I've spent twenty-five years locked away," she pointed to the castle turret, "like a princess in a fairy tale, only the fairy tale always had you lurking in the background, the grim reaper my father told me would cause my demise."

Tristan's mouth narrowed to a slash. "I have some control here, but there are forces I cannot control. And I will not risk you being smashed by my enemies."

He snapped his fingers and the tide rushed over,

engulfing them and crashing into the castle. The outer walls crumbled beneath the onslaught of the waves.

She saw not a castle crumbling from forces he could not control, but Tristan himself, ruthless and determined, his sexual intent overshadowing her as fiercely as the tidal wave.

Nikita looked at him and his expression shuttered, but she caught a glimpse of his sorrow, as opaque as mist.

"Why?" She tugged at his arm. "Why are you so overprotective?"

"Because I cannot bear for you to die again, as you died while I was in purgatory of the Shadow Lands."

Niki searched his tightened face. "You saw my death?"

"I felt it. I felt your spirit ebb, and that of our son." He placed a hand over his heart. "It was like all the energy had left me, Nikita. And I could do nothing to aid you. I died all over again that day you perished," he said quietly, refusing to meet her gaze.

He turned his head and regarded the horizon. "Lupines live a very long time, but they are still fragile. But there is a way for you to become immortal, as I am."

She felt boneless with shock. "Are you serious?"

"Yes. It is not a simple matter. It requires a choice." Tristan turned back to her. "The choice will be yours. I cannot force you into it. But if you choose to become immortal, then nothing would ever harm you again."

Nikita gripped his arm, her emotions in a lather. She wanted to remember, wanted to erase the deep sorrow radiating from him, but she also needed time and space. "I'm not like the sand castle, Tristan. And Lupines are not fragile as humans. I am wolf, and I have defenses. And despite the fact that I'm naïve in some ways…"

She flicked out a hand and let her claws emerge. Confidence filled her. "I have my own natural defenses. My wolf is smart, and she's very protective of me. My father, brothers and my twin taught me well."

His expression remained inscrutable. "A wolf offers flimsy protection against the darker forces I have encountered, Nikita. You are indeed naïve to think that your wolf can handle such evil."

The insult stung deeply. Though her temper was rising, she retracted her claws. "Nice of you to have faith in my abilities. It's a wonder you even abducted me, if you think I'm a weak Lupine who can barely hold my own. Maybe you should look elsewhere for a mate and a lover. Try a Lupine dating service. I've heard they work wonders, even for sour wizards."

She stood and walked off.

Tristan suddenly materialized at her side. "I am not a sour wizard, my sweet. I am a man who is worried about protecting my mate. And I did not abduct you."

Nikita gave him a pointed look. "You carried me off and I had no say in the matter."

"You were ill! Dying! I saved you!" He dragged in a deep breath, clearly frustrated.

"Then, thank you. If I'm not your prisoner, then let me return back to my home. Nia and Aiden can care for me."

"Nia and Aiden are not at your home. They are at the Mitchell Ranch, and they are quite preoccupied…with each other." Tristan softened his voice. "All of your pack now lives with Aiden's people. The ranch has been closed. Nikita, nothing is the same as when you left."

Nothing. She was naïve. You can't go home again. You don't belong there and the home you had is no longer there. She envisioned the ranch, wind rustling through the dead grasses, the ghosts of her past swirling around like dead leaves…

"There's no place like home," she whispered.

Tristan looked distant. "The Wizard of Oz. A very good movie."

A lump clogged her throat, but she would not surrender to tears. There was no yellow brick road or a way back for her. She would not cry in front of him. "If I no longer have a home there, then I can make a home elsewhere."

"You can, my sweet. I had hoped…you would make one with me."

The vulnerability in his voice caught her attention. Niki turned to see a shadow enter his gaze. And then she felt a cold rush of power, so frosty that her stomach squeezed tight. Tristan's expression hardened. He swore quietly.

A blonde woman of ethereal beauty approached them. Wearing a red bikini that was more dental floss than cloth, she was tall and model-slim, with eyes green as moss and a full, sensual mouth. But she radiated no warmth, and her beauty seemed otherworldly and chilling.

I know her. Nikita shivered.

The blonde stopped before the sand castle they had abandoned.

"How quaint." The blonde woman looked amused. "Trying to recreate the past, Tristan?"

"Mara," he said, his deep voice growing distant.

Niki's blood went cold. Faint recognition filled her.

She knew this woman, perhaps from that long-ago life, and felt the coldness radiating from her like the blast of an air conditioner upon her damp skin. A shiver skated down her spine. Power pulsed from the woman in small, sharp blasts. Tristan had the same power, but his power felt like a warm, comforting blanket on a winter's night.

This woman was frost personified; the bite of ice when one lay shivering in the snow...

"What do you want, Mara? Whatever it is, I will not grant it." Tristan stepped in front of Niki, as if shielding her from the woman's view.

But Mara peered around Tristan. "Darling, don't be such a stuffed shirt wizard. I heard through the Fae grapevine that you found your Nikita and I wanted to say hello."

Niki did not smile. "You've seen me. Good-bye."

She wanted to be far, far away from this woman. Gooseflesh broke out on her bare arms. Sensing the threat, her wolf growled, fearful of Mara's intentions.

"My mate is correct. You have seen her. Now leave, lest you face my wrath." Tristan flung out his arms and stepped forwards.

Power sizzled in the air, and his dark eyes turned a glowing, ethereal blue. Tristan seemed to grow in height, his mouth curled in a vicious snarl, his fangs descending. The raw fury of his magick undulated through the air in invisible ribbons, crackling and snapping.

Nikita shrank back. Please...stop.

And then he turned, saw her and his expression grew stricken.

Tristan's eyes turned brown once more and he

resumed his normal appearance. Whatever normal was.

"I'm sorry, my sweet. When you are threatened, I tend to overreact," he murmured, cupping her cheek with one warm palm.

"Oh, how very endearing." Mara clapped her hands, but her face remained cold and impartial. "Tristan, you are smitten. Delightful."

The Fae waved a hand. "I'll be on my way. Have a good morning!"

Nikita's heart did not stop racing until the woman was well down the beach. Tristan growled slightly, then relaxed as he turned to her. "Are you all right?"

She managed a nod. "I've never seen such a display of your power."

He searched her gaze. "You fear me."

Who wouldn't? "I'm a little overwhelmed."

"I would never hurt you, Nikita. Never." His face tightened. "I would give my last breath to protect you."

Tristan's hand dropped to his side. He looked lost and distant once more and she inwardly sensed him pulling away. "You need more time. I should not have brought you here, into the open, where that one could find you."

"You can't shut me away like I'm some buried treasure, Tristan." She fisted her hands. "I'll admit, that...witch...scares me, but I won't hide from her, or anyone else. I've done enough hiding in my life, forced into it because my family was trying to protect me from being abducted, and destroyed, by you. If it were up to me, I would have lived free and wild as a wolf."

"You always were courageous. That has not changed."

Courageous? Her? Far from it. I do a good job pretending, that's all.

He turned back to the hotel. "I can sense your distress. Let's return to the room, so you may rest."

Rest? She wanted to explore, not remain trapped behind four walls as she had been before. "No. I'm not an invalid." She studied the wash of foamy surf curling upon the shore and then gazed into the horizon. A red and white flag upon a white buoy floated on the gentle waves. She'd seen that flag in movies and books.

"I want to go snorkeling. I've never been in the ocean before."

Tristan stared. "Now? After Mara has seen you?"

"Wait until she sees me in a red bikini. I've got bigger boobs than she has."

Tristan's jaw dropped and desire flicked in his gaze as he glanced at her chest. "Indeed."

"If you're not going with me, I'll go alone. I'm not a porcelain doll you can lock away, Tristan."

"I wish I could," he muttered. He gazed up and down the beach as if searching for trouble. "Come with me."

Half an hour later, changed into a red bikini Tristan had conjured for her, and carrying a dive mask, snorkel and flippers, she ran from the shore into the surf. It was chilly, lapping gently at her ankles.

She glanced backwards at Tristan, following her. He'd changed into swimwear as well. It revealed a lot more than the black tunic and trousers and boots.

A lot more.

A shiver raced down her spine. Gods, he was sexy. Hot, hot, hot as her twin would say. And as cute and hunky as that other wizard, Xavier, had been in a green

Speedo that accented his muscled body and his very impressive package, Tristan was ten times more male.

His muscled chest boasted a triangle of black, wiry hair and his arms were firm with muscle and sinew. The black swim trunks were modest and hugged his lean hips and came to mid-thigh.

A faint memory tugged at her—the silky hair on his thighs rubbing against her legs as he lay naked atop her, fisting a hand in her long hair while he moved deep inside her, whispering a promise: "I will be inside you so deep, my sweet, that whilst I am gone, you will remember my cock claiming your tight cunnie, and long for the day I shall return to love you again."

She felt arousal bite, sharp and sweet. Nikita bit her lip.

He looked at her with a knowing smile. "Does my body please you, my sweet?"

Oh no, not going there. Her shoulders lifted in a casual shrug.

His expression grew hungry as he studied her with a smile. "You look most lovely in that bathing attire. Very…fetching. I shall have to stick close to you as your protector to fend off all the lusty males."

His grin grew wicked. "Very close."

The only lusty male in sight was Tristan, whose bathing trunks had suddenly developed an interesting tent. Cheeks heated, she tore her gaze away from his groin and ran into the surf, heart beating fast.

He was at her side instantly. "Be careful of the riptide. It is to the left of the rock and quite strong."

"I can swim," she muttered.

As she waded further out to the coral rock the clerk at the hotel's shop had told her about, Niki attached her mask and snorkel and began to swim in clumsy, big strokes.

Dad had taught her and Nia to swim, but his lessons had been brief. She never had much opportunity to use the pond on the ranch where other Lupines loved to splash and play.

She put her face into the water and saw the coral rock, and dozens of yellow and blue fish gathered around it.

So lovely. Enchanted, she swam among the blue fish, who swam upward as if to greet her. She waved her hand through them. They unfurled like a ribbon, as if her movements were hypnotizing them.

I could stay here forever.

She could hold her breath a long while. After tossing aside her snorkel, Niki sucked in a breath and dove deeper to investigate the fish. She waved a hand and the fish swam toward her, surrounding her like fans at a rock concert. Maybe this was part of the magick the wizards shared with her—a new ability to call animals toward her.

Time to test it out. She envisioned a big tarpon swimming toward her. Once she'd watched a fishing show on television, and the huge fish fascinated her. Niki flicked her fingers out toward the depths.

No tarpon. Instead, she saw several strands of brown seaweed floating in the water. It snaked toward her and with a sudden flash of movement, one curled around her neck, pulling her downward toward the left of the rock.

And the riptide, to suck her further out to sea.

CHAPTER 4

This could not happen.

Tristan stared, dumbstruck, as the rope of brown seaweed curled around Nikita's neck. With her fingers, she struggled to escape as it pulled her toward the rock. Then he shook free of the shocked horror filling him.

The seaweed tugged her toward the left of the coral rock, where she could hurt her head and drown. And then to his relief, he saw her shift into wolf. She snapped at the seaweed, and freed herself.

Good girl. He swam toward her, but the wolf paddled away, then broke the surface gasping for breath. Tristan waved a hand, creating the illusion that Nikita the woman was still snorkeling in the safe zone.

To his dismay, he felt the tug of the rip current. Nikita panted, swimming hard against it.

His heart pounding hard, Tristan willed the waves to calm. Mara had power over the elements, but so did he. Dear goddess, he might have lost her.

The ocean smoothed to mirror-flatness as he swam toward her. Tristan wanted to materialize them both inside their room, but too many Others were on shore. Too many eyes, and he wasn't certain if Mara's were among them and would follow.

He must tread cautiously, and then get Nikita the hell out of here.

The wolf paddled alongside him, not whining or whimpering, her gaze alert. He could feel the rapid pounding of her heart, but she hid her fear well in wolf form.

Her wolf was her best defense, he realized, one she had used to escape the woes of her sheltered existence.

Finally, his feet gained the sand. Nikita sprang forward, cutting through the surf, and then collapsed upon the wet sand. He immediately sent a tendril of magick through the air to mask her appearance so she looked more like a large German shepherd than a wolf, then he sank down next to her, his fingers fisted in her thick fur.

Good girl, he silently told her. You were correct. You do have effective defenses in wolf form.

Her gaze flipped up to him, and her tail thumped against the wet sand.

A group of Skins, including a lifeguard bearing a bullet-shaped red preserver, darted forward. Tristan pushed back his wet hair. "Thank you for your concern. I am fine."

Murmurs of relief came from the assembled Skins. He did not see Mara. Tristan sent a mental suggestion outward to the Skins, urging them to return to their former activities. But the lifeguard did not budge.

"You chanced that rip current to save a damn dog?" The lifeguard looked disgusted as the crowd drifted away.

"My dog." Tristan hugged Niki tight. "My best friend."

Several female sighs of appreciation sounded, followed by nods of respect from several Skins. As the crowd dispersed, the lifeguard frowned.

"Dogs are not allowed on this beach." The man gave him a severe look.

Fuck you. The words did not leave his mouth. Instead he waved a hand. "You did not see this."

"I did not see this," the Skin repeated.

"You will return to your lifeguard stand and daydream about Baywatch."

"I will return to my lifeguard stand and dream about fucking the women in Baywatch."

Nikita stood, shaking off droplets from her soaked fur. Tristan dropped to his knees and cupped her muzzle in his hands.

"You've had enough trauma for one morning. Let us go upstairs so you can rest."

As they walked along the beach to the far end to access the hotel entrance, two Skin women in bikinis sighed in admiration.

"So sweet! I adore it when a man loves his dog that much," one gushed.

"Do you think he's single?" whispered her friend.

Niki stared at the women and uttered a low growl, baring her fangs.

Hiding a smile, he gave her a reassuring pat. "Come, my sweet." Then he nodded at the startled Skin women. "Good day, ladies."

When Tristan and Nikita were far enough out of sight, he created the illusion that Nikita came out of the ocean and went into the hotel. Then he dematerialized them to their penthouse. Nikita shifted back to Skin.

For a moment, she stood there in the nude, then she conjured clothing.

You have no need to worry about me staring at your nudity. I am still too shaken to notice. I could have lost you. Again.

Her mouth thinned to a slash as she faced him. "What were you doing?"

Tristan stared. "Saving you."

"I could save myself. I told you, my wolf is smart."

"So smart she knows how to avoid a rip current? Or enchanted seaweed that tries to drown her? Without me to protect you, you could have been badly injured."

"I can protect myself, Tristan. I'm not made of glass."

"No, but you are mortal and flesh and blood and you can get hurt! That rope of seaweed was enchanted and tugging you down to drown you!"

She shook her head. "I can't even have a small adventure. I know it was enchanted. I enchanted it by mistake. It happened when I tried to call forth a tarpon." She lifted her shoulders. "The magick must have spilled over to the seaweed. So I shifted into wolf and freed myself. No problem."

"No problem?" He took a deep breath. "You're naïve if you think you called forth that seaweed, Nikita. Our powers do not work that way. It was dark enchantment caused by something else, most likely Mara. I am most displeased with you. From now on, you will not swim in the ocean nor will you go near the water."

Eyes huge, she looked at him. "You're worse than my family ever was, smothering me like this. Is that what you want, Tristan? Put me away in a box and take me out when you want me? Keep me hidden away?"

"Go shower," he said curtly. "You have sand in your hair."

She stumbled off to the bedroom, and shortly after, he heard the shower running.

Tristan waved a hand and removed all seawater from his body, drying his clothing. His magick was much more efficient than a shower.

He went to the window and stared at the ocean.

Deep inside he ached. He could have watched her slip away from his fingers like sand, and failed her yet again.

And now she didn't want, nor need his help.

Now was the time, while he could still communicate with Gideon, for contact was forbidden in the Shadow Lands.

Murmuring a chant, he traced another protective rune on the window.

A minute later, a tingle rushed down his spine, warning of the other wizard's arrival. Tristan turned to see his friend standing before him. Dressed in his customary red tunic, with red trousers and boots, his long dark gold hair tipped with crimson, Gideon, the Crimson Wizard, did not look happy.

"I know." Gideon held up his hand as Tristan started to speak. "I should have warned you when I discovered she knew you were with Nikita. But she means no harm. She only wanted to wish you both well."

"Mara tried to drown Nikita. That is an offense I cannot forgive."

"It was not my sister. Trust me, Tristan, she has gotten over her feelings for you." Gideon raised his dark eyebrows. "She has had more than nine hundred years to do so. That particular torch she carried? She extinguished it long ago."

"Then who else would wish to harm Nikita?"

"You're the Silver Wizard, Tristan. You have many enemies, like the rest of us." Gideon snapped his fingers and a crystal ball appeared in his palm. He peered into it and his forehead wrinkled.

"What?" Tristan demanded.

"I cannot see. The future is cloudy, my friend." Gideon twirled the ball in his hand and his long hair billowed in the breeze it created. "It means your future, and Nikita's, is tied to all of ours."

Tristan leaned against the armchair, his thoughts secret and guarded. He glanced out the window, noting that a storm gathered on the horizon. The waves began to toss to and fro, and beachgoers scampered for the hotel as the storm approached.

He knew what was causing the storm on this sunny day. When two members of the Brehon gathered, and their emotions lathered...

Not good.

"Perhaps it is best you return Nikita to her pack, my friend. I know what you were promised..."

"What?" Tristan stared at the Crimson Wizard as if Gideon had suggested he toss Nikita back into the churning surf.

"I warned you to guard your heart. Create your longed-for heir with her, but do not fall in love all over again. You will have to eventually give her up, for she cannot remain in Tir Na-nog more than ten days. You saved her mortal life with the potion, but the effects will wear off and she will die unless she returns to Earth."

"Unless she chooses to become immortal and drinks the potion of the Blooded Moonflower."

Gideon stopped twirling the ball, his gaze hard. "Danu gave you permission for that, but Nikita may not choose to remain. Do not interfere with Nikita's fate, Tristan. She could be the downfall of us all if you do. You are not in this alone."

Xavier had said the same thing, but not with that doom and gloom warning. Tristan scowled, his temper rising.

"I will never give her up simply because you are afraid of the future. You need to watch your damn whore of a sister and keep her away from my mate."

"I am not afraid. And my sister is not a whore. How dare you call her that!" Gideon's eyes flashed red, signaling the rise of his powers.

Outside, thunder crackled and rain pelted the windows. Oh, this was going to be good. He did not spar often with Gideon. It had been a long time and he needed to unleash his pent-up anger and frustration.

"For a fifteen-hundred-year-old Fae wizard, you are sorely lacking balls." Tristan flipped him the finger.

"That's it. First you accuse my sister of being a whore and now you insult me." Gideon hefted the crystal ball, and it turned a glowing crimson, crackling with energy.

Gideon flung it at Tristan. He dodged and the glittering sphere smashed into a vase filled with lilies, blowing it to shards. The pungent smell of flowers laced the air, along with the metallic scent of pure power.

Growling, Tristan lobbed back a silver ball filled

with his power. Gideon ducked and it crashed into the wall, blowing a giant hole into the pretty wallpaper and making the room shake.

"So that is it, eh?" Gideon conjured another ball of power and threw it at Tristan. It hit him square in the chest, but did no damage.

None of them could hurt another. It was the way of the Brehon.

"Your aim sucks," Gideon jeered as Tristan lobbed another energy ball at the wizard.

This one did not hit Gideon, but crashed into a glass pitcher filled with ice water. Water splashed over Gideon, soaking his red tunic and his face. Sputtering, he glared at Tristan.

"Chill out," Tristan shot back. "Have you not learned anything in fifteen hundred years?"

"You're a fucking waste of breath."

"Out of millions of sperm, you were the fastest?" He flung an energy ball at Gideon again, his temper sailing out of control because deep down, he knew Gideon was right.

Nikita could not be his, permanently, unless she drank the potion. And the price she'd have to pay for becoming immortal might be too much for her and she would return to Earth. He would have to give her up, for the only other way he could remain with her in Tir Na-nog permanently would be if she died. And he could not bear that sorrow again.

The bedroom door opened and the love of his life rushed out, clad in a bathrobe.

"Stop it," she cried out. "Stop fighting!"

Nikita flung a glowing white sphere at the energy balls. The sphere engulfed them and made the silver and crimson balls vanish. The sphere gently floated in the air, glittering like a Fourth of July sparkler. And then it burst like a balloon. Dozens of white and purple lilies floated in the air, then dropped to the carpet.

Tristan and Gideon exchanged glances. He softened his voice as he spoke to Nikita.

"My sweet, do not fear. We do this type of fighting from time to time. We cannot hurt each other. It is harmless."

She sighed, seemingly with relief. But Gideon was not relieved. He stared at her.

"She has your powers. Son of a bastard elf, Tristan, she has our powers!" Gideon wiped his forehead with the sleeve of his tunic.

He gave a humorless smile. "Our powers, turned to flowers."

Outside the storm quieted, now that they no longer fought.

Staring at his Nikita, he felt a sense of awed wonder he had not experienced since becoming the Silver Wizard. He and Gideon fought with energy balls often in Tir Na-nog. It relieved boredom and there was no harm in it, since they could not physically damage the other. The goddess Danu had ensured no one wizard could rise in power above the others.

But none of them could vanquish the other's power, either. Nikita stared at the lilies on the carpet. They slowly faded, and Tristan's gut churned. Her power had not lasted. A grim reminder that what lay inside her could not last, either, and when that happened…

He must get her out of here.

Tristan bowed his head at Gideon. "Gabhmoleithsceal,

my friend," he said in the formal words of the Brehon.

"Gabhmoleithsceal, my friend." Gideon apologized and bowed as well.

"I shall take care of clean-up," Tristan offered.

The Crimson Wizard nodded at Nikita. "My lady." He jerked a thumb toward the balcony. "Tristan, a moment alone."

A balmy ocean breeze lifted the strands of his long hair, making the silver glint in the sunshine. Tristan braced his hands on the railing. "What is it?"

"Crown Prince Alexander of Clan Drakon, one of your dragon shifters, was pulled into the Shadow Lands by his great-grandfather, Drust, when the prince was about to take on four red dragons he believes assaulted Emma, Alexander's friend. How the hell could Drust pull him into the afterworld?"

"When Sebastian was serving me he exchanged blood with Alexander in an oath of loyalty. Sebastian's blood contained the magick I instilled in him to allow him to travel back and forth between this world and the afterworld."

"And with the blood exchange Prince Alexander could also travel back and forth between this world and the afterworld." Gideon's gaze grew suspicious. "I believe you suggested this blood vow."

He blinked. "What is wrong with a dragon blood vow? It cements friendships and ties when one dragon leaves a clan to join another."

"And that portal is the one you created when Sebastian was serving you."

"Yes."

Gideon stared. "You said you would close that portal after you freed Sebastian from his service to you."

"I changed my mind and left it open for Sebastian so he could visit Drust in the Shadow Lands." Sebastian had used the portal as a gateway from Earth to the Shadow Lands and then to Tir Na-nog during his years of service to Tristan.

"That was kind of you to allow Drust to see his beloved great-grandson. Not wise, but kind. Most unexpected."

Tristan's smile grew grim. "I did not do it as a kindness to Drust. I did it so Sebastian could tell Drust how I endowed him with more gold after his marriage, and how close we have grown. Sebastian is like a son to me. He is quite grateful to me for all I have done for him and Skylar, his mate. And he will not visit Drust any longer because, as I reminded him, his life is in this world, not the next."

And the one report Sebastian had given him was quite eye-opening. Sebastian had said Drust grew quite angry after Sebastian praised Tristan. Drust told him to never trust Tristan, for "you're my blood, Sebastian, not that silver-haired bastard. I'm your family, not him. You owe him no loyalty. He's trying to take over my family. If I could get out of here, I'd smash his face in."

Tristan had found his enemy's weak spot, and planned to strike him there. Hard.

"What games are you playing, my friend?" Gideon asked slowly. "Do not trifle with Crown Prince Alexander. Force him to leave the Shadow Lands and get him back home. It is one thing to meddle in the affairs of a silver dragon like Sebastian, but interfering in the life of the heir to the Drakon dragon clan is another. Alexander is destined to marry and mate with Princess Sabrina from Clan Ciamoth."

Tristan shrugged. "Would I interrupt true love? If it were true love?"

"You would strike at the heart of your enemy for revenge." Gideon folded his arms. "You suffered a terrible death, Tristan, but you were made immortal by our goddess, Danu. You must forgive and forget."

"I can forget my death. And the torture I suffered." He stretched out his hands, watching the wolf claws emerge from his fingertips.

"I can never forgive Drust's actions in the vision I saw afterward." His body tensed, and the wolf claws sharpened. "After King Emer had me executed, he ordered my head mounted on a pike on the castle wall. Drust stole my head and waved it before a crowd. In triumph."

"Visions are a tricky thing, Tristan," Gideon warned. "They are not always clear."

He forced the wolf claws to retreat. "This one was. He gloated over my death. And I am certain Drust caused Nikita's death, and the death of our babe, something I can never forgive. He killed my son before he was born. Killed him so I would have no descendants, no legacy on Earth."

In the Shadow Lands, he had a plan to crush Drust's dearest hope beneath his boot heel. Embittered, Drust would suffer the most demoralizing defeat and never escape the Shadow Lands, never have the hope of ascending to Tir Na-nog and finding peace and the chance for reincarnation and eventual reunion with his kin. While he, Tristan, continued to be both guardian and judge of the dragons, and remain in close contact with Drust's family.

Gideon held up a hand. "Your revenge is your affair, Tristan. I cannot interfere. But find Prince Alexander and return him to his family so the marriage can take place."

He gave Gideon an innocent look. "Of course I will. I do adore weddings."

With a warning glance at Tristan, the Crimson Wizard vanished.

Tristan went back inside. Niki sat on the sofa, clutching the lapels of her robe, still staring at the carpet, scented with the sweet smell of lilies.

"I did that."

Tristan went to her and placed his hands upon her shoulders, giving a gentle squeeze. He drank in her scent, spices and fresh lilies and everything his heart wanted.

"As I told you, you have our powers. The potion you drank contains droplets of my blood, and the blood of the Brehon. Our blood contains our powers."

He waved a hand and the room was restored to rights, as if his battle with Gideon had never happened. Tristan went to the sideboard and took the little knife sitting by a bowl of fruit. He cut his finger. Silver blood welled up. He went to the vase still filled with lilies, dripped one droplet upon a tight bud and it burst into full bloom.

Her gaze widened.

"And that is what is inside me?"

"For now. It is what saved your life from the parvolupus disease." The cut flesh healed and he set down the knife.

"But it cannot last. The energy I conjured, the flowers...they are gone."

"Yes." His chest went tight as the realization dawned in her eyes.

"And when the power inside me dies? What then?"

Emotion clogging his throat, he managed to find his voice. "Then you die as well."

CHAPTER 5

What irony. Tristan had saved her, but it could not last. How long did she have to live?

Utterly drained and shaken, Nikita climbed between the covers of the freshly made bed. She, the wolf who had hidden away, now possessed a great and terrible power.

Nikita stretched out her fingers and stared at them. A power she did not want, nor understand, that would ultimately destroy her.

What other surprises did Tristan have in store?

"You failed to tell me about this," she said, fighting a sense of unreality.

"I was going to."

"Verbal ability is a highly overrated thing in a guy, and it's our pathetic need for it that gets us into so much trouble." She sighed. "Sleepless in Seattle. Becky was right. But then again, she never met anyone like you."

Tristan materialized on the bed. "I am sorry for fighting, and for alarming you."

Niki stared at her hands, which began to shake. "Why am I so exhausted?"

"The power you expelled. The first time you use it, it drains you. The same happened to all of us after we ascended to the council of the Brehon. For us, we replenish our energy differently. For you, sleep is required."

His sensual mouth turned down. "Rest now, and when you awaken, I will explain it all."

Instinct told her that he would not move until she stirred. For once, she felt glad of his presence.

Niki closed her eyes, willing herself to dream. Instinct also told her the past could be recreated in dreams and she needed to know what they had shared, needed to know before she faded into dust.

Knowledge is power, she'd often told Nia, her twin sister.

She began to dream....

She saw a woman lying upon an enormous canopied bed, velvet hangings adorning the posts. Her face was in shadow, but the woman writhed in pain, her hands over her belly. Another young woman wiped a wet cloth over the patient's sweating forehead. She was shapely, but plain. Camilla. She knew this somehow, that Camilla had become a good friend to her before the woman's mate had died. Camilla insisted on caring for her when the pregnant woman grew too large and ungainly to move about.

But all Camilla's ministrations were useless. The woman on the bed was dying. The poison she had drunk, innocently thinking the cup held a magick potion to help her baby grow strong in the womb, was seeping into her bloodstream. Her senses dulled by grief over losing her mate, the pregnant woman had failed to use caution. She had no male to protect her, no family to watch over her welfare. She was in tremendous pain and gasped for breath.

She was all alone. Niki's heart ached with pity for the dying woman.

Attendants stood nearby, looking helpless and grief-stricken. Niki watched as a tall, rugged man, his long black hair tied back, strode into the room.

Not Tristan, but another. Her heart pounded as she recognized the man.

Drust, his best friend and betrayer.

Drust went to the woman holding the wet cloth and pushed her aside. "She cannot be saved. Tristan's heir will die with her."

"No," the woman said, tears streaming down her face. "It cannot be. Why, Drust? She already lost her mate. She was innocent in all this! You said you wished to make up for Tristan's death when you gave me that potion to help her baby!"

Then the pregnant woman on the bed gasped and screamed her last. They pulled the sheet over her face, but first Niki caught a glimpse of the dead woman...

It was her. She had died, and the child she was to bear, Tristan's son, had died with her...all because his former best friend had caused her death with a potion that contained poison.

Gasping, she rolled over, moaning, sensing she had this dream before. No, no. Someone stroked a cool hand over her forehead and the vision faded.

"Sweet dreams," a deep voice murmured, and she knew it was Tristan. "Dream of us, my sweet. Only of us."

And then the familiar dream she'd experienced before began, as it always did, with her pacing the long, protected walkway behind the battlement of a stone castle…

She could see the turret close by, with a door she could access if she had to run and seek safety.

Sounds of war raged in the distance. Nikita's heart pounded with fear as she gazed beyond the fields to the forest where the fighting raged. The day had dawned cold and wet, and the battle had moved closer to the castle. For weeks he had been at war, fighting to protect the land and those he loved. But the enemy was strong.

Her love was out there. Would he return?

He must return, for she would die if he spilled his life's blood upon the battlefield.

Tristan. His name was Tristan, the guardian of Castle Baldwin, and lord and protector of shifters.

So dedicated to his people, not only Lupine, but all shifters, for the Fae had enthralled all shifters, making them into little more than servants. Emer, the Fae king, liked her mate, and had granted him title of the land and the castle.

But Tristan, and the other Lupines, were forbidden to hunt in the forest unless they asked permission from Emer.

This is not freedom, Tristan had told her, lying in their bed and stroking her hair after their love play. "If I must war with the Fae, so be it." He had placed a warm palm upon her bare belly. "For you, and the future of the child you will bear."

"I'm not with child," she'd protested.

He had smiled. "Not yet. But soon."

A shiver went through her at the heated promise in his eyes. Nikita had placed her palm over his. "You made a promise to me on our mating day, Tristan, a promise to me and our future young. 'I will always put you above all others, and your needs first.' Can you not appoint someone else to lead the war if it comes to that? Drust has much knowledge of war and strategy. He would make an excellent general."

He had gone silent, his gaze distant. "Let us not talk any more of war, my sweet. I am cold and need your arms around me."

As always, he'd silenced her worries with his mouth, and made fierce love to her, making her forget all reason.

That was two months ago, and now the inhabitants of Baldwin Castle, and all shifters, were at war with the Fae. Tristan, her mate and her love, lead the battle cry, despite her concerns.

Now as she walked the battlement, a cold wind made her shiver, despite the fur lining her gown. Worry needled her, as sharp as the piercing wind, even though Tristan was powerful. He held the looks of a youth, and possessed the age and wisdom of an elder. Once she dared to ask him how old he was and he had laughed.

"Older than you, my sweet," he had told her. "Old enough to remember the time when dragons were plentiful as the fish swimming in the sea. But you are my first love, my only love."

And then she heard the triumphant horns sound, and relief made her shoulders sag. Nikita peered at the gray horizon and saw a silver dragon take flight toward the castle as the troops began to emerge from the forest. Joy turned to a new worry.

Turning, she started to flee for the safety of the turret, but the dragon was swift. He landed on the roof, folded his massive wings and waited.

She sighed. "I know."

The silver dragon smiled, showing rows of wicked, jagged teeth. His tail swished back and forth like a cat's. Drust, Tristan's best friend and his ally in the war.

"I'm not supposed to be here. Drust, let me pass."

Blinking, the dragon did not move. Anxiety filled her. Perhaps the dragon had bad news to share.

"Shift back to your human form so you may speak to me," she directed.

The dragon did not.

Frustrated, she scowled. "Then do not remain silent! Tell me! Is Tristan hurt?"

Drust shook his head.

Sighing with relief, she pointed to the ground. "Go fetch him, and bring him to the chamber straight away. He will be hungry and thirsty. Go!"

The silver dragon stretched his wings and flew down to the ground. As she scurried to the turret, she peered over the side and saw the dragon lift into the air again, this time bearing a rider upon his back.

Tristan would not only be hungry and thirsty. He would be furious.

Nikita hurried through the castle until she reached a large chamber. The heavy wood door stood open to show a fire crackling in the hearth. The chamber was a bedroom. The same bedroom she'd visited each night.

Near the fireplace were two carved chairs and a wood table. Upon it were two large basins, one filled with water, and a stack of clean cloths. A trencher filled with fruit and a joint of beef were next to a goblet filled with ale. A bench was near the table.

She paid no heed to these pieces of furniture. Her

interest remained in the massive bed covered with furs. The furs were to keep warm in the drafty castle, but she had him to heat her body from the inside out.

The dragon rider strode into the room in silence. Nikita stood near the bed, watching him. Standing over six feet, he was strong and handsome. His eyes were dark as night, and his black hair brushed against his shoulders.

The warrior crossed the room to the fireplace. He unbuckled his sword belt and then carefully set it upon the table. It remained in easy reach. Always the warrior, never allowing his weapon to be far from him. He could fight in Lupine form, but the Fae were clever, and riding Drust gave Tristan an advantage in a war filled with flying fairies and sprites.

He washed the dirt and grime off his face, then dried it with a clean cloth. Removing his shirt, stained with the blood of others, he turned to her, the strong muscles of his broad shoulders gleaming in the firelight.

"You finally returned home, for you won the battle," she told him.

"I always win. Drust is a strong dragon, and one cannot defeat an army led by a dragon."

"But you are his rider, and his warrior. You are their leader."

A crooked smile touched his sensual mouth. "Your flattery will not distract me, my sweet."

Her pulse skipped a beat at the look on his face. "Distract you? From what?"

"You disobeyed me," he said softly in a tone that brooked no disobedience.

Nikita blinked. "Did I?"

Tristan took the cloth and dipped it into the warm

basin of water. He began scrubbing the blood and dirt off his chest. Nikita sighed with relief, seeing he was not wounded. There were a few nicks and deep purple bruises, but nothing serious. As he scrubbed his armpits, he studied her.

"I told you to never show your face where the enemy can see you while I am gone."

"Drust told you I was pacing the battlement." She knew the dragon would, for the shifter confided in Tristan.

"He worries about your safety much as I do."

Quivering with sensual anticipation, she watched him wash his arms, the cloth stroking over strong muscle and sinew. So handsome and virile, this man of hers.

"And I told you, I cannot cease worrying and watching for you while you are gone."

Next, he sat on the bench near the table and removed his boots and stockings, and then he stripped until he was nude. He washed his thighs, belly and buttocks, running the cloth slowly over his skin.

He gave her an intent look as he washed his genitals. His other weapon, which had slain her with such pleasure after their first joining.

Throwing aside the cloth, he turned to her. "You are stubborn, wench."

Nikita smiled. "One who is wearing too much clothing."

"Take it off." His voice was soft and steely, but passion fired his eyes.

"Are you not hungry?"

"Aye. Hungry for you."

The heat of battle fired his blood, and he needed her.

She would be his second conquest this day, but a willing one.

Slowly, she shrugged out of the gown, letting it puddle at her feet. Nikita removed her shoes, underclothing, and stockings. He watched, his dark gaze intent. From a thick nest of black hair at his groin, his sex swelled.

He was a powerful man, a warrior who killed, but he would not hurt her. She knew this. Even when his lovemaking grew fierce and rough, he never hurt her, for he had made a promise.

She lay back on the bed, her arms open wide, her legs splayed in invitation. His gaze darkened as he stared between her thighs.

"So beautiful," he murmured. "Pink as a rose, wet with dew."

Placing a knee on the bed, he kissed his forefinger, then pressed his finger to her cheek. Nikita smiled as memory stirred. Upon their first meeting, he had made the gesture, a symbol of his feelings from the start. It was his first gesture to her before they made love, and his last when he left her to fight yet again.

With a soft growl, he lay upon the furs and took her into his arms, capturing her mouth with his own. He forced his tongue past her lips, and she trembled beneath the insistent pressure of his kiss. Though she had been a virgin before he claimed her, she knew how to please him and teased his tongue with light flicks, enjoying his groan and the way he quivered in her arms. Niki kissed him back with equal fervor, glorying in the feel of his damp, hard flesh pressing her against the furs.

Too long they had been parted.

He tore his mouth away and feathered light kisses down her neck, licking her earlobe. He pressed a kiss to her shoulder, working down to her left breast. Her warrior licked the cresting nipple and a bolt of lightning shot between her trembling thighs. Nikita moaned as he suckled her, his fingers drifting between her legs. The gentle strokes made fire come there, and she writhed with pleasure.

She needed him inside her, now.

He raised up and looked at her, his gaze smoldering. "It was a hard battle, well fought, and my blood fever is up. My need of you is so fierce, I cannot be gentle."

In answer she spread her thighs wide. "Take me."

With a low growl, he parted her slick folds with trembling fingers and then positioned his sex at her soaked entrance. Nikita shivered with excitement. Snarling, he thrust deep inside her. She gasped, her fingers digging into the muscles of his shoulders. Always, the first time he entered her he met with resistance, as if she resented the intruder who claimed her body, her heart. And then her female flesh grew soft and welcoming, and eager to receive him.

Going still, he looked down at her, expression filled with concern. "Am I hurting you?"

"Never." She writhed beneath him. "But I shall hurt you if you delay any longer."

The smile upon his face was filled with satisfaction, and a gleam of mischief. Then his expression turned intent as he began to move, driving hard and fast inside her. She gripped his shoulders and wrapped her legs around his hips, feeling his flesh slap wetly against hers. And then she felt the climax shimmer in her loins and Niki arched back and screamed as he took her.

Shouting, his head thrown back, the cords on his strong neck straining, he poured himself deep inside her body, claiming his victory.

They lay upon the furs in each other's arms, as he stroked her hair. A feeling of deep unease mingled with the pleasure, and she shifted her weight, wincing at the soreness between her legs, and the discomfort of muscles she had not used for a while.

"You're mine. No one else will ever have you." His dark gaze was fierce, filled with passion.

"No one," she whispered. "I'm yours, always."

I love you.

The emotion was so intense, her chest hurt.

He took her into his arms and made love to her again, slower this time, and when she cried out her completion, he joined her, shouting her name as he pumped his seed deep inside her.

Afterward, Nikita drowsed on the furs, filled with contentment, refusing to examine the unease winking deep inside her, like a torch in the dark distance.

He smiled and placed a warm palm on her flat belly. "You are in heat and I believe we conceived our son today. We shall have our babe at last, my love, the babe you have longed for, the son who shall carry on my legacy."

A babe of her own. A child, created in love. Her lover was strong and virile. It had not taken long for him to impregnate her. She already could feel her womb quicken with tiny, new life.

He leaned over her, and rubbed a thumb over her still crested nipple. "I can see you now, your belly big with our child, and then suckling our son. He will be a fine, strong lad."

Niki laughed and playfully swatted his hand. "You forget I must give birth first. I have heard that is less than pleasant." She smiled, though dread filled her as she recalled the whispers of the midwives in the castle. "Some women have died birthing their firstborns."

The passion faded from his gaze, replaced with intensity. "I will never allow anything to happen to you, my sweet. Even if I must leave you, you will be safe. You are my heart and my soul, and I would die without you."

"Don't you dare ever leave me." She reached out for him, her lover, her life, the one who came to her every night, who claimed her body and her heart.

And then as he reached for her, the tenderness in his expression turned to sharp panic. Something grabbed him from behind, something with sharp and wicked claws. He screamed in pain and fought, but the unseen thing kept dragging him, hurting him...

This time, the dream did not turn to mist. She could see clearly.

His face bloodied, wearing his customary black tunic, and leggings, her mate stood on a wood platform. One eye was swollen shut from beatings. They had poured salt into his wounds, the bastards, to ensure he would keep bleeding and would not heal. The black-clad executioner flanked Tristan on bloodied platform.

A tall man with long silvery-blond hair sat on a throne behind Tristan. He was dressed in blue robes, his cold eyes green as glass. He tapped the armrest of the throne.

"I give you one last chance to confess, Tristan Kearney. Tell us where the dragon eggs lie and you will be set free."

Nikita broke through the crowd and reached the platform, her fingers reaching up to touch his. Chains rattled as Tristan stretched out his hand to her.

"Tell them, my love," she begged. "Tell King Emer what he wishes, and return to us. I need you. We," she put a hand on her bulging belly, "need you. Must your son grow up without a father?"

"I love you," he whispered, reaching out a hand to her. "I shall love you through eternity, Nikita. Heaven and hell may never separate us. Stay strong for the sake of our son."

"Tristan, please…confess. Do not forsake me or your child! Beg mercy from Emer and he will grant it. Stay with me."

Tristan closed his eyes and she felt his resolve, and his regret. "I cannot betray nor forsake our people, Nikita. After my death, they will rise and defeat the Fae."

"And you would forsake me for a cause? I matter not to you?"

"Not true. I do this for you, for our child, so he may have a future as a free Lupine, and not be enslaved to Fae."

"You do it to become a martyr," she told him, bitterly. "What of the promise you made to me on our mating day? I promise to put your welfare above all others. Think of me, Tristan. How am I to live without you?"

"Think of the greater good, and what this means for our people."

"The greater good?! What about me? Our child? Our life together?" She stared in stunned disbelief as Emer's men dragged her backward, away from her mate, her love, her life. He cared not for her, only for the great, almighty cause.

She begged him with her eyes, but he turned from her.

"Tristan? One last chance. Do you confess?" the king called out.

Tristan raised his head and faced Emer, his chains rattling. "Never. Our people will win this war, and be free of your tyranny, Emer. All shifters deserve to live in freedom, not enslaved to Fae."

The king's mouth curved into a cruel smile. "Very well." He signaled the executioner.

They chained Tristan to the poles and stretched out his arms, forcing him to face the jeering crowd of taunting Fae.

And then the black-robed executioner stepped to a wood table covered with a cloth. He pulled back the cloth, revealing a row of sharp instruments. The man selected a hook and approached.

Tristan paled.

The Fae executioner ripped open her mate's tunic, exposing the taut muscles of his back. She remembered caressing those muscles as he moved inside her, smiling down upon her as they made love and created the babe inside her belly.

Sunlight gleamed upon the wicked curve of the hook as the executioner raised it again, and then slashed…and pulled…

Tristan cried out, his eyes wild… "Nikita," he screamed. "Nikita!"

"No, please! Don't leave me, you promised to never leave me!" she shrieked. "Don't leave me!"

Don't leave me! You promised…

She awoke, screaming, clawing at the bedcovers in panic. She had seen in brutal reality the agony suffered by her mate, had seen how he died in horrific pain…

"Nikita!"

Two strong arms surrounded her, pulling her against a hard, warm chest and the beating heart of an immortal wizard. A beating heart…she tried to center her scrambled thoughts, push away the terror. His heart still beat. He was alive.

Sobbing, she clung to him as he stroked her hair. "Oh Nikita," he whispered brokenly. "My sweet. Do not dream of losing me. I am here. I am here."

Murmuring soothing words, he held her tight as she curled her shaking body around him, fear coagulating in her veins, her stomach in knots. When at last she lifted her tear-streaked face to gaze upon him, he looked at her with sorrow.

Tristan gently wiped away one tear with the edge of his thumb. His touch felt soothing and cool to her flushed skin.

"You promised," she whispered, fisting her hand in his shirt, grief forgotten amid the raging sense of betrayal. "We had a life together. I remember it well now. We had a lovely life and a passion and fire each time we made love. We had a child I was to bear you. You promised me on our wedding day that you would always be there for me, for our children, that I would come first, before all others. And you broke that promise."

CHAPTER 6

She had remembered the passion and the fire in their relationship.

Nikita also remembered the betrayal and the lies. Heavy with regret, he watched her leave the bed and stand by the window.

"I had hoped we would have more time together before you recalled that time and what I said to you," he told her, joining her.

Niki folded her arms and stared at the ocean. "You warned me. The most powerful and emotional memories surface first. Breaking a mating promise...that's a very emotional memory, Tristan."

"I did not break it. I put you first, Nikita, and our child."

"You put war first, Tristan. Your ego first, as you flew off to fight." She pressed a shaking hand to her temple. "I can still recall the cheers as you flew away on Drust to fight the Fae. Mighty Tristan! Our savior!"

Anger flashed in her blue eyes as she turned to face him. "Their savior, while I was left in the castle, wondering if you would return to me. Wondering if the Lupine I promised to honor and obey and share my life and my body with, would ever do the same. I was pushed into shadow, the shadow of doubt and fear, knowing you'd placed yourself in grave danger! I had no future!"

Guilt stabbed him but he pushed it aside. The cause had been noble, and the shifters had won after he had died. "You had no future without war, for what future is it for shifters to live under the thumb of the Fae? King Emer was determined to keep us enslaved. We could not hunt on our own damned land without his permission! We were forced to serve them, to till the soil of their farms. We had no freedom to raise our young, to form packs."

He drew in a deep breath. "I did not enter the Drakon War lightly. It was not for my ego, as you think. It was to rally the clans and the races of shifters to overcome Emer's forces."

"I begged you to rally them with Drust leading the forces. He was dragon and would have made a good general. And you jumped upon Drust's back and flew off, and from that moment, the war was all yours."

She stood, arms folded, looking as severe and accusing as she had hundreds of years ago. Ah the irony of being scolded for something he had done in a past life. Tristan shoved a hand through his hair.

"I want to go home," she said. "Now."

Damn. "You cannot."

"Fine, I have no home. I'll remain here."

"You have to accompany me to Tir Na-nog. You have no choice."

He paced the room. "The potion I gave you changes your cell structure, and it saved you. You must come with me to Tir Na-nog to renew your body and purge the potion in four days, or you will die."

Whirling, he narrowed his eyes. "A very painful death, for no mortal can endure the blood of the Brehon and the magick of the dragon's heart, and survive for long here in this world. Or the Shadow Lands."

Niki stared at him with huge eyes. "Maybe you should have let me die of the parvolupus disease. I would have been better off."

Fury filled him. In two strides he was at her side, his fingers upon the soft flesh of her upper arms. "And watch you die? Never! I swore I would do everything, anything, to save you from that godsdamn disease!"

"You failed to save me centuries ago because you weren't there." Her voice broke. "If you'd been there, I would have lived. I would never have drunk the potion, for you always brought me everything. All my food, my water, you checked everything because you feared someone poisoning me. But you weren't there and I missed you so much, so very much...."

Grief, guilt and shame rushed inside him like the ocean tide. He released her arms, feeling as destroyed as the crushed sandcastle she'd conjured on the beach. "I was not. I am so sorry, Nikita."

Blinking hard, she turned from him. And then she spoke in a quiet voice. "Drust was responsible for the potion. I saw it in my dream. He was very pleased to see I was dying, and our child with me."

Tristan went very still. "What else do you remember?"

"I was given a magick potion that was supposed to make our baby grow stronger. I'd had a little bleeding and was worried. Instead, it contained poison." She took a deep breath. "Drust had obtained the potion himself from a Fae…to kill me and our child."

Deep inside he knew Drust was responsible, but Tristan lacked the magick to see clearly into her past after he had died. He had only seen a cloudy vision of Nikita's death after he'd become the Silver Wizard.

All the Brehon could not clearly see their own futures or the past or the future of their loved ones. The goddess Danu told them it was to keep them focused on their duties.

You will pay, Drust. You will live forever in shadow, your name forgotten through the ages.

Silently, he vowed to proceed with his plan for revenge. He would crush the dragon in the afterworld and Drust would always walk alone.

Just as Tristan had walked alone all his time in the Shadow Lands.

Tristan fisted his hands, recalling the agony of his torture and execution. Helpless and powerless, his fate at the whim of those who tortured and executed him.

I will never be that helpless again, never without the kind of power that makes me feel like that. I will always be in control. Always. And I shall not lose Nikita again, ever. To the last drop of my blood, I will see you are safe, Nikita.

"And you will never be there for me again, will you?" She traced a rune on the window, the same protective rune he had drawn.

He doubted she was even aware of what she did.

"You are the Silver Wizard, guardian of shifters.

You have responsibilities and duties that will always take you from my side. You wish to become my lover again, and father a child with me, but you will leave us alone once more."

"I will always watch over you. I will never allow anything to harm you or our child," he said softly.

She sniffed. "Skype via wizard style doesn't cut you out for Father of the Year, Tristan. You only care about your powers as the wizard and your damn responsibility to save the world."

Tristan had always prided himself on control, but the thin thread he held regarding Nikita was beginning to fray. "It is not all I care about, and if you are not careful, my sweet, you will find out. You are sorely testing my patience and you do not want to see me angry."

He felt the rise of his powers, felt his irises begin to glow ice blue. He heard Nikita's heart beat faster, but she held her ground.

"And what are you going to do to me, Tristan? Abduct me? You already did that. Punish me for making you angry?"

"There is one thing I have not yet done," he said in a deep, low voice. "I've been patient, but my control goes so far. I am more than a wizard who judges shifters. I am a wolf who has desired his mate for more than nine godsdamned centuries, a wolf who needs you to claim you in the flesh."

I want to bury myself so deep inside you that nothing will ever part us again.

Niki lifted her chin. "Why? All you ever cared about in the past were your duties. They came first. Not me."

Tristan strode over to her, and clasped her chin with one hand. "To hell with my duties," he snapped, and he kissed her.

Nikita had never in this life kissed a man before.

So she could not imagine it would feel like this—electrifying, sending currents of heat through her body.

Moaning, she snaked an arm around his neck, clinging to him. He tasted like fire and hot cinnamon, and the darkest, richest chocolate. He tasted like all the sensual dreams of her most forbidden fantasies.

He would do more than make love to her. He would consume her.

Tristan tunneled his fingers through her hair and bent her backward. She could feel the urgency behind his mouth, the hardness of his body pressing against hers, the rigid length in his trousers against her soft belly.

This would not end with a mere kiss, but with fierce lovemaking.

No.

It was but a whispered thought, laced with fear. I'm not ready for this. Her memories of the past were one thing, but the present was quite another. She reminded herself that she didn't know this man—this wizard.

Dizzy with longing, she pressed her fingers to her temple as Tristan released her. His gaze had turned to onyx.

He wanted her badly, and he would take her, and take her again. And again. She was powerless to prevent it.

Judging from the hot throbbing between her legs, her body did not want to prevent it. *I was made for this, for love. Not to be hidden away like a fungus in a basement.*

Panting, he tore his mouth away from hers. "You shall be coming into your heat soon." He traced a line over her mouth, swollen from his fiery kisses. "I must restrain myself, lest I fall into a mating fever."

"But you are the Silver Wizard."

Tristan kissed the corner of her mouth, and she shuddered with need. "I am still Lupine deep inside, a man who craves the touch of his mate and longs to bury himself inside her."

She was innocent, but no fool. "You must have had many lovers over the centuries."

His eyes glowed ice-blue with power. Though she felt vulnerable with his obvious rise of his power, she sensed he would not use it against her.

"Many lovers, but never for more than one night. They meant naught to me but a fleeting pleasure. My heart always belonged to you, my sweet. Always. As your body belongs to me."

Nikita sputtered. She lifted the long mass of her hair. "I'm Lupine. I don't see a mating mark there indicating you're my mate, Tristan. Do you?"

"Not yet," he said softly, his gaze gleaming with intent. He traced a line down her neck and the mere touch made her shiver with anticipation. "I shall enjoy placing mine there, my sweet."

Then his expression turned hard. "But not here, and regretfully, not now. We must leave this place. It isn't safe."

She dreaded where he would take her next. In

this world at least, she felt a small modicum of control.

"Where to?"

Tristan picked up her hand and brushed a soft kiss against her knuckles. "North Carolina, to see a dragon shifter who once served me in Tir Na-nog. I released him from his debt of servitude and he now lives happily here on Earth with his mate, Skylar. His name is Sebastian."

He dug into his trouser pocket and withdrew a slim wallet, fishing out several large bills. Her eyes widened. "That's the tip for the maid?"

Tristan frowned. "Is not five hundred dollars enough? Should I leave more?"

She rolled her eyes. "I should get a job here."

Snapping the wallet shut, he shook his head. "You will never have to work, my sweet."

"And how am I supposed to occupy my days? Knitting? Watching reality shows? Or more movies? I'm sick of watching movies."

"Keeping me busy in bed will occupy all your time." He flashed a wicked grin, and she threw a pillow at his head.

Then he grew serious and held out a hand. "Come."

Did she have a choice? Her stomach tightened as she placed her palm into his.

Nikita felt the familiar tingle down her spine as Tristan clasped her hand and waved a hand, dematerializing them. Her mind went gray, and then they suddenly stood outside a large stone castle.

"Sebastian's home," he told her, kissing the back of her hand. "Sebastian is Drust's great-grandson."

"And he's your friend? Drust's relative?" The descendant of the dragon who betrayed you and had you killed? Had me killed, along with our baby? Niki shook her head. "I'd hate to see what your enemies look like."

She wondered what this compound would hold. More false friends? Or worse, enemies who would love to see her suffer because of Tristan?

"You are one se-xy sexy dragon."

Sebastian ran a hand over his mate's diamond-scaled body and grinned. "Let's get scaly."

His love code for "let's make love in dragon form."

As he shifted to his own dragon form, he covered Skylar's glittering body with his heavier weight. Sebastian's silver scales glinted in the sunshine of the castle yard. He loved doing this when the courtyard was quiet and everyone else was busy, this time with a picnic in a local park.

He slid his silver body over hers. Sebastian found her small, wet slit and pushed inside.

Ahhhh. Amazing.

After the months they had been true mates, he still shuddered with immense pleasure each time they came together, either as dragons or in Skin form.

He rode her hard and fast, as Skylar turned and snapped at him with her fangs to hurry it up, she was getting close, so close....

With a roar, and a burst of flames streaming from his mouth, he climaxed, spilling his seed deep inside his mate as he heard her high-pitched roar in answer and she reached her own satisfaction.

Shuddering, he collapsed atop her, and licked the

back of her long neck, smoke pouring from his nostrils, and hers.

Damn, that was good. So good.

A loud pounding came at the front door. Sebastian raised his head, ever cautious and wary for his mate's safety. He bared his fangs and blew a little fire over the already burnt lawn.

He was protective.

It came with the territory.

Gently he disentangled himself from Skylar, slowly pulling out and ruefully glancing at his long, slightly rigid penis.

In Skin form, his dick never looked so good or so big.

Sebastian shifted back to Skin and conjured clothing as Skylar did the same. He held out a hand to his mate, the regal princess who ruled over this clan. In her long, dark-red velvet robes, she looked amazing. Every inch the princess.

He didn't care what she wore. Skylar was breathtaking in any form, any clothing.

"We should answer that," she told him solemnly.

Sebastian knew this, for he had felt the telltale tingle down his spine that announced the presence of sheer power. "It's Tristan. I don't know why he's knocking. Usually he just shows up."

Taking her hand, Sebastian walked with her to the door. Skylar had a butler, but on days like this, when Sebastian preferred to have her alone, she gave him time off.

Taking a deep breath, he opened the door.

Tristan stood on the limestone stoop. The Silver Wizard was a foot taller than himself, dark and intimidating. Power crackled around him like the sizzling current from an electrical line. But instead of his normal black clothing and severe look, the wizard sported...

Trousers? Sebastian blinked and exchanged glances with Skylar.

Not only trousers, but a casual green polo shirt and... Sebastian glanced downward. Docksiders.

The wizard had a protective arm around the pretty, plump blonde at his side, who offered a shy smile. Judging from the smitten, tender gazes Tristan kept showing the blonde, this was the ONE.

It was about damn time. Tristan's got a girlfriend! Tristan's got a girlfriend!

Not a girlfriend, you fire-breathing moron. Tristan's voice echoed inside Sebastian's head, using the telepathic link they had shared for more than a century. She is my mate. My Nikita.

Well, are you going to make introductions or just stand there like a love-struck dope?

Tristan growled. Watch it, dragon. Respect. I am still your judge.

Oh yeah? I can still fry your hairy ass.

Not as much as I can fry your scaly ass.

Sebastian laughed, totally delighted. He realized with a start how much he had missed their sparring when he'd lived in Tir Na-nog, awaiting his next assignment on Earth.

Tristan cleared his throat. "My lady Nikita, may I present Princess Jewel d'Arield'Auberge au Rhagos and her consort and mate, Sebastian."

"That's it? I'm just Sebastian?" the dragon asked with a mock scowl.

"Oh pooh on the formal titles. I'm Skylar," his mate said, sticking out a hand.

Nikita shook it. "I am so pleased to meet you. Thank you for seeing us."

Polite and sweet. Sebastian squeezed Skylar's hand, immediately liking this Lupine. He wondered if she could hold up to Tristan's immense personality and power. That wizard was like a bulldozer on an anthill.

"Come inside, please. I'll make some tea," Skylar told them.

Sebastian stepped aside as Skylar escorted Nikita into their home. As Tristan passed, Sebastian caught his arm.

I suspect this isn't a social call.

Patience, dragon. I will reveal my true purpose soon, but for now, I wish Nikita to experience something she's never had before.

What? A ride on a dragon? He grinned. I give nice rides.

Tristan sent a little current energy zapping at his buttocks.

Sebastian winced. Ow!

Not dragons. Friendship.

As the Silver Wizard walked past him, Sebastian wondered about Nikita.

When they were settled inside the formal living room, drinking the tea Skylar served, Skylar turned to Nikita with a bright smile. "So you're Tristan's lover."

Tristan choked on his sip of tea and Sebastian laughed. Nikita turned red. "He is, er, my past mate."

"Oh." Skylar was blissfully unaware of the scathing look Tristan aimed at her. "Your ex."

"Not quite," the wizard said tightly. "My mate from when I was mortal. It is a long story, Skylar."

Skylar immediately looked contrite. "I am sorry if I offended you."

Tristan waved a hand. "No offense taken."

Reaching over, Sebastian squeezed his mate's hand.

Nikita looked around the room. Seeing the photos on the grand piano, she gestured. "May I?"

Skylar nodded. "Those are photographs of my family, and Sebastian."

As she perused the photos, Nikita's gaze went to the oil painting hanging above the fireplace.

"Drust." She stared at the portrait as if haunted. Then she walked over to the portrait and touched the gilded frame.

"You know him, er, knew him?" Sebastian asked. He exchanged troubled glances with Skylar.

"I remember him well." She looked at Tristan, who sat tall, foreboding, his expression shuttered. "He was Tristan's best friend."

Whoa. This was new. "I knew that my great-grandfather fought with you in the war, but not that he was your best friend."

"I never wanted to tell you before, because I know how you honor your family, Sebastian. But Drust not only fought with me in the war." Tristan looked solemn. "He betrayed me to the Fae King, and caused my torture, and eventual death."

Sebastian set down his teacup and it rattled upon the bone china saucer. "Sweet dragon's blood. Why and how did this happen?"

"I was hiding from King Emer's soldiers in a house Drust owned on the outskirts of the kingdom. I had just hidden the dragon's eggs that would provide enough magick to tip the balance of power for shifters and help us win the war. Drust informed the king's men where I hid, and that I knew the location of the eggs."

Tristan's expression tightened. "In return for my capture, Drust received one hundred thousand pieces of gold."

"He sold you out for money?" Shock and shame filled Sebastian. In the times he had visited his great-grandfather in the Shadow Lands, the old man never said anything. He showed no interest in the riches he had lost after he died, only in preserving family history and 'having you remember me, so I do not fade into shadow forever.'"

"I don't understand. If Drust did this, then why is our clan dedicated to serving you?"

"Drust's eldest son, your grandfather, established that bond to ensure all of Clan Drakon would never suffer as a result of Drust's betrayal. I do not have the power to punish the innocent, but he wanted a guarantee, so I accepted his oath of loyalty and service."

Deeply troubled, Sebastian felt his chest tighten. Drust had been a good teacher when he'd visited him in the Shadow Lands on his way to Tir Na-nog to serve Tristan. The old man had been so damn lonely, too.

"There has to be some explanation. I can't see my great-grandad doing something so heinous."

Tristan and Nikita exchanged glances.

"He also caused my death, and that of our unborn son when Tristan and I were mated centuries ago, before I was reborn to who I am now." Nikita spoke in a bare whisper. "Seeing him here, it makes me remember the pain we suffered."

Whoa. Sebastian swallowed hard as he studied Nikita's sad expression. "I have no desire to make you feel pain. But why would he do that?"

"To eradicate any chance of my having a legacy and descendants." Tristan joined her over at the portrait. "He once told me that my ego did not deserve an heir."

"Sarcastic, just like him." Sebastian went to the painting and touched it. "I'll take it down. I'm sorry, Tristan. I didn't know this about him."

"You are not your great-grandfather, Sebastian. You have much honor, and I treasure our friendship." Tristan told him.

Sebastian nodded, his throat tight. "Remove it, Tristan. Replace it with a painting of flowers."

"Or another dragon," Skylar added. "Anything but Drust. I don't want that man's likeness in my house any longer."

The bastard didn't deserve to hang in a place of honor. Or have any place of honor.

Tristan seemed to consider. He waved a hand and the portrait of Drust vanished, replaced with a glow-in-the-dark velvet tapestry of dogs playing poker. Skylar laughed and Sebastian groaned.

"Seriously dude? Can't you at least replace it with flowers or a nice landscape?"

Grinning, Tristan waved his hand again and this time a stately and beautiful oil painting of a dragon in flight hung on the wall.

"Is there anything else we can do for you, Tristan?" he asked.

"Yes," Tristan admitted. "But first, it would be nice

to partake in some of the normal activities you enjoy with Skylar."

Sebastian's eyes widened as he thought of the one thing that preoccupied them. Holy dragon's breath. What the fuck, Tristan? You getting kinky on me?

Tristan frowned. "Not that! I thought we could go to dinner."

"Dinner." He nodded. "Dinner is good. I bought a bar near here, fixed it up so the clan could have a steady source of income. You guys like burgers and hot dogs?"

Nikita looked as if he'd just offered her jewels. "Love them."

He'd used the word bar, and judging from Tristan's suspicious expression, the wizard thought Sebastian meant a place filled with lowlifes and rats gnawing on pizza crusts.

Tristan insisted on driving, much to Sebastian's chagrin. He had visions dancing in his head of his brand new Lexus turned into a chariot, or worse, ending up in a ditch.

But the wizard drove with expert skill, one arm hanging out the window, as Nikita sat shotgun. Sebastian watched them with feelings of amusement and trepidation.

When Tristan began singing "Sugar" by Maroon 5 in accompaniment to the radio, Sebastian had to bite back a smile. Damn if he didn't slay those lyrics. Had a nice voice, too, though Nikita kept stealing incredulous looks at him, especially when Tristan gave her a pointed look as he sang, "Won't you come and put it down on me?"

Each time he sang that, Nikita replied in a firm voice, "No."

Each time, Sebastian chuckled, and got a little warning zap in his buttocks as a result.

After they'd parked and gone inside the bar, Tristan looked around with appreciation.

Yeah, I spent a lot of money fixing up this place. Skylar loves coming here to watch games, and I wanted a restaurant where she could kick back and relax, be free from the pomp and circumstance surrounding her when she's holding meetings with our people.

"Nice," Tristan murmured aloud. "A good place to watch the Bowl that is super."

"It's called the Super Bowl, and that game is long over, Tristan," Nikita corrected, sliding onto a stool at the long, polished metal counter. "Get with the times."

Skylar paled, as if she expected Tristan to zing a little energy at Nikita for contradicting him in front of others. But Tristan's gaze twinkled. "Are you accusing me of being out of touch with sports, my sweet?"

She tapped one finger against her cheek. "Yes. But you are cute, so that makes up for it."

And then Nikita smiled, and the sweetness and wholesomeness in that smile made Sebastian's breath hitch. Lovely, yes. But there was a teasing innocence that was refreshing, and judging from the way Tristan drank in her gaze, the way he stared with longing at her, there was something special there.

Something special that went back hundreds of years.

She wasn't afraid of Tristan. No cowering, not even the quiet respect Skylar afforded the Silver Wizard.

Nikita treated the wizard like an equal. How refreshing that must be for Tristan, Sebastian mused. Often when he was in Tir Na-nog, awaiting Tristan's next assignment, Sebastian had seen his deep loneliness. With only the three other wizards as equals, it had to be pretty damn lonely, knowing everyone you encountered was either terrified of you and wanted to avoid you like leftover squid supper, or wanted to suck up to you for something.

Tristan shot him a look. *You love squid.*

I hate squid. Even deep fried, it's mushy and fishy. Every time you served it to me and said it was a treat, I wanted to barf. And you're reading my mind again. Stop it.

You never told me. I would have seen you had something much more suitable. Like leftover cow patties.

Sebastian laughed. When Skylar gave him an odd look, he cleared his throat and called for the bartender.

Tristan and Nikita ordered two domestic beers and four cheeseburgers, rare. Sebastian went with the usual fare for himself and Skylar: two imported beers and four burgers, well-done.

As they sipped beer and waited for their dinner, Sebastian explained the process of renovating the bar and expanding it to include an outdoor patio for summer and spring.

"We're even doing pizza delivery, as soon as we find a competent driver," he told them.

Tristan sipped more beer. "I'm looking for a new job," he deadpanned. "I could deliver pizzas for you."

Laughter erupted from Nikita. "He would be your fastest delivery guy, too. Imagine, Sebastian. Pizzas delivered hot in sixty seconds or your money back."

Tristan's mouth quirked in a rare smile. "Gives a whole new meaning to fast food."

He and Nikita clinked their beer bottles. Fascinated, Sebastian stared at them, delighted with this whole new side of the wizard. Playful and relaxed.

It's about damn time someone made you laugh, Tristan. You've been too damned serious lately. You're so gloomy you'd make an outing at an amusement park seem like a day at a funeral parlor.

As Sebastian went to open his beer, it sprayed all over his shirt. Sputtering, he set down the bottle and saw Tristan sporting a sly grin.

Skylar kept staring at Tristan with avid fascination. When he raised a brow, she blushed. "I'm sorry. It's your hair. With the silver tips, it's so...interesting."

An impish look came over Nikita. "He really should cut it. He looks like a hippie."

"I've always worn my hair long," Tristan protested.

"You should try something different. Maybe pull it back in a ponytail. Or a man bun." Nikita raked her hands through his hair and he made a purring sound.

Then she pulled it up into a ponytail, secured it with a clip Skylar gave her, and Sebastian laughed. Tristan looked so resigned, he almost felt sorry for the guy.

The Silver Wizard glanced at the wide screen television and then down at his clothing. "No Skins here, only shifters. It's safe. We need proper attire for this, my sweet."

He waved a hand and clothed himself in a red and white baseball shirt and jeans, and then suddenly Nikita wore a baseball cap upon her head. She laughed as she tugged off the cap. "The Yankees? Tristan, please. My team is the Red Sox."

"As you wish," he murmured, and changed the logo on her cap.

She put it on and their food arrived. They ate, watching the baseball playoffs. Nikita took little, dainty bites of her burger, sometimes pausing to eat a French fry from Tristan's hand. Absorbed in the game, she gestured, shouted and shook her head, much to his amusement.

"So you like baseball?" Sebastian asked Nikita. He swallowed a bite of burnt hamburger. "You're a sports fan? I think Tristan was into sports nine hundred years ago. Gladiator games, maybe tussling with a samurai or two. He's got the man bun down pat for being a samurai warrior."

The wizard shot him a dirty look and removed the clip from his hair. It spilled down his shoulders. Tristan handed Skylar back the clip.

"I've spent a lot of time alone in my apartment, with the television for company. I grew to enjoy sports. It felt like I was almost there, cheering on my favorite teams," Nikita said, her gaze centered on the wide screen above the bar.

Skylar exchanged a look with Sebastian, who turned to Tristan.

It's a long story, dragon. Nikita's family hid her away to keep me from finding her. There is a prophecy in the family that made them fear I would take her away and kill her.

Sebastian blinked. You? You're tough, but not a monster. What a stupid prophecy.

Then the wizard gave a real smile. Thank you.

On the screen, the batter swung, and the umpire called him out.

"Strike? Strike? He's out? Are you insane?" Niki stood up, waving a fist at the wide screen. "He was safe, damnit. Safe! Drop dead, you stupid jerks!"

Face flushed, she suddenly pointed a finger at the television screen.

Skylar gasped and Sebastian felt his heart drop to his stomach.

Holy dragon droppings.

The opposing team had all fallen down, as if they were all dead.

Horror filled Niki's expression as shocked gasps rippled through the bar. "Oh dear goddess, what did I do?" she whispered.

Tristan stood and flicked a hand, and the players all stood up, looking stunned, but normal. The television announcer was saying something about a sudden heat stroke.

"I'm sorry. I'm so sorry." Huge tears swam in Nikita's blue eyes. She hiccupped and looked miserable.

Tristan pulled her against him. "Hush, my sweet. It is all right. Everything is fine."

He gently kissed her cheek, then her mouth, and kept making little soothing sounds, even as the television monitor showed that everything was fine: the players kept playing and the audience no longer gasped in stunned shock.

Tristan had set everything to rights. The Silver Wizard stroked Nikita's hair, his gaze filled with sympathy.

"My poor Niki," he murmured. "You did not know. It is not your fault."

Then he looked at Skylar and Sebastian. Skylar kept gripping his hand, squeezing so tightly that Sebastian winced.

"Nikita has some of my powers," Tristan said slowly, "and does not yet know how to control them."

Sebastian felt a stab of deep pity. Nikita was Lupine. She'd only wanted to come to a bar and feel a sense of normalcy, with a beer and a burger, watch a baseball game.

Not zap the opposing team with a stream of power that toppled them to their knees.

They finished their meal, with Sebastian desperately trying to make small talk about the improvements Skylar had made to the compound, and how the clan was moving on to other economic opportunities. But Nikita looked woeful and Tristan's expression remained grim.

Finally, Tristan pushed back his plate. "Thank you for dinner, Skylar and Sebastian. We should return to the compound so we can talk."

Meaning: I'm getting serious now.

As they started to leave the bar, Skylar took one look at Nikita, who kept staring at the polished bar.

"Pleasure before business. You're our guests and we rarely have visitors these days. I need a mani-pedi afternoon." Skylar turned to Nikita. "Girls' night out, only during the day."

"What is a girls' night out?" Nikita asked.

"When we leave the men to discuss boring things like sports and ruling the world, and we paint our toenails bright pink." Skylar hooked her arm through

Niki's and Sebastian had never loved her more. "You and me, Niki. We're going to gossip about men and dragons, and have our nails painted and drink wine just like a pajama party."

Nikita brightened. "I've never been to a pajama party. My twin sister, Nia, has often spent the night and we've watched television, but Nia was always too busy to do girl stuff."

"Well, you'll love a mani-pedi. First thing I did in restoring the castle was add a day spa. We'll do the whole routine, even a massage."

Tristan and Sebastian smiled. Sebastian silently applauded his mate for her generosity in making Nikita feel normal again.

As the women chattered and climbed into the back seat of the Lexus, Sebastian glanced at Tristan.

"You can't coddle her. Or protect her from everything," Sebastian said softly. "She is a very unique Lupine, Tristan. But she is her own person."

She is indeed special. The wizard's gaze went soft as he stared at Nikita.

That is what love does, Sebastian thought with grim amusement. It makes the most powerful wizard into a slave. I wonder if he knows it?

I am not a slave, Tristan responded, irritably. I am a Lupine who has longed to see and touch his mate for hundreds of years. Nikita and I were married in the Dark Ages, before I became the Silver Wizard.

Sebastian fell quiet on the ride back to the castle. He wondered what the wizard wanted from him. And what would be the cost this time?

Tristan felt Sebastian's worry as clearly as he felt his own mate's anxiety lessen, the more she talked with Skylar. He sent tendrils of calming energy into the air.

Sebastian would be upset enough when he found out the real reason for this visit.

As they pulled up to the castle, he looked around with appreciation. The compound was breathtaking, with sweeping views of the valley below the beautiful gardens and proud stone buildings that housed the people. The castle was fashioned from blue limestone, with towering walls and circular turrets. Wide, open windows were cut into the two turrets on the castle, probably designed to allow a dragon to fly inside. Green plants and flowering bushes grew around the castle.

They went inside to the formal living room. Plush burgundy chairs and a leather sofa were arranged before a rock fireplace large enough to roast a pig. Vases of fresh flowers sat on the polished tables. Skylar had turned the castle into a home.

Their mating had been a good choice, he thought. And the outcome of Sebastian's last assignment, for he had assigned the dragon to teach Skylar all about becoming a dragon.

Sebastian had black curls that spilled down to the collar of his starched white shirt, angular features and burning blue eyes. The silver dragon tattoo that indicated he served the Silver Wizard, as did the rest of his family, curved from his neck down to his right shoulder.

Skylar: ah, there was a rare jewel. She was, in fact, a royal blooded jewel dragon, with waist-length curls of brown, ash, blonde and red tumbling down her back.

She had a light dusting of freckles across her cheeks and moved with a certain regal bearing.

"Would you like anything to drink?" Skylar asked, ever the polite hostess.

Her mate, on the other hand, cut to the chase before they could even sit down.

"What do you want from me, Tristan? Another two hundred years of indentured servitude?" He softened the words with a smile.

But Niki sputtered. "You enslaved him?" She turned with an accusing look at her mate.

"It was that or watch the Shadow Wizard turn him into dragon dust. I saved your pretty ass, Sebastian."

Sebastian now grinned broadly. "My mate would say it's an ass worth saving."

Then his smile dropped. "Why are you here?"

"I need a favor."

Sebastian blinked. "You, the mighty Silver Wizard? The man who turned me into a tiny dragon, only as large as an alligator, and made me live in scales for fifteen years, so a woman could kill me and cut out my living heart? Yeah, Wiz, I'm all about doing you a favor."

"It does seem rather drastic," Tristan agreed. Then he drew Nikita forward, his hand resting possessively on the small of her back. "This is what you did, Sebastian. Your dragon's heart created a potion that saved my Nikita from death."

Tristan glanced at her. "My sweet, why don't you go with Skylar and start on your spa day while Sebastian and I talk?"

Skylar looked worried. "Is this about Alex?"

Nikita turned to her. "Who is Alex?"

"A dragon shifter," Tristan cut in before Skylar could answer. "Sebastian's cousin, Prince Alexander. He is missing."

Sebastian's mouth tightened. "My cousin, who's enamored with another woman and not the one he's supposed to marry. I hope the hell he didn't run away."

"He is in the Shadow Lands," Tristan told him.

Nikita frowned. "I thought only the dead could enter the afterworld."

"There was a little glitch." He gave her a gentle smile. "Go, enjoy yourself. I shall explain everything later."

When the women had left the room, he and Sebastian sat on the sofa.

Awe filled Sebastian's blue eyes. He hoped the dragon would agree to his proposal, for he needed his permission.

One simply did not take a knife to a dragon's mate and hurt her, even if one was the Silver Wizard.

"So… I saved Nikita's life? With my dragon's heart, before you made me whole and mortal again?"

"Without your dragon's heart, I could not have made the potion, for giving our blood would not be enough to keep her body corporeal and admit her to Tir Na-nog. I am taking her there through the Shadow Lands. It's the only way Nikita can access the afterworld without dying."

"And while you're in the Shadow Lands, you're going to convince Alex to come home, right? He's got to marry Princess Sabrina soon and if he doesn't show his face at the palace, Sabrina's father, King Horace, will regard that as an insult. It could break the truce between the clans. Ole Horace is a stickler for protocol and formality."

"Alexander is a stubborn dragon." Tristan was diplomatic. "Xavier visited him and told me Alexander does not wish to return. I cannot force him back, for in doing so, I could damage his earthly body. He must return of his own free will."

"I was afraid of that. Alex phoned me recently and told me he doesn't want to wed the princess. He wants to marry for love." Sebastian stared at the photograph of himself and Skylar. "I know what that's like. I would not want to marry for anything but love."

Tristan watched his former servant's expression. "Did you know Alex gained access to the Shadow Lands only because of the power of your blood? He had the ability to be a Shadow Jumper, but it was muted. With your blood, it became powerful."

"Damn! I didn't know or I'd never have changed blood in the formal oath."

"It is not your fault, Sebastian. Alex is reckless and impulsive."

"No more than I was."

"True," Tristan agreed. "You dragons are often such."

"You've got to get him out of there."

"I shall. But this is why I need a favor."

Sebastian narrowed his eyes. "You're not going to hurt Drust, and get your revenge?"

He chose his words with care. "My first concern is getting Prince Alexander out of the Shadow Lands and home, where he belongs."

True enough.

"How can you talk him into it? Alex is pretty damn stubborn. He could stay there forever."

"Unless he is convinced his family loves him and needs him back."

Sebastian snorted. "Good luck with that. My uncle, the king, sees Alex as a stud to procreate and unite kingdoms. But maybe you can send me."

"No. You are needed here if you and Skylar wish to make that baby you've both longed to conceive. But a token from you, a blood sacrifice to convince him that he is loved and needed, will suffice."

"Anything you need. Alex and I have been close since childhood. He's pulled me from scrapes time and again. I'd do anything for him."

"Good. Then I shall require one of your mate's scales, which, unfortunately, I will have to remove from her skin. While she is conscious."

He let the words sink in. It didn't take long, for Sebastian bolted to his feet. "Son of a fucking lizard!"

Ah, the dragon was a little upset. Tristan crossed one leg over his knee.

"You touch her, and I don't care if you are the fucking Silver Wizard, you are fucking dead."

"I'm immortal and you can't kill me," he said without irony. "So will you sit down and take a deep breath?"

No use. Sebastian paced, his gaze whipping to the portrait on the wall. Tristan let him pace, let him work it out. Sebastian was devoted to Skylar and he sensed his torment.

He turned, and Tristan saw his pulse finally return to normal. "Why Sky? Why not me? Take my scale to free my cousin."

"It will not work because your scales aren't as strong," he said bluntly. "And a sacrifice from your mate, made willingly, would convince Alexander more than anything that he is loved and cherished, for you already shared a blood bond with him."

"How badly will it hurt? Will she be maimed? Does she have a choice in the matter or are you going to tie her down, dig it out of her and do whatever the hell you please?"

"She has a choice. She can say no. The choice is entirely up to her. I merely did you a courtesy by informing you, because I know the protective traits of shifters." Tristan stretched out his hands and stared at them ruefully. "Myself included. But I have the means to replace the scale with something that will not only make her whole again, but endow her with powers she has never before had. She will be nearly invincible."

As Sebastian digested this, he added softly, "Stronger than you."

The dragon waved a hand. "I don't care about that. I care only about her getting hurt. So this would be an extra layer of protection?"

Tristan nodded.

Understanding flashed in the dragon's eyes. "That's the real reason you want the scale. It's not just for Alex, but to give Sky protection that will make her undefeatable when she is dragon."

Though he smiled inside at his friend's insight, Tristan didn't blink. "Perhaps."

"Okay." He gave a deep breath. "I'm not crazy about the idea, but it's up to Sky. I'm game if she is. And I do love Alex. He's critical to the clan. I know Drust loved seeing me and having me visit and he's so damn lonely, but Alex has to get free from there. I bet Drust is coaxing him to stay just to have someone to talk with."

"Your great-grandfather is selfish."

"He's in purgatory. He was pretty damn bitter last time I saw him."

And he will become even more bitter when I am finished with him.

Sebastian gave him a level look. "I don't blame you for hating Drust's guts. But that's in your past and Alex is our clan's future. However, if Sky says no, I don't care if her scale can spring that whole frigging clan of mine. No is no. Deal?"

He smiled. He'd always respected Sebastian for serving him without complaint, and for his loyalty, but he respected him even more now. "Deal."

"Let's tell her now; let her make the choice."

"No," Tristan said. "Let them have their girl time. Skylar needs it as much as Nikita."

The dragon looked surprised, then gave a wry smile. "Damn, I have been hogging Sky all to myself, huh?"

"A natural reaction among mates. Come. Grab a beer and show me around the compound while they get pampered."

Two hours later, after Sebastian had not only taken Tristan on a thorough tour, but also enlisted his help in repairing a broken limestone wall, Skylar and Nikita emerged from the castle. Nikita looked much more relaxed, her blue eyes shining as she greeted them. He kissed her cheek, needing to ground himself by touching her soft skin.

Skylar's expression was troubled when Tristan finished explaining to her what he required. Nikita looked ill.

"Is it truly necessary?" Nikita asked. Then she bit her lush lower lip. "I'm sorry. You wouldn't ask if it were not."

His mate's reaction pleased Tristan. She was beginning to trust him.

"You can say no, Skylar. There will be no retribution."

Tears formed in Skylar's eyes. "I don't know what I would have done if you hadn't restored Sebastian after he died, Tristan. Anything you wish, it is yours. And Alex is needed by his clan. He is the heir. He is the future of uniting Clan Drakon and Clan Ciamoth."

Sebastian kissed his mate. "You certain about this, sweetheart?"

Skylar nodded. "Let's just get it over with. Now. The longer I wait, the more scared I will get."

"I wish I could administer something to make you feel no pain, but unfortunately, if I do that, it will alter the scale."

He looked at Sebastian. "It is best that you not witness this, Sebastian. Your natural instinct will be to protect your mate, and strike out at me. In doing so, you could seriously injure Skylar. Why don't you take Nikita for a little ride?"

As Skylar shifted into her dragon form, her diamond scales glittering in the sunshine, Tristan felt his former protégé's worry, but it was mixed with trust.

Sebastian went to the large yard and shifted into a silver dragon. He looked back at Nikita, who laughed as she climbed on his back.

"Hang tight," Tristan called out. "Enjoy. It is better than a ride on a roller coaster."

When they soared into the sky and were out of sight, Tristan turned to Skylar. Her huge emerald eyes reflected trepidation.

"I will not lie, Skylar. This will hurt like hell, but only for a moment, and when I finish, you'll be stronger than ever. Strong enough to resist not only disease, but any other dragons trying to defeat or injure you."

Skylar grinned, showing rows of jagged teeth, and nodded.

Tristan gritted his teeth and took out the crystal he had snipped off Xavier's hair. Then he removed a small silver knife from his pocket, and coated it with coldfire, the most cleansing, and potent of fires. Only with coldfire could he penetrate Skylar's diamond scales. The coldfire would numb the area, but only slightly.

Coldfire, his most potent power.

"One, two," he murmured. "Three."

He sank the blade into the chink between Skylar's scales. She roared, fire pouring from her mouth, and inside his mind, he heard her human scream. Tristan winced and dug. No time for emotions. He worked quickly, cutting and dropping the bloodied diamond scale on the lawn. He summoned his powers and turned Xavier's crystal into a new scale, glittering in the sunlight. Coating it with coldfire, he gently placed it upon her bloodied skin. It melded to her skin, and snugly fit against the other scales.

Stepping back, he murmured a chant and placed a calming hand on her body. And then watched, transfixed, as the sparkling glow from Xavier's crystal engulfed her body. Skylar's roar of pain turned into a howl of joy. Oh yes. Feel the power. Skylar would now be practically invincible in dragon form, unable to be defeated by even the most powerful dragons.

Trust. He trusted Sebastian with his beloved's life, and he trusted Sebastian's mate with such incredible magick.

Finally, the glow vanished from Skylar's body. She turned and looked at him, her eyes shining as he put the bloodied diamond scale into a protective bag and slid it into his pocket. And then she shifted back, and conjured clothing as Sebastian landed with Nikita. As soon as Nikita slid off his back, Sebastian shifted to Skin, conjured clothing and rushed to Skylar's side.

"Wow." She beamed at Tristan. "That hurt like hell, but only for a moment. The rush of power after? Holy dragonfire, it was almost as good as an orgasm!"

Tristan laughed, greatly relieved to see her in good spirits.

"What's almost as good as an orgasm?" Sebastian demanded.

"My touch with women, Sebastian. It is almost as potent as the pleasure you give your mate," Tristan told him.

Sebastian growled and fisted his hands, and Nikita giggled. "Tristan, please. Stop poking the dragon in the cage."

Skylar cupped her mate's cheek. "Easy, big boy. I said almost."

Judging from the way they gazed at each other, it was time to leave. Tristan slid an arm around Nikita's waist and held out his hand to Sebastian. "Thank you, for everything."

Sebastian looked surprised as he shook his hand, but

Skylar gave a shy smile as Tristan kissed her cheek. "Thank you, Tristan. For everything."

Tristan pointed to the back of the compound. "That back fence is most sturdy now. And you shall not have to worry about intruders or attacks. I warded your entire compound with my magick. It will not fade."

Nikita said good-bye as well. Tristan waved a hand and they dematerialized.

When they materialized seconds later, she looked around with a stunned expression. "I can't believe it."

He had taken her back, to her home, where the portal was to the Shadow Lands.

The Blakemore Ranch. He knew she would not like what she saw.

For everything, all she had known her entire life, was gone.

CHAPTER 7

Nothing was as she remembered.

Tears blurred her vision as Niki walked around the lodge. The entire ranch had a feeling of disuse and even the fresh aroma of pine wafting from the nearby trees had vanished, replaced with the acrid stench of old smoke and ashes. The cabin where Nia had lived was gone, burnt to the ground.

"Aiden burnt it because he did not want to take chances with the parvolupus disease and your lab," Tristan told her quietly. "Then Xavier destroyed the remains with coldfire to ensure the disease would never again infect anyone or the land itself."

"Gone? That quickly?" she whispered, staring at the overgrown pasture, the corrals where horses had once pranced and played.

Weeds grew around the lodge, and as the wind rustled through the trees, she could almost hear them sigh with regret.

"I had asked Xavier to handle any problems with Lupines in my absence and when he discovered what Aiden planned, he helped. It was for the best."

For the best. Her childhood home, her refuge, gone.

"My parents' graves…"

"Are still in the forest."

Tristan watched her quietly as she went to the ruined shell of her twin's cabin. "My things…"

"I'm sorry, my sweet. I salvaged your pajamas, and Nia asked Xavier to save jewelry plus the electronic files on your laptop and all the family photographs, but everything else was destroyed."

Everything gone. Her computer. Her diary, where she'd jotted down notes about the ranch and trying to find a cure for the disease. Her lab, all her brothers' things that she had kept in the closet to remind her of family—like their favorite baseball mitts—gone.

Even the stuffed wolf she'd had as a child. One ear had been missing and a glass eye gone, but she'd put it in her armchair, for it comforted her on nights when she was so lonely and could not run herself as a wolf.

Niki sifted through the ashes, not caring that her hands got dirty, not caring that Tristan stood by, watching her. Her life was…gone.

Nothing was hers anymore.

"Please go away; leave me alone," she told him quietly. "I need some privacy."

"I cannot. It's too dangerous."

Exasperated, she dusted off her hands, scrubbing away tears with a fist. "Dangerous? What, something will rise from the ashes and destroy me? A phoenix with rabies? There's no one here and I'm already broken, Tristan. Can't you give me a few damn minutes to mourn? Stop coddling me as if I were made from glass."

He looked away, his body tense, and she realized he had changed his clothing back to the black tunic, black

BONNIE VANAK

leather pants with the laces, and the soft doeskin boots. It made him look dark and dangerous again, and reminded her of his status as the Silver Wizard.

Powerful and immortal, a being not to trifle with. But she steadied her nerves. If she never asserted her needs, then she was doomed to become little more than the mild, obedient Lupine she suspected she'd been all those centuries ago. She would never be locked up again, unable to pursue her own dreams and passions.

Once she dreamed of having a mate who would love her and set her needs above all others. They would have children, and the children would have children, and as she grew old and contented with her mate, their grandchildren would play at their feet.

Nikita looked at the ruined land. That dream seemed as dead as this ranch.

"Tristan, please give me privacy."

Finally, he nodded. "I will be over by the trees so that I can still keep my eye on you."

When he walked away, she combed through the charred remains of the cabin, sifted through the ashes. Maybe her wolf was still here...perhaps she could salvage a small part of it, a keepsake.

A few minutes later, she realized the futility. Niki stood and fisted her hands. Anger was better than tears and grieving. She had grieved enough when the disease took away her family and all of the pack's males. Logically, destroying the cabin made sense.

But a small part of her cried out for the past. Her past, not the one she had shared with Tristan, but her past in this life.

She was not going to cry, no, not in front of him. Gathering the shreds of her dignity together like a tattered cloak, she walked down the path to where he sat beneath the sheltering branches of a shady oak tree.

When she saw what he was doing, she smiled a little.

Flicking its bushy tail, a squirrel ate a nut Tristan had held out to him. Then the animal saw her, scolded them and raced up the tree.

Niki flopped onto the grass beside Tristan. Her grass. Her property, and Nia's. No other grass would ever feel the same, for it would not belong to her legally. Suddenly she felt exhausted, her muscles trembling with fatigue.

"Is that how you pass the time? Feeding prey?"

Tristan flipped a peanut shell into the air and caught it. "I like animals, and squirrels are not prey for me. Not any longer."

"You don't hunt in wolf form? What about the night you saw me by the bonfire pit?"

He snapped his fingers and the peanut shell vanished. "The night you were so terrified of me that you tried to run." His gaze went smoky. "You need not fear me, Nikita. I would never hurt you. And no, I do not hunt prey. If I do, it is to give the kill to a Lupine."

She stared at the lodge, remembering the laughter of women, the times when she had come out of hiding to address the elders and play with the children. "This was my home. I have nothing now."

"Not nothing. I did ask Xavier to save this."

Tristan reached behind him and brought forward a battered stuffed wolf, missing one glass eye, one ear chewed off.

Overwhelmed, Niki cried out and hugged the toy.

His expression guarded, he watched her.

She caught a wistfulness in his gaze, as if he wished to be the stuffed animal.

Emotions churned inside her. She felt torn, for she wanted to trust and draw closer to him, yet she feared his power and his ruthless streak. But he had not pressured her. Yet. He had not pushed her into sex, though it was obvious from his tension and the hungry way he kept watching her that he desired her very much.

And then what, once he had claimed her, made her his mate? He wanted to sire a son, probably to replace the son they never had in their past life. And the biggest question of all remained unanswered...what would happen to her and the baby? Would he abandon them as he had before?

Words were words. Tristan had uttered vows of devotion centuries ago, and put war before her needs. Would he put his responsibilities first now? Surely he must, for he was a being of enormous power and duty.

She had nothing to guide her except dreams from the past, and her own instinct. But for now, she was grateful he had done this small favor.

"Thank you," she told him, squeezing the toy. "This means so much to me. Silly, because it's just a toy."

"Nia wanted to come herself, but Aiden would not allow it, for he feared the disease might still linger on the property. She told Xavier about that stuffed wolf. I told him to save anything of yours that had sentimental value and could not be replaced."

Sensing he felt almost jealous of her affection for the stuffed toy, Niki set down the wolf. "Long before I experienced my first shift into wolf, I used to pretend Jax was a real wolf and we'd go hunting. I'd sneak out at night when everyone was asleep and take Jax with me and prowl through the forest."

"I know. I watched over you during those times."

Startled, she stared at him. "I sometimes felt I was not alone…"

"You were not. I stayed hidden, for I had no wish to frighten you. But I would not see any harm come to you. By the time you grew old enough to shift, I no longer visited, for your senses were developed enough to warn you I was near."

And that was when she had fallen into real trouble and eaten the berries that nearly caused her death, which had made her father gamble everything to secure Pandora's Chest. She, Nikita, had caused the curse that fell upon the ranch.

So many choices and regrets. Niki plucked a strand of grass, her throat tight.

A cool breeze rustled the branches overhead, making her shiver, despite the sunlight dappling the pines. The squirrel Tristan had fed scampered down the trunk, and landed on his shoulder, waving his tail. Tristan conjured another peanut and fed him.

She was glad to see wildlife return to the ranch, for since the disease, many animals had pushed back further into the deep woods. Perhaps soon the wildlife would take over the ranch. Maybe it could be a refuge for the creatures. Certainly it was depressing as it stood now…abandoned, as haunted as a ghost town.

"Must we go to the Shadow Lands? If this potion you gave me won't last and I'm going to die unless you get me to Tir Na-nog, then why not simply zap me there?"

His jaw tightened as he petted the squirrel, which had jumped into his lap. "You cannot be 'zapped' into the afterworld, Nikita. Unless you are dead. The Shadow Lands offer the only safe passage for you."

At least he would be with her.

And then she caught his tension, as clear as his scent change, for his delicious aroma of spices and cedar changed to bitter almonds and cold metal. What was the reason for it?

She caught another scent, now, that made her stomach roil. The coppery, slick scent of blood. She had scented all that the day Tristan was executed.

"Are you going with me?"

"I will be with you as you enter the Shadow Lands." Torment filled his gaze as he stared at the distant lodge. The squirrel jumped off his lap and ran off.

"What's wrong?"

"It is not a place I wish to revisit, Nikita. The Shadow Lands for me are...filled with dark memories."

Sweat beaded her forehead. At least she would not be alone. She reached for the wolf and hugged it again, feeling her world tip on its familiar axis. Death did not terrify her, but the process of dying certainly did. Not for the first time that day, Niki wished her twin, Nia, was here, squeezing her hand and telling her all would be well.

"You went there after you died?"

He nodded.

"Was I ever in the Shadow Lands? When I died?"

"No." He avoided her gaze. "You went directly to Tir Na-nog. Eventually when I became the Silver

Wizard, I was not permitted to have any contact with you, not until you were reincarnated."

"Why? Why did I go there and you couldn't see me?"

"It was...part of my agreement with the goddess when I became the Silver Wizard. Contact was forbidden so I could concentrate on my duties to all shifters as their judge and guardian." He gave a soft smile. "If I had you in my arms in the afterlife, I would surely have neglected all my duties."

"When must I go? Can't I have more time...perhaps visit Nia?"

"No. Even now your body is growing weaker. You have little time until you collapse. Once you enter the Shadow Lands, you will be a little stronger, but eventually the potion will wear off. And the danger that followed you to the hotel is growing closer. This forest may be cleansed of the parvolupus disease, but other dangers lurk."

Tristan's jaw tensed. "There are Fae present nearby, and I know not if they are friendly. I doubt it."

She reached out with her senses, but scented nothing except the familiar aroma of pine, the stench of charred wood and the smells of woodland animals. And Tristan, whose aroma remained dark and deadly. Nikita listened intently, but heard nothing, either.

"If there were Fae, I would detect them. I know every inch of these woods, and if Others are present."

"There are Fae able to cloak their scents. They can blend with the woods and move through the air like blowing leaves. You would not know of their presence until they strike."

"The Fae who watch over the woods are benign."

123

"Not all Fae are benign, Nikita." Tristan stretched out one leg and folded his arms across his broad chest. "I thought you would have remembered that from your past life. Mara is but one Fae who presents danger."

Even an unfriendly Fae on familiar territory was better than the unknown dangers lying ahead in the Shadow Lands. She looked around at the trees, the grass, the gravel pathway and the distant mountains, and shivered. "I'll take a Fae, even Mara, over going through that portal. I'm scared." There, she admitted it.

"You must trust me, Nikita." He ran a finger down her cheek, a bare caress that made her shiver. "The portal entrance to the Shadow Lands is only the beginning of your trials. In the Shadow Lands, there are certain tests you must undergo that I cannot help you with."

"What kinds of tests? Physical?"

"Tests of courage, inner strength, and moral character. It is the way of the Shadow Lands, to aid the lost and wandering souls of Others who wish to move on to the next level."

"I'm not a lost soul. I know where I belong." Then she looked around the deserted ranch and felt the grief return. "Actually, I don't know where I belong anymore. Everything has changed."

"You belong with me. You always have," he said quietly, his gaze growing distant once more.

"Maybe we had a connection once, Tristan. I was your mate, yes, I'll admit I am remembering that part of my past life. But how can I belong to you when I have barely lived in this life? I've spent twenty-five years hidden from you, fearing you would appear and kill me. I can't simply accept that you're supposed to be my mate. We're in the 21st century, and women have choices now, even Lupines like me. This isn't the old days."

"In the old days, life was simpler. I miss those days." His expression grew stormy. "I took what was mine and no one questioned my choices."

Maybe someone should have, and then you wouldn't have ended up on King Emer's execution block. Niki bit her lip. He could probably read her mind and she did not want to argue. Tristan had now had hundreds of years to traverse the territory of the afterworld that was all unknown to her.

Once the unknown had presented an exciting challenge; indeed, it was one reason she'd enjoyed running as wolf at night. But now that the grim reality of this journey had arrived, she was just plain scared. He held all the cards.

And yet if she remained here, refused to go, she'd die. I'm too young to die. I haven't even experienced life. I need to stop thinking the worst, and step out and have a little faith.

Then Tristan's wistful voice spoke inside her mind: Have a little faith in me, Nikita. I told you that night when I carried you into your apartment, I would not harm you.

Setting the wolf down, she looked directly at him. His dark gaze seemed unfathomable and dark as night. This wizard could snap his fingers and conjure clothing from thin air, or lay a trail of destructive coldfire that would strip life from the land. And he fed squirrels peanuts. He was a study in contrasts.

She took a deep breath. "All right, I will go with you. I don't want to die. I'll return to your home and become your lover again, and bear your son if I must. And then what happens? Do I stay there with you?"

His gaze was solemn as he looked at her. "No. You cannot remain in Tir Na-nog longer than ten days, unless you drink the potion of the Blood Moonflower and become immortal. And the babe we will create will become immortal as well."

Jaw working, Tristan fisted his hands. "I will admit to being selfish, Nikita. I want you at my side, always, as my mate. But equally so, I never want anything bad to happen to you and the babe we will conceive. It would...kill me to see you die all over again."

His quiet concern touched her. Immortality sounded like a most tempting option. To never die, and never again have the grief of knowing her child died with her, or that their child would never die, either. "What's the problem with that?"

"Drinking the potion comes with a terrible sacrifice."

"And?"

He opened and closed his fist. "You will never be allowed to see your family again. You must remain in Tir Na-nog. With me."

Niki's heart squeezed tight. "Never see my twin again?"

"No."

"Never even visit for a brief while? Never see my pack again? Or visit Nia and Aiden when they have children?"

"No."

Tears filled her eyes. "What kind of choice is that? You or my family?"

"It is the way of the afterworld, Nikita," he said

gently. "But the choice will be yours. But I will become mortal as you so we may have ten days together to create our babe, ten days to relive what we lost. And if you decide against drinking the potion, you must return to Earth and I will return to my responsibilities as the Silver Wizard."

Life as a single mom? No mate at her side. "This sounds terribly one-sided. You get your heir and I get to raise him alone, even if I become immortal, because you'll never be home."

Tristan stood, pulling her with him. He towered over her, and his physical presence reminded her of his immense power and strength. He could crush her like a bug if he chose. "We shall have more time together and can live together in my home in Tir Na-nog if you drink the potion. If you don't, you will return to your pack at the Mitchell Ranch and be there with them. Aiden and Nia will ensure nothing happens to you."

His expression tightened. "I trust Mitchell, and your sister loves you. I shall watch over you, always."

Her fate was lined out just as it had been from the time of her birth. She hated this. Always she'd longed for love and passion. And now, to learn she could experience one, but not the other unless she lost her family, left her empty and embittered. Always she'd longed for adventure and to travel and experience life. Each time she watched a movie or read a book, Niki had wistfully imagined leaving the ranch and sailing across the world to indulge in other cultures and countries.

Tristan restricted her life as much as her family had. Perhaps that's what the prophecy truly meant—he would kill her dreams, not her physical body.

"Seems the only choices I have are pretty damn sucky. But can I have an hour to say good-bye to my ranch?"

"Of course."

He seemed so polite, and distant, she wondered if she'd offended him with her assertions. But she refused to be a meek doormat, without a mind of her own. Hadn't she been stripped of enough choices while living here?

Nikita raised her arms and summoned her magick. Feeling the familiar tug in her belly, and the delightful tingle race down her spine, she smiled.

And shifted into wolf.

Her senses exploded as if someone had tossed a bucket of cold water into her muzzle. Invigorated and exhilarated, she felt like a super wolf, able to leap up one mountain and forge onward to the next.

Tristan's gaze softened. "You are so beautiful in wolf form, Nikita."

Tilting back her head, she gave a long, low howl, expressing all the emotions she'd felt since Tristan had spirited her away from her home. Sadness. Joy at walking on the beach. Fear and sexual excitement. The latter had her pawing at the ground. He was right. She was coming into her heat soon, and her wolf wanted to run wild and free…and mate.

Run wild and free, yes. Mate…no. How could she raise a child when she hadn't even lived as an adult herself, yet?

I can escape him. I can find a way. But he's right for now. I can't stay here or I'll die. Death is not a good option.

Scenting a rabbit nearby, she turned her head and

bounded down the pathway, toward the old barn and the bonfire pit. Chasing prey was the best way to distract her wolf from the sexual urges shooting through her.

"Nikita, wait!"

But she paid him no mind. Blood hummed in her veins as she darted through the woods, crashing through underbrush, leaves crunching beneath the heavy tread of her paws. As wolf, she felt an energy her body in Skin had lacked.

She bolted up the mountain, ignoring the fact that suddenly her legs felt leaden and heavy. Still, she pressed on, needing this, needing to feel normal.

Even though deep inside, she knew this was not normal. She was losing strength again, even as wolf.

The scent of rabbit grew stronger and suddenly she saw it, a plump one, quivering by a tree. Nikita had no desire to kill the woodland creature. She merely thrilled to the chase.

A chase that was slowing down, for she could not run any longer. Niki loped toward the prey.

The rabbit suddenly shape-shifted before her eyes. Gone was the scared, quivering mammal, replaced by a creature out of her worst nightmares.

It was as long as a rattlesnake, with a slimy red body and razor sharp teeth lining its jaw. It looked like a worm, but it was as thick as a log. Hissing, it struck at the tree and sank its fangs into the oak.

The tree withered and died before her astonished eyes.

Snarling, she backed away, slowly...

And howled as the steel claws of a trap snapped around one of her back paws. Niki pulled in vain, her wolf instinct overriding the sensible human knowledge that the action would only tear her flesh. The steel jaws of the trap held her in place as the worm slid toward her. Jaws opening, it reared up, its yellow slitted eyes almost like a dragon's.

"NikitaaaaaBlakmore," it hissed.

She howled louder. Tristan! Tristan!

"You will die in the Shadow Lands," the worm hissed. "You will never become Tristan's mate."

Snarling, she snapped at the worm as it drew closer.

And then Tristan appeared at her side. He stood, powerful and strong, and pointed a finger at the worm.

"Be gone!" he roared.

The worm vanished into a shower of dust.

Whining, she sat back on her haunches, unable to shift back into Skin, the pain lancing through her back paw. Mingling with the pain was a deep confusion. What had happened to her beloved forest? Her land? Tristan said the forest was cleansed, but clearly, something evil had taken hold of it.

She collapsed, unable to stand the pain any longer. Lying on the ground, twigs and leaves in her fur, her sides heaving from the force of her panting, Nikita stared up at the darkening sky. Tristan was right. There were dangers in this world, and not only from her body growing weaker. Even her wolf provided little defense against such powerful forces.

She might as well have been on a strange ranch, in strange woods. This was no longer her familiar home turf.

Kneeling down, he stroked her head. "Nikita, I told you to wait for me. Why did you not listen?" he said, and there was disappointment twined with the concern in his voice.

130

Tristan snapped his fingers, and the trap vanished, along with the stinging pain. He laid a hand upon her bleeding paw and warmth spread through her. He healed her, just as when she'd fled from him in fear, the great and terrible Silver Wizard. With a gentle hand, he examined her body.

"No damage." He stood, his relief evident. "You can shift back now."

Niki shifted back into Skin, but lacked the strength to clothe herself. Shivering, feeling stupid and weak and ashamed, she curled into a ball.

She was growing weaker, just as Tristan had predicted.

Sighing, Tristan waved a hand, clothing her in jeans and a long-sleeved cotton shirt and boots. Finally, the awful chill left her bones.

"T-thanks." Her teeth still chattered. "Wh-what was that thing?"

"A death worm." Tristan pulled her close, running a hand down her back, and she relished his body heat. "They are a manifestation from the Shadow Lands. Ancient Others with tremendous powers can summon them at will."

"Why was it after me?"

She felt his chest rise and fall in a deep sigh, as if she'd exasperated him. "I told you, Nikita, I have enemies. They would do anything to hurt you, for it would hurt me. They use dark magick to manifest creatures like the worm. There are many more in the Shadow Lands that you may encounter. There is great danger and you must never drop your guard. Stick close to me at all times."

"What kinds of other creatures?" She lifted her head

131

and peered upward at the tree tops. "Giant spiders?"

"Sometimes. Only those spiders do not spin webs of silk, but a corrosive hemp that burns mortal skin." Tristan's voice deepened and took on an ominous note. "Most spiders are harmless if you do not irritate them. But others are more evil. Some are merely malicious. In the Shadow Lands, deceit is common. The most plump, delicious-looking fruit can hide maggots. A cute, fuzzy kitten masks a Grimoira, a ten-legged creature with needle-sharp fangs that spit poison."

"Good thing I'm a wolf. I don't like cats and I can live without fresh fruit."

She was proud that her voice remained steady, since she shook inside.

It felt disconcerting to realize that the land she'd known her entire life, her refuge, had turned into a murky maze filled with hidden danger. Her wolf had roamed these woods without fear, with confidence, relishing the freedom night brought. Now she wasn't certain if something worse than that horrid worm lurked in the forest. And the more she heard of the Shadow Lands, the less she wanted to go there.

His expression softened. "There are many delights there as well, and Others who choose to live there instead of moving on."

"Why would they stay?" This surprised her more than the dark creatures he'd mentioned.

Tristan gazed into the distance, his eyes growing thoughtful. "In the Shadow Lands are memories of life on Earth, and those memories are strong. It is what makes the Shadow Lands so compelling and disturbing. One can relive one's death, or a love lost. All who pass there must come to terms with their actions on Earth.

For some Others, it's too overwhelming. They may choose not to remember that a loved one or a friend or a family member is no longer with them. They can recreate those happy times in the mists of memory. And get lost there."

"Like living in a perpetual dream."

Tristan nodded, still gazing at the jagged mountain peaks. "It is not uncommon for someone to remain in the Shadow Lands for many years until he can find peace and self-acceptance."

He spoke in a low voice, and instinct told her he was speaking of himself.

"You had regrets after you died, didn't you? Memories you had to purge."

She was careful not to probe about their life together before his execution. But his expression darkened.

"I have done my time and passed on, Nikita. Do not ask me about it again."

He stood and brushed off his leather pants. "Come. It's time to depart before something worse targets you and you are too sapped of strength to fend it off."

"Maybe it's safer here."

"It is not safer for you. Even now your body, both in Skin and as wolf, is growing weaker. If you remain here, the potion will begin to break down your cell structure, and destroy you from the inside out." He frowned. "I swore long ago I would never again permit myself to allow anything to harm you, and I will protect you with every ounce of my power. You accuse me of keeping you in a box, but rather a box filled with comfort than the dangers you just faced. Will you now listen to me?"

"A box can be a coffin. And ignorance is not bliss,

Tristan. You could have warned me more about those…things. I'm not stupid."

"No, you are not, but you are innocent. In more ways than one. You cannot remain here much longer."

"Great choices. If I stay here I die. If I go into the Shadow Lands, I'll get attacked by giant things with teeth or disgusting maggots. I'll take what's behind door number three."

"There is no door number three." Tristan held out his hand. "Come."

She did not take it. "Why are you doing this to me, Tristan? You said you had moved on. Why didn't you choose another? A Lupine who would be only too happy to become your mate in Tir Na-nog and bear your son."

An ethereal glow ignited his eyes. "You are the only one for me, Nikita. Having you back in my arms was the only request I made when I became the Silver Wizard. I wanted nothing else. Not riches, nor a glittering palace made of silver, nor power. Just you. You were promised to me ages ago. And it is time to fulfill that promise."

"And I get no say in the matter? We're not living in the Dark Ages anymore, Tristan. I have choices!"

"You do. You can remain here and die an agonizing death."

"You could have let me die in my own bed, with my sister near me," she whispered.

His jaw turned to stone. "No. I swore I would not let you go or allow you to come to any harm. I swore to not force you, Nikita. But I will not allow you to remain here to turn into a puddle of rotting flesh."

When he put it that way…

Darkness began to fall upon the ranch as she reluctantly placed her hand into his. Tristan led her down the mountain, back to the bonfire pit and the scum-covered pond. Seeing the pond filled her with sadness. Once she and Nia, in rare moments, had splashed and played here, their privacy fiercely guarded by their protective older brothers. Those innocent, happy times were few, but she'd cherished each one.

Now they were distant memories. Would she relive those in the Shadow Lands as well as the darker memories? Niki thought of the deaths of her family, and all the ranch's males, and shuddered. She had no desire to step back into the past and relive every single, anguished moment.

Blinking, she stared down into the dark, algae-covered depths of the pond that had been crystal clear when she and Nia shared a few precious hours here as children.

"This is my family's pond. I swam in it with Nia when we were young."

Tristan gave her a solemn look. "It's the entrance to the Shadow Lands. This is the only way you may access Tir Na-nog."

She stared at him. Was he nuts? "It's a pond."

"There are many such entrances. This one has been here all along on your land."

Heart pounding, she stared at the murky water. Moonlight cast an eerie silver glow upon the mirrored surface. It was quiet in the forest. So quiet.

Tristan removed the diamond dragon scale from his pocket and murmured a chant. Waving his right hand, the water suddenly turned white, with swirls of silver, a spinning vortex like a wormhole she'd seen on Star

Trek. Wind blew at her hair and a chill raced down her spine. He stood in the wind, his long hair blowing back, his expression implacable in the eerie glow of the light water.

Then he tossed the diamond dragon scale into the water. The scale vanished, and the water returned to normal.

"What…was that?" she asked, her voice trembling.

"I sent the dragon scale into the Shadow Lands to a safe place where I may retrieve it later." He looked at her solemnly.

"Your magick is that powerful?"

"Of course. Are you ready, my sweet, to cross over?"

Suddenly she wished her twin were here to give her advice. Nia always knew what to do. Nia, the stronger twin.

And you walk alone now. Nia has her mate.

The thought pierced her with sadness. She glanced at Tristan. All her life she'd feared this wizard causing her a painful death and that fear was hard to fully set aside. It was like being told as a child to fear flames because they could burn you to death and then being asked to build a campfire. But he was the only one who could guide her through the darkness.

I don't want to die. I feel like it's time for me to finally start living.

"Jump into the water and it will pull you to the other side." Tristan's voice deepened. "And then we shall walk through the Shadow Lands and access Tir Na-nog."

His home, the place where it was prophesized she would become his bride and die. Fear rippled down her spine. Everything unknown stared her in the face. She was about to enter the afterworld, a place Others went only when they died. Her natural instinct balked at jumping.

"I can't do this."

He held out a hand, his dark gaze intent. "I promise I will not let anything happen to you. This is the only way for you to reach Tir Na-nog, to live, Nikita."

Where they would create a baby, a baby with an absent father. A baby, who would tie her to Tristan for life. If the prophecy didn't come true and she didn't die after becoming Tristan's bride, she could never find another mate because any other Lupine would be too afraid of the Silver Wizard's power…and his claim on her.

She continued to hold his gaze. All her life she'd been pushed around, shoved into a dark corner, never allowed to show her true face. If she capitulated now, she might as well return to being the ghost of a Lupine she'd been all her life.

"Then if I am to do this with you, Tristan, I want…I need…a promise as well."

He said nothing.

"I will do as you ask, go with you through the Shadow Lands to your home and bear your child, if you promise I will come first for as long as we're together. Meet my needs, and put me before your other concerns. Your wizardly duties. At all costs."

Doubt filled her. He had not placed her first in their prior relationship, and now he was the almighty Silver Wizard, guardian of their kind. Asking him to set aside his duties and responsibilities was like asking the wind to stop blowing.

"You know not what you ask, Nikita."

An ominous note threaded through his deep voice.

"I know very well what I'm asking. Is it a deal? Or do I remain here, and slowly die?"

He sighed, a sound filled with sorrow. "I cannot bear that."

"Then choose."

"Yes," he said quietly. "I promise to put your needs before all other concerns, Nikita. Now, will you go into the portal? You have little time left before your body succumbs to the effects of the potion."

Strength was rapidly leaving her body. Niki knew he was right. But all her Lupine instincts resisted jumping into the water and the unknown.

"It's so dark," she murmured.

Tristan waved a hand. "Is this better?"

The water had turned crystal-clear blue, lit as if from within.

"I could quote from the Titanic." Twisting her hands, she stared at the depths. "But I'm too scared."

"Then I shall. I won't let go, Nikita. I cannot go with you, but I will never let go." He picked up her hand and brushed a soft kiss against her knuckles. "Titanic. I'm your Jack. Promise me you'll never let go, Nikita. You will survive. You must."

"I'll never let go. Just like Rose didn't," she whispered. "But damn, I'm so afraid that if I jump, I'll die. I don't want to die."

"I promise you will not die, my sweet. Jump. Jump and I'll be with you in spirit."

She jumped. Just before she was sucked under, she saw Tristan standing on the shore, his expression filled with regret.

"I'm sorry, my sweet. I cannot go. You must make this journey alone."

And then the current sucked her down, into the blue depths.

CHAPTER 8

It was amazingly blue, so blue she wanted to die.

This was death, Niki thought, struggling to breathe. Blue surrounded her, the brilliant turquoise of a thousand clear oceans, pressing against her skin. She lost air, and gasped. On the verge of panic, she looked up and saw a brilliant white light, a circle of energy cutting through the thick turquoise.

Tristan spoke inside her mind. "Just breathe. Relax. The first time is like being reborn. Let it happen. Your body will adjust."

But fear clogged her veins. She couldn't suck in enough air, all the water and the pressure closing in around her. She was going to die.

She felt the whisper of a kiss undulating through the water, and then it touched her mouth, as if his thoughts gave her breath. As she took in air, calm replaced the panic. He kept kissing her as they ascended through the water, sending fresh, clear oxygen into her lungs.

Niki swam upward, toward the pulsing white light, and then broke the surface.

Bright sunlight gleamed overhead in a clear blue

sky. The pond was an exact replica of the one on her land, so precise she wondered if she were still home, on Earth. She started to tread water and realized her feet touched the sandy bottom.

She emerged from the pool and stood on the banks. If these were the Shadow Lands, then they looked oddly safe and beautiful. Her clothing was dry, her body and hair dry as well. Anger churned inside her as she saw Tristan leaning against a tree. Dressed in his customary black, he studied her.

"You lied. Before I jumped, you said you'd be with me."

"Not precisely. I told you I would be with you in the Shadow Lands, and here I am."

"Bastard," she whispered. "Semantics."

Tristan sighed, and his hand trembled as he shoved it through his long hair, as if her words agitated him. She had never seen him this shaken before and wondered what had caused it.

"I knew you would not go without me, but I could not accompany you. It is forbidden. Everyone must make the journey alone to the Shadow Lands, just as everyone dies alone." He detached himself from the tree and strode toward her. "Even I did."

"Lying ruins your credibility, Tristan. What other lies have you told me?"

"It was not a lie. I told you I would be with you in the Shadow Lands." He spread out his arms. "Here I am."

But where was here? "All I did was half-drown. I never left."

"Not quite. You are in the Shadow Lands. When you first cross over, everything looks like what was dear to you on Earth. But it is not Earth." Tristan dragged in a deep breath. "Close your eyes."

She did.

"Open them."

Niki looked around in sheer awe. The forest, which had resembled the one on her ranch, had now changed to trees featuring colorful yellow and crimson leaves tipped with silver and gold.

Dozens of green and blue dragonflies danced in the cool twilight air, their wings beating furiously. They circled her, playfully drawing near and then darting away. She laughed and twirled.

"It's like a welcoming committee. I adore dragonflies."

"They're Fae," Tristan said solemnly. "Fairies. Watch out. Some bite."

But she was too enchanted to pay him heed. Niki stretched out her finger and one landed upon it. And then she felt a sharp nip.

"Ow!" She stared at the fairy, who showed two very long, needle-like fangs, crimson with her blood.

Niki shook her finger and the fairy flitted away, the sound of its high-pitched giggle echoing in its wake.

"There is beauty here. I created the illusion of sunlight and the blue sky to make the Shadow Lands less foreign to you upon your entry." Tristan joined her, his hands behind his back. "There is ugliness as well. Danger. Some comes from creatures, like the fairies, who have chosen to stay here and embrace their dark side. Do not leave my side, Nikita. I must guide you through this. I will aid you as I can, but each Other's journey is highly personal, based on what they need to purge and forgive. My powers are diminished here and

142

I may not be able to protect you as much as I can on Earth."

Fear skated down her spine. Tristan looked darker, and more menacing. The customary black tunic and black leather pants looked muddied and stained, and his doeskin boots bore brownish stains.

Blood?

"If your powers are not as strong, how can you find Alex?"

"I already found him. I have visited Drust, incognito, and seen his great-grandson." Tristan's expression darkened. "And after I send Alexander home, I shall have my revenge upon his ancestor. That power was granted to me long ago."

"And you waited all this time for revenge? Why?"

"Because you came first. You, and your needs. And your safety."

"What happens now?" She felt on uncertain footing, as if she were crossing a pretty but roaring creek, on wet, wobbly stones. One misstep and she could fall down into the raging waters.

"The Shadow Lands manifest your deepest desires and your darkest fears." He paused, lacing his hands behind his back. "That is what makes them so damn dangerous. You must take care at all times, Nikita. You are not dead, but you are not among the living anymore. The dead appear as corporeal flesh, but they are only spirit. Still, they can hurt you. There is great magick here."

His eyes were cold, nearly lifeless, not sparking with the faint teasing humor that she'd grown accustomed to. Dark bristles shadowed his taut jaw. The beard stubble made him look even sexier, but also edgier and more dangerous.

"Since this is your first time here, and things may seem overwhelming, think of a place you would love to visit and we shall be there."

Closing her eyes, she envisioned a long, sandy beach, windswept and slightly cool, with sea oats waving in the breeze.

When she opened her eyes, they were standing on the sand. Behind them the ocean seemed to stretch endlessly onward, and the beach curved around in a giant horseshoe shape. They were in a large cove, with luxurious waterfront homes on one edge of the horseshoe, and a lighthouse and pier on the opposite side. But the skies were leaden with clouds and the air felt cold and lifeless.

Niki turned and looked toward the mainland. A gray, weather-beaten hotel read "Sandy Shores Inn." The building was a 1910 two-story Victorian house that had been converted to a bed and breakfast.

Tristan looked around.

"I've always wanted to visit a beach in Maine," she explained. "And this inn looked quite lovely from the website. They serve homemade waffles with whipped cream and chocolate, and sausage and eggs for breakfast."

The smile he gave her was not amused, but grim. "Beaches and housing in the Shadow Lands can be deceptive."

They began to walk on the sands. Sunlight peeked out now and then from the clouds, glinting on the tawny sand, picking out flecks of brilliant quartz. She looked at the houses peppering the shoreline. And then she stopped with a sudden realization.

Some of the houses had the quiet charm of

beachfront homes she'd seen along Maine's shoreline. But others...

They were built at crazy angles. One was upside down, one built on a slant that made it nearly impossible to stand straight.

"As I said, the beaches here can be deceptive, especially after one first enters the Shadow Lands."

She went to the water lapping at the shore, and tested it with one finger. Cold, just as she'd imagined.

"Since you are the only true living mortal here in the Shadow Lands, there will be...creatures...who are attracted to you and your life force. Most will be merely curious. Some will want to devour that life force."

"I'd like to see the inn." Her voice sounded a little shaky, but she kept her gaze centered on him.

They walked up the wood steps of the inn. The view was splendid from the second story porch, but in the distant water she saw a floundering shape.

"It's a whale." Delight filled her. "I wish I had binoculars."

Suddenly a pair appeared in her hands. Not questioning the gift, she held the glasses to her eyes.

Horror pulsed through her.

It looked like a whale, but this creature was no gentle mammal eating krill. It was as large as a house, and had jagged dagger teeth. It rose out of the water and snapped at a bird flying overhead. The helpless bird struggled, and then vanished into the maw of the sea animal.

Her heart was heavy as she lowered the glasses. Tristan looked at her quietly.

"You're right. Nothing here is as it seems." Nikita's hand shook.

"In Tir Na-nog, the whales are simply whales and the homes are all whatever you wish. But here, you share space with Others who work out their own pasts, dreams…and tormented nightmares."

She'd had enough nightmares on Earth, thank you very much. But he'd created sunshine and blue skies, so perhaps she could create beauty as well. "I want to explore. Are there mountains here? I've always longed to go camping in the mountains."

"Yes, but the mountains can hold danger. Rockslides, if you are not careful."

"Well, what about another beach?"

"We need to press on," he said tightly. "This is not adventure land, Nikita. And time has a habit of trapping you, if you find a place soothing to your spirit." He picked up a seashell on the railing and held it to his ear.

The contrast between the mien of the dangerous wizard and the boyish expression on his face as he closed his eyes to listen to the seashell was incongruous.

Fascinated, she looked at the planes and angles of his sculpted face. So handsome. Relaxed as he was now, without the constant guarded look he wore, he drew her like a lodestone. Perhaps this was the Tristan who had enchanted her in the past, the man/wolf who had captured her heart and refused to release it.

"What do you hear?"

"Stay connected all the time for only twenty-five drachmas! Unlimited talk and text on the ancient world's fastest smart phone."

Tristan set down the shell. She smiled, but the grim laugh rumbling from his throat was as ominous as the behemoth creature in the ocean. Then he squinted at the sky and his expression grew grimmer.

He nodded at the steps. "Come."

His pace was quick and hurried as she followed him down the stairs. When they reached the sands, thunder rippled through the air.

"Don't look back," he advised.

Of course she did.

The pretty, scenic inn had crumbled into dust and then vanished with a pop, as if clearing the air it had inhabited.

Niki's stomach pitched and roiled. "We were just there."

"Things dreams are built upon are not always stable. Since you are not dead, nor immortal, what you conjured cannot remain there long."

At least she had Tristan as a guide in this unknown land. As they walked the beach, Tristan once again laced his hands behind his back, looking lost in thought.

"First, fairies that bite me and then beachfront inns that crumble. Isn't there a place we can go that's a little more fun? Maybe a nightclub with great dancing where I can wear designer shoes? Now there's a fun fantasy."

Instead of answering, he bent down and scooped sand into his palm, then let the grains spill through his outstretched fingers. Terrific. He ignored her. She might as well be a shadow.

And then she noticed the tension gripping his broad shoulders and how his fingers trembled as he released the sand.

Dropping to the sand, she sat and hooked her hands around her bent knees to watch him. Niki gentled her voice. "What happened to you here in the Shadow Lands?"

"I spent much time here, Nikita. It was painful. I kept reliving my life, over and over, until the anger consumed me like fire."

He turned and she saw a long tear in his tunic, jagged and stained, as if with blood. "And your execution?"

It must have been too horrid to bear.

Tristan nodded. "Not the way I died, but the look in your eyes, and knowing I was leaving you. It was hell."

She sensed an enormous struggle taking place within him. Her own spirit felt weighted by it. The air felt leaden, sullen, and the blue sky suddenly became overcast. The pretty white lace of the surf turned an ugly gray.

"This place, it's beautiful, but it's as if there's an aftertaste infringing on my wolf's senses." She glanced upward at the darkening clouds scudding across the sky. "I'm not sure that's the right word...does my mood affect the weather?"

"Yes. Part of it, I fear, is me." His rueful smile did not reach his dark eyes. "I am immortal, but the mortal part of me, buried deep inside, remembers how powerless I was at my torture and execution, and how I had no power here. I swore I would never again feel that sense of helplessness again. I would like us to journey as quickly as possible to where we must go."

"Then show me the way. But let's have a little joy as we journey there." She touched his arm. "I have no desire to make you relive painful memories, Tristan. If

Others choose to remain here and not progress to Tir Na-nog, then they have found a way to have happiness here. Wouldn't you like that as well?"

His full mouth twisted into a wry smile. "I would like to get to Alexander as soon as possible. That is my wish. And we must get you to Tir Na-nog by nightfall."

She glanced overhead at the sun.

"Time has a way of slipping away here in the Shadow Lands. A day here is like three on Earth. But when the sun sets, if you are not in Tir Na-nog, you can turn into shadow forever."

Tristan turned and snapped his fingers. The beach turned into a thick forest of pine and oak trees. Sunlight dappled the ground, but there were no sounds of wildlife, no birds singing in the limbs overhead.

Tristan started walking.

What choice had she? She followed.

Her clothing had changed as well, from jeans and a plain shirt to a long, flowing purple gown. Soft velvet shoes clad her feet. Niki put her hand to her head and realized her hair was bound in a snood.

Was this the way she'd looked when she'd died 900 years ago? Or had she herself conjured this clothing out of some inner need to connect with a past she barely remembered?

They walked about a quarter of a mile through thick forest, following a pathway strewn with tiny stones. The stones hurt her feet a little, but she didn't complain. She was far too fascinated by this place.

"One question. Are my brothers and my father and mother here? Will I see them?"

Her dearest wish.

But he shook his head as he kept walking.

"Your mother resides in Tir Na-nog. Your father and brothers chose to be reincarnated."

Maybe she could see her mother, the woman who'd died giving birth to her and her sister. The thought crawled through her mind like a fat spider, spinning a web of more questions and more concerns.

She'd started to ask another question when a six-legged giant spider stepped out from the trees and blocked their path. Had she conjured it? Had it leapt from her mind? Big as a horse, the spider reeled back and hissed, showing white fangs that dripped a grayish liquid.

She'd barely had time to scream when Tristan lifted a hand and the creature burst into ash. Niki shivered. Even here, he wielded much power. He turned, and his mouth narrowed. "Guard your thoughts, Nikita. Here, thoughts can turn into reality."

"I didn't mean to think of...that."

"Think happier thoughts," he said dryly.

"Fine. I'll think of my mother. If I can conjure things like...that thing...from my imagination, then why can't I conjure my mother? I want to see her, Tristan."

"Conjuring objects from your imagination is one thing, and people are another. People have free will. You cannot snap your fingers and have them appear before you."

He spread out his hands. "I tried it many times when I was here, and you had died. It did not work. I tried to conjure those I had lost, like you, and my parents, to help me overcome the terrible loneliness. It did not work. Even Drust has found that out, for he longs for connection to his family."

He stood, arms folded, looking powerful and

150

immortal. "It is impossible to create even a good illusion of ones you have loved, and lost when you died. Come, we must press on."

"Why can't you zap us to where we need to go? Or conjure a car or at least horses?"

His gaze went distant. "Because there is something you must experience first. I am forbidden from taking you directly to our eventual destination."

That sounded quite ominous. She wanted to question him further, but saw the implacable set of his jaw. She shivered, and as he turned his back to continue, Niki remained quiet.

They stopped to rest beneath the shade of an oak tree. At least it looked like an oak tree. Niki glanced up and saw plump red leaves suddenly turn into fruit.

"Can we eat that? Or will it turn into a giant cacti or something deadly?"

Tristan followed her line of sight. "Yes, this tree is safe."

"How do you know?"

He stood and ran his hands over the tree. "It has good energy vibrations."

He stood and plucked two apples, handing her one. She bit into it, watching his expression. He was as remote as the distant clouds.

"This is a place of memories and the reason why I do not like coming here."

Even his speech and mannerisms had changed here, becoming more formal and stilted. He turned the apple over in his hands. "There are some memories that I do not wish to recall. Even the disaster that was our mating day."

Niki paused in chewing. "Disaster?"

"Not the day itself, but the wedding night." To her amazement, his tanned skin grew ruddy.

"Tristan Kearney, almighty Silver Wizard, are you blushing?" She shook her head. "What, did I ravish you senseless?"

"I was an ass."

She searched his expression. "I think I remember a little of it. I've had dreams of the wedding, anyway. It was lavish, and you drank a lot."

"You should not try to remember, Nikita." He finally bit into the apple. "It was not pleasant for you."

A tingle raced down her spine. She sensed this was of great importance. "If we are to be together, Tristan, then I wish to remember."

"No."

"Then I'll try to dream of it myself."

"No!" He set down the fruit upon the soft grass. "I do not wish you imagining something that could turn into a frog or a spider again. Lie down and close your eyes."

When she did so, Niki heard him murmur some strange words and then she fell into a dream.

She was lying in a large canopied bed, the red velvet drapes tied back to the posts with silk ribbons. The castle room was drafty, and the fine white silk night rail she wore provided flimsy protection against the cold. Nikita did not care.

It was her wedding night, and she awaited her groom.

Tristan Kearney, earl of Baldwin castle, was King

Emer's most trusted advisor. Their mating had been arranged by Emer himself. And along with his virgin bride, Tristan would receive the vast forest territory her family had owned for generations. The woods were filled with game, and King Emer enjoyed hunting there upon his white stag, bounding through the forest as his huntsman blew the silver horn.

Nikita suspected Emer, king of all the Fae, had arranged the match because he wanted a claim on the forest, and would find a way to coax them from Tristan.

Her groom was handsome, a tall Lupine with dark hair reaching down to his shoulders, a strong, muscled body and eyes black as night. When he walked, all the ladies in the court whispered of his sexual prowess, for he was known to be an excellent lover.

"He has a prick larger than most rods," one Fae lady-in-waiting had gushed. "Those wolves know how to use it, too."

Niki only hoped he would be gentle with her. Her mother had assured her that Tristan would make love to her in Skin, and with his Lupine knot he might even tie with her the first night, for it happened often with mates. The knotting increased the pleasure for the female.

She looked forward to that part of her mating.

But where was he? She had retired an hour ago. Yawning, she curled up and went to sleep.

When the creaking of the wood door to their bedchamber awoke her, the tall candles had burned halfway down. Her handsome groom stumbled inside the room. She caught the scent of spirits and her nostrils twitched.

He had been drinking. Nikita had dreaded this more than their initial joining, for Tristan was not prone to hard drink, and the king adored strong drink and insisted on his lords drinking with him. Watching him with wariness, she realized Tristan had spent time celebrating his wedding day without her.

Did he care more for politics and enlisting the king's goodwill, even on their mating night?

"Good evening, my sweet. I apologize for my tardiness, but the king had my ear for a long while, and I could not break away."

Tristan paused and lit more candles. Nikita wrinkled her nose. Tristan had wealth and could afford to waste the precious tapers, but she wanted darkness, not light.

With lithe grace, he strode across the room. He might be inebriated, but even so, he moved with stealth, as quiet as his wolf. She had seen him hunting in the forest, taking down a deer, breaking the creature's neck before the animal even caught his scent.

Tristan stared down at her, hunger flaring in his dark eyes. "You are most beautiful, Nikita. My Nikita. My mate. But you are wearing far too much clothing."

With a low growl, he tore off the sheer, pretty nightgown, ripping the delicate material. Nikita shivered, suddenly filled with dread. He would tear into her as well, but she had hoped for more gentle consideration.

Tristan shrugged out of his clothing. Nude, he stood before her. Flickering candlelight showed the angles and planes of his muscled, hard body, the dusting of dark hair on his chest, his long, strong limbs...

And...that.

His penis, thick and long, jutting out from a nest of black hair at his groin.

Her mother had warned that sex would hurt briefly, but her mate would be patient and gentle, as all male Lupines were.

Tristan turned to her, his dark gaze caressing her as she hugged her knees, staring at him. Then he sat on the bed, drew her into his strong arms and kissed her. He had kissed her before, briefly, chastely.

This was different. He swirled his tongue over her lips in little, expert strokes, making every cell in her body tingle. Moaning, she wound her arms around his neck, enjoying his deep, hungry kisses. She could taste the strong ale he'd consumed, and his own delicious, unique taste, like the finest wine.

Tristan tore his mouth away and she fell back upon the bed. He caressed her bare skin, palming her breast. He ran his hand down her thigh and felt between her legs. Nikita squirmed, uncomfortable with his fingers probing her, for it reminded her of the humiliation she had suffered this morning at the hands of the king's personal physician.

"You're wet," he muttered. "And tight."

The wetness came from the oil her maid had insisted she apply.

"It will make the joining easier, my lady," she'd said.

Even though her own mother had insisted she come to Tristan with nothing upon her skin but her own scent, as Lupine tradition dictated, Nikita had remembered the whispers of his largeness and applied the oil.

He swept his hands over her body, caressing her breasts until she sighed with passion and blushed,

155

knowing her nipples were growing hard beneath his expert touch. This was the lovemaking she'd eagerly anticipated. Just as suddenly, he dropped his hands. She sensed a sudden tension within him as a fierce glitter entered his gaze.

"I cannot wait. You have driven me mad. You are mine," he growled.

Then there was no time to think or even breathe, for he was parting her legs and pushing that rigid part of himself into her. Grunting, he gave a powerful flex of his hips and drove deep inside her.

She screamed at the burning pain.

He thrust twice, and she felt the warm wash of his seed flood her womb. Panting, he collapsed atop her.

Stunned, hurt and grieving, she lay beneath him. This was marriage? Mating a male who had no consideration for her, no tenderness?

He pulled out of her torn flesh and she winced. Then he rolled over and lay prone upon the bed.

Fast asleep.

Drunk.

Tears clogged her throat. A drunken mate on my wedding night. I deserve better.

But she was no weak Skin, to whimper and bewail her fate. She was strong. Lupine. Slow rage built inside her.

Nikita slid off the bed and went to the washstand, washing gently between her legs, bathing away evidence of her blood and his seed.

She tossed down the cloth with a look of disgust.

And then, stretching out her arms, she called upon her magick and shifted into wolf. Tristan might reach for her several more times this night, as her mother had warned, but he would have to dance past one weapon she intended to use well.

Her teeth. Watching her husband sleep, she bared her fangs and slunk off to the shadows behind the wash basin.

Perhaps an hour, or two, had passed when he finally stirred.

"Nikita." Tristan raised his head from the bed. "Where are you, my sweet?"

From the shadows, her wolf watched him in silence.

He raised his head and rubbed at it. "Ow. I drank too much."

Then he stood and looked at the blood-stained sheet. "Shit," he muttered.

Tristan whipped his gaze around. "Nikita? My sweet, please, do not hide from me. I am sorry."

He walked toward the washstand. "Nikita, my lovely mate, please, come out. Do not be frightened. I am so sorry for how rough I was with you."

Sorry? You shall be sorry.

Growling, she sprang out at him, and sank her teeth deep into his right thigh. Tristan yelped. She released him and then backed off, still snarling.

Does that hurt? Now you know what it feels like to have someone make you bleed.

Ribbons of bright red blood streamed down his leg. Tristan clapped a hand over his privates. His penis, smeared with her virgin blood.

"Nikita, my sweet. I deserve that and more." He gave her a contrite look, almost boyish. "But please, for the sake of the children we shall have, if you are going to bite me again, can you aim slightly lower?"

He stuck out his foot. "This is safe enough."

157

Her wolf watched him with caution.

Wriggling his toes, he pointed to them. "Nice foot. See? Very tasty."

Inside the wolf, the woman relaxed a little at his charming smile. He did not yell at her or strike.

Then Tristan shifted, so swiftly she barely had time to blink. He advanced, a powerful and muscled timber wolf. Her own wolf, recognizing the scent of her mate, whined.

Instinct warned her to turn, let him do what he would. He was male, her mate, and much stronger.

He did not mount her. Instead he crossed over to her front and licked her muzzle. And then he did the most extraordinary thing. Tristan rolled over, displaying his belly and his privates.

It was the most vulnerable position a Lupine could show to another, for she could easily tear his throat out. Her gaze went to his sheath and balls. Or other things.

Shaken by this trust, she shifted back into Skin and walked to the bed. Nikita climbed into it, watching him shift back as well.

Tristan sat on the bed, blood from the bite wound trickling upon the bedsheet. What irony. The sheet stained with virginal blood would be stained with his blood as well.

He rubbed a hand over the dark bristles on his face. "That did not go as I had intended. I had planned to woo you gently, and coax you to lie with me, not act like a rough brute. I was drunk. There is no excuse for my crude behavior. I beg your forgiveness, my lady."

Nikita said nothing, only watched him.

"If you are willing, and please Danu, I hope you are, allow me to show you what pleasure our joining can give you. I promise," he touched his finger to his lips and then touched her cheek, "that I will not hurt you again. Please, Nikita."

He was her husband, her mate. She had little choice. But seeing the tenderness in his gaze and his chagrined expression, she gave a little nod.

Tristan lifted her hand to his mouth and brushed a soft kiss against her knuckles.

Then he made love to her again, his time with his hands and lips and he was gentle, and patient. Pleasure filled her and this time her screams were not from pain, but ecstasy as she cried out his name and clung to his broad shoulders.

Afterwards, she lay in his arms, stroking the damp hairs upon his chest.

"Better?" he asked.

She nodded.

He sighed, and rubbed his cheek against the fall of her long hair. "I am such a blasted fool for mistreating you that way. And I regret that I must hand off the sheet from our bed to the steward tomorrow, to show proof you were pure."

Tristan snorted. "Damn stupid Fae tradition that King Emer insists upon for all his noblemen. We Lupines have no need of such archaic and primitive rites."

She raised her head. "There is no need. King Emer knows I was a virgin."

Tristan frowned. "How?"

"The exam he ordered." Nikita pulled away from him, sat up and plucked at the covers. He stayed her hand.

"What exam?"

Furious heat ignited her body as she recalled the shame and humiliation. "The one King Emer insisted I have to prove I was a virgin, and worthy to become your mate."

Tristan went very, very still.

"It is normal, I suppose, in these circumstances. You're a high powered official in Emer's court mating with a commoner Lupine who is rich only because my family owned land. My mother tried to protest, but Emer's physician said there would be no marriage if I refused."

"What did they do to you, Nikita?"

She didn't dare to look at him as her voice dropped to a bare whisper. "They made me lie upon a table, naked, and put a sheet over my body, and spread my legs. There were ten members of the court there as witnesses. The Fae physician looked at me...down there. He touched me...it was unpleasant."

And it had hurt, though not as much as when Tristan had taken her. What had hurt more was the laughter of the assembled noble men and ladies, looking on as if she were an animal.

Only the sound of his harsh breathing filled the cold room.

"And then?"

"Emer himself came into the room. He wanted to personally...see."

She could hear Tristan's increased heartbeat, feel his gathering rage as his scent changed. "He dared to look at you?"

"It wasn't the looking as much as what he said." Tears pricked her eyelids, but she refused to cry. And Emer was their king, their ruler. She had little power.

He was Tristan's friend, and Tristan was his closest, most trusted advisor, the lord of all shifters.

"Nikita." Tristan clasped her arms very gently, brought his face close to hers. "You are my mate now. My life partner. You need not be ashamed, but I must know everything. What did that bastard say?"

At the swear term, she blinked in surprise. And then she searched his eyes and saw the real concern there, amid the rage. Nikita touched his face, tracing the aristocratic lines of his cheekbones. Tristan came from noble blood and she was only a commoner, but in that moment, she felt she could trust this Lupine, aristocrat or no. He would never hurt her.

"He looked...at my private place and laughed." Shame pricked her. "And said, 'Look at that. Fresh wolf cunt.'"

Tristan's fingers on her arm tightened.

"And then they all laughed."

A low growl rumbled from deep in his throat. Tristan released her arms and sprang off the bed, pacing back and forth. "That fucking bastard. That bastard! How dare he insult you, my mate!"

With a snarl, he picked up one of the pretty silk pillows from the bed and threw it across the room. Claws emerged from his fingertips. He raked them down the thick tapestries lining the wall, shredding one. "I should tear his throat out."

"Better his throat than the tapestry. It is a very nice tapestry."

He looked at her, and gave a harsh chuckle. "My Nikita. You are a treasure."

She was not alarmed at his fury, but relieved at his protective streak. Perhaps she did come first in this mating, as his vows had stated. But then fear filled her as well, for Emer was a powerful Fae king with the might of the Fae army behind him. The Fae ruled over shifters like Lupines.

"I daresay you are not the only Lupine who wishes to rip out his throat. The fathers and mothers of all virgin Lupines who must endure this new, brute tradition would agree with you," she told him.

Dying candlelight gleamed upon his skin, shadows dancing over the muscled flanks as he strode across the room and joined her in bed. She was accustomed to his nudity by now, and it felt natural. More natural than the binding clothing, the thick gowns required by Emer's court.

"All Lupines are required to this barbaric ritual? Since when?"

"Since King Emer made a law for shifters, all shifters, more than two moons ago." Nikita shook her head, bemused. "Have you truly been so blind to the needs of your people, Tristan?"

Guilt touched his expression. "I have. Too long I have been in Emer's court, away from my own people and their woes."

"We have little power. Especially not the commoners, Tristan. The Fae rule over us and do as they please."

Her mate's body tensed, as if he came to a new realization. "Our lives belong to him. Drust warned me, but I refused to listen, hoping things would change. Hoping I could change them, since Emer respects me."

Tristan shoved a hand through his thick, dark hair. "I was a fool. Emer respects me not at all and respects our people even less. He leaves us no privacy, strips away our dignity as it pleases him. We deserve better. We deserve to be free to hunt upon our lands as we please, not wait for permission, and form our own packs instead of living as Emer dictates. Lupines should not be mixed with other shifters."

He cupped her face with his strong, warm palms. "You deserved better, my sweet. I am so sorry you were forced to endure such humiliation. It was not me who ordered that procedure. I would never request that of you."

As he curled his arms around her, she heard him say words that made her blood turn cold:

"One day, we shall be free of his tyranny, even if it means war."

CHAPTER 9

Niki awoke, her mind refreshingly clear instead of muddied as most dreams left her. She slowly sat up, and saw Tristan watching her with a guarded look.

"It was war, then."

He nodded, hugging his knees. "Our wedding night opened my eyes, Nikita. You opened my eyes. I had failed to realize the brutality of Emer's reign, the indignities our people were forced to suffer."

The dream hadn't been as much about the initial joining of their bodies, but the joining of purpose. Niki gave a humorless laugh. She, who had only wished to mate with the handsome Tristan and raise a family, had ignited the spark inside him that began a war that ultimately destroyed them both.

She stretched out her hands and wriggled her fingers.

Tristan's brows knit together. "What are you doing, my sweet?"

"Studying my hands. They don't look like the bloodied hands of a warmonger."

"They are not. They are the hands of a woman I wish to make my mate again, in this life. Let's forget the past, and start anew."

But she could not forget the past, for in doing so, she disrespected all they had shared, all those hopes and dreams the old Nikita had kept alive. And though he spoke words of purpose and passion, his deep voice carried a note of hollowness and he made no attempt to draw close to her.

"Start anew, when you still have the same mindset, Tristan? I am flesh and blood, with dreams and hopes of my own. We had a life as mates, but you died."

"And I am immortal now. I am the Silver Wizard, with immeasurable powers. You need not worry about me."

"Worry about you?" She scrambled to her feet. "I'm worried about me. You want to have sex with me and then go charging off on your duties as wizard, locking me up like a prisoner to keep me safe."

Blue flickered in the darkness of his eyes, signaling the rise of his powers. "When I make love to you, Nikita, you will be a willing prisoner...in my bed. I plan to keep you there for a long time until you beg me to stop. Or not stop."

A wicked smile touched his sensual mouth. "It is a good thing I have a very sturdy bed with a thick headboard that will not break when it bangs against the wall."

Headboard banging sex. Oh wow. Her wolf howled with sheer female need as Nikita studied his muscled form and the thick silk of his hair billowing in the breeze. Tristan, after that first awful encounter, had been an expert lover in the past, and her dreams of their time together in bed had left her aware and aroused to the point of pain.

But that was a different Nikita. She was not afraid to

state her needs. "Fine. Then let's do it. Right here. Who needs a bed?"

He blinked. "This is a place that tests the will of all, including immortal wizards. And if I touch you, my control may shatter. I cannot make love to you until I am mortal, unless I use protection and prevent conception."

His deep voice went husky. "And I do not wish your first time to be as brutal as I was in the past, my sweet. But if I touch you, lust will win over my control. I will not be...gentle."

"I'm not fragile or made from glass, Tristan. I'm also not the naïve Lupine of nine hundred years ago. I can handle whatever you dish out."

"Can you?" he asked softly, the blue of his eyes growing brighter, signaling the rise of his power. His nostrils flared, as if he scented her rising desire.

"Or you are suggesting I conjure a battery-operated boyfriend to deal with my frustration?"

Barely had the words left her mouth when a flesh-toned vibrator in the shape of a penis appeared in her right hand. Niki's eyes went wide. Goodness, it was six inches long and round as a fat sausage. Startled, she clasped the bottom and triggered a switch.

The vibrator began jerking from side to side.

He gave her a pointed look. "And you wish me to compete with that?"

"If memory serves correctly in nine hundred years, you have nothing to worry about." The BOB began growing until it was a foot long. Then longer.

Tristan scratched the rough bristles on his firm chin. "This is quite entertaining. Are you trying to set a world record?"

The vibrator suddenly began to sprout little green wriggling tentacles that licked the air. Tristan raised a dark brow.

"I read a very bad erotic romance not long ago," she admitted, feeling her face heat. "It was a freebie."

"It certainly did stay in your imagination," he murmured. "I hope you are not into monster porn?"

"Please. I have more taste than that. Getting impregnated by a wizard is enough of a challenge. I have no desire to climb into bed with a T-Rex."

Niki threw the BOB to the side. It began twisting and growing, and forming teeth. Dear goddess! It grew into a lizard-like shape...much like a baby T-Rex. Tristan flicked a finger at the BOB and it vanished with a soft poof.

Humiliated that her dark fantasies had surfaced, she picked up the apple and resumed eating it. At least fruit was safe. Apples...not bananas.

Suddenly the apple turned into a large yellow banana. Choking, she drew it out of her mouth and set it down.

"This place is dangerous," she said in a shaky voice. "I can't even eat fruit."

"What do you wish, Nikita?" He sounded tired.

Love. Love me the way I need to be loved, as if I'm the only Lupine in your universe and there's no one else claiming your attention. Put me first and make me your world. I've been so lonely for so long, as if I've lived in a vacuum.

I want to travel the world, see sights, have adventures with someone at my side who will be my best friend, my lover, my mate.

But she knew his answer. He could not love her.

Care for her, feel affection, yes. Put her needs first? He'd promised that. But love, the deep kind that her twin shared with Aiden, the binding love that sealed together Lupine mates as they went through life, making babies, raising a family and watching their children grow, and then their grandchildren?

No.

He was an unreachable immortal and as the Silver Wizard, he must focus on his duties to judge and guard all shifters.

No matter how much she wished it was otherwise. Unless she agreed to give up her life as a mortal Lupine, and stay with him in Tir Na-nog, never seeing her own family ever again.

Looking down at her elegant gown, and the glittering threads of the bodice, she felt a sense of new purpose. "Did I die in this gown?"

Tristan didn't look at her. "It was your burial gown."

"Then enough of this." She closed her eyes and imagined herself as a strong, capable female warrior, one who would not allow anyone to poison her or her child.

When she opened her eyes, she wore tight fawn trousers of supple cloth, a matching fawn vest made of soft doeskin, and a long-sleeved silky blouse, gathered at the wrists. Her hair was bound back in a ponytail. In her right hand was a bow and slung over her right shoulder was a quiver filled with arrows.

"Like a female Robin Hood," she murmured. She cleared her throat. "I'd rather be the Sheriff of Nottingham. That's it then."

Niki cleared her throat and quoted from the movie she'd seen, "Cancel the kitchen scraps for lepers and orphans, no more merciful beheadings and call off Christmas."

Tristan did not even blink. He was too busy staring at her legs.

"Robin Hood, Prince of Thieves. Alan Rickman was a splendid actor, a terrific Sheriff of Nottingham."

"I do not know about Robin Hood, but those trousers are most becoming on you." Desire ignited his dark eyes as he lifted his gaze to her startled face.

She flushed beneath his hungry gaze. "You've seen my bare legs before."

"Not like this. Not in the Shadow Lands, where everything, including my own lust, is amplified." He scrubbed a hand over his face. "Though the gown was distressing because it was your burial shroud, I prefer gowns. Although they do make you more accessible when I wish to take you."

"Wish to take me!"

His gaze gleamed. "Do you remember the mirror image when we first entered the hotel, Nikita?"

How could I forget?

Curious, she studied him. The deliberately relaxed pose could not disguise the tension in his muscles…

This was a land of danger, but one of fantasies as well. "What is it like having sex with you?"

His gaze grew intent. "Sit down close your eyes, my sweet. When I pleasure you with my touch, it will be quite intense. You may pass out."

As her eyelids lowered, she felt him touch her. All over, his hands caressing and exploring, as if her skin were bared to him. Nipples tingling, she moaned, feeling him gently thumb them until they became diamond hard.

She felt his mouth, warm and firm and commanding, upon her own and sighed, opening to him. His tongue lazily thrust inside, an invitation. She moaned as he deepened the kiss.

And then he drew away and she felt his hand skim down her belly, dip into the waistband of her trousers.

He put his hand between her legs.

Shocked and aroused, she opened her eyes and saw him leaning against a tree.

He hadn't touched her at all. Had distanced himself from her in fact. Yet the pleasure now pulsing between her legs, growing more and more intense, felt quite real.

It was magick. He was using his powers to make it feel as if he touched her with his hands, and now teased and stimulated her sex. Oh wow, it felt like his long, skilled fingers were sliding between the slick wetness of her cleft, then lightly stimulating her clit. Rubbing, stroking with gentle, expert moves, making every muscle in her body tense with pleasure.

The tension between her legs built higher and higher until she collapsed, screaming as the pleasure exploded into orgasm. Stars burst behind her eyelids and she gasped for breath.

For a few moments, she struggled to regain her lost composure, wondering if she would ever be the same again.

CHAPTER 10

A slow smile curved Tristan's handsome face.

"Was it good for you, my sweet?"

Good? Toe-curling, mind-bending amazing.

"That," she dragged more air into her lungs, "was how it was with us in bed?"

"A mere taste of it," he said softly.

The experience left Niki deeply shaken. She'd always known Lupines were sensual, but the impact of his magick touch had left her panting for more. And she didn't want this, didn't want him to give her such intoxicating pleasure that it clouded her mind to all else.

Trying to control her breathing, she held out a hand. "Give me a moment."

He waited, his gaze heavy-lidded.

The wizard had woven a spell of sensual magick with his kisses and his fiery passion. He held a mysterious, sexual power over her that could turn her into his willing slave, making her forget her own dreams and hopes.

How was she supposed to leave him when she craved his touch again like a drug?

"Was it like that between us all the time?"

"Most of it. I was quite lusty and you were most desirable." His look grew dangerously intent. "As you are now."

"Seems like a one-sided experience," she shot back. "You make me fall to pieces and you stand there as if none of this affects you."

His mouth narrowed. "Do not judge me, Nikita. I am quite affected, which is why I cannot physically touch you here and now."

Then he turned abruptly, but not before she caught the frantic pulse beating in his neck, and the interesting tent in his trousers.

She was not alone in this desire, it seemed. Tristan wanted her as badly. It should be reassuring, but she wondered what would happen if he surrendered to his own passion.

He studied the sky peeking through the thick covering of trees. "Come, Nikita. We must hurry. We are spending far too much time in these lands."

I already came, she thought humorlessly.

Trying to tamp down her desire, she followed him.

But she needed to know more about this mysterious wizard who turned her world upside down and showed her a glimpse of such incredible passion. He was immortal, yet felt desire. Showed it.

She navigated over a large, fallen log and jumped down. "If you're immortal, how can you have sex?"

Tristan stopped and turned, the look on his face almost comical.

"You said everything in the Shadow Lands is not corporeal since they are dead. And yet you are living, you have a beating heart, you have a body and you have…" Her gaze dropped down to his groin. She looked away, flushing.

"Yes, I have one of those as well and it works quite well," he said dryly. "Too well, for it has a mind of its own." He glanced upward. "We have a long way to go yet. We must not delay."

As he began walking again, he kept looking around, scanning for danger. But her curiosity would not be denied. She had dozens of questions and he had not answered many.

"But how can you have a functioning body? If you wish me to drink this magick elixir so I can become immortal, I need to know the basics. I'm a science geek, Tristan. I need to know how things work."

Tristan held back a low-hanging branch so she could duck beneath it. "We wizards are as corporeal as your pack, Nikita. When I was made the Silver Wizard, I underwent a transformation, as you will, except you will not have my powers. I was made corporeal again, and the powers endowed in me allow me to live in Tir Na-nog as flesh, not spirit. The elixir of the Blooded Moonflower helps maintain our immortality. It is the only food, if you will, we require. And when you drink it, you will become immortal as well."

"Like a human tasting ambrosia in the Greek myths becomes immortal. So the elixir is the food of the wizards as ambrosia is the food of the Greek gods?"

A faint smile touched his mouth as they navigated past another fallen log. "Yes. Except we wear better clothing and we are much less capricious with our powers."

The smile dropped. "It is forbidden for me to share

my seed with a mortal, for it contains part of my magick and my powers as the Silver Wizard. I cannot make love to you until we reach Tir Na-nog and my home, where I will become mortal again for the ten days you are with me."

He turned and started through the forest again, and she walked at his side this time, not behind. Tristan kept scanning the forest, as if looking for something.

By drinking the magick elixir, she could become immortal as well, but lose her family.

Tristan told her to get to the crystal cave where Drust hid Prince Alexander, they had to walk through a desert filled with hidden traps. Like a minefield, she thought, as they eyed the treacherous terrain ahead. Nostrils flaring, she looked at the long plateau of tawny sand. Like the deserts of Egypt, it seemed a giant sea of sand, no end in sight. Her wolf, already uncomfortable with the stale air, the heat and the smell of old blood, whined.

Down girl. I don't want to venture here, either, but it seems we have little choice.

As they stepped upon the sand, Tristan glanced at her, his expression guarded. "There are dangers below and above this desert, but the greatest danger is within."

"Would you mind being more specific?"

"I can say no more."

"You sound like a Chinese fortune cookie."

"I have been told that before," he agreed.

The cryptic warning didn't boost her self-confidence. Greatest danger from within? What did he mean and why couldn't he elaborate? She'd have been better off with a Magic 8 ball or consulting her daily horoscope. Maybe it meant she had to find the internal spirit to set herself free. Tristan had mentioned that this was her journey.

Not his.

The crackling aura of his power became more visual. Before, it had manifested as a flicker around him, a faint silver aura much like the glint of a mirror on a cloudy day. Now it was like full sunshine hitting a mirrored surface, and she found it difficult to gaze at him.

He walked apart from her, hands laced behind his back, his arrogant chin held high, his shoulders straight. She reminded herself that even here in the Shadow Lands, he was a being who held magick far beyond hers. No matter that he'd been her lover and mate in a past life, and wished to claim her again.

The promises he'd made earlier dimmed in light of this drastic personality shift of this remote, powerful being. As if the wizard had replaced the Lupine who remembered her from his previous life, and wanted her as his mate again.

She suspected it had to do with remembering his time here before.

The sands seemed to stretch on forever. Every once in a while she'd see a flicker of a mirage, like a watery reflection in a pond. Some were sharper than others. They would appear, then vanish.

Making small talk, she chattered about a science book she'd read on biology and plants.

He gave her a level look. "Concentrate on where you step, Nikita. Less chatter and more awareness."

Gone was the endearing "my sweet." She had never heard him be this critical.

"I am aware. I'm very aware of how moody you've become."

They walked for what seemed like a long time before they came upon an outcropping of trees like nothing she'd ever seen. Stubby trees with peeling gray bark, their limbs outstretched in sinister shapes, like arms ready to pull her aside.

"Avoid those trees," he told her.

She did not hesitate to heed his warning. A sulphuric odor clung to them, and her wolf whined again.

When he stopped, his power pulsing like a beacon cutting through the night, she swallowed hard. Show no fear.

Instead, she softened her tone. "What is it, Tristan? What is it about this place that makes you so edgy? You have power enough to overcome everything."

"I am not edgy. I am the Silver Wizard. And I have no need of your flattery."

"Tristan, the Great and Terrible Wizard," she mocked, resenting his curt tone.

"Nikita, I am in no mood for games."

Giving a shrug that hid her resentment, she skipped ahead. "Then stop acting so surly as if we're walking through quicksand. I've been cooped up my entire life in a basement and I'd like to explore. This is a desert, but you said the Shadow Lands are filled with manifestations of magick. The Shadow Lands aren't so bad if you can control your thoughts and your dreams. It's not pleasant, but..."

Barely had the words fled her mouth when the sand opened beneath her feet. She spilled downward, into a long, dark tunnel. Her wolf howled in fright.

Down she fell, about ten feet, until unexpectedly she

went sprawling into a square, dark room. And then the opening above her turned into a pane of glass, closing across the box.

In abject panic, she hurled herself up at it, uselessly. Her skull collided with the glass, stunning her, and then she fell hard to the floor.

Panting, she looked at her prison. No more than 5 x 5, it was a cage with black walls, the only light coming from above.

Her greatest fear had manifested itself. She was trapped and alone.

When she had been confined to her apartment, Niki had left each night, roaming the ranch woods as wolf. Only the open sky and fresh air had soothed her wolf, had enabled her to remain in the apartment each day.

Now, imprisoned in this box, her wolf began to howl. But she could not shift. Her magick was useless in the Shadow Lands.

Claustrophobia squeezed her like a vise. She fought to catch her breath, to not hyperventilate. You're trapped, Niki. Trapped in this box, as you were trapped in your basement apartment for your entire life.

She scrabbled for logic in the face of her fear: Tristan wouldn't leave her here. He wouldn't.

You will stay here and no one would find out, or care.

No one will know the true you, because your entire life has been non-existent. You're a ghost. Trapped. No freedom.

No.

"Tristan," she screamed. "Help me, please!"

She looked upward through the glass ceiling and saw him standing above her, arms folded, gazing into the distance. Couldn't he see her? Hear her screams?

"Help me," she begged, pounding on the ceiling.

But he didn't even look at her.

His impervious stance told her that he was indifferent to her needs, just as he'd been nine hundred years ago.

Whatever held her in its grip was torturing her, causing excruciating mental agony.

She could not breathe and she could not summon her wolf, the beast that always gave her strength in times of crisis and anguish.

Then a gentle, deep voice spoke inside her mind, pushing aside the clanging of her thoughts. Focus, Nikita. You can do it. Do not fear. Look within. You are strong and brave. And I will not let you be forgotten. But you must help yourself.

She stretched out her hands and pushed at the ceiling, which seemed now to be lowering upon her. She felt the crushing weight as much as the lack of oxygen.

Panic squeezed her lungs. She began to thrash helplessly, gasping for air and wasting what little she had left. No. Stop it! Get a hold of yourself.

Look within.

Centering her concentration, she closed her eyes and stopped pushing at the glass ceiling. She focused on all the good things about her basement apartment: its safety and quiet and cool, clean familiarity. She had in some ways enjoyed the years of living on the ranch in relative isolation from the pack. She'd loved the elders who fussed over her and treated her like a favorite grandchild. She recalled the love and affection of her father and brothers. The joy of running wild and free as wolf at night. She could do that in her mind, if she just concentrated. And the walls would fall away.

Nikita traveled further in her memory, feeling the deep, binding love of her identical twin. *Nia, I miss you so much.*

The glass ceiling continued to descend, pressing her down into the floor of the box, trying to incite her to fresh panic.

Niki refused. She took a deep breath. *Miss you, Nia, but I'm so happy you and Aiden are together. You deserve to be happy, and deserve a good Lupine like him. You're both strong leaders and will serve our people well.*

I'm strong, too, but I've never had the chance to explore what I can do, because I've been afraid all my life and trapped by a prophecy that the wizard might find me and destroy me. Well, he's found me now, and I'm on a great adventure.

Trapped in a damned box instead of my apartment!

But at least I'm not at home. I'm traveling! Maybe not officially—there's no stamp on my passport, but at least we bypass the long lines at customs and immigration.

The thought struck her as wildly ironic and funny. She laughed, and forgot about everything except the absurdity of the situation. And then she stared upward, still laughing.

Fine. I can stay here, take a nice nap. No prob.

The glass ceiling vanished, and she found herself on the sands near Tristan once more. His back to her, he seemed to study the squat trees.

"Tristan," she whispered.

No response.

"Look at me," she ordered. "Damnit, Tristan, stop ignoring me. I called to you and you didn't help me! I felt like I was dying!"

He turned and Niki gasped. He started to raise his hand to reach for her, and then it dropped to his side. He did not look at her, seemed to look past her.

Silver-colored blood trickled between the fingers of his clenched fists.

Niki went to him, reached for his hand. He jerked it away, but she grabbed his wrist. So cold, like death. She unfurled his bloody palm and winced at the cuts made by his nails.

"Talk to me," she urged. "Please. Why did you do this to yourself? What's going on, Tristan?"

When he finally spoke, he sounded broken. "It was the only way I could stop from reaching for you. It is forbidden for me to come to your aid when you face your darkest fear in this world, when the struggle isn't against creatures you can manifest like the spider or the worm, but yourself. You had to find your own way out of that box. If I had helped you other than by giving you encouragement... I could have lost you forever."

And then she understood what it cost him to watch her struggle and panic, caught in the grip of the trap fashioned by her deepest fears. To feel powerless and helpless to aid her, just as he felt powerless when he was held prisoner by the Fae, and eventually executed. Niki lifted his hand to her lips and gently pressed a kiss to his wounded palm.

The bloody lacerations faded.

Surprise flickered in his eyes. "Why did you do that?"

"To thank you, and heal you. Every Lupine needs the power behind a simple touch, Tristan. Especially when they feel lost and hurt inside, and helpless."

"I am not Lupine. Nor helpless." He pulled his hand away and the impartial coldness returned to his demeanor. "Do not make the mistake of thinking me that way, Nikita."

"You were Lupine once. You were like me, like Others, in a past life."

"No longer. The Shadow World holds not the dangers for me that it does for you." He laced his hands behind his back once more. "I've already paid the price when I was here hundreds of years ago, and finally learned to free myself."

She was in another world, and each step carried unknown dangers. She needed connection in a world fraught with uncertainty.

"Then show me the price you paid, Tristan. It will help me to reconnect with you."

He gave her a quick, startled look. "Here? Now?"

Giving a philosophical shrug, she went on. "I can't think of a better time or place. You came here after you died. Show me what it was like for you. I need to know what you endured."

She spread out her arms. "I feel as if none of this world affects you."

"It once did," he said quietly. "You do not want to see what happened. You already watched me die, once."

"I do want to see." She gathered her courage. "Because nothing, absolutely nothing, could be as horrible as watching them torture and then kill you."

A cynical look entered his eyes. "Very well."

Tristan waved a hand and suddenly she was transported to a dark forest. She saw him, wearing the clothing he was executed in, wandering among the trees. Blood streamed down his face and his clothing was stained with it.

"Nikita!" he screamed. "Nikita! Nikita!"

Her own name, shouted over and over again, cut through her like a blade. Then the dream-Tristan sank to his knees, rocking back and forth.

He shifted into a silver wolf. The wolf, his fur matted with blood, lifted his head and howled, the sound so piercing it hurt her eardrums. Niki winced and plugged her ears with her fingers. She could not bear to hear it.

Tristan waved his hand and the image vanished. The fine angles and planes of his handsome face tightened.

"You have seen what I endured, Nikita. Now you know."

"That was your life here after you perished? For how long?" she whispered.

"Days, perhaps. Or weeks." He squatted down, scooped sand into his palm and let the grains fall through his fingers. "My time here was like an hourglass. An hourglass marking each minute, each second, in a hell I could not escape. Not a true hell, but a hell of my own because I lost you. And I will not lose you again."

Tristan stretched out his hands. "I am the Silver Wizard, and I have the power now to keep you safe. And once we enter Tir Na-nog, we will come together again in passion as it was before, and create a baby to replace what we both lost."

He might as well have been making a speech to an

audience for all the authority in his tone. He wanted to command her fate, as much as he'd wanted to command the army that fought in the Drakon War.

She sensed he hid behind his power and might, and the mask of imperviousness because he didn't want to fully share himself or care about her that deeply again. Niki felt her chest tighten. Love screwed things up because loving someone could really hurt. Her own love for her identical twin, who had worried about her leaving, had trapped her in that basement as much as fear of the prophecy had.

But she wasn't a vessel for his pleasure, or his purpose to create a child. She was living flesh and blood, with dreams and hopes of her own. Sex, yeah, she longed to be intimate and swept off her feet into an erotic bliss she'd never experienced. But not left cold and alone afterward, with no one to share her life with, no mate to be there for her, to grow old with, and watch their grandchildren play.

It was as if he guarded his heart against her. She thought she'd grown closer to understanding him, but that glimpse inside him barely flicked the curtain.

The wizard was a cement wall, and she'd had enough brick walls surrounding her.

She sat on the sand. It was neither hot nor cold. It was neutral, like Tristan's expression, when she felt only frustration and grief that he'd shut himself away from her after the little glimpse she'd seen of how much he had cared.

"We must go." He looked around. "It is too dangerous here. You are too vulnerable in the open."

No use protesting. Tristan, looking grim again, pressed onward. Scrambling to follow, she tried to quiet her rapidly beating heart, certain it was audible.

They left the outcropping of stubby, distorted trees and entered the open sands once more. Niki's head felt foggy and her thoughts cloudy with anger and frustration. Clouds rolled in overhead, reflecting her darkened mood.

He glanced upward and then back at her. "The weather is changing. I did not do this."

"It's probably me. Watch out, because it will storm next, with the way I'm feeling."

"Control your emotions, Nikita," he said tightly. "They will not serve you well here and you are still alive, not a spirit manifestation like the Others here. Negative emotions will attract negative beings eager to siphon away your energy."

Barely had they gone more than one hundred yards when a thick mist rolled over the sands. Tristan immediately tensed. "Get behind me."

What now? Could it be worse than becoming trapped inside her own mind, in a box that held her captive?

And then the mists cleared and all around them sprang up a rich, green forest. Dead leaves swirled at their feet and the air was ripe with an underlying smell of decay. And I thought the desert was bad...

Tristan's nostrils flared. "Stay back."

Mist rolled through the black trees and then the wisps of fog took shape. Four creatures, the size of large grizzly bears, stood before them. With black pits for eyes, red slashes for nose and mouth, and spindly bodies of gray flesh, they looked like a nightmare sprung to life.

Tristan glanced back at her.

"Not me," she screamed. "I imagined vibrators with tentacles, not this!"

"Nikita Blakemooooore," one creature hissed, showing razor sharp claws. "We have come for you on the bidding of our mistress. She wants your beating heart."

"Nikita, conjure a weapon," Tristan snapped, spreading out his arms to shield her.

But her horrified mind could only imagine the plastic toy swords she'd seen her older brothers play with as children. Instantly a plastic sword appeared in her trembling right hand. Trembling, she held it outward, hoping plastic was effective in this world.

The wraiths moved forward, and then rushed past Tristan, aiming for her. Niki fought them with the short blade, but succeeded in stabbing only one. It vanished soon as her sword sank into its chest.

It seemed the material of the weapon did not matter, only her aim. Filled with more confidence, she slashed at the creatures as they tried clawing at her with their razored hands. She sliced off one hand, but it regenerated.

"Aim for their chests," Tristan shouted, as he cornered one wraith.

"You cannot destroy us, Silver Wizard!" it sang out.

"I may not destroy you as the Silver Wizard, but I can fight you as a Lupine."

Tristan shifted into a large silver wolf. Snarling, he leapt at the creature, which backed up against a tree. Jaws snapping, he tore apart one wraith, who vanished with a loud pop of air.

But as he turned for the other, it picked up the silver wolf by its neck.

A bone-chilling snap rang through the stale air as the creature broke Tristan's neck. The wolf tumbled downward onto the forest floor.

No! Shock immobiled her.

Then panic and grief squeezed her insides. Tristan, oh Tristan, you can't be dead!

She saw the wolf rise, its head at an awkward angle. It was alive…with a broken neck. No time to contemplate that, for the wraith advanced.

Snarling, she lifted her sword and started to rush the creature, which swiped at her with dry, dead razor claws.

Then the wolf shook its head, straightened his neck with an audible pop. He lunged forward and sank its teeth into the creature's hindquarters. It screamed and tried to shake off the wolf, but Tristan tore its leg off. Slimy yellow fluid gushed out onto the forest floor.

The wolf lunged for the creature's throat and tore it apart. The wraith vanished with a howl and a rushing of air.

The sword trembled in Niki's outstretched hand as the wolf shook its mighty body and loped over to her. Tristan shifted back to his Skin form, clad in his customary black. The forest vanished, leaving them standing in the desert again.

"Mara must really hate me," she said in a shaky voice.

"Hate is a mild adjective," he murmured.

"How could Mara control these…things…here?" What kind of power did the Fae possess to be able to conjure wraiths from the afterworld?

"She must have sold her soul to the Keeper of the Dark Lands, a Dark Fae who holds a key to this world and can send other creatures to torment Others. It's the only explanation." Tristan rolled his head, cracking and popping bones. "Damn, that hurts."

Nausea roiled in her stomach. She dropped the sword and watched it vanish. "He broke your neck."

"Yes, but as I said, I'm immortal. And I have a tough neck." He winked at her, but she could not even summon a smile.

This world was far too scary. How could she even get out of here?

Glancing again at the sky, he nodded. "We have enough time. I could not affect your journey until you faced your darkest fear. I am allowed now to transport us to a safer location, closer to Drust."

Tristan drew a pattern in the air and a doorway suddenly appeared. Taking her hand, he walked with her through it.

The dark forest was gone. She stood in a quiet glen, as peaceful as the one back on her ranch. Birds chirped in the oak and maple trees, and in the distance, she heard horses whinnying.

"Where are we?" she asked.

"It is an illusion I created to keep your emotions happy, and the negative energy away. Like a bubble surrounding us until we reach Drust's cave."

"How did you manage to leave here, Tristan? What's the secret to finding a way out? Can we truly get out of here?" She looked around, deeply rattled.

"We can, just as Prince Alexander can return to Earth. Come Nikita, we must continue walking. I know the way."

He started down the gravel pathway cutting through the glen into the woods. Soon they were in another forest, only the sunlight dappled the trees and the air was less heavy here.

She took a deep breath. Wow, she felt winded lately. Was it this new area they now walked?

"I just saw this...thing...break your neck. You may be immortal, but I'm not and I'm scared. I need to know what happened to you here."

"What happened to me here is not something I wish to discuss."

Niki pulled at his arm, stopping him. "I need to know, Tristan. I have a pretty big decision facing me and I need facts! How do you expect me to move onto the future with you, to have a life with you as an immortal, with our child, when I don't know all of your past, especially the past when you were stuck here?"

His gaze shuttered. "You have a point. If it will help you make your decision about taking the potion..."

"It will."

Instead of answering, he bent down and touched his hand to the earth. Tristan took a fistful, and let the dirt spill through his fingers, as if grounding himself. Then he stood and dusted off his hands.

"I was drowning in self-pity, Nikita, totally consumed in my own misery, thinking only of what Drust had taken away from me. I longed to make him suffer as I had suffered. And then I conjured a suit of armor and phantom dragon soldiers to fight, soldiers who resembled Drust. It became pointless."

He drew in a deep breath. Staring at the horizon, he seemed lost in the past. "I needed to heal my broken spirit and find peace. I needed...purpose. I met two Lupine shifters who had died in the Drakon War. They were even more lost and wretched than I. Using the knowledge I'd gained in my time here, I helped to guide them through the Shadow Lands."

"You found a new purpose," she said gently, watching his body stiffen with tension.

Tristan stretched out his hand and drew a pattern in the air. Marveling, she watched as a vision—like another mirage—appeared before them—a shining gold gate wreathed in green leaves.

"After helping five of them, I realized my actions manifested the hidden gate to access Tir Na-nog. I could have stepped through it and left this world behind. But I did not." He glanced at her, and then closed his fist. The vision of the gate vanished.

"I could not leave them behind, but the gate would only allow entrance for a few moments at a time."

"You sent them through instead."

He nodded and waved a hand again, manifesting a silver sword in his hand. "I was a mere mortal who had died, so it was not forbidden for me to help. I taught them to fight the evil manifestations of their negative energy, and each time they succeeded, the gate appeared again. I sent through many shifters, Lupines, cougars, bears." He gave a rueful smile. "Even dragons. I helped create worlds for them in here where they could learn to deal with their innermost demons, conquer them, and then move on to the next plane."

Tristan stepped forward and sliced at the trees, which suddenly vanished. She stared in amazement.

They were at the beach again, the beach she'd longed to visit. Only this time it was peopled with Others, sitting on lounge chairs, or swimming in the ocean. Children built sand castles at the shoreline or played with bright red beach balls.

The dark coldness was gone. This was the beach she'd longed to visit, and explore.

She shot him a questioning look. "This is the beach I wanted to imagine."

"And you could not imagine it thus until you conquered your innermost fear."

He shoved the sword deep into the sand. "I told you that one cannot conjure loved ones here, Nikita. Not their actual spirits. But it is possible to create a vision, a hallucination if you will, fashioned from your heart's desire. And when I was finally ready to move on, I created one for myself. Look."

She turned in the direction of his pointed finger. The people on the beach suddenly vanished, but for a woman, a man and a child. Then her heart stilled in wonder and sudden grief.

At the shoreline, the dark-haired little boy, clad in a black tunic and black leggings, ran up to greet the waves and then ran back, laughing. The tall, handsome man with shoulder-length black hair caught him up in his arms and hugged him tight.

Tristan.

The woman turned her head slightly to regard them and smiled.

It was her.

"You created us. As a family." A lump clogged her throat.

"It was a vision of a future I could not have in the life I left behind, but perhaps I could have in the next life," he said quietly. "A dream I clung to, and that gave me the reason to finally move on, so I could choose to become reincarnated and find you again in another lifetime."

She stared at the dark-haired little boy, clinging to his father, who swung him around, and then kissed his cheek.

A fat tear rolled down Niki's cheek. Another. Dark clouds scudded across the sky and suddenly raindrops began pelting the sand. But the trio at the shoreline did not vanish. They remained in the rain, the golden-haired woman who sat on the sand, watching the adoring father and his laughing son.

Tristan picked up the sword again and the scene vanished. They were back in the forest again, but raindrops still splattered the ground, running in rivulets down the tree trunks to puddle on the loamy earth. He waved a hand and the sword vanished.

Very gently, he reached out and wiped away one of her tears with his thumb. "Do not cry, Nikita. I did not tell you this to bring you distress."

She pulled away from him, unable to deal with the sudden bout of grief for what they had both lost. They could have lived a good life together, raised a child who would grow strong and happy. But it was pointless to regret.

She'd had enough regrets in her current life.

"That damn Drakon War. It killed too many good people," she whispered. "And too many dreams."

"As with all wars, it was not black and white," he said diplomatically. "It created new dreams. In the end, the shifters won their freedom. The war forced all shifters to unite, something dragons were not doing. It was the unusual friendship I shared with Drust that led the dragon clans to work together as they should."

And Drust betrayed that friendship. The torture

Tristan suffered had been excruciating, but the betrayal was as well. "How long were you here, Tristan?"

"I stayed until the war ended and our people were free. After, Danu appeared to me. The goddess told me she had seen my courage, and my sacrifice. I had a choice. I could ascend to immortality as the Silver Wizard and become the guardian of shifters, or I could remain in Tir Na-nog."

His powerful shoulders tensed and his jaw became like granite. "After being powerless as King Emer's captive...it was beyond my wildest dreams. Emer was long dead, sent to the Dark Lands. I could not avenge myself upon King Emer, for he was out of reach. But Drust, oh, I thirsted to have my revenge upon the one who separated me from you, who sold me out for gold."

The Dark Lands, the Hell for Others. She wondered why Drust hadn't gone there, too. She didn't like the intensity of Tristan's expression, as if his revenge took precedence over all else.

"What about your dream of being reincarnated so we could be together again?"

"She told me it was a possibility, but there was no certainty, for you have free will and it could take a while."

A while? Try 900 years. The goddess must have an odd sense of humor.

"I coaxed from Danu a promise." His voice grew husky. "In exchange for becoming the guardian of all shifters, I wanted only one thing. I needed to become your lover, and the father of your child. All the power in the world meant nothing to me if I could not see you again, Nikita. And so I became the Silver Wizard, and I began the wait for you to return to me. Nine hundred years I have waited for that promise to be fulfilled."

Her chest grew tight again. "A very long time."

"I would have waited another nine hundred years to hold you in my arms again."

Niki reached out to him, to embrace him, hoping this time he would not shut her out. She needed the contact in this cold, dark place and she longed to comfort him for all his past torment. He stiffened and drew back.

"No. I must not. Not here. If I touch you, all my control will shatter, Nikita. I want you so badly that I dare not risk it." His voice trembled slightly.

He shifted into a magnificent silver wolf, the size of a small Shetland pony. Ice blue eyes regarded her coldly.

The wolf nudged her forward.

Fighting her welling emotions, she kept walking. Maybe he'd shared his past anguish, but he certainly wasn't allowing her close now. Tristan had become a stranger once more.

Being in the presence of a wolf triggered her own Lupine instincts. Nikita called upon her magick and tried to shift.

No use. She had to maintain her human form.

A heavy weight settled on her chest. She was alive and Lupine, yet walking in the realm of the dead. No longer did she have the solace of the wolf that always kept her centered and calm. Or of the guardian who'd once promised his heart to her centuries ago, but now thirsted for revenge upon Drust and seemed as distant as the stars.

She wondered if he'd ever pledge it to her again.

CHAPTER 11

Gray skies and sullen clouds darkened the skies as they proceeded through the Shadow Lands. It felt like they had walked for hours through the forest when, finally, the trees cleared and they came to a jagged mountain.

The entrance to a cave was set in the mountain. Tristan shifted back to Skin.

"Drust," he muttered, his voice rich with satisfaction. "He is hiding Prince Alexander here."

Niki stared at the dark opening of the cave. "Why have you waited all this time for revenge, Tristan? How long has Drust been here?"

"Centuries."

"And you want to do this now, when you need to get me out of here?"

"You are the reason we are here, Nikita. You suffered as much as I did because of Drust's betrayal. He was not merely responsible for my execution." Tristan's voice trembled. He waved a hand and a vision appeared in the air, as opaque as mist—herself and Tristan, walking with their arms around each other in a green meadow, watching a dozen children run and play.

"He took away all our dreams and hopes of being a family, of living in peace and growing old to see our grandchildren."

Emotion clogged her throat as he waved a hand andthe vision vanished. "There are always new dreams." Deep inside, she wondered if this revenge was more important than she was to Tristan.

Tristan gazed down at her. "Yes. We will have another future together. But he caused my death, Nikita, and made me feel powerless and helpless. He murdered you, Nikita, and killed our babe in your womb and I could not help you. That is something I could never forgive."

Ancient screams echoed in her mind, a memory from the past. But they weren't her screams.

She closed her eyes, seeing Tristan, his body torn and bleeding, the agony he suffered as they tortured him to find out where he'd hidden the dragon's eggs. He had remained steadfast and never told the Fae. Even as the king's executioner picked up the knife and spread his legs apart to reach for his manhood...

Moaning, she hugged herself. "What they did to you, my poor Tristan."

"Do not be distressed, my sweet," he said gently. "That is in the past."

Fierce resolved filled her. "I don't just want him to suffer because of what he did to me and how he took everything away from us." She felt hatred consume her. "I want him to suffer because of what he made you go through."

"He will."

Confidence filled his deep voice. He pulled himself straighter and she saw the aura of power around him grow stronger. Tristan walked over to a towering oak tree near the cave entrance. Dropping to his knees, he dug in the earth and pulled free the diamond dragon scale she'd seen him previously toss into the portal leading to the Shadow Lands. Dusting off his trousers, he returned and handed her the scale.

"This is the key to sending Prince Alexander home. Stay here. I must see what Drust is doing. I will be back."

Then the Silver Wizard shifted again, this time into a black raven, flying into the cavern.

Dread filled her as she clutched the dragon scale. A few moments later, the raven returned.

Tristan shifted into Skin. She handed him the scale and he walked into the cavern.

Niki followed, her stomach tightening with dread. She had no desire to confront the dragon who had caused her death.

Jagged spikes of white crystal dangled from the ceiling. The walls were pure white crystal as well. After the staleness of the desert, the air here felt cooler and smelled fresher. A tangy scent of charcoal and sharp sandalwood teased her nostrils.

Ancient senses stirred within her, along with memory. This was Drust's unique scent from when he roamed the earth as a fierce dragon.

In the middle of the cavern in human form, Drust sat in a wooden chair at a simple wooden table. No other furniture was present. Papers were strewn over the table, and a quill and inkstand rested there as well. Overhead, a fly buzzed lazily around before landing on a stalactite.

Drust pushed back the chair and stood. He looked

corporeal, but as Tristan had informed her earlier, he was only a spirit.

Unsmiling, he faced them. Certainly she had never expected this—to find a powerful silver dragon in the afterworld, who looked nearly as menacing as the wizard who'd taken her captive.

Once Tristan and Drust had been close friends, formidable to those who opposed them. Tristan's sharp fangs had sliced flesh and Drust's fire had burned those unfortunate enough to be in its path. Now, as she looked at the Silver Wizard and the silver dragon, she knew they were bitter enemies.

Drust had short, black hair and a close-cropped beard and mustache. He had the most intense blue eyes Niki had ever seen, burning and searing. He resembled his great-grandson Sebastian, but in looks only. For Sebastian was handsome and charming and had a sunny disposition.

Drust was dark, brooding and intense. The thick gray hooded cloak he wore was shapeless, flowing down to his bare feet. His mouth thinned as he glared at the wizard.

"Tristan. Why are you here, to torment the dead or replenish your energy? Are your powers so diminished here that you are as ineffective as you were when we broke bread on Earth?" Drust's deep voice carried an edge of contempt.

Tristan offered a grim smile as his aura pulsed bright silver, as if to refute Drust's words. Niki could barely stand to look at him. Power crackled and hummed in the dull, stale air.

"I have no need to replenish my energy. I could turn you into charbroiled barbecue for dinner, but for the fact that I detest lizard meat."

Ignoring the jab, Drust turned to her.

"Nikita." His voice was deep and echoed through the cavern.

Tristan pulled her closer and his lips curled back in a snarl, showing his fangs.

"Down boy," she murmured to him. "I can handle him."

"I last saw you several hundred years ago," Drust said, and for a moment he looked deeply pained.

Nikita tried to quiet her pounding heart. Drust should scare her. His searing intensity warned her that this was no dragon to trifle with. But he had betrayed Tristan, causing his death. Hers. And their unborn son's.

And that last thought stirred her, roused her anger.

"I should have gasped my last breath cursing you," she said in a low voice, advancing towards him. "I should have cursed you for turning Tristan over to King Emer simply so you could gain more gold. Cursed you for killing my child."

Niki curled her right hand into a fist and slugged Drust.

The dragon shifter reeled backward, blood welling from his cut lip. Niki flexed her fingers.

"You bastard," she screamed, shaking with rage. "You murdering bastard!"

Crystals hanging above them trembled and the walls of the cavern shook, as if her wrath were an earthquake.

The dragon's shoulders slumped. "I deserve that," Drust told her.

The admission stunned her. Tristan frowned as he glanced at her.

Giving a grudging laugh, Drust touched his mouth

and the cut healed, and vanished, along with the blood. "You have turned into a fighter, Nikita. But you did no real harm to me. One heals quickly from injuries caused by another in this world, but not as quickly from the injuries within."

He went to the table and sat with a weary sigh. The fly that had hung on the stalactite flew downward and landed on a piece of parchment. Another joined it, both crawling on the fine beige paper.

The dragon shifter swatted at them with no real effort.

"True enough." Tristan's expression grew stormy. "I could cause an injury within you that would never heal. One that would tear apart that organ you once called a heart."

"Even here, in my quiet place of respite, I am plagued by flies...and sharp-tongued wizards."

"And I am plagued by a dragon who betrayed me and caused my death," Tristan shot back.

Drust heaved a deep breath. "I did not betray you, Tristan. I told you when you first saw me here in the Shadow Lands. But you chose not to believe me. Each time you came here on the anniversary of your death to taunt me, you refused to believe I was not the one who turned you over to the Fae king's men."

"I had proof it was you, dragon. I saw the letter you wrote to Emer, telling him where I hid, telling him I knew where the dragon eggs were hidden."

The dragon shook his head in denial. "What does it matter? You will believe what you wish—that I am guilty of everything and I caused all your suffering."

"Not only mine, but my Nikita's as well." Tristan snarled. "And now at last she is back with me, after all these centuries."

Drust glanced at her and his mouth curled into a smile. The smile vanished, replaced with a cynical look.

"You finally have your Nikita back again as your mate, eh Tristan? Had I known this, I would have bought you a mating gift—a supply of Viagra. You are more than fourteen hundred years old. It must be difficult to maintain an erection at your age."

Unsmiling, Tristan stared back. "It's even harder to maintain one when you are dead, dragon."

"I may not have had sex in centuries, but at least I am not a randy wolf. Does Nikita know of your sexual conquests since you have been parted? All those women in your bed who shared your cock? How faithful to her memory were you, wolf?"

The words stung, even though she knew Drust said them to taunt the wizard. She knew that Tristan had taken many lovers over the centuries. But hearing someone actually say it brought an unpleasant visual to her mind. Tristan's wolf surfaced as sharp claws emerged from his fingers.

"Those women meant little to me. I gave them pleasure and they gave me pleasure as well. I never gave them anything else, and they did not expect anything."

"If you'd truly loved your mate all these centuries, Tristan, why did you seek pleasure in their beds? Wasn't the memory of Nikita good enough?" Drust mocked.

"My sex life is none of your concern, dragon." But she could see the strain around his mouth, and sense the gathering tension within him. Above the dragon, a huge crystal stalactite began to drip. Tiny droplets of crystal-clear water formed a puddle near Drust.

The stalactite smashed downward. Drust leapt aside just before it reached his head. The dragon blew a breath and red flames melted the man-sized crystal.

"It takes more than that to harm me here in the afterworld, you sly wolf. I'm already dead."

"Do not underestimate me. Just because you are living in the Land of Shadow does not mean I cannot make you suffer," Tristan snapped.

He opened his fist and a tremendous ball of silver fire flickered there. Tristan closed his fist and the energy ball vanished.

"Enough of this. I am here to take Prince Alexander back to the world of the living, where he belongs, so he may marry the Princess Sabrina and unite Clan Drakon and Clan Ciamoth."

"Alex doesn't want to marry her and he's not here." Drust leaned back, folded his arms.

"Liar," Tristan said softly. "I know exactly where he is, and what you have been doing with him. You have fed him all your knowledge and all your tales of honor and glory. You have made him promise to remember you, so your name will live on in history You made him your companion because you are so lonely at night your spirit screams for a friend, for anyone to converse with."

His smile grew dark. "Even a lowly black raven, who came to visit you, sat on your shoulder and saw all. You stroked his feathers and you called him friend, as you once called a Lupine friend before you betrayed me to King Emer, you fucking bastard."

Drust stared at Tristan, his jaw dropping, and stood,

nearly knocking over the chair. "You spied on me? You knew I was here, with Alexander, all this time?"

"I told you to never underestimate my powers, dragon. In life…and in death." Tristan's tone went deep with warning. "You have no business dealing with the living."

Drust stiffened. "You're an arrogant sod, Tristan. Haven't changed in centuries. Becoming the mighty Silver Wizard has only made you more high and mighty. My great-grandson is my blood, my business, you fucking wolf. Now get the hell out of my home."

Tristan ignored him. Nostrils flaring, he walked to the back of the cavern where another entrance had been cut into the mountain. "Prince Alexander, come out of there."

Nikita rubbed her hands, feeling suddenly cold. Pins and needles stabbed at her feet. She wasn't certain if the pain was from the emotions pulsing here in this cave, or something else.

A tall, handsome, dark-haired man entered the main cavern. His aura glowed bright silver, pulsing with threads of pure red. Out of all the creatures she'd seen in the Shadow Lands, he glowed the brightest.

It must be Alex.

Clad in blue jeans and a grimy gray baseball shirt, he stared at them. His silky black hair was clipped short and his lean cheeks and tight jaw were clean-shaven. He had blue-green eyes with thickset dark brows pulled downward into a scowl as he studied Tristan.

Drust joined his great-grandson and put a hand on his shoulder. "Alexander, I told you to keep to your studies. This has nothing to do with you."

But the crown prince shook off Drust's hand and approached Tristan without fear.

"What are you doing here? You, the wizard who refused to help my Emma."

The wizard's look was severe. "You cannot remain here, despite your ability. You are a Shadow Jumper, Prince Alexander. You are one of the rare Others with the ability to go back and forth between Earth and this world when a portal is opened, but that doesn't mean you can stay."

Niki went to the table and sat down, her legs feeling rubbery. She had no idea Shadow Jumpers existed, but such magick must be quite powerful.

The prince looked guilty. "I wanted to visit my Pops."

Drust's expression softened as he gazed at his great-grandson. "I am glad of your company, Alex, and I still have much to teach you."

Tristan shook his head. "Having the ability does not mean you can merely use that power as you wish. You have been jumping back and forth between worlds, using the portal I left open for your cousin Sebastian. I am taking that ability away from you unless you promise to never come here again."

Tristan's voice hardened. "There are great consequences to Shadow jumping. The more time you spend here, the less your attachment becomes to your world."

"I can't return yet. Not now. He's been teaching me, telling me ancient battle strategies in how to deal with the dragons who hurt my Emma."

"She is not your Emma," Tristan said gently.

"She's my best friend." Alex scrubbed his face with

both hands, his expression haunted. "Four red dragons jumped her in the woods and assaulted her before I could reach her. They could have killed her."

"Yes, but they did not."

Alex seemed to consider. "I'm a dragon, and I protect my own. You don't protect us. You're the all-powerful, all-mighty wizard and yet you let them roam free!"

The wizard only looked pained. "I am sorry about that, Alexander. I could not interfere with her fate. And it is not my duty right now to punish the dragons responsible for that evil. That I must leave for another time."

Secrets flickered in Tristan's dark eyes. Tristan was the Silver Wizard, guardian and protector of all shifters, including dragons. If it was not his duty, then whose duty was it to deliver justice?

"I can't lose Em," Alex whispered. "I don't wish to marry Sabrina and I will not rest until I find the red dragons who assaulted Em."

He gave Drust a fond look. "After Pops pulled me in here, he promised to help me learn to sharpen my battle skills in Skin and in dragon form. Pops told me he was an excellent warrior back in his day."

"All will work out as it should, Alexander. Trust me in this. When you prove yourself worthy, you shall win love. Now, are you ready to return home?" Tristan asked.

"I'm staying a while longer." Alex leaned against the wall and folded his arms. "Let them find another to marry the princess and became a stud for the kingdom. Why should I?"

"You have family who love you, Alexander."

Tristan's gaze went distant, as if seeing something from afar. "And you will find love of your own, a special love, if you listen to your heart."

The prince shook his head. "My family cares only about my title, not me as a person. It was only with Em that I felt I could be myself and not the prince." He glanced at Drust. "And here as well, with Pops. Give me a damn good reason to rush back there."

"There is this." Tristan removed the dragon's scale from his tunic pocket. "Your cousin's mate, Skylar, sacrificed this scale for you, as proof you are much needed on Earth. You have family there, family like Sebastian and Skylar, who love you. A clan who needs your leadership. This is no life for you here among the dead."

Alex took the scale and turned it over in his hands. Blinking, he looked up, his gaze filled with awe. "Sebastian did this for me? He allowed his mate, his greatest love, to have this taken from her?"

"Your cousin would do anything for you," Tristan said gently. "As his mate would. They agreed to sacrifice the scale to show you how precious you are to them and your clan."

The wizard glanced at Alex's ancestor. "Once Drust would have done the same for me, and I would have done it for him. We had that kind of bond as well, long ago, but it was broken."

Drust looked away, guilt etching his expression.

"Sebastian must be very worried about me to allow you to do this to Sky. She's his heart and soul." He turned the dragon scale over in his hand. "Did it hurt her?"

"Yes. But I replaced the scale with a crystal one,

courtesy of the Crystal Wizard. Skylar now has impenetrable diamond scales that no weapon may pierce."

Alex gave his first real smile. "Thank you. I'm sure that will ease Sebastian's mind. He's always worried about protecting her."

"A trait that comes with male shifter mates," Tristan murmured, his gaze flicking to her. "Are you ready to return home now?"

"I wish I could stay here a little longer. My Pops is the only one who has the patience to work with me to teach me ancient history, share stories of our family's lineage, and how to fight like a warrior with honor."

Honor? Nikita laughed. Suddenly very weary, she propped her chin upon one fist. "Your 'Pops' has no honor, Alexander. He was responsible for killing me in my last lifetime, and my unborn baby."

Alexander's jaw dropped. Drust shook his head. "Do not listen to them, son."

"Of course I won't. It's not true." The dragon prince turned to Drust. "Tell me it's not true."

Drust did not reply, only shook his head, looking ashamed.

"You killed her? And her unborn baby?!" Face expressive with shock and grief, he stared at his great-grandfather.

"That is what Tristan believes."

"Did you?" Alexander demanded.

"I was responsible for her death," Drust said quietly. "It was my fault."

"All this time you droned on and on about dragon honor, and you killed an innocent? A babe in the womb, and a pregnant woman?" Alexander burst out.

"Alexander, wait," Drust began…

"Your great-grandfather also betrayed me and caused my torture, and execution." Satisfaction etched Tristan's expression. "I daresay he failed to mention that tidbit in your lessons about ancient history."

Alexander stepped back, lines of strain bracketing his wide mouth, his jaw rigid.

"You're a bastard, Pops," the prince whispered. "You told me that our family lineage was honorable and now I find out that you betrayed Tristan, your friend? What honor is that? You told me to be a dragon prince I must never tolerate liars or those who would betray. And you did this?!"

Niki wanted to feel satisfaction at the guilt on Drust's face, but she did not. She only felt pity and sadness. To be rejected by one's own family must be shameful.

She wriggled her fingers, worried about how they seemed to be losing feeling.

"Alexander, it is not as you think," Drust said. Then the dragon's shoulders sagged. "You will not believe me, either."

Alex looked dully at his great-grandfather. "You are dead to me. Dead to all of us at Clan Drakon. I will enact this into law upon my return. No one will ever remember you, or tell tales around the fireplace of your great deeds because it's all bull. All of it."

Then the crown prince turned back to Tristan. "I'll go home. I never want to come here again."

Drust roared, flames shooting out of his mouth and covering the cavern wall. He reached out a hand to his descendant. "Alexander! Do not leave me here alone!"

Ignoring him, the prince walked up to the cavern wall, flattened his palm and closed his eyes. Suddenly an archway appeared on the rock. It looked like a doorway shrouded in mist. Alexander stepped back.

"I will close the portal after you use it, Alexander. It is too dangerous to leave it open any longer. You, and only you, can enter it once, and the gate will close," Tristan told him.

"Thank you," the prince said quietly. "Thank you for reminding me of the importance of family."

He gave a disgusted look at Drust. "Some family, anyway."

"Alex," Drust whispered. "Do not forsake me, son."

The dragon prince did not look back, but jumped into the portal. Tristan waved a hand and chanted, and then the portal closed.

Tristan palmed the dragon's scale with a look of tremendous satisfaction. "Your memory will turn to dust, dragon, as it should have centuries ago. Your kin has no loyalty to you. I command their loyalty now. Skylar gave me her dragon's scale to save her cousin from her own free will. They, too, now know what a murdering bastard you are."

Naked fury showed on Drust's face. The dragon snarled, his hands turning into claws and Nikita instinctively drew back, though she was a safe distance away. Drust turned his head and breathed fire at Tristan, but the flames did not touch the wizard.

"You took away everything from me, you fucking wolf." Drust came toward him.

Tristan growled and then shifted into wolf.

Drust shifted as well, into a silver dragon the size of

a small pony. Evenly matched in weight and muscle, they rushed at each other.

Snarling, they clashed, the enormous silver wolf and the silver dragon, clawing and biting. Tristan gained the advantage and tore at one of Drust's scales.

If the wolf tore out the damned dragon's throat, it would not be enough. She watched the fight with satisfaction, but deep inside, something nagged her that this was wrong. Did Drust truly kill her? Memories were made of shadows, it seemed.

The dragon bore great gouges on his scales. Her desire to see Drust hurt began to fade.

They could be locked here for days, weeks, ages, and there would be no resolution. Just as Tristan had spent too much time wandering these lands, locked in his own self-pity and misery. When would it end? This cycle of violence and anger?

Tristan said time had a way of warping in the Shadow Lands. How long had they been here? She had no way of knowing inside the cavern and she remembered Tristan's dire warning that they must get to Tir Na-nog soon.

All she knew was that she felt weaker, much weaker, since arriving at Drust's cavern. Niki glanced down at her arms. They seemed to be growing red. Odd.

"Stop it!" she cried out. "I don't want you to get hurt, Tristan!"

The wolf and the dragon broke apart and Tristan immediately shifted back into Skin. Drust turned back into human form, but instead of the solid body he seemed to project, his body looked less corporeal.

He was badly injured, while Tristan didn't even bear a scratch.

"Relax, Nikita. I am not injured." He turned to Drust. "It is time you fully paid the price for your betrayal of me, and murder of Nikita and our babe."

Tristan smiled grimly and waved a hand, transporting them to a scene straight out of her worst nightmare.

His past, and hers. The execution block.

CHAPTER 12

They were standing in a replica of the courtyard of the castle of King Emer. Tristan stood upon the same wooden platform where he had breathed his last breath.

Only this time it was Drust, clad only in gray leggings, his chest bare, his arms stretched upward. Thin ropes circling his wrists were looped around a hook on the pole, keeping him captive.

For centuries, he had waited for this moment and the justice Danu had promised to him. "You shall be avenged of the one who wronged you, Tristan," she had told him long, long ago.

He only possessed the power to exact revenge on those in the Shadow World who had wronged him.

Nikita, sitting on a green throne draped with vines and leaves, an exact replica of the one King Emer had sat upon as he watched Tristan die, looked pale and wan. Her skin was growing ruddy.

"Fear not, my sweet. This shall not take long." Tristan stepped close to Drust and clasped his throat. Though the dragon was not flesh, he could make him feel mental pain.

Exquisite pain.

Oh, he would not torture the dragon, and have Nikita watch and sicken her, reminding her of the past. But he would inflict on the dragon the mental anguish of waiting...

The horrid anticipation as the cloth hiding the sharp instruments was unfolded, and the executioner held up each gleaming piece and announced what he would do to him...

He brought his face close to Drust's. "Have you ever felt the agony of waiting for the whip to slice your skin? For a metal hook to tear into the muscles of your back, and the eventuality of knowing those who torment you will take your manhood away from you, in front of a jeering crowd, as your beloved watches? You try, oh you try, so hard to keep your silence, but then your screams become a song, and you pray for death."

"I am sorry, Tristan." Drust looked at him with dull eyes. "We were friends, once. Brothers in arms."

"An apology a little late, dragon. We were friends, until the day you betrayed me. Emer told me he gave you one hundred thousand pieces of gold in exchange for revealing where I hid. He showed me this in prison and laughed, and then he brought me here as his executioner ripped my flesh open and made me scream again, and again..."

He should feel triumph at finally having justice. But only emptiness settled in his chest. Deep inside, he knew this was wrong. It would give him no peace.

No. He must pay for hurting my Nikita and our baby. Tristan waved a hand to summon a hook in his palm.

He opened his hand.

It was empty.

Summoning all his magick, he tried again.

Nothing.

Tristan stared at his empty hands as Nikita sat on the throne, her head buried in her hands.

Horror pulsed through him, and knowing dread. Tristan looked at his former best friend. "You did not betray me."

Drust closed his eyes. "No. Just as I told you, I did not turn you in to the king's soldiers."

Tristan reeled. This made no sense. Gods, what had he done?

He waved a hand and the ropes holding Drust captive vanished. The dragon shifter slumped downward, sitting on the platform. Gray mist began creeping along the courtyard, hiding it from view.

The gray mist of shame.

"I never would have betrayed you, Tristan. Someone else did, and blamed me to make your torment even worse. They are responsible for writing that letter and signing my name to it." Bleakness showed in the dragon's eyes. "I was away at a meeting with other dragons, rallying them to fight with us. By the time I discovered what happened and returned, you were dead. And I blamed myself for not giving you a place more secure, a place where no one would find you."

Tristan glanced at Nikita, worried about her paleness, the shadows beneath her eyes. "Nikita remembered in a dream that you gave her the potion that killed her."

"I did. I begged for a potion from Mara to help

Nikita. She was bleeding and in danger of losing your babe. But someone poisoned it and she died."

"Who?"

"I don't know." Drust shook his head. "Perhaps Mara."

Mara, who was still alive. The bitch.

"I did not know. I looked into the past, and saw you," Tristan felt shame and horror creeping through him at the thought of wanting Drust to suffer as he had. "All these years… I thought it was you."

Drust sighed. "You kept insisting I was guilty and I was guilty, in a way. I failed you, Tristan. I failed our friendship and our brotherhood when I failed to keep you hidden and safe. I wanted to keep your mate and babe safe as well, and I failed in that."

He waved a hand. "This, more than anything, is why I have been stuck here, unable to move on."

But it made no sense. Many of his visions were clouded, but the one of Drust holding up his severed head had been most clear.

"I saw a vision. You holding my severed head up before a crowd and shouting." Tristan's jaw tightened. "In triumph."

"Visions from the past are always clouded when one is dead," Drust said ironically. "I did take your head from the pike on the castle wall, where Emer had it mounted. I flew down and retrieved it. If I could not save your body, then your spirit would live on…in the people and our cause, the cause you wanted to win, Tristan."

He blinked.

"It hurt me so badly to see what they had done to you, my friend. To know that the Lupine whose bond I cherished, whose courage never ceased, who sacrificed so much for all shifters, not just his people, had met with such an end. I wanted to fly over the king's castle, blow fire upon all who resided there. But I knew that was not the way to win the war. I took your head, and I showed it to the troops, who had grown disheartened with your death. I shook it at them as a rallying cry, 'Let his death not be in vain! Honor him with your lives.'"

Tristan went still, his stomach knotting, his throat burning.

"And then I buried you, in a place of honor, where Emer's soldiers would never find you. A warrior's burial. Fit for a king."

He could barely speak for all the emotion tight in his chest. A deep silence fell between them. And then Tristan remembered the good times he and Drust shared, fishing in the lake near the castle, dining in the great hall, hunting for prey in the forest.

"Thank you," he said quietly.

Drust's eyes were wet. He scrubbed at them with a shaking fist and then his mouth twitched in a ghost of a smile. "It was a rather large grave, for you always did have a big head."

"You always did accuse me of that," he recalled, needing to break this tension between them. "At least you found my head in one piece. The other pieces were scattered to the four corners of the kingdom. I imagine they were hard to find."

"And I had no time for a scavenger hunt," Drust joked back. "Especially trying to find your lost manhood. It was so small, it would be like hunting for a needle in a haystack."

"Larger than yours, dragon."

"Have you ever seen a dragon's penis after we shift? Much larger than a wolf."

"But Lupines can knot during sex and we can deliver much more pleasure to our mates."

Drust grinned. "I missed you, Tristan, my friend. I missed our sparring, and your humor."

The smile dropped. "Will you forgive me for failing you, and your lovely mate? For not protecting her and your child?"

Tristan's chest tightened. "No, my old friend. I failed you. I should have trusted in our friendship and our bond and not in watery visions of the past nor an evil Fae king's words."

The dragon reached out to offer his forearm for Tristan to clasp in the way of warrior brothers.

The humility in Drust's voice reminded Tristan of the other times when they had broken bread and fought together. "I forgive you," Tristan told him quietly, and felt something ease in his chest at last.

"Tristan," Niki called out. Her voice seemed feeble.

Turning, he looked at Nikita and felt fresh horror.

Time had a way of slipping away from you in the Shadow Lands. And in his thirst for revenge against Drust, he had neglected the most important thing in the world.

Nikita.

The magick potion that saved her life, that enabled her to venture through the Shadow Lands, was wearing off.

Her skin had turned a mottled red. Her hair was nearly all silver and her feet…he rushed to her, seeing only shadows where her toes had been.

Tristan reached for her right hand. Her fingernails had turned to crystals.

He had wasted an entire day pursuing his vengeance against Drust. If he did not get her out of the Shadow Lands and to the safety of Tir Na-nog by sunset, she would fade into shadow.

Forever.

CHAPTER 13

She felt weaker than she'd ever felt from the parvolupus virus. Niki struggled to stand from the opulent throne, and collapsed upon the wood platform.

I have no toes, she thought in a daze, staring at her ankles. *Maybe this is a dream and I'll awaken. What did you do to me, Tristan?*

The wizard rushed to her side, anguish tightening his expression. "Nikita. Oh my Nikita, I lost track of time. The potion is wearing off."

"You promised to always put my needs before all others," she whispered. "And once more, Drust and the war came first."

He looked at Drust. "I have to get her out of the Shadow Lands before sunset and to Tir Na-nog. She cannot walk. Will you help us?"

Conjuring his gray cloak once more, Drust rushed over to them. His gaze turned troubled as he looked at her and then upward at the sky.

The sky, which had started to grow darker.

"The Crystal Gate is closest," he said. "I have taken many dragons there, acting as their guide. Take her to the Crystal Gate."

Already she felt the strength leaving her limbs. Instinctively she knew if she remained, she would be forever lost.

Tristan clasped her hand, his mouth trembling. "Not an option. She could have passed through that gate prior to her body changing. Now, she cannot get through. She is neither flesh nor spirit, but turning to shadow. My only chance of saving her is to get her through the Dark Gate before sunset."

Drust's blue gaze flicked to Tristan. "Not a wise option. The Shadow Eaters gather at twilight at the Dark Gate. You don't have much time if you are to take her. The gate's location is always changing from one day to the next. But I know a way there for this day."

"What are Shadow Eaters? They don't sound good," she asked. *Not that this is much better…*

Tristan turned to her. "Cannibals. Consumers of flesh and guardians of the Dark Gate at night. At night in this world, the Dark Gate turns from the gate granting access to Tir Na-nog into the portal where the damned are forced to enter the Dark Lands. Hell."

Nikita felt her stomach pitch and roll.

"Your flesh would be quite a delicacy, Tristan," Drust pointed out. "If you dare risk it, and you're caught, they will eat you alive. They can't resist mortal flesh, and immortal flesh is like steak to a starving man."

He gave him a level look. "Take the dragon's scale."

Tristan nodded and craned his neck skyward. "We may need it as a diversion. We have only a little time. The Shadow Eaters appear only at dusk."

"Unless someone tells them."

He cocked a dark eyebrow at his friend. "I gather

you will not do so, and put your own spirit at forfeit, Drust. I will not tell if you do not."

"Fine with me."

Tristan lifted her into his arms. "We must hurry."

Niki had never felt so weary in her life. Time seemed clouded here and yet the passage of the day was clearly marked by the sun traveling across the sky. It hung lower now, but Tristan assured her they were close to the gate.

Walking ahead of them, Drust entered a forest of stubby, twisted trees. The very ground beneath them seemed torn and dry and cracked, as if it was cursed.

And then she saw ahead a pool of water, only this one was a deep, clear blue, like a fresh water spring.

"The water changes at night," Tristan murmured. "And when it comes time for a soul to pass through, the water turns to fire."

Remind me to bring an extinguisher. The thought did nothing to cheer her, or push aside the constant feeling of trepidation. Though no one else was at the spring, she sensed a presence.

Drust pressed on until they reached two trees that stretched almost to the sky. "The gate," he announced.

As Tristan set her gently down on the ground, Drust turned and looked at them. "Before we do this, my old friend, allow me to help you find the one who did betray you, and killed Nikita and your child."

"I am damn certain it was Mara, for she was jealous of Nikita. It is a delicate, diplomatic matter I shall have to handle myself. But thank you," he told Drust.

Tristan waved a hand and the pool of water became like fire. "It is time, Nikita," he said solemnly.

But instead of the relief she'd expected, the hairs on

her nape saluted the air. Tristan released a low curse. They all turned at the crackling of branches underneath heavy footsteps.

Someone had indeed betrayed them, for stepping out from the trees were not two, but four Shadow Eaters. They turned avidly towards her, their whispers stinging her ears.

"It is far too soon for them to arrive. Someone alerted them to our presence." Drust backed away.

"Mortal," one whispered. "Flesh. *Fresh flesh.*"

It grinned, showing sharp rows of jagged teeth stained with old blood.

It headed straight for her.

CHAPTER 14

Even her worst nightmares could not compare to the horror of the keepers of the Dark Gate. Drawing on all her strength, she struggled to remain standing.

The Shadow Eaters were skeleton-thin, with skin like desiccated liver she'd once eaten, so thin she could see the ribcages and joints of their bones. Red eyed, they had serrated teeth and the foul stench emanating from them smelled like rotting flesh.

"Let me distract them with this," Drust told Tristan, holding out the dragon's scale.

The dragon boldly walked up to the first wraith. "Let us pass. We offer payment, and it is not the time of the Dark Gate to manifest itself as the gate to the Dark Lands."

One took the diamond scale from Drust, turning it over. "It has power," it trilled in a thin, nasal voice. "Such power, with the blood and living flesh still attached. We crave flesh."

Another wraith looked at Drust with its cold, empty eye sockets. "For your payment, you may pass."

The four wraiths examined the scale and began to argue over tasting it.

"Hurry," Drust urged. "They're distracted."

But as they started for the pool, the wraiths looked up and hissed. "Not the rest of you. Only the dragon."

Drust hesitated on the edge of the pond. "The girl, at least, goes with me. The scale is for us both."

A wraith stretched out a long claw. "We shall take the wizard. He is immortal and holds much power. Very tasty."

"Go," Tristan yelled, and then he pushed Drust.

Light exploded before her eyes as the dragon entered the gate. As Tristan went to push her into the water, she struggled against him. "Not without you!"

"No! Go, Nikita, before they discover your mortality," he hissed.

But she dug in her heels and then the wraiths surrounded them. One yanked Tristan backwards as another gripped her wrist. Gorge rose in her throat. She struggled against retching from the stench of the wraith.

Tristan conjured a knife and sliced his arm. The four Shadow Eaters stilled.

"My blood and my flesh hold immortal power. Take me," Tristan roared.

The wraith holding Nikita captive released her as all four converged on Tristan. They pulled him downward, opening the red slits of their mouths.

And they began to devour him alive. Tristan screamed.

Heart beating like a war drum, she looked around for a weapon, for anything to draw them off. Panic made it difficult to breathe. *Think, think!*

Flesh. They craved flesh. Searching the ground, she found the knife Tristan dropped.

This must work.

One Shadow Eater began to gnaw on Tristan's arm. He struggled harder. And then his wild, tormented gaze met hers.

She felt an anguish and pain so deep, it was as if the Eaters consumed *her* alive, not Tristan. And then she knew he had suffered this before.

Many times.

No!

"Nikita." Tristan's voice was hoarse. "Do not give them what they crave, lest you release a beast. They will never forget the taste of mortal flesh, and will hunger for it all their days."

But she could not stand by and wring her hands while this courageous wizard, who had done so much to aid her, was torn apart. Even if his body would mend, what about his spirit?

Danu, make my hand steady and my aim quick. Give me the courage to do this to save him.

Niki bit her lip to stifle the scream. The cut was swift, and on target. White-hot pain lanced her as she sliced off her pinkie. She ran toward the four wraiths. One straddled Tristan and was about to consume his face. Her wizard bellowed in agony as another began to tear into his leg with sharp, jagged teeth.

Then all four stopped at the scent of her blood, looked up and swiveled their heads toward her.

"Flesh. Sweet, living flesh," one crooned.

Niki tossed her finger away. The wraiths, eager for the treat, rose off Tristan and raced after it. With her uninjured hand, she pulled him upward.

Silver blood streamed down his face. Half his nose was missing, his lips were torn and bloodied, and his earlobes were ribbons of flesh. He ran/limped with her toward the blue pool.

"Together," he said. "Where you go, I go."

"Together," she told him. "Where you go, I go!"

They jumped into the pool, and water washed over her in a soothing blanket.

It did not burn, nor hurt. All she felt was the same whooshing sensation as when she'd fallen into the pond back at her ranch. But this time, she was not alone. Tristan kept a secure grip on her hand and the comfort of his touch grounded her.

When they landed, it was upon a soft bed of the greenest moss she'd ever seen. Niki blinked hard, woozy, but the pain of her finger had vanished. She felt stronger and healed.

She wriggled her fingers. All of them were on her left hand and all had turned back to flesh. Niki looked at her arms. They were normal skin tone. It was as if she'd never cut off her finger. Tristan too, had healed.

"How did this happen?" she asked.

"In the afterworld of Tir Na-nog, one is easily healed."

But flickering in his eyes was the darkness she'd glimpsed before the Shadow Eaters descended on him. The memories could not be as easily healed.

"You should not have done that."

The distant note back in his deep voice, Tristan looked as remote and forbidding as he had in the past. The Silver Wizard had returned, pushing aside the Tristan she had known who watched over her steps.

"I would not see them tear into you. Again." She

picked up his smooth, healed hand and kissed each knuckle. "I could not bear it. It was worth the agony of my pain to distract them."

And then something inside him seemed to crumble, like stone walls collapsing on a sturdy tower.

"Ah, Nikita." He sounded broken as he smoothed back her hair, kissing her now healed and restored finger. "My poor, brave Lupine. You gave yourself to save me. A blood debt that I cannot repay. An act that will have dire consequences in the future, I fear. You are a true warrior princess of old."

She touched his healed mouth. "No. I'm Niki, a Lupine of this century. Not a warrior princess. But a Lupine who will not abide another's suffering."

Her voice went soft. "Especially yours."

For a moment he stood there, rubbing his cheek against her hand, his eyes closed. Then he straightened and looked like the Silver Wizard once more. Tristan pointed to the forest.

"The entrance to my home is there."

"Where is Drust?"

"He has gone ahead on his own journey. Come, my sweet."

They walked a few yards before reaching the gate. The portal was more of a fairy gate, with mossy green tree limbs arced to form a long tunnel. A glowing yellow and green light pulsed at the end. Enchanted, she glanced down at the stepping stones that led to the light. Each one was framed in green with runes scratched upon the surface. The air smelled of pine and fragrant musk. Her wolf senses pricked with awareness, but no sense of danger loomed here.

Only a deep peace and dawning feel of excitement.

"It's like coming home," she marveled.

Tristan nodded, his mouth tight. "My home."

But not hers. She belonged to the land of the living, and could not remain here for more than ten days with him, unless she drank the potion of the Blood Moonflower.

Clasping her hand, he walked with her to the gate. Warm, fragrant air washed over her as they traversed the stepping stones. There was no tugging sensation, nor the horror and panic she'd felt when she'd nearly been sucked down into the swamp waters in the Shadow Lands. Nothing but a feeling of utter peace and joy.

When they cleared the gate, she saw a stretch of golden meadow, and a distant forest. Birds sang as they flew overhead, and she saw a crystal clear stream cutting through the meadow.

Tristan turned to her, a soft smile on his handsome face. "Welcome home, my sweet."

She had no memory of this place, yet her wolf senses tugged playfully, urging her to shift. "Can I turn into my wolf here?"

He nodded. "Lupines are granted a brief stay in Tir Na-nog, but only as wolf. I granted this to Kyle and Arianna when they needed to heal. But because we are here, in the magick of my home, you may assume whatever form you wish—Skin or Lupine."

Niki poked his arm. "Shift with me. Let's run!"

The change came over her swiftly, so fast she was barely aware of it. But unlike shifting to wolf on Earth, here her senses were already empowered. The grass smelled ripe and the air was pure and cool against her nose as she raced across the field.

Looking backward, she saw a silver wolf, large as a small pony, hot on her heels. Giving a joyous yip, she dodged and darted through the meadow, thrilling to the chase. Her instincts recognized the silver wolf as one who would never hurt her, for he was her mate.

Niki saw a translucent bubble floating on the wind and gave chase, her jaws snapping, her paws thudding hard against the ground. The bubble exploded, releasing a tiny sprite, who darted around her muzzle like a blue-green, blinking firefly.

"Welcome, Nikita," it trilled.

"You talk?" she asked. "But you don't bite, or do you?"

A high pitched giggle came from the sprite. "No, I don't bite."

Wait. She was...talking? Holy wolfsbane, she was having a conversation with a sprite...in her wolf form!

She ground to a halt and turned, and Tristan collided with her, toppling her to the ground.

Niki pawed at his face. "Get off me, wizard. You're heavy."

Grinning, showing rows of sharp teeth, he dodged her claws. "I'll be upon you heavier yet," he said.

The image came to mind, Tristan naked atop her, moving as he thrust deep inside. Startled, she rolled over and stood, shaking off her coat. "This is too strange. I'm a talking wolf. Like a cartoon!"

"It's the fantasy world of my homeland." He stood and nuzzled her throat. "Would you like me to murmur sweet words into your little pointed ear?"

She stuck her tongue out at him.

He shifted back and lay in the grass, laughing as she

nipped at his hand, and then licked his face. "Stop it, you're tickling me," he said, still laughing.

Niki shifted back to Skin and imagined herself in a flowing pink gown, with starlight sequins rimming the hem. She sat beside him as he stretched out, gazing at the sharp blue sky.

Gone was the wariness, the ever-present slight tension gripping him since the moment he'd swept her into his arms back at her ranch and spirited her away. No more faint lines of strain bracketing his mouth, stamping his dark eyes. It was as if arriving at his home had peeled away a protective layer to show the vulnerable Lupine beneath.

Yet still burning in his gaze was the ever-present passion she'd glimpsed from their first meeting. Tristan slid his muscled arms around her and gathered her close.

Niki cupped his smooth cheek, glad to see the shadows vanished from his eyes. "You look different. Younger."

"I feel as if I've been asleep, or dead, for nearly a thousand years. And now, here with you, my blood is pumping again and my heart is beating. I'm alive." He pulled her closer, smoothing back the masses of her tangled hair with a hand that shook.

Nikita marveled at the tremor, at the tender vulnerability etched in his expression, and the wonder, as if he saw his world anew.

"I'm alive and everything is whole again, and dancing with color. I can smell the lilies in the field, and hear the wind moving through the trees from miles away. Not because of my magick and my immortality, power bestowed on me to be the guardian of shifters, but because of you, Nikita. You've breathed life into my dark soul. You took away this cynical, cold bastard and turned him into a man once more, a man who longs for your touch, for the whisper of your kiss."

He lowered his mouth to hers, barely brushing his lips across hers. It was a light, teasing touch, a taste of what was to come.

Trembling with her own excitement, she tensed, reaching again for the control that always dodged her heels. As if he sensed this, Tristan pulled away and gazed down at her.

"Let go. Don't try to control it." He kissed her again, framing her face with his warm hands. His mouth tasted like the most exotic wine tinged with her favorite chocolate. Dizzy with need, she kissed him back.

All her life she'd been under someone else's control, heeding the instructions of her family, and then, of her identical twin. Never before had she allowed herself to release her innermost inhibitions, even when she ran wild as wolf in the forest. Always there had been a leash of restraint, wary of what might happen if she lost herself in the moment.

She'd been too fearful of the future, too wrapped up in the possibilities of her own demise, to truly enjoy life. Now, in Tristan's arms, Niki knew she had nothing to lose.

Trusting him wasn't easy, but he'd promised to never hurt her. So she leaned into him, cherishing the pleasure coursing through her veins, the way he seemed so tender, and yet raged with a fire only she could extinguish.

Niki relished the power she held over him, not for the sake of power itself, but for the pleasure she could give this immortal. She knew what they'd shared in the past had been unique and priceless.

"Come. My cottage is through those woods." He stood and stretched out his hand.

Taking his palm, she walked with him toward the forest, ignoring the nagging voice inside her warning this would never last, for it could not.

Warning her to never hand over what she'd guarded all these years.

Her virginity.

CHAPTER 15

Tristan's cottage, tucked away deep in a wooded glen, filled her with awe. Two stories high, it was hewn from rough timbers, but upon entering, she saw the most comfortable modern furnishings. The living room had a blue silk striped sofa, and there was a wide screen television hanging over the river rock fireplace.

In the back was a wide wood deck with a splendid view of the creek wending through the woods, and another meadow that showed a vista of jagged purple mountains.

"Heaven," she sighed.

"Home. Each of us is allowed to create a home however we wish."

"Why didn't you create Castle Baldwin?"

He spoke quietly into her mind. *Castle Baldwin was where we spent many happy hours, my sweet, but it was also a place of blood and death. I wanted this, our heaven away from the castle, to be my home. Do you not recognize it?*

Niki went to the fireplace and ran a hand over the mantel. It tingled beneath her palm, as if the memories had come to life. "Our cottage in the woods you had built for us, as our special retreat from the world. Except you updated it with modern furnishings."

"The Dark Ages were rather bleak when it came to interior design."

He took her hand and led her into the single bedroom. The king-sized bed was fashioned from thick oak limbs.

Good thing I have a sturdy bed.

She glanced at him and saw his knowing smile. Nikita blushed, knowing what he planned to do with her in this room…

Tristan sat on the white comforter and patted a space beside him. "It is quite comfortable, my sweet."

"I'm certain it is."

"I would ask you to test it out, but we will be spending plenty of time here later. I plan to keep you very busy in my bed." A roguish grin touched his sensual mouth.

A tingle of anticipation rushed down her spine. Niki's palms sweated and she scrubbed them against her clothing. Trapped in bed with Tristan for ten days, making love…

He crooked a finger at her. "Come here."

She stood between his opened thighs and braced her hands on his shoulders, feeling tensile muscle and bone beneath his clothing. So hard and so very male. Tristan took a lock of her hair and twirled it teasingly around his finger.

"So beautiful," he murmured. He released the lock of hair and splayed his fingers on her hips and then gently squeezed. "So very plumb and ripe, like a tasty peach."

Then Tristan cupped her face and kissed her, his

tongue teasing and light at first, and then going deeper. Nerve endings screaming for more, she leaned into the kiss, craving those long, lazy strokes of his tongue. Her nipples turned diamond hard and blood pooled low in her loins.

He broke the kiss and his smile was filled with wicked promise.

"A small taste of what I plan for later, but not to your mouth." His smoldering gaze flicked down to the space between her legs.

Nearly boneless with desire, she turned away, knowing he could not love her until he was mortal. She went to a door and opened it and gasped with delight. Dozens of gorgeous gowns hung in the closet. Sifting through the clothing, she found a violet gown that seemed lighter than air and felt like satin against her fingers as she stroked the fabric.

Tristan joined her and pointed to the shoe rack. "All designer shoes and styles and all will fit you perfectly."

"You're going to spoil me like crazy."

Tenderness edged out the hard male lust on his face. He grazed his thumb against her lower lip, stroking with a languid grace that warned this male would be lethal in that bed of his. All her female hormones cranked up and Niki realized with a start that he'd been right. She was coming into her heat.

"I want you to be happy here, Nikita, and have everything you desire."

She turned from him, fighting her own rising desire, and went to the other door. Niki opened it to the most luxurious gold and white tiled bathroom, featuring a glassed-in shower with twin jets and a gleaming bone-white toilet.

Tristan watched her quietly as she turned back to him. "You have no need of a bathroom."

"Until now." He returned to the living room and she followed. Tristan pulled open a door on the cabinet near the fireplace. He removed a flask and then uncapped it. Blue, glowing liquid swirled in the vial. He stared at it, his gaze troubled.

"When I drink this, I will lose all my powers. I will be as weak as I was nine hundred years ago when Emer's men tortured me."

A shadow crossed his face. "I took all the precautions for this moment, Nikita. This cottage, this world around us, has a protective spell that keeps the blood pumping through our bodies. As mortal Lupines, you and I cannot venture past the boundaries. If we do, we shall both die.

"I warded my homeworld with powerful magick to fulfill all your hopes and dreams." Tristan looked wistful. "I wished to create a world where you could learn to love me as you once did nine hundred years ago."

Her throat tight, she touched his hand. "I remember that world before it turned into dust. It was a good life, Tristan."

The blue liquid glowed brighter, sparkling now. He swirled the vial again. "I gave you the protection of my body and my magick when I rescued you from the parvolupus virus, my sweet. But my powers will be limited once I take this. I will be nothing more than a mere Lupine once more."

A mere Lupine? "You never were only Lupine, Tristan. You were powerful as mortal, powerful enough to lead an army to fight the Fae. And I am not the helpless Lupine I was nine hundred years ago." She stroked his trembling hand with a gentle caress. "I want to experience this with you, experience all you want to show me."

A faint smile touched his mouth. "My courageous Nikita. Always the spirit of a wild wolf." He looked down at the potion.

"Bottoms up," he murmured, and drank, grimacing.

Astonished, she watched the subtle glow of silver ringing his body vanish. The silver tips of his hair turned dark and a jagged scar appeared on his firm chin. He staggered backward and sat on the sofa.

"That was not nice," he muttered. "I feel so damn weak now. I hate being weak."

Niki sat beside him and touched the scar with a trembling finger. "I remember this mark. You got it after your first battle in the Fae Wars."

"It vanished when I became the Silver Wizard. I am not immortal now, Nikita."

Tristan smiled, but there was a tired look about him, and purple smudges beneath his eyes. "I must rest, my sweet. Draining my powers is arduous."

This powerful being, who never slept, was now as vulnerable as she was. The thought troubled her as she lay on the bed with him. Tristan stretched out, one hand above his head.

He closed his eyes. She watched him, her chest hollow. *Oh Tristan, part of me wishes I could replace what we lost and stay with you here forever, creating the family we were denied. And the other half that never experienced life wants to just run away and be free.*

Niki rolled over to her side and closed her eyes.

And fell into the past, as she had before.

236

Only this past brought her to the executioner's block. Tristan was on his knees, staring wildly at her as she rushed to the platform.

Sorrow pierced her, such anguish that she sobbed. Her mate, her beloved, was going to die in agony. She would never see him again. Two of King Emer's guards came and grabbed her arms to tug her away from the platform.

A promise from him, her beloved…he would hold fast to it and never break it, even through the centuries…

"Promise me, Tristan," she cried out as they dragged her away. "Please, promise me we will be together again, in another life, another time. I cannot bear to live without you. You are my only love."

"Nikita, my sweet." The anguish in his eyes would haunt her for the rest of her days. "I promise. I will find a way to return to you. I love you forever. I will love you…"

A glint of sunlight on steel as the executioner's hook descended. She could not watch, but his screams sliced through her. *Tristan, my Tristan, my only love. I will never love another man. Come back to me somehow, some way. Don't leave me, please don't leave me…*

And then it was over and he screamed no more.

Niki awoke, panting, her heart racing with panic and grief. Beside her, Tristan stirred. His eyes flew open. Dark brown, she thought, tears trickling down her cheeks. In their life together, they had been a deep, clear blue.

"My sweet Nikita, what is wrong?"

She hugged him tight, fearing if she let go he would die, as he had more than nine hundred years ago. She had made a promise in her heart, a promise she'd never broken. The Nikita of the past knew this, and guarded her heart well.

"I remember now. I know why you came to me back at the ranch, why you saved my life. It wasn't for your own purposes. You were fulfilling your promise."

"Yes," he said quietly.

"You promised me. You promised we would be together again, and that's why we're together now." She clung to his wrists. "All this time I thought it was because you simply wanted a child, a baby to create your legacy. It was me all along who made you come back."

Gently, he stroked a finger over her trembling mouth. "Do not weep, Nikita. I am here with you now, as I was then, as I am, forever."

For a moment she clung to him, and then she wiped her eyes with the linen cloth he handed her.

"And we can be together, always, as a family, if you choose to drink the potion made from the Blooded Moonflower."

His voice was distinctly neutral, but she saw the faint hope flicker in his eyes. It was too much for now. Tristan or her family? How could she choose?

She didn't have to choose until their time together had ended here.

"What now? Is there anything to eat in your magick cottage?"

"Are you hungry?" he asked.

"Very much so. I haven't been until now."

"A side effect of mortality," he said cynically. "I am quite starved. Get dressed and I shall take you to dinner."

"There's a restaurant here in your home?"

"Only the best for you, my sweet." He winked at her.

A while later, they were seated outside at a round table in a clearing in the woods. Sprites hovered overhead, their brilliant iridescent green and blue lights twinkling amid the gathering darkness. Golden light glowed softly from the lanterns hanging from the trees and the single candle flickering on the tablecloth. A shaft of bright moonlight dappled the pines overhead.

Tonight she'd chosen a silk gown of deep violet, embroidered with silver thread on the hem and sleeves and silver ballet slippers.

In a black suit, white shirt and a red checked tie, Tristan looked like a young business executive, except for his shoulder-length hair.

And the air of age shimmering around him, even in mortal form. He looked no older than 30, until you looked deep into his eyes and saw the shadows of his haunted past.

Tristan leaned over and clasped her hand. "Does this please you?"

"It's lovely. How did you…"

He gave an elegant shrug. "I created a world I thought you would like, my sweet. I wanted us to have a real date, just as mortal Lupines would."

"Mortal Lupines would spend their first date running in the woods, catching rabbits and belching."

His dark eyes widened. "Truly?"

She laughed, glad to see she could tease this powerful wizard. "No. I went on a couple of dates, in Nia's place. They were nothing like that."

"Did these Lupines respect you?"

She smiled at his deep, protective tone and the frown wrinkling his forehead. "Yes. They were guys, but they didn't try anything. It was just movies and dinner. One date took me to a rodeo. I really liked that. I didn't get out much, as you know."

"And how does this compare to those dates?"

He sounded the tiniest bit anxious, and that shredded the last of her shyness. "This is beautiful, Tristan. I adore the fairy lights."

He beckoned to a sprite, murmured some words and the sprite flew away. Moments later, soft music filled the air.

Nikita laughed, recognizing the song. "The theme song from Titanic?"

"One of your favorites," he said in a husky voice, leaning forward. "I know all of them."

"Why? Have you been stalking me?"

She asked this in a light, teasing tone, but deep inside, she wondered how Tristan managed to know so much about her in this life. His knowledge of her in their past life she understood. *But I am not that Lupine any longer. She is gone, far gone.*

Solemnly he picked up her hand and laced his fingers through hers. "Never. I respected your privacy."

"Then how did you know this was my favorite song?"

His hand left hers and he looked guarded.

"No secrets, Tristan."

He picked up his wineglass and took a sip of the sparkling liquid. "In conversation with Danu, she informed me that your mother knew all about you. She's always watched over you."

Nikita nearly choked on her own sip of wine. "My mother? She died shortly after I was born!"

"I know. But she never stopped loving her girls."

Tears clogged her throat. "What else can you tell me?"

"Each time you sang this song, it filled her with music. She knew how much you adored this song, just as she knew how you enjoyed the challenge of your studies in biology and science. Your mother was most proud of you."

She dared to ask the question what she'd wondered about since she'd jumped through the portal into the Shadow World. "Can I see her?"

Regret filled his expression. "In another life, perhaps."

Though disappointment filled her, she was glad her mother had cared. "Tristan, why were you talking with the goddess about me?"

He ran a finger down the stem of his wineglass. "To seek final permission to bring you here, to my home. It is forbidden to mortals. Though she had granted my request long ago when I became the Silver Wizard, I needed one last assurance."

He looked directly at her. "I would never do anything to harm you, my sweet."

She folded her hand over his. "I know that, now."

"I did discover a few secrets about you, and your

twin." An impish light danced in his dark eyes. "You two are gifted with extraordinary Lupine powers, as happens in the rare twin births."

"I doubt it. I've never felt it."

"The power has yet to manifest itself, for you are but a young Lupine. When you turn older, your powers will increase."

Their meals arrived. Nikita dug into her prime rib with great enthusiasm. It seemed fresher and more delicious than any other meal she'd ever tasted. As they ate, Tristan talked about cases he'd had in the past as the Silver Wizard, and about his favorite Lupines. Kyle, the ranch hand to Aiden Mitchell, was one of them. Kyle was half Lupine, half Satyr, who was fiercely loyal and had walked alone for many years before meeting his mate, Arianna.

After dinner, they strolled back through the woods using the stepping stones cutting through the woods. Each time her foot landed on one, it chimed a note, and lit up. Delighted, she ran back and forth over them, as he watched with a smile.

When they went inside his cottage, melancholy came over her. Dining with him brought back memories of the Lupine she had loved long ago. And too well she remembered the pain of watching him die, and soon, she would have to part from him all over again unless she chose to give up her family forever. It wasn't fair, but life wasn't meant to be fair.

Tristan touched a lamp on the bedside table and it lit up with a soft golden glow. More magick. Tonight, she needed to create a special magick of her own with him.

Niki turned to him, clutching a handful of his white silk shirt. "Don't leave me. Make it so we'll always be together in memory, Tristan, and I'll always carry part of you inside me. Tonight, make me yours."

He searched her face. "Are you certain you are ready for this?"

She nodded.

Tristan had assured her he would never hurt her, and deep inside, her heart cried out for this moment. She trembled as he pressed a finger to his mouth and then to hers. The whisper of a kiss, the same gesture he had made on that long-ago wedding night.

"I promise I will be gentle this time, my sweet, and give you as much pleasure as possible." He brushed a kiss against the corner of her mouth, then placed his warm, calloused palm against her flushed cheek.

Niki smiled and rubbed her cheek against his hand. "And I promise I won't bite."

Laughing, he pulled her into his arms, where she belonged, where she had always belonged. He kissed her lips, then feathered little kisses across her cheeks. He dropped one singularly sweet kiss upon her nose.

Then he took her mouth, gently probing against her lips with his tongue, until she parted for him. His tongue danced against hers, and she met his urgent thrusts with bold ones of her own. She knew this dance, though she was innocent, for her memory urged her onward. The dance he would initiate when he joined their bodies as one.

Tristan feathered tiny kisses against the warm skin of her throat, licked the curve of her earlobe and lightly bit. Such a tease.

Pulling away, she studied the pulse throbbing in his neck. "Biting me, wolf?"

"Paying you back for our wedding night, wench." He cupped her breast and lazily stroked a thumb across one hardened. "I plan to pay you back in ten times the pleasure."

Moaning, she clung to him, her fingers digging into the hard muscles of his shoulders. He nuzzled the space on her neck where he had placed his possessive mating mark all those centuries ago. Her skin was untouched. That would change when he turned fully wolf and marked her, she thought with dizzying pleasure as his hand slid up to cup her breast.

Everything consumed her in a whirlwind. Niki shuddered as he slipped her gown off her shoulder, baring her breast. He put his mouth on her nipple, swirling his tongue in hot circles, working wicked magic across her shivering body. He was a powerful wizard who belonged to shifters, but now, in her arms, he was hers. Exclusively hers.

She bent her head to the crook of his neck, and ran her tongue along his warm skin, tasting him. Beneath her tongue his skin tasted slightly salty, mingled with the sweetest wine and it reminded her of that other time and place, when their first time together had been crude and hasty.

He was not in a rush now. Indeed, Tristan took his time arousing her. She grew impatient, not he.

Drawing from her inborn sensuality that was wholly Lupine, she slid the gown free of her body, and it spilled at her feet. Through the opened window the breeze fluttered the gauze curtains and caressed her now-naked skin.

Desire glittered in his dark gaze as he gazed upon her nudity. "You are so beautiful, lovelier than the vision I've held close to my heart for more than nine hundred years."

Tristan shrugged out of his suit jacket, undid his tie and sat on the massive bed to toe off his shoes. When he was divulged of all clothing, he stood before her, in quiet pride, tall, his muscles gleaming in the candlelight, his phallus erect.

Her eyes widened, not in maidenly shock, but in fierce need as she beheld his rigid length. Noticing her stare, Tristan's gaze twinkled.

"Do you like what you see, my sweet? What are you thinking?"

"I am thinking that I must have been quite mad to bite you that high on your leg on our mating night all those years ago. Or very accurate with my mouth because I truly could have done considerable damage and made you into a eunuch."

He laughed. "I trust you," he said teasingly. "Do you trust me?"

His gaze grew solemn. "Do you, Nikita?"

She nodded.

Tristan cupped her face with his hands. "I promise you, Nikita, I shall be faithful to you all my days. Even if you choose to remain mortal and return to Earth, I will never have another woman in my arms but you. You are the only one for me. I have waited 900 years for this moment to be one with you, and I would wait another 900 to have you back in my arms."

His tender pledge made her heart ache and her throat tighten. "Being with you now makes me forget all the pain of our past. Make it vanish forever, Tristan. Make new memories with me, ones I can carry with me through the ages."

"I will," he whispered.

Skin to skin. Nothing between them. No barriers. Seeing his naked, tanned flesh stretched over muscle and sinew, lowered all her inhibitions. Here, with her, Tristan was no longer a powerful wizard, nor a phantom from her past. He was living flesh and blood, a man who had longed for her, had waited for her.

What woman could say her lover, her mate, waited nearly a millennia for her return? To laugh with her, hold her in his arms and make love to her and whisper his undying fidelity?

With a small intake of breath, she touched him. Fingers trailing hesitantly at first over the silky hairs of his forearm, up to the curve of his bicep and then the muscles of his broad shoulders. Tristan remained absolutely still, letting her explore. To have this magnificent male at her power, to do with as she pleased...she was in control.

Her fingers lightly grazed his flat abdomen, exploring the valleys and curves of his ripped torso, then she went lower.

A single stroke along the rigid length of his erection, straining upward from a nest of black curls at his groin.

A single droplet, like a tear, leaked from the rounded tip of his penis. She touched it and he trembled.

Niki brought her finger to her mouth and tasted him. Slightly salty, with a hint of honey.

His scent shot through her like liquid heat, arousing the most female and feral part of her wolf. Tristan smelled like fresh air on a summer day, newly hewn grass, cool water tumbling down a mountainside. She had always been more comfortable in wolfskin than human skin because only as wolf could she run free, escaping the confines of her luxurious basement prison.

And then he gave a little mysterious smile and kissed her, cupping her bottom and squeezing and kneading. The hard, rigid length of him pressed against her soft belly as his mouth worked magick upon hers—reminding her that she was not in control after all. This wizard had enchanted her with his sensuality, and his devotion.

Everything whirled around her: sensation upon sensation, the slickness of their fevered bodies pressing together, the mingling of his warm breath upon her flushed skin, her trembling fingers pressing against bone and hardened muscle.

Tristan swept her into his arms and laid her gently upon the turned down bed. The soft golden glow of lamplight shone upon his naked skin.

He drew her to the bed's edge and parted her thighs, staring intently at pink flesh made wet, not by oil, but her own arousal. Then he put his mouth on her.

She went rigid, shaking with pleasure, screaming out his name as his tongue swirled and licked over her clit, then slowly stroked between her wet slit. The ache became pummeling tension with each delicious caress. Niki gathered fistfuls of sheets in her hands and arched her back as his teasing strokes became more urgent. And then the tension riding low in her loins increased and she shattered, crying out and arching her back.

Dark gaze glittering, he raised his head and wiped his mouth with the back of one hand. "You taste more fragrant and sweeter than the most honeyed fruit, like sweet nectar sliding down my throat."

He gently pushed her fully back upon the bed As she scrambled back to lie against the pillows, he moved over her trembling body, stretching out her arms and lacing his fingers through hers. This was it, then, no going back.

She never wanted to go back, not into their past. This moment was exquisitely theirs, here and now.

Tristan edged his lean hips between her thighs. Bracing his weight on one elbow, he took his rigid penis in hand, guiding it to her sleek heat. Breath tore from her throat as he pushed gently at her swollen, soaked folds.

"Look at me," he told her softly.

And then he was inside her, joining them fully. She winced at the slight stinging pain. Tristan raised his head, his smoldering gaze locked to hers. Amid the primitive possessiveness there swirled such tenderness that her breath hitched.

"Are you all right, my sweet?" He pressed a gentle kiss against her forehead.

Niki reached up and cupped his cheek. "I am, my love."

He smiled and his expression grew intent as he began to move, his thrusts taking on new urgency. Blood sang through her veins as the pleasure intensified. A bead of sweat gathered on his forehead and then dropped upon her breast, as sparkling as a tear in the sunshine.

Erotic pleasure gathered low in her loins as he plunged into her over and over, and she felt another orgasm claim her.

He collapsed upon her trembling body. Emotionally overwrought, Niki stared over the taut curve of his muscled shoulder, tasting the salt of her tears, breathing in his rich, cedar and pine scent, feeling the cooling breeze through the windows dry the sweat on their joined bodies. His head dropped into the curve of her neck as he panted, his chest rising and falling.

Awash with pleasure and sensual lassitude, she stroked his damp hair. Tristan, her greatest love. Bonding with him in the flesh had proven erotic and given her a sense of belonging she'd sought all her life.

But she knew it would not last. For in less than ten days, she must return to the mortal realm.

And he would remain here, forever.

CHAPTER 16

Tir Na-nog was like a fantasyland where all her dreams could come true, except for finally meeting her mother, and she'd set aside that disappointment. For twenty-five years, Nikita had lived life as a shadow in a basement, and now Tristan showered her with attention. He seemed determined to make her happy.

All the adventures she'd always longed to experience were at her fingertips, made possible by the wizard who made her burn with desire. He took her water skiing at a blue lake, expertly maneuvering a fast little boat as she skied. Pearl-colored dolphins leapt out of the lake as she passed, and peacock blue fairies skimmed the water, leaving glistening trails of fairy dust in their wake. She and Tristan went hiking in mountains that resembled the jagged peaks of Colorado she'd always longed to visit. They explored and traveled, all within the boundaries of his world. They even sipped chicory coffee at a small outdoor café in a city just like the French Quarter of New Orleans, but for the fact the coffee was served by a pink-haired ballerina who danced her way over to their table, coffee and beignets in hand.

On their fifth day together, they went to a beach in his home territory. It was complete with a turquoise ocean, a hot yellow sun shining in the blue sky and a Tiki Bar. Fairies, acting as waiters, flew back and forth to serve tropical drinks with little yellow umbrellas.

Lounging in a lavender bikini (her favorite color) on a beach chair next to Tristan, she read an historical romance novel that had long gone out of print. Tristan had a library bigger than the lost one at Alexandria, and anything she desired to read he could find. She poured through science journals she had never been able to access and biology papers about Lupines and their cell structure, and the magick within them.

Yesterday they had spent a quiet afternoon at the cottage. He read the writings of Socrates while she indulged in Hawking's A Brief History of Time.

Once in a while he would look up and talk about a passage, and they'd argue about philosophy. Each time she brought up a point, he'd counter expertly.

For each point he won, she had to lose a piece of clothing.

And when she was fully naked, he stripped as well. He took her by the hand to the bed and they made the headboard slam against the wall as she clung to him and screamed.

One could not win a philosophy argument with this ancient wizard, but the penalty for losing was very sweet.

Nearly as sweet as the view of him now. In navy swim trunks, his muscular torso bared, his shoulder-length hair gleaming blue-black in the sunshine, he sat in the chair beside her, reading a stack of papers. Once in a while he sighed and shook his head.

They had only ten days together and he still had his mind on the job? "I thought you were on vacation, wizard."

He studied her through his mirrored sunglasses and she could see the reflection of her annoyed expression. Tristan set down the papers on the sand. A sudden breeze blew at them and the fairies tending to the bar flitted off, frantically trying to catch each one.

"I was catching up on routine reports. They can wait."

Feeling a stab of guilt, she had been reading, after all, she smiled to make up for her bitchy look. Niki set down her novel. "The job never ends, does it?"

"No. But I wish to make you happy, my sweet. Tell me if anything I do displeases you. I wish to be your lover, more than that, I wish to be your friend again."

Deeply touched by this flash of humility from the powerful Silver Wizard who could obliterate a city with the flick of his hand, she touched his hand. "I could use a friend. I don't have girlfriends. I have only Nia."

He swung his trim, muscled legs over the lounge chair, and sat facing her, bracing his hands on his knees. "Tell me about your childhood. What did you like to do together?"

Again, he touched her. Tristan could have diverted the conversation away from her sister, knowing the choice ahead of her.

Stay—and never see her family again.

Or see her family again—but never be with him.

For a few moments, she talked about how she and Nia learned to swim in the pond at dusk, guarded by their brothers and their father. At night when they grew older, when they could, they would shift together and run through the woods, twin wolves loping through shadowy glen and thick forest, as the silver moonlight lit their way.

"Then we'd return to my apartment, change in PJ's and eat chocolate puff cereal while watching movies. Nia always preferred romantic comedies and I liked crime dramas, especially the parts where the CSI team analyzes the crime scene."

"Ah, your love of science." He removed his sunglasses and picked up her abandoned book. "Is this about the science of love?"

Grabbing the book back, she playfully swatted him with it. "It has great love scenes in it."

A forest green fairy with midnight wings zipped over, bringing him an elegant silver and black envelope. He opened it.

Tristan handed her a black and silver invitation. "My people, the ones here, are giving a fairy ball tonight in your honor, to welcome you here."

She read the delicate script. "I thought we couldn't leave the bubble shield encasing your home territory because we're mortal."

"We can't. They're holding it at the ballroom of my mansion on the far reaches of my territory."

She dropped the invitation into her violet and white striped beach bag. "You have a mansion?"

Tristan reached into the cooler at their feet and withdrew a shiny red apple. He bit into it, munched and held the fruit out to her. She sighed with pleasure as she sampled it. The fruit was sweeter here. Everything tasted amazing.

"A small one. Only one hundred rooms."
"What?"

"You should see Gideon's mansion. His is larger than the state of New York."

"That's a whole lot of cleaning staff," she murmured.

"As you've seen, my sweet, my home is vast. I warded it with magick to enable you to have anything your heart desires, including a formal ball." He leaned forward, his gaze twinkling. "I remember how well you enjoyed such gatherings in our past."

"And how do you know what's your territory and what infringes on another wizard's?"

"I'm a wolf. I know every inch of what is mine." He took the apple from her. Holding her gaze, he slowly licked the spot where her mouth had touched. "I enjoyed tasting you last night, my sweet. And perhaps after the ball, we shall enjoy a different sort of dessert."

She flushed with sensual anticipation and sipped her rum runner. It wasn't alcoholic, but tasted just as sweet. She didn't need rum to get drunk here on Tir Na-nog. All she needed was to gaze at Tristan to feel intoxicated, all her inhibitions lowered.

But she couldn't have him longer than their ten days together if she wanted to see her twin again. She felt stricken at the thought. He leaned forward.

"You look distressed. Do you wish to attend this ball? If you do not, let me know."

"I'm fine and the ball sounds lovely. I've always wondered what it would be like to attend a formal gala and wear a long gown and pretty shoes."

"I want to know what makes you happy, Nikita." A shadow crossed his face. "We have so little time together here, I want to make it as special as possible."

Her throat tightened. "You've already made it very special."

For a moment they gazed at each other, and in his dark eyes she saw shadows of the past that still lingered. Niki wished she could erase that pain, those memories.

Sex drove them away. She kissed him, feeling his mouth move under hers. Then he drew back and beckoned to the fairies. A rainbow-colored fairy zipped over to him and hovered.

"My lady Nikita and I wish to be alone."

Nodding her tiny head, the fairy zipped away. Dozens of fairies left the Tiki Bar, darting away on gossamer wings.

Tristan stood and tugged at her hand. He led her over to the thick blanket on the sand where they had stretched out earlier after swimming.

His gaze burned as he tugged her down and kissed her, running his long fingers through her hair. Beneath the bikini bra, her nipples hardened.

He kept kissing her, and then with his right hand, skimmed the bare flesh of her belly until reaching her bikini bottom.

Suddenly shy, she looked around. "Tristan…"

"Hush. It's all right."

Tristan pulled aside the fabric and slid his fingers lightly across her sex. Niki moaned as he stroked in long, teasing caresses.

"You're so wet," he murmured.

The exquisite friction of his hand against her soft, moist cleft made her body tense with anticipation. He increased the rhythm.

Niki pumped her hips upward, desperate for release.

She stared up at him, his mouth curling into a tender, yet very male smile.

"I need you." She took in a deep breath. "Tristan…"

"No." He kissed the corner of her mouth. "This is only for you. My pleasure can wait."

Crying out as orgasm seized her, she arched upward as he caught her mouth in a tender kiss.

Tristan kept kissing her as he withdrew his hand. He pulled away, his gaze dark, his look intent.

"I love watching you come," he said softly. "Your eyelids growing heavy and your sweet little mouth panting, and that flush upon your soft skin."

Nerve endings still pulsing with pleasure, she glanced at the impressive tent in his swim trunks. "It was rather one-sided."

His gaze gleamed. "I am saving my strength for later. Sometimes the anticipation of a moment is almost as sweet as the moment itself."

"Then you'll need a cold hosing in the ocean to tame that monster."

He looked down at his erection and gave a dramatic sigh. "It is most eager to be with you again, and does not like the word 'no.' I shall have to douse it a while."

Standing, he tugged her upright and ran toward the water. She followed him into the ocean, laughing as he splashed her. Being here with this wizard made all her dreams come true. Each moment rolled into the other with blazing swiftness, until the joy inside her made her feel full to bursting.

But what of her twin? To never see her again? And now that she was finally freed from that basement, and could walk in the open among her pack, what of them?

To never run free and wild as wolf with the pack, but remain here on Tir Na-nog.

A prison is still a prison, even if it is lovely.

Niki would not think of that today. *I'll think of that tomorrow.* Shades of Scarlett O'Hara and *Gone with the Wind.*

For tomorrow, even here in the sweetness of the heavenly afterworld, would come soon enough.

Fairy dust glittered in the air as their coach pulled up into the drive of Tristan's white-columned mansion. The black and silver coach, pulled by four flying silver unicorns, had sailed through the air from the cottage in the woods, over glen and glade. Nikita had hung out the window, staring below at silver trees shimmering in the moonlight, and the green, blue and yellow lanterns hanging from each limb to light the way as a mark of honoring them as Tristan rested a possessive hand on her thigh.

A silver-haired Fae in a black and silver uniform opened their coach door and helped her descend. Sounds of violin, cello, harp and flute filled the air and lights blazed inside the mansion.

Tristan climbed down from the coach and thanked the Fae, and then took her hand. "Everyone is inside, waiting for us."

His sensual gaze caressed her like a stroke of silk. "You look lovely."

She twirled. The amethyst gown embroidered with silver stars came to a low V in the bodice and had capped sleeves edged with silver thread. Her matching high heels had diamond buckles and swirls of diamonds in the back, and felt like down upon her feet.

But Tristan took her breath away. In a black silk tuxedo and white shirt with tiny silver buttons, he looked dashing and sexy. Lifting her hand to his mouth, he kissed it.

"Shall we, my lady?"

As they entered the mansion, a footman clad in black and silver opened the door for them. He had short, stubby arms. Nikita thanked him and he nodded and flashed a huge smile.

"Welcome, my lady Nikita," he uttered in a deep growl. "We have waited many long years for your visit."

And then she did a double take as she gave him a second glance.

His yellow eyes were reptilian slits and his mouth filled with short, pointed rows of teeth.

As they cleared the door and entered the vestibule, she asked Tristan. "Is that a dinosaur?"

"Saul, a T-Rex shifter, who reduced his true form in order to serve as footman," he murmured, taking her gloved hand. "He is one of the few of his kind here, so I gave him a permanent job at my mansion, where he could mingle with others and feel accepted. This is the eternal land of youth and beauty, and we shifters have been around for a very long time."

"No wonder you worried about me reading dino porn. You worried the competition had a head start on your seduction games," she whispered back, grinning.

Tristan threw back his head and laughed. He squeezed her hand tight.

Then they were entering the grand ballroom,

standing atop a sweep of stairs with a polished silver banister lined with green vines, and violet and silver roses. Two fairies, their translucent wings beating the air, hovered on either side of them. Then their bare feet touched the marble floor and they transformed into human form, standing about five feet tall.

One black-haired with lovely sloe violet eyes, and one golden-haired with green eyes. Both wore pink tulle dresses with garlands of pink roses.

The dark-haired fairy turned to her and curtseyed. "Welcome, my lady Nikita. And Tristan. We are most honored to host this ball for you. I am Genita." She handed Niki a silver rose.

It smelled as fragrant as a cup of her favorite cinnamon tea on a cold winter's night. Niki thanked her.

The golden-haired fairy curtseyed as well. "I am Belleora, my lady. Welcome. We are so pleased you could join us."

Belleora handed her a violet rose and Nikita thanked her. The aroma of bacon wafted from the rose. As she blinked in startled amazement, Tristan laughed and the fairies smiled.

"You are Lupine, my lady," Belleora trilled. "A rose that smells of your favorite food can smell no sweeter."

"Now, my sweet, open your palms and let the roses rest there," he instructed.

She did and with a shimmer of iridescent sparks, they transformed into dragonflies, which flew off in a blaze of glitter. Niki laughed. "It's lovely! Thank you," she told the fairies.

A seven-foot tall majordomo in silver and black livery stood at the top of the stairs. "My lords, ladies and gentle folk, and folk of fang and claw, I bid you to welcome our honored guests, Tristan, the Silver Wizard, and his lovely lady Nikita!"

Guests waiting below broke into loud applause.

The majordomo suddenly shifted into a silver dragon the size of a small car. He breathed and instead of flames roaring from his mouth, fairy dust blew over the crowd below. Then the dragon beat his wings and flew, circling above the crowd, nearly touching the domed ceiling. He did a series of acrobatic flips and twists in the air, drawing gasps of wonder from the crowd.

Taking her hand, Tristan escorted her down the steps. As her feet touched each stair, it lit up with an ethereal blue light and played a musical note.

"Cedric is an ancient, a dragon from before even my time," he told her. "He does everything in a theatrical fashion."

When they reached the bottom of the stairs, the crowd lined up on either side. Round tables covered with lavender and silver linens dotted the ballroom, and the dance floor looked to be made from parquet. Upon a raised dais, a twenty-piece orchestra of pointy-nosed goblins clad in tux and tail played.

"Goblins are notoriously lazy, but here they produce the sweetest music," he said.

He gazed at her, his face expressive with both desire and concern. "As the guests of honor, we are expected to open the ball with the first dance."

Aware of the curious gazes of the Fae, and shifters, she felt her stomach tighten. So many eyes upon her, the one who had never even gone to a formal dance.

"I don't suppose they would be content with something I saw on *Dancing with the Stars*?"

He offered a tender smile. "I will lead, if you will, my sweet, and your steps will never falter."

She had trusted him to bring her this far. Why not continue the journey?

At her nod, he slid one muscled arm around her waist, the other clasping her raised hand. A waltz. She had seen this enough times in movies. She could do this.

As Tristan swept them around the ballroom, she fell into his steps, her feet not tripping, and she laughed for the sheer enjoyment of the moment. At last, she danced in an opulent ballroom and wore a lovely gown, with starlight shining down upon them as they danced.

In his arms, she felt so secure and safe and cherished.

I could stay here forever.

You cannot, unless you never wish to see your twin again.

The thought cut through her joy like a knife slicing through butter. She pushed it away, determined to make the most of this, her first dance with Tristan.

He leaned closer and whispered into her ear. "I shall enjoy a different dance with you later, my lady."

Heat suffused her skin. Fingers tightening on his firm, muscled shoulder, she let him sweep her away, just as he'd swept her away at the ranch, swept her into a new and strange and exciting world.

Applause sounded as they finished their dance. She curtseyed and Tristan bowed. The T-Rex shifter who had acted as footman at the door called out, "Well done!"

Silence draped the ballroom, and she saw the slight

disapproval on the faces of other guests. Some Fae protocol broken?

The hell with that. This was her dream, and in her dreams, everyone, even lizard shifters, were treated with utter respect.

Nikita left Tristan and went to Saul. She took his tiny, clawed hand and curtseyed to him. "Thank you, for making me feel welcome."

She kissed his cheek.

Saul went beet red and then another round of applause broke out in the ballroom.

When she rejoined Tristan at their table, he leaned back, his eyes focused only on her. As if they were not among more than a thousand guests in his enormous ballroom.

He leaned forward and covered her palm with his. "Thank you for acknowledging him, Nikita. Saul has often felt left out at affairs like this. His upbringing was rather...crude."

"No one should feel left out." She remembered the loneliness in the basement when her twin, as pack leader, went running with the others and she was forced to remain behind.

Tristan stroked her fingers in a slow caress. "You always did treat all with fairness and diplomacy. From the simplest peasant ogre to the highborn, you looked upon them equally."

As dancers took to the floor and swirled around them, she noticed Fae with silver hair and Lupines who looked half-human, half-wolf milling about the guests and asked him about them.

"Everyone takes the form that pleases them when they wish. Here, one does not worry about shifting accidentally in front of Skins. Only in the Midnight Kingdom can shifters assume their true form and mill about freely from city to city," he said.

She'd heard of vague tales of such a kingdom, where Dark Fae and shifters co-mingled, and their magick was most powerful, and dangerous.

"I thought that place was legend," she remarked.

"It is truth." Tristan nodded as a blue fairy in shimmering tulle flitted by and trilled a greeting.

Another fairy flitted over, offering them a silver tray loaded with delicacies. She selected a sea scallop wrapped in bacon and bit into it with a sigh of pleasure. As she ate, several Others came to their table to greet them.

Tristan greeted each one with warmth, spending several minutes inquiring about them, his concern obvious. Yet even in mortal form she felt the aura of his power ringing him like a lighthouse beacon, where the others were pale moonlight in comparison.

Out of the corner of her eye she saw a tall, bearded man clad in a blue velvet tunic, cobalt leggings and doeskin boots. He stood on the sidelines of the ballroom, looking at the scene with brooding eyes.

"Drust," she said, touching Tristan's arm. "I'm going to ask him to dance. He looks so lonely."

Tristan kissed her cheek. "Enjoy yourself."

When she went to him, the dragon shifter looked wary and startled. Nikita offered a wide smile.

"I seem to recall a time when I danced at many great balls in Castle Baldwin, and one such dance was with you. Would you do a kindness and dance with me?"

Drust bowed low. "It would be my pleasure, my lady Nikita." Then, in a lower voice, he added, "I owe you much more than a mere dance. It is my greatest wish that I could make amends some day for failing to watch over you and safeguard you from harm after Tristan died."

He danced with effortless grace, twirling her around the ballroom, her skirts flying out, but he kept her at a courteous distance. Her fingers tightened on his shoulder.

"Are you settling in here? This place is heavenly, but I can imagine it takes some adjusting after the Shadow Lands."

"The Shadow Lands were hell for me," he confessed, expertly cutting a turn. "The land can turn the hardiest of souls, the strongest of men and dragons, inside out. Only those with truly strong spirits, and courage, survive past their memories to move onward to Tir Na-nog."

"Tristan was pained while we were there," she admitted. "He must have suffered much."

He looked down at her, his look expressive with regret. "He had the memory of you to guide him here. You have always been the only one for him, from the moment he saw you in the market square two years before your mating day. He told me, 'Drust, look at that lovely Lupine. See how gentle and yet spirited she is? She is the one for me. I know this.'"

Nikita blinked. "According to my dreams, which are memories, ours was an arranged match. He scarcely knew me. He knew of my father's landholdings, and the forest-rich territory. That is why he mated me."

Drust laughed, a deep sound that held much amusement. "Did you ever stop to think who did the arranging, my lady? Tristan cared not for territory. Or licking the white ass of that foul bastard, Emer. He wanted you. He would have given anything to have you, anything to make you happy. You had given away some of your wares to a group of Lupine children who went hungry and ignored by Others. He said to me, 'Drust, she is so lovely. Each time I see her my heart feels lighter. She is the woman who can make me the Lupine I know I can become, if she is by my side.'

"Your true beauty was not your looks, but your soul. He recognized this, and knew you belonged together. It happens at times with Lupines, this soulmate recognition. It happens far less with dragons."

A warm tenderness came over her as she glanced over at Tristan, talking with Saul. And then new memories surfaced, the flower garden Tristan had planted for her when she wistfully mentioned longing to see the blue wildflowers each day. How he had moved her entire family into the castle at his own expense when he caught her crying one night because she missed her kin. And how he'd taught her to read, when she longed to become educated.

Tristan had always been there for her, but she did not recall his little acts of kindness and love.

"He never told me."

"Men are stupid in that way. We did not dare to be perceived as weak and ruled by the heart, not when the Fae were constantly breathing down our necks. But he knew you were his. I always wanted to find my true mate. I was mated twice and never did find her."

He swept her past a table filled with Fae drinking and laughing. "But you had Camilla. You loved her, from what I can recall."

"I loved her, but I was busy upon the king's business

and had little time for her. Once she told me she felt less than a female because she'd failed to give me children. I tried to assure her I had six strong, healthy children and did not need another. I tried to make her feel accepted, but it was a long and difficult road."

She felt sympathy for Camilla, who had been loved and did not feel it.

"Is Camilla here in Tir Na-nog?"

Drust shook his head. "I have not seen her neither here, nor in the Shadow Lands. Shortly after the end of the Drakon War and there was peace between shifters and the Fae, I caught her with a lover, and banished her."

"Oh Drust!" She pulled back a little and studied him. "I'm so sorry."

He shrugged. "I did love her, but I would not tolerate such a betrayal of trust." The dragon laughed. "Ironic, isn't it? Betrayed by my mate, and all these centuries Tristan believes I betrayed him. Betrayal is an ugly thing, my lady."

The dance ended and he gave a courtly bow to her curtsy. Then he formally escorted her back to her table and pulled out her chair.

Drust took Tristan's empty seat, his gaze sweeping over the crowd. "It feels odd to be among this many after so many centuries of forced solitude. I do not know if I like it."

She touched his hand. "This is a land of dreams, Drust. You should learn to experience joy once more. If not for you, I would have been in real trouble."

"The Shadow Lands are no place for one such as you with a gentle and innocent heart," Drust said. "For me, they were painful, yet comfortable. They were a place to contemplate my life, and my death."

Curious, she studied him. "How did you die? Was it a great battle?" She imagined Drust's chest pierced by a lance or him gasping his last breath as he fought to defend his territory.

He grinned. "Carriage accident. Not very noble."

They laughed a moment. Then the dragon stared again at Tristan. "Tristan could have left you to journey through the Shadow Lands. He walked that path again because he would not see you walk it alone. And he was forced to remember all the torment he suffered while there."

Another shifter asked her for a dance, and Nikita ended up on the floor dancing for a long while. Finally, with excuses of needing to sit, she returned to her table. By now Tristan and Drust were talking, walking the perimeter of the ballroom. Hands hooked behind his back, Tristan listened as Drust talked. Once in a while he lifted his head and laughed at something the dragon shifter said. Memories blazed back—good ones. Utterly content, she let herself drift into one—before the Drakon War began. Tristan with his best friend, Drust, went fishing in the lake near Castle Baldwin as she and Camilla, Drust's mate, watched Drust's children from his first marriage scamper over the meadow next to the lake.

Camilla was plain-faced, but good with the children, and she had a quiet air about her Nikita had found refreshing. Camilla kept her company when Tristan and Drust were sent off on a raid for King Emer.

Nikita watched the children, her chest tight. She had confirmed today her suspicions.

"They seem so frail," she mused. "And yet they run and play as if they were indestructible."

"A trait among children, lost to us as we age. Do you want children, Nikita?" Camilla asked, handing her a cup of wine.

Nikita smiled and set the cup down. "Yes. It is my dearest wish." She pressed her hands to her belly. "I think that wish may be coming sooner than I had hoped."

Camilla hugged her tight. "Congratulations. Drust and I were never able to conceive on our own."

She blinked at the wistful look on her friend's face. "I'm sorry."

Camilla shrugged. "I have Drust's children from his first marriage to care for, and they are like my own. It will suffice."

But to never carry the child of a man you loved, it must be heartbreaking, she had thought. And then she looked at Drust, who gazed at Camilla with the same tenderness Tristan displayed to her, but Camilla did not return the look.

Tristan's deep voice broke through the memory. "My sweet, are you well? You look lost in thought."

She smiled and accepted the silver goblet of punch he handed her. "Just thinking of the past."

Maybe Camilla had taken another lover because of her inability to give children to Drust. The dragon admitted he had little time for her.

Would the same happen to her if she chose to remain on Earth as mortal? At least here, she would see Tristan often. Give him a chance to be a real father.

The thought deeply troubled her.

They remained at the ball for a few hours, mingling with the guests, dancing, but always keeping an eye on each other. On the carriage ride back, she studied him with sweet anticipation.

When they arrived back at the cottage, he dismissed the coach and the coachmen, and they flew off into the night. Taking her hand, Tristan led her into the bedroom.

Once inside, he loosened his black tie, unbuttoned his jacket but then stilled, his gaze heavy-lidded with desire. In the soft golden glow of the bedside lamp, Tristan could have been a billionaire CEO returning from a late night benefit, ready to tumble into bed with his wife for a long bout of lovemaking before rising with the sun to assume his business duties.

Only this was a fourteen-hundred-year-old wizard who dispensed justice by obliterating shifters who did evil. Such a burden on his spirit.

She went to him, grazing her thumb along his stubbled jawline. "I had a great time tonight. It was amazing meeting all those shifters from your past."

He picked up her hand and kissed it. "I have lived long, Nikita, done much, but loved only one woman— you."

He rubbed her hand along his bristled cheek. She wished she could erase the haunted look in his eyes. This was the heavenly afterworld, but turning mortal must have triggered memories Tristan did not wish to recall.

"I love you as well, Tristan."

He looked up, a flash of hope on his face pushing aside the darkness.

"I have always loved you deep inside, but the part of

me that remembered the pain of your death, and how I was left alone, refused to recall it. All those nights after you died, I would curl up on my bed and weep. And I would wish for one last time running with you beneath the moon as wolf, one last touch of your lips against mine as Skin."

She slid her arms around his neck and reached up to kiss him. He lowered his head to hers, and the kiss was sweet and brief, not the drugging kisses he'd showered upon her in the previous days.

Tristan cupped her face with his warm palms.

"I want to fall into you like water, drown myself in you. I want to dive into you so deeply the memory of you will carry me through the centuries to come. Being immortal and patrolling the mortal plane is lonely, Nikita. Watching all your friends die, loathing to grow close to anyone because you will outlive them, or they could embark on a dark path that forces you to kill them so that others may live."

She stared into his dark brown eyes. "Tell me what I can do to ease your pain."

"Be with me tonight. Run with me as wolf, as we once ran when we were mates on Earth. I want to feel the wind against my face and hear the beat of your heart as you race with me beneath the moon."

His eyes closed as he kissed her knuckles, one by one. "With you at my side, the loneliness is vanquished. The darkest nightmares in the Shadow Lands, not knowing if I would ever hold you once more in my arms, were a living hell. When the grayness in the Shadow Lands threatened to swallow me until all I could hear were my own screams and remember the pain as they tortured me and the guilt I felt at leaving you, I would run as wolf and pretend you were running alongside me. Only the memories of you pushed the darkness away a little."

Deeply touched at his confession, she kissed him.

They left the cottage and went outside. Nikita lifted her arms and called upon her magick and shifted into wolf. Iridescent sparks swirled around her, as lovely as fairy dust.

Sensations rushed at her, the smell of water in the creek behind Tristan's home, the sounds of fairies dancing on the wind, the feel of the earth beneath her paws.

The large silver wolf standing beside her looked at her quietly in the moonlight. And then they bounded off for the woods.

Racing after him, she yipped with sheer enjoyment, snapping at the glowing green dragonflies darting in and out of the woods. Silver moonlight spilled down upon them, and she could taste the scent of prey hiding in the bushes.

But tonight her hunger was not of wolf, but woman.

They ended the chase at a small glen deep in the woods, near a bubbling creek. White orchids and lilies grew amid the green mosses and grasses. Tristan shifted back to Skin. Still nude, he padded over to a flower. She shifted back to Skin and watched him pluck it and then inhale the fragrant scent.

He held it out to her with a solemn look.

"Will you be my forever mate, Nikita? I ask much of you, for if you decide to remain mortal, you could never choose another mate to grow old with or bear other children with. No other male would be interested in you."

The mating mark. Her breath caught. The mark a male Lupine gave to his female, to show to the world she was his. It diffused the lust of other males. They would never be sexually interested in her.

But she could not imagine having sex with anyone but Tristan. And if she could not have him as her mate, then she wanted no one else.

He claimed her heart, always. She accepted the lily and inhaled its fragrance.

"Yes. I will be your mate."

He kissed her then, his mouth tasting like the sweetest wine and honey. As he drew back and cupped her face with his warm palms and pull her closer, the lily spilled to the ground. He kept kissing her, long, drugging kisses as he skimmed a possessive hand over her backside, and then pressed her closer. The rigid length of his erection dug into her belly. Tristan broke the kiss.

"Get on all fours," he told her.

He looked feral and wild as his wolf. For a moment, fear flickered through her. Permanently Tristan's.

Tristan slid a hand around her neck. "Only you, my sweet. You are the only woman I shall ever love, for eternity. When the stars cease shining and the moon fades, there will be one light in the sky and it will be me, burning with love for you."

And then the hunger for him returned and her fears evaporated beneath the power of his touch.

Only his.

Still naked, she dropped to the ground on her hands and knees. In the gleam of moonlight his eyes glazed with lust.

He was in full mating frenzy. Biting her lip, she

surrendered to the fevered passion. She opened her legs wide in the traditional mating position and braced herself.

His heavy body settled atop her, the edge of his cock nudging her soaked slit as he wrapped muscled arms around her waist. He nuzzled her neck, and then dragged his tongue over her sensitive skin. Tristan kissed and caressed her until she felt ready and open. Wriggling her bottom, she spread her legs open wider as the moonlight caressed them both.

"Now," he murmured.

He pushed his penis deep inside her body. Her cry of pleasure was silenced under the penetrating thrust of his tongue as he turned her head toward him and kissed her. She wanted more. Her feminine tissues clung to his cock as he hammered deep inside her, their wet flesh slapping together.

Tension filled her loins as he squeezed and kneaded her hips, riding her hard. Then Tristan fisted a hand in her long hair and slammed into her even harder.

Turning her head, she watched his incisors sharpen and lengthen. Tristan gently turned her head aside, nuzzled her throat. She moaned as his cock pushed deep inside her and stilled.

"Now," he growled.

Sharp teeth sank into her neck. Niki cried out. Pain flashed through her, along with an erotic throbbing in her loins far more intense than anything she'd ever felt.

Then he licked the wound, his tongue dragging slowly over her sore skin. The stinging pain faded, replaced by intense pleasure. Nerve endings screeching with sensation, she moaned and pushed back against him, undulating her hips. He grunted and kept thrusting, harder and harder, each push of his cock rubbing against her sensitive tissues.

"Come with me," he panted, wrapping his arms around her waist, sealing her to him.

She let go, the pleasure bursting deep inside her loins as he penetrated deep. A long, low howl ripped from him as his powerful body shuddered behind her, his seed spurting hotly into her womb, each ejaculation causing new ripples of pleasure that stroked into small orgasms, sending waves of fresh pleasure inside her.

They collapsed to the ground. But he did not pull out. She felt his cock thicken inside her.

The mating knot of Lupines.

Tristan rolled them onto their sides, his arms possessively wrapped around her, anchoring her close. After a few minutes, he eased out of the tight clasp of her body. He lay on his back on the soft, damp grasses, and pulled her into his arms, the sweat from their bodies sealing them together.

For a while, they simply lay together, the sound of their ragged breathing filling the air until her breathing slowed and she could finally think straight.

He skimmed a gentle hand over her belly. "We made a baby tonight."

Raising her head, she glanced down. "How do you know?"

"I can sense it." He kissed her again.

Tristan's child. And she was now his forever mate. Overwhelmed with joy, Niki pressed her hands to her belly. She would have a child, a child to raise and care for, a child to watch grow, and guard.

Her mother had died giving birth to her. Joy turned to ashes as she curled up next to Tristan, tunneling her fingers through the hair on his chest. "What if something bad happens?"

Tristan's gaze became fierce. "I will not let any harm come to you or our child, Nikita. I promise, you will both be safe. I pledge you the protection of my body and my powers as the Silver Wizard."

His voice trembled a little. "I will not lose you again."

Such devotion in those words, and in the kiss he gave her. Tristan pulled her closer and stroked a hand tenderly over her belly.

Tears clogged her throat, partly from joy and partly from dread. She dreaded their time together ending.

For then she must choose.

Stay with him here, forever.

Or go.

CHAPTER 17

Never had he experienced such tender bliss.

Not since he'd walked the earth as mortal had he known such joy. The days passed from one to another in a rush of erotic pleasure and sweetness, for Nikita was in his arms at last.

Mine, he thought in a possessive rush of pure male satisfaction, gazing down at his sleeping bride.

He'd filled his cottage with all the most luxurious items she could ever want, even the chocolate cereal she and Nia had loved to eat. He pampered her with dinners fit for immortals, and in the mornings, brought her breakfast in bed, teasing her mouth with the strawberries he dipped in fresh, clotted cream.

Now, on the ninth day of their allotted time, Tristan felt a pang of impending loss. One more day with his Nikita, and then he must return her to Earth.

His forever mate.

The potion in her veins that had allowed her entry to Tir Na-nog had long worn off. She was mortal once more and could live a long life as Lupine on Earth.

The protective bubble encasing his property and his

276

home that allowed them both to dwell here as mortals would vanish after sunrise on the eleventh day.

When that happened, his powers would return, but Nikita would wither and die before his eyes, banished to the Shadow Lands. And she still had not made up her mind about taking the elixir that would allow her to dwell here, with him, forever.

Losing her would be too painful to bear.

He must not think of those dire consequences, but live in this moment. Time was too precious for them both.

Tristan lounged in bed, enjoying the luxury of silk sheets and Niki's warm, soft body cuddled against him. Propped up against two fat pillows, he scanned his tablet, knowing he still must keep tabs on his charges.

Stirring, she lazily opened one eye. "Is that an iPad? In Tir Na-nog?"

"It's a tablet. It has voice recognition software, and works off a cloud. It's how I can track Others and make notations on their activities."

She sat up, pulling the sheet over her breasts. Tristan caught a glimpse of smooth, pale flesh and his sex stirred.

"Can you see any shifter on Earth with that?"

Nodding, he set the tablet down to reach for her, but she grabbed it.

"Show me my twin sister," Nikita said, speaking at the tablet.

"I am sorry, but I do not understand twisted titter," the tablet chirped in a frilly female voice.

Tristan folded his arms across his chest and grinned at the adorable frown puckering Nikita's forehead.

"Nia the wolf. Show me Nia the wolf."

"*Beowulf,* an Old English epic poem consisting of…"

"No! Show me Nia and Aiden."

"I am sorry, I do not understand Need An Apron. Would you like to find cooking classes?"

He doubled over laughing as Nikita threw the tablet on the floor. "It's useless."

Still chuckling, he reached over and dropped a single kiss on her pouting cheek. "It is my tablet, programmed for my voice, my sweet. Let us forget electronics."

With dawning hunger, he pulled the sheet down, exposing the perfect curve of one rounded breast. "I have much better, and more enjoyable, activities for you."

Her eyes went dark and her skin flushed the prettiest shade of red. "Do they involve your mouth and my body?"

"Of course," he murmured, leaning over her.

She glanced at the sunlight dappling the trees outside the window. "You promised to take me on a picnic today."

"Do not worry, my sweet," he murmured, his usual arrogance returning. "This shall not take long."

With deliberate care, he traced a line over the swell of her left breast with his tongue, enjoying her little shivers of pleasure. Tristan swirled his tongue around her nipple as Nikita threw back her head and sighed. He took her nipple into his mouth and suckled gently, knowing the exact amount of pressure to deliver the most exquisite pleasure.

As she moved restlessly beneath him, he threw back the sheet and moved over her. Fisting a hand in the tangled masses of her long, silky hair, he nudged her plump thighs open with his hips, his erection hard and throbbing. Tristan drove into her hard, groaning as his cock made contact with her warm, welcoming heat. Nikita moaned and wrapped her arms around him as he began moving deep inside her.

As he'd promised, it did not take long, for he was too aroused, but she cried out and squeezed around his driving cock. She'd always been like that, he thought in a haze of passion. Nikita had been in perfect rhythm with him, even when he'd been too eager and could not wait to reach his own pleasure.

Tristan stared down into her face, loving the way she climaxed, eyes wide open with dazed pleasure only he could give her. He let himself go with a loud groan, spurting deep inside her.

Panting, he rested atop her, his grip on her hair loosening as she idly stroked the muscles of his back.

The erotic pleasure shuddering through his body faded, nudged aside by mingled feelings of sorrow and alarm. *I can't live without her. Not after having her here at my side, like this. Each day waking up with Nikita in my arms, each night falling into her. How can I live without her in my life?*

You must. You are the Silver Wizard and your duty is to your people. You cannot have her here in the afterworld and you cannot stay with her on Earth. And how can she give up seeing her family? You know how close she is to her twin.

For the first time since his death and his ascension to being the Silver Wizard, Tristan wished he'd refused the job. Duty first, always. In his past life, and now.

Having experienced a taste of happiness and fulfillment in his woman's arms, he wanted more.

Don't fall in love again, Gideon had warned. *You have only ten days in Tir Na-nog with her.*

Ten days. It might as well be ten minutes, for all his longing.

Ten thousand years would never be enough with his Nikita, his beautiful wolf.

She touched his face as he braced his weight on his arms, so as not to crush her. "What's wrong? Your eyes…they're changing colors again, Tristan."

He slid off her and turned away, knowing eyes changed because of his growing sadness.

"It is nothing, my sweet." Bending his head so she could not see his eyes, he kissed her hand. "We should get dressed."

He wanted her affection.

Her heart.

You cannot fall in love again.

A hard knock sounded upon the cottage door. Frowning, he looked out the bedroom window and his heart dropped.

Gideon, the Crimson Wizard, stood outside. His fellow wizard would not interrupt his time alone with Nikita unless it was urgent.

Tristan frowned and slid out of bed, pulling on a pair of black sweatpants. "Shower, my love. Gideon is out front."

He strode with impatience to the front door. Gideon was the last wizard he wished to see.

Your sister is the one who killed my Nikita, and betrayed me.

But one did not make such accusations lightly, and for now, Nikita was safe here with him. He would deal with Gideon and Mara later.

Dressed in a crimson tunic, red leather pants and red boots, Gideon stood outside, arms folded across his chest. His gaze swept up and down Tristan and he gave a disgusted sniff.

Tristan shut the door behind him and leaned against it. "Why do you look like you have something permanently shoved up your ass? And why the hell are you interrupting me?"

"You've done it, wolf. Exactly as I warned you not to do. You've fallen in love."

He stiffened. "No."

"Don't deny it. It's all over you. On your face, your hair… I can smell her on you like perfume."

"Sex," Tristan growled, "does not equate to love."

Gideon sighed and looked backward over one shoulder. "X!"

The Crystal Wizard appeared, took one look at Tristan. "Wow. Look at you."

Tristan gave his friend a contemptuous look as he studied Xavier's white jumpsuit, studded with sequins. "You should talk. Are you in one of your Elvis moods again?"

But Xavier ignored the jab and turned to Gideon. "Damn. He's done it. He's fallen in love, just as you feared."

Truly irritated now, Tristan scowled.

"Dude, your eyes." X opened the door and pushed him inside to the hallway, where a large gilded mirror hung on the wall.

Gideon joined them. The trio stared at Tristan's eyes.

They were not bright, electric blue with the surge of his powers, nor the usual dark brown. They were a clear, deep blue.

As blue as the days when he'd walked the earth as a mortal.

Tristan touched the mirror with a wondering hand. "They have not been thus in more than nine hundred years," he said in awe.

"She's making you Lupine again, Tristan." Gideon's voice rang out with ominous warning. "Get rid of her, before it turns permanent and you're lost to us."

Leaning against the hallway table, Tristan folded his arms across his bare chest. "It is not permanent. I had to alter my body chemistry and lose my powers to impregnate her."

Gideon stabbed a finger in his direction. "Changing your body chemistry to become temporarily mortal, to beget an heir, yes. Your hair and your body are as they were in mortal times. But your eyes are always dark, except when your powers flare. They are the window to your immortal soul."

Dread snaked through him as Tristan turned back to the mirror. His friends were correct. He *was* turning mortal again. And if this continued, he could become permanently damaged.

"You know what happens to us when we lose our powers, Tristan."

Shuddering at Gideon's words, Tristan touched the mirror. With tremendous power came tremendous responsibility. In exchange for their magick and being guardians of Others, the wizards had pledged to the goddess Danu that they would never lose their magick by giving it to another. If they neglected to request her permission, they would suffer the consequences—the wizards would turn into Shadow forever, ghosts wandering the Shadow Lands.

Danu had given him permission to create the potion that would save Nikita, and allow her entrance here. But it was a temporary sharing of power only.

"You're going to Hell," X offered helpfully. "In a handbasket."

Palm trembling, he touched his face. An ugly thought flashed through his mind. He would become immortal again, but if she chose to stay on Earth, he would be obsessed with protecting her. And his job as the Silver Wizard was to protect all, not merely Nikita and their babe.

If he became so distracted with Nikita on Earth, and failed to adhere to his duties, would the goddess strip him of all his powers?

Banished from Earth and never able to see Nikita again? Left helpless to protect her and shield her from all harm?

He scowled at X. "I am not. I have not chosen to share my powers. This is merely a side effect of becoming temporarily mortal." He turned from the mirror. "It will not last."

Gideon's expression turned hard. "She's probably pregnant already, Tristan. Get rid of her."

Once Nikita leaves here, she will be vulnerable to your damned sister again. Mara killed my Nikita once. She will not do so again.

"Do not interfere with my business, Gideon. You have enough trouble of your own." He fisted his hands. "I want from you a promise that you will keep Mara away from Nikita once she returns to Earth."

The Crimson Wizard blinked and Xavier whistled. "Why?" Gideon demanded.

Tristan chose his words with care. "I do not wish

Nikita to be plagued by someone from her past who will cause her distress. And your sister is a powerful Fae who can be…annoying."

Something flickered in Gideon's gaze. "Very well. I promise. I will make sure Mara does not come near Nikita. She is an ancient, but her interest in your woman is mere curiosity, Tristan. And if it means you may focus on your duties as the Silver Wizard instead of worrying about Nikita, I will be most glad to do it."

"Good. Now…" Tristan narrowed his gaze. "Why the hell are you here?"

"Danu has called a formal convocation to discuss Drust. You must attend."

Damn. The goddess rarely called them all together and her commands could not be ignored. He looked at them. "Why now? Is it that important?"

"I asked her for this convocation. You know the matter of Drust is important, Tristan. The dragons are growing more and more out of control and someone needs to keep them in line." Gideon suddenly looked weary. "We will need their strength and their unity in the future."

He could not argue that, for Drust's great-grandson, Prince Alexander, was proof of how headstrong dragons could become.

And proof of how powerful as well.

"When?"

"This afternoon, at dusk." Sympathy filled Gideon's expression. "I am sorry, my friend. I asked her to delay the meeting, but she insists on today. You have until twilight to be with your Nikita, and then you must return her to Earth and the mortal realm."

"I'm to have ten full days." Stricken, he stared at his

friends, his fellow wizards, who had sacrificed their own blood to bring Nikita to the immortal realm.

Gideon cleared his throat. "The goddess cut your time short for this meeting. If you wish the full ten days with Nikita, you forfeit the meeting...that's not a wise choice."

Duty first. Always.

X looked at him with sympathy. "I'm sorry. It sucks. I wish you could have more." Regret flickered in his eyes. "I wish we all could have more. But this is the price we paid for becoming immortal."

The price we paid. The irony slapped him full in the face. He had demanded of the goddess the chance to find his beloved Nikita again, and impregnate her with his heir so his legacy would not die. When the executioner's blade had taken his life, he died knowing his Nikita, and their babe, would live. But when she'd died along with the babe, his purpose in the afterworld had died as well.

He wanted a child of his own blood, his line, more than anything else.

But he failed to realize he'd wanted something even more precious—Nikita in his arms forever.

He could not remain here in their blissful utopia forever, nor could he be with her on Earth, walking as a mortal. Their destinies took them in separate directions, unless she took the potion.

His friends looked away.

He must abide by the goddess's dictates. "Very well. I will give her up and allow her to return to Earth, but I was promised ten full days. Nikita must have one more day to make up her mind about taking the potion and joining me here, forever."

"I cannot see how the goddess would not grant that, when she did promise ten days," Gideon admitted.

He was the Silver Wizard. His personal needs came last. Tristan straightened. "I shall be there."

Closing the door as they walked away, he leaned against it. Nikita came into the room, toweling her hair. "Did you meet with Gideon? He had better have a good reason for interrupting your time with me."

Heart heavy, he went to her and gently wrapped his arms around her. *I will miss you so much. So much. Every day I go without you near me, I will die another death. But I must. I made a promise.*

He had promised her, as well. But the greater good, and his duties, came first.

Tristan laid his cheek against her hair. He could say the words weighing on him since the moment he'd poured the magick potion that saved her life and enabled her to accompany him into the afterworld.

"I love you, my sweet Nikita," he whispered. "I never stopped loving you, and I shall love you for all eternity. You have my heart, always."

Nikita pulled away, searching his face, her mouth wobbling. "What's wrong? You look as if you're about to die all over again."

He brushed a kiss against her forehead. *It feels that way.*

Through the opened windows, a thrush sang in the trees. Wind-tossed leaves skipped over the stepping stones leading to the cottage. The air felt cool and smelled of earth and pine, but inside he was so damned cold, he wondered if he'd ever be warm again.

"What do you wish to do besides your picnic, my

sweet? It's a gorgeous day out. Let's make the most of it and do whatever you desire."

"You're talking differently, too." She cupped his face. "I know speech patterns, Tristan, as much as I know biology and plants and Lupines. Something happened. What did Gideon tell you?"

"It doesn't matter." He trailed a finger over her lips. "Today is for you and me only. Let's go on the picnic I promised you."

Her eyes were wet, but she offered a faint smile. "Like you told me we used to do?"

He nodded. "Pack a basket with food and wine, and I'll get ready."

The spot he'd chosen was breathtaking.

Turquoise waters spilled over the waterfall, frothing the pool below, which was lined with mossy trees. Birds sang in the trees. Lemon-yellow water lilies floated lazily on the pool's surface as blue iridescent dragonflies landed on the pads and then flew off.

As Tristan set down the basket and she spread out a blanket upon the grass, Niki had the vivid recollection of being here once, long ago.

"It's a recreation of where we used to picnic, near Castle Baldwin," she told him.

Tristan bent down and swirled his forefinger in the water. "Tir Na-nog is whatever we wish, my sweet, especially for the wizards. All of us are allowed to create worlds of our imagination and choosing. I created several such areas where my memories were happiest."

She stepped onto the stones in the shallow end of the pool, delighted to feel them beneath her feet. Not slippery or slimy, but soft as down.

"Of course I added my own enhancements." Tristan stretched out on the grass and picked a yellow daffodil, twirling it between his fingers. "I remembered how you once fell after walking on those stones and I caught you."

Joining him, she took the flower and playfully swatted his face with it. "And then I pushed you in."

He grinned. "We were both quite wet, and cold."

Then his gaze turned dark, pupils dilating against the blue of his irises. "I found a most interesting method of warming you, my sweet. But let us save that for after lunch. I am hungry."

They feasted on fried chicken, a joint of beef and fresh figs grown from the tree outside his cottage. Clear white wine sparkled in the goblets she'd packed as they toasted each other. Secrets seemed to swirl in his eyes, but she did not press him.

Today was for creating new memories. She did not want to ruin this wonderful time and what little time they had left with uncloaking his secrets.

Niki leaned over him and pressed a kiss against his mouth. They kept kissing, hands roaming over each other. And then Tristan stood and pulled her with him.

Kissing her still, he backed her against a thick oak tree.

He lifted her up against the tree, his gaze wild and haunted. Whether his feelings stemmed from their past or their doomed future, she did not know. Niki opened her thighs as he settled between them. Tristan shoved up the hem of her flowered skirt.

"I want to fly into the sun and burn with you, burn so brightly your light will never extinguish. I want to bury myself in you so deep, you'll never let me go. I want to sink inside your soul, so we will always be one and nothing will ever part us again, neither time, nor death. No matter what happens to us, we shall always be together as one."

Guiding himself inside her, he sank deep, his cock like soft steel pushing into her. Niki winced and then sighed, wrapping her arms around his neck. He began to thrust hard, whispering into her ear as she closed her eyes and clung to him.

He fisted a hand in her long hair, tilted her head back and kissed her throat as he pumped hard and deep inside her in long, lingering strokes that made her gasp. Niki raked her nails down the strong muscles of his back as he took her. She cried out, wrapping her legs around his lean waist.

Each graceful, powerful move of his hips increased in tempo growing faster, a melody to the harmony of his deep grunts and her sweet sighs. Tristan nuzzled her neck, sweeping his tongue across the tender flesh.

"Open your eyes, Nikita," he commanded softly. "See me. Only me, my sweet. I am a part of you as you are a part of me. You own my heart. I shall never give it to another. I never did."

He moved faster and faster, his dark gaze pinning hers, his eyes smoldering with fierce passion. "You shall always be mine. I am forever yours. Nothing, not even the power of destiny, will ever separate us."

He shuddered inside her, his cock jettisoning hot seed, and she screamed as sensation shot straight to her core. Shaking from the power of her orgasm, Niki felt herself float upwards. Then she realized it was not the pleasure nor her imagination.

They were indeed flying.

They soared skyward, toward the sunshine punching a hole in the clouded sky. The sky was so blue it hurt her eyes through the tears, and the freeing sensation of flying made her giddy. Tristan kept ejaculating inside her, each pulse sending new little quivers of orgasm through her. She clung to him, wanting to soar into the sun, never letting go.

"Look at me, Niki," he said, sounding broken. "Look at us, and remember this moment well."

She stared into eyes, his expression filled with tenderness and desire.

"Do not look down."

Niki glanced over his shoulder and froze. Oh dear...

They were higher than the tallest trees, floating upwards like balloons. Tristan's cottage was a microdot on the green landscape.

Her grip around him tightened. "Don't let go of me, Tristan."

He stared down into her eyes, his gaze haunted. "Soon I must, my beloved."

Slowly they floated downward to the ground. When her trembling feet touched the grass, she sagged against him as he separated their bodies.

"That was exhilarating. So freeing!"

Tristan tunneled his fingers through her long hair. "Such adventures we can experience together, my sweet, if you remain here with me. For all your life you have been sheltered and hidden away. Here, safe with me, you can truly live."

Her euphoria faded. If she remained here, she would

still live within the confines of the heavenly afterworld, never able to return to Earth and her beloved twin.

He rubbed his cheek against hers, in the way of wolves rubbing their muzzles against each other. "I do not wish to pressure you, Nikita. I know you will be giving up much to remain here, including your sister."

She did feel pressure, but not from his words. She had fallen for his seductive ways, caught in the sensual snare of his erotic lovemaking, not the phantom dreams that teased her while on Earth, but the very real touch of his hands, his mouth.

The Silver Wizard had woven a spell around her as effectively as if he'd trapped her in a cage. Niki knew if she left him, the taste of his mouth moving subtly over hers, the feel of his cock deep inside her, would become nothing but memories.

And having experienced the very real pleasure he could deliver, she did not want any more memories.

She wanted the living, breathing Tristan, making love to her each night.

They dressed and returned to the blanket and rested, gazing at the sky. Tristan kept staring at her, his expression sad.

"What's wrong?" she rolled over.

"We need to return."

Niki went to gather the picnic items. He shook his head. "Leave them."

"Why? Aren't we returning to the cottage?"

Tristan touched her cheek. "My Nikita. I wish…how I wish…"

Something was very wrong. "We have a day left."

"No." He glanced at the setting sun. "We have only this moment."

Her heart pounded with dread. "You told me we had ten days. Today is the ninth day!"

"We were granted ten days, but Gideon has called for a convocation of the Brehon with the goddess Danu, on a matter of great importance." His eyes closed. "I must assume my immortality again to meet with her."

"And then you're returning to me." But her heart began to pump hard, as she saw the answer in his face.

"I cannot. I know not what she will ask of me, and I cannot stay with you as an immortal. You are far too tempting. You consume my thoughts, my every waking moment."

Suddenly she saw her life as it had been in the past. "Because your duties come first. Not me. Just as before."

Pressing a hand to the slight swell of her belly where she suspected their child grew, the child conceived in love, she felt her throat close tight with emotion. "You're sending me back."

He gave her a solemn look. "I must."

He went to a bed of flowers near the pool, and snapped one off. The flower was crimson, and glowed like stardust.

Tristan fetched the cup he'd drunk from, rinsed it in the pool, and then added water and the flower. He drank.

The silver suddenly returned to the tips of his shoulder-length dark hair, and the blue vanished from his eyes, leaving them brown once more. A silver aura ringed his body, pulsing with power. Gone too, was the scar from his face, the mark that she had stroked idly in bed, listening to the beat of his mortal heart while he held her close.

292

Tristan her love was gone, replaced by the immortal wizard.

"When I return you to Earth, you will be naked, for you must enter there as naked as the day you were born. I will ask Gideon to make arrangements for you with your pack. You will not be alone, my love."

"Don't go."

"I must." He gave her a steady look and spoke quietly. "Have you decided yet about drinking the potion? We could drink together."

For all their time together, Tristan had shown her the power of making her dreams come true. She craved his touch in bed, and cherished every moment they shared. But the thought of leaving behind her family, the only life she had ever known, hurt her heart.

She hesitated. "If I choose to drink this potion, and become immortal, will our baby become immortal as well? So we can be a family?"

"Yes." He went very still.

"But I will never see my other family again. My wolf pack." Her voice broke. "Or Nia."

"No. As an immortal you will have to reside here, with me, in Tir Na-nog. You cannot cross back and forth. Everyone must pay a price."

"And you paid the greatest price of all," she whispered. "You gave up your chance to be reincarnated with me so we could be mated and raise our children together. When am I going to be first in your life, Tristan? Only if I drink the potion?"

Tristan framed her face with his large, warm hands. "You always were first in my heart. I came back to you, Nikita. I honored our promise to be together again. I could never break it. Yes, I wanted a child, a babe of my blood to carry on my name, but I wanted you, needed you more, as you needed me."

"You never left me." She put a hand on her chest. "You stayed with me, here, always. But I need more than a memory of your love. I need you."

"I will always be there, in your heart." He placed a palm over her rapidly beating heart. "If you choose to remain with your pack on Earth, I will always give you the protection of my magick. If you needed me for anything, you need only call upon me and I will be at your side. I will never let anything happen to you again, my sweet."

"Tristan, may I have a day to consider? To be with my sister again, and make my decision. Just one day?"

He closed his eyes. "One day. I can grant you one day, but no more. I will come to you in one day with the potion, and it will be your choice to drink. Or not."

"It's so hard to give up my family. I love Nia so dearly. But I want you and I to be together. To be a family, and have the chance denied to us in our last life."

Tristan opened his eyes. He glanced at the sky. "Forgive me, Nikita." He kissed her hand, his expression tormented. "Please return to me. I cannot force you into doing what I wish. The choice is yours. But if you decide to remain a mortal, take good care of our babe. I shall watch over you as I can. You will be safe with your sister and her mate."

But I can't have you as my mate. I can't have what I want the most, a child conceived in love, yes, but a baby to raise with his father. Tears swam in her eyes. "Tristan, please, don't leave me."

Mist swirled around their ankles as he stepped back.

Tristan's mouth worked as if he struggled with his feelings. He was the mighty Silver Wizard and had to remain strong.

The mist snaked upwards, covering everything but his face and the anguish there.

"I love you," he whispered, as the vision of him faded into mist. "You have my heart, forever."

And then the mist closed in on him and he vanished from her sight.

CHAPTER 18

An immortal's heart could not break, so he had been told when Danu had made him the Silver Wizard. Yet here he sat, his heart shattered like pieces of fragile glass.

Tristan regarded his fellow wizards around the enormous round table in Xavier's home in Tir Na-nog. Caedryn, the Shadow Wizard, Xavier, the Crystal Wizard, and Gideon, the Crimson Wizard. They met in the Crystal Palace, Xavier's home, for the crystals in the palace gave them the most ability to foresee the future. Once they had met on neutral ground, but they were long past egos and concerns about the others' powers.

Danu had never visited them here. She sat at the round table, her emerald gown spread delicately around her, its starlight patterns glittering. A fairy circled her, light glinting off the coppery sheen of its wings. The fairy settled on Danu's shoulder. Tristan knew this fairy was Danu's assistant, who remembered everything. The keeper of memories.

The goddess spoke, her voice as sweet and clear. "Gideon requested this formal conclave to address the matter of Drust, the dragon shifter who has entered Tir Na-nog. Gideon has formally petitioned me to bring Drust to Tir Na-nog…and elevate him to the position of the Brehon. A fifth wizard, to rule over the dragons and guide them."

Tristan stared at the goddess and then looked at Gideon, feeling as if someone had whacked his knees with a tree limb. "What? I am the guardian of dragon shifters."

"And they have grown out of control, Tristan. You know this," Gideon said quietly. "While I was taking over your duties as you were escorting Nikita here, I dealt with them personally. They are powerful and require much time. Your hands are full with the other shifters."

The two others shot him questioning looks, but said nothing. To give up his power over dragons? Impossible. The very territorial wolf inside him growled at the thought.

"Drust is a dragon, true, and one who has sacrificed much. He was my friend when we were mortal, and quite courageous." Tristan struggled to keep his voice even. "But it takes years, perhaps centuries, to fine tune the abilities one requires to be a wizard to rule over Others."

"We all had mentors," Gideon pointed out. "I was your mentor, and you did fine."

He didn't like it. Didn't like giving up one bit of control. True, his thirst for revenge against his friend died upon learning Drust did not betray him nor kill Nikita in her former life, but making him a wizard, an equal?

"He was your best friend once," Danu said softly,

297

the goddess gazing at him kindly. "You were two formidable warriors, fighting for a noble cause. If Drust becomes the fifth wizard, the guardian of dragons, you will mentor him."

And then he recalled their friendship, the times they flew through the sky together, working as one, defeating many Fae. The battles they won had turned the tide against the Fae, and united all shifters.

"It would take some adjustments," he said diplomatically.

Finally, Caedryn, the eldest among them, spoke in a deep voice.

"What has this OtherWorlder done, my lady, to deserve such responsibility?"

Danu nodded at Gideon. He stood and braced his hands on the crystal table.

"I obtained the records of Drust's actions in the Shadow World. Drust has remained in there for centuries to mentor other dragons, so they may access the portal to Tir Na-nog and avoid being consumed by the Shadow World. He has acted as their guardian in the afterworld, and aided them so they could become reincarnated once more. He has shown exceptional courage, selflessness, and...." He looked directly at Danu as he spoke, "mercy. Such is the way of the Brehon."

The goddess seemed to agree. "The time of dragons has passed, and the time of man has reigned. But among OtherWorlders, the dragons are endangered. It is Gideon's belief, and I hold fast to this as well, that dragons are a special race who require their own guardian and judge. They need guidance from one of their own."

Danu stretched out her hands and a crystal ball appeared in her palm. "I approve the election of this fifth wizard. However, I leave the final decision up to you. I will leave so you can cast your votes."

Waving a hand, she tossed the ball into the air. It split into four sections.

Each section slid over to one wizard.

Danu vanished. Tristan toyed with his piece. He waited.

Xavier was the first. He squeezed his piece hard in his right hand, and suddenly an ethereal emerald glow pulsed on his skin.

Tristan held his breath. One 'yes' vote.

Slowly, Gideon did the same and a crimson glow pulsed on his skin. That made two.

Then Caderyn took his piece and shifted it to his left hand. Tristan watched, his thoughts secret and guarded.

The Shadow Wizard shifted his piece to his right hand and squeezed. A grayish glow surrounded him.

Three yes votes. He was the decider. He thought about the strenuous extra responsibility he would assume in mentoring Drust. There would be little time left to visit Nikita, to check on her welfare. So little time, when he already watched their few days together vanish.

Love or duty? Which would he put first?

Drust would make an excellent guardian. But I am too filled with emotion to think clearly about this enormous decision.

Tristan pushed his piece of the globe away. "It is finished, my lady. I am postponing my vote."

She appeared before them, saw the glowing right

299

palms of the other wizards. "What reason have you, Tristan?"

Disapproval rang out in her sweet voice. But he knew her, knew her wisdom, and he knew she liked directness and honesty.

"I returned Nikita to the mortal plane, back to her family and her twin, whom she loves very much. She requested one more day to make her decision regarding consuming the Blood Moonflower nectar, and becoming my immortal mate." He gave her a level look. "I gave her the day you took away from us to call this meeting."

The three others looked stunned. Danu did not. A little smile touched her rosy lips. She had always liked his directness and his boldness in dealing with her. "Go on."

"I will decide upon Drust's fate after Nikita has made up her mind." He smiled ruefully. "My mind is too muddled to cast a vote now."

Something flickered in the goddess's eyes. "You have fallen in love with her all over again, Tristan. I see it on your face, my son. You were warned against this. It could be your greatest downfall."

He shrugged to hide his concern. "If falling in love is such sin, then half the world would be in trouble. But perhaps there would be less bad poetry and more sports channels."

The other three did not even move, though Xavier's mouth quirked slightly upward.

Danu looked at him and laughed, the sound like tiny silver bells. "You always did amuse me, Tristan. Very well. I will grant you one more day. But no more."

She regarded them all with a grave look. "If you

decide Drust is to become the fifth wizard, he shall need much of your teaching to guide his people. And a special gift to keep them in line."

She opened her palm and a delicate blue flame flickered on the surface. "Coldfire. Much more than any of you have the ability to summon. Drust would be known as the Coldfire Wizard, the fifth wizard of this conclave."

His chest tightened as the others went still. They knew what this meant, as he did.

"My lady, why such tremendous power? Are the dark times you warned us about approaching sooner than we believed?" Tristan asked.

A little warning would be nice. But he didn't joke about this, for it was too serious. If Drust became the Coldfire Wizard, he would help them form a formidable force to fight evil. They would have a greater chance. Remembering the horrors of war, of seeing his comrades struck down by the Fae, Tristan felt divided in half.

His decision was no longer a matter of simple duty in teaching a new wizard to guide and judge dragons. It was teaching a wizard who could help save thousands of lives.

If Nikita chose to remain mortal, he would have less time to spend with her on Earth.

Danu looked grave as she closed her palm. "Dark times are coming for OtherWorlders, indeed, and all must be prepared. It is so, and the dragons shall need a good, just guardian to unite them as one force to defeat evil."

"Their magick is most powerful," Caderyn murmured, and Tristan knew then that the Shadow

Wizard's vote had been cast only because of this reason.

With a little nod of her head, the goddess dismissed Gideon, Caderyn and Xavier. But she beckoned for Tristan to stay. He remained at the table, watching her with a guarded look.

One never knew what the goddess wanted…

"Tristan, of all my wizards, your heart needs mending the most. This is why I granted your request when you ascended to being the Silver Wizard. But beware, Tristan." Danu folded her hands on the table. "Do not interfere with Nikita's fate, for you will suffer the consequences."

"My lady." Tristan bowed his head and the goddess vanished.

He went outside into the bright sunshine, a great weight settling on his heart. He missed Nikita dreadfully and it was not even hours that they had been apart.

How was he to endure life without her?

CHAPTER 19

One day to make up her mind. Love or family?

Freedom and adventure, or a life with Tristan and the family she'd been denied in her last life.

Time had proven elusive and fleeting in Tir Na-nog, and here on Earth, she knew it would pass all too soon

Niki closed her eyes, longing to hold onto the last image of Tristan. She felt a gentle breeze touch her cheeks, ruffle her hair.

When she opened her eyes, she realized she was back before the pond that had been a portal to the afterworld. It seemed so very long ago when Tristan had brought her here.

Weeping, she sank to the grass and buried her face into her hands. A shiver raced down her spine. Niki raised her head.

She was nude. Tristan had warned she must arrive back on Earth as naked as the day she'd entered it.

And then her sharpened Lupine senses detected the scent of a familiar, dear wolf. Hastily she wiped her eyes and turned her head.

A mirror image of herself raced toward her. Niki stood as her twin collided with her and then wrapped her arms around her waist. She closed her eyes again and relief filled her.

"Niki, oh, thank the goddess you're alive, and well." Nia hugged her tightly and then released her, scanning her face with obvious anxiety. "He didn't turn you into a pumpkin or make you do weird things?"

Flushing at the thought of the things they had done together—things that one could not share with a beloved sister—she shook her head.

Aiden, her twin's mate, approached with a blanket. Aware of her nudity, she covered her breasts with her hands. But he averted his gaze and only draped the blanket over her shoulders.

"I was told you'd need this." He gently kissed her cheek. "Are you ok, Niki?"

She nodded and clutched the blanket close. "Who told you? Tristan?"

"No. We got a message from Gideon, the Crimson Wizard, that we'd find you here." Aiden rubbed a hand over his smooth chin. "He told us to bring you warm clothing, and then let you rest after you had a big meal. No shifting for twenty-four hours."

"Scary guy," Nia murmured. Then her twin gave her a long, thorough look. "You okay, Niki? You look like you've been through hell."

"I have. The real thing. Well, almost." Not wishing to fret her sister, she hugged her again. "But I'll be fine now."

Just a-okay, even though my heart is broken because I have to decide between freedom as a mortal and having you in my life, or returning forever to Tristan as an immortal and being imprisoned in Tir Na-nog, as sweet as that afterworld is. I know what a prison is like.

It can be a basement apartment with all the luxuries you gave me, or a heavenly afterworld where all my dreams can come true. But I'm forbidden to leave, so it's still a prison.

Here, I'm finally free from that coffin of a basement and I no longer have to hide as a shadow.

But I love Tristan and if I remain here, he'll become the shadow in my life, and that of our child's. How can I choose?

She looked around. "It feels as if I've been gone forever. Longer than a week."

Nia wrinkled her nose. "A week? Try two months."

Two months! But Tristan mentioned time was different in the afterworld.

Aiden gave her an even more critical look. "You've changed, Niki."

Then he exchanged a glance with his mate. "I'll get the golf cart."

"I'm not crippled. I can walk," she protested.

But as she started to accompany her twin along the pathway leading from the pond, her legs shook badly. Niki leaned on her sister.

"I don't know what's wrong with me," she admitted. "I feel wobbly, like a newborn colt."

Aiden drove up in the golf cart. He took another look at Niki, climbed out and then swung her into his arms. Very gently, he placed her in the back seat and tucked the blanket around her. "Just rest," he murmured. "We'll have you home in no time."

Home. It sounded heavenly, yet she no longer knew where she truly belonged. She'd felt most at home with Tristan, back at his cottage in another dimension, another world.

But how could she leave her twin forever? Leave the life behind as a wolf?

Aiden turned. "You need an airlift, too?" He swung Nia into his arms and strode with her to the shotgun seat. Giggling, her twin hooked her arms around the alpha's neck, her gaze growing soft as she regarded her mate.

Theirs was a good match, Niki thought. She was glad of it, glad her twin found such joy with Aiden, though her own heart remained empty and broken.

Perhaps when she settled in with the pack, this grief would ease. She put a hand over her belly, instinct telling her a tiny life grew there.

They headed up the pathway to the drive. Aiden's big pickup truck sat there. As she started to get out, Aiden quickly intervened.

He scooped her up again and Nia hurried to the truck, opening the back door of the cab. Aiden set her inside and looked at her with worry in his dark eyes.

"Your scent has changed. I know what that means." He turned to Nia, who gasped.

"OMG, Niki, you're pregnant."

Niki bit her lip, tensing at her sister's worried look and Aiden's dawning anger. "Yes."

"Tristan is the father." This from Nia.

"Yes."

"Son of a bitch!" Aiden slammed a hand against the truck's exterior. "That silver bastard forced you, I'll..."

"It was of my own free will," she interjected. "He didn't force me."

Nia clasped her hand. "Honey, you can tell us the truth."

Niki laughed. For their entire lives, they'd feared the

wizard and his power, and knew the prophecy said Tristan would destroy her. Nia probably thought nothing good could come of the wizard abducting her and that Niki had lied out of shame, or for another reason.

"He was my mate in another life."

"I know. He told us that when you were dying and he saved you." Nia still looked worried. "But that was another life, honey. He had no right to take you away from us."

"He had every right." She sighed, remembering the promise she'd coaxed from him all those centuries ago. "I'll tell you everything, but first, let's go home."

Wherever home would be in the future, she had yet to know...

Tristan dematerialized, appearing in a dark forest in Tir Na-nog. Drust sat before a roaring fire, staring into the flames.

Clad in the same cobalt blue and silver tunic and trousers he'd worn when they had been mortals, the dragon looked healthier and more relaxed. His feet were clad in tawny doeskin boots. Glancing up and seeing him, Drust gestured to the rock beside him and Tristan sat.

"You have met with the goddess and she told you what she desires." It was a statement from Tristan, not a question.

Doubt clouded Drust's piercing blue eyes. He gazed around. "Danu wants to make me into a wizard of enormous power. You hold the deciding vote."

"Yes," he said, watching him. "It is a rather big decision. I have not yet cast my ballot."

Drust looked down at the ground. "Do you think me capable? For all these years, you thought I betrayed you and you didn't believe me."

"I am sorry, Drust." Tristan opened his palms as he once did hundreds of years ago, to show he held no weapon. "I was mad with rage and grief at losing Nikita and our child, and the thought of revenge burned hard."

He took a deep breath and released it. "The price you pay for love is very steep at times."

"Indeed," Drust agreed. He poked at the ashes with his stick. "I do not deserve such an honor to be a wizard like you."

"It is not as much of an honor as you believe. It is a rather large responsibility. You will have powers equivalent to mine."

His old friend looked at him in the face, his gaze stricken. "If I am given this power, I want to use it for good, to aid my people. They are lost, Tristan. Lost and constantly squabbling. And I wish to aid you as well, when you need me."

His voice trembled and Drust struck a fist upon his knee. "I was not there for you in the past as I should have been. It is my biggest regret. I wanted to save your Nikita and instead, she died under my watch. That is inexcusable."

Tristan felt a stab of pity for the dragon shifter. "If I do this, Drust, if I agree to allow you to become the Coldfire Wizard, what would be your greatest desire?"

Power was a tricky thing. But power used for the right reasons...

Those broad shoulders sagged and Drust rubbed a

hand over his short, black beard. "I know not if I will be a good guardian for my people. I want them to have the best guardian possible. But if this means I can save more of them from destruction, and stop the fighting that has broken out among the clans, I will do it. If...you will teach me. I want to learn from the best."

Tristan nodded. "Just as you taught me in the past to fight while we flew together."

"Except your aim with a spear was always a little off, wolf." Drust grinned and then looked intent. "If this is to be, Tristan, I beg you one boon."

He waited.

"I want to help you in your greatest hour of need. Anything you need from me, whatever I can do, call upon me."

For a moment he felt a prickle down his spine as if the dragon's words were prophetic. But he dismissed it. He was the Silver Wizard and Drust would be a new wizard, barely able to harness such tremendous power.

"I will." Tristan smiled. "I would be most pleased to teach you, my old friend. And thus, you have sealed my decision."

He reflected. "The dragons have grown dangerously out of control, and with their tempers, they can be dangerous. They must learn to work together."

"We dragons can be ill-tempered." Drust sighed. "Like my great-grandson, Alexander."

Tristan braced his hands on his knees. "I have other duties to attend to, but I will return to your family and restore your lost honor, Drust. I will tell them that you did not betray me, nor did you cause the death of my Nikita."

"But I did, in a way." Guilt flickered over Drust's

face. "And the memory of it caused me to remain in the Shadow Lands. Only by helping you and Nikita to the Dark Gate did this guilt ease a little."

"It is in the past. I promise, I will help you overcome that memory. You have a long road ahead of you, Drust. Coldfire carries a tremendous power," he warned. "It can shock the dying back to life, and kill evil with a single blast of that ugly dragon's mouth of yours."

Drust grinned. "Dragon breath?"

Then he sombered. "Tristan, how can I be responsible for such tremendous power? I know nothing of this."

He clapped a hand on his shoulder. "I will teach you, my friend."

Reaching into the flames, Drust picked up a burning ember. "How will I become this wizard? I'm not corporeal now. How will she make me corporeal? Will it hurt?"

Like a bitch. "It is a secret rite of passage all wizards must endure," Tristan said diplomatically, but he rubbed his chest, remembering his own ritual when he became the Silver Wizard.

They stood and Tristan shook his hand. "Welcome to immortality. Be courageous."

Drust grinned. "If you can do it, so can I. I am stronger than you."

"Dragon breath."

"Wolf bait."

Tristan stood, and closing his eyes and using his magick, called upon Danu. The goddess appeared and he and Drust bowed before her. Tristan rose.

"My lady, I have made my decision. I cast the final

deciding vote, and I agree that Drust should become the fifth wizard." He took a deep breath. "The Coldfire Wizard."

Danu gave a little nod. "I am most pleased, Tristan."

She turned to Drust. "Coldfire is a tremendous power. It can indeed bring the dying back to life. I will teach you how to use it, Drust. Tristan cannot show you how to harness this as a dragon. He will be your mentor in using your other skills."

Secrets danced in her eyes and he wondered what her ultimate goal was, for the goddess always had a purpose.

"My guards will arrive shortly to escort you to the sacred cavern where the ritual to make you into the wizard shall take place," she told Drust.

Then with another little nod, the goddess vanished.

Tristan looked at the dragon shifter. "Good luck."

With a friendly punch to his shoulder, Tristan left. He dematerialized to Earth, resisting the urge to check on Nikita.

By now she was safely ensconced with her twin and Aiden, secure in their pack.

But he did have a score to settle concerning her fate, and her safety, and it was time at last to confront Gideon on his murdering sister…

CHAPTER 20

Two hours after her return to the ranch, Niki was having trouble adjusting to life back on Earth, let alone life in a pack.

On Aiden's ranch, everything ran like clockwork. She'd been given a room in the lodge near her sister and Aiden, but despite the fact that Nia was just down the hall, Niki had never felt so alone.

Even on a ranch surrounded by Lupines, her own people. Aiden and Nia had combined the Blakemore and Mitchell packs and made them into one strong family.

But she still felt like a stranger.

To keep herself busy, and keep the nausea in her belly under control, she embarked on a project to take all the family photos of her family and scan them into the computer, and then put them into an album. She also studied the history books Gideon had sent to given Aiden to give to her, books crammed with stories and etchings from the days when she and Tristan had lived, and loved, as mates.

After a light lunch of crackers and ginger ale, she turned the pages of parchment and studied the etchings.

One in particular caught her eye. It was of a tall, slender Lupine. She was stately and handsome, but had an ethereal quality about her that was not Lupine. Niki read the caption under the image.

Camilla, mate to Drust.

Her friend, who had laughed with her, had shared confidences with.

They had grown close, as Tristan and Drust had. Camilla had been a good friend who kept the loneliness at bay.

Her stomach grumbled, reminding her that she had eaten little today. Closing the book, she stood. Niki headed for the kitchen in search of something more substantial than crackers.

Pregnancy as a Lupine was a bitch, she thought humorlessly, hunting through the refrigerator for raw meat. As Lupine she craved meat, but her hormones had affected her body. It didn't help that she was still adjusting to the high levels of gravity, and that food here tasted heavier and different than in Tristan's home world.

Niki found a package of raw chopped meat. She removed it and put it on the counter, deciding to fry a rare hamburger. Unfortunately, her stomach clenched. Bolting for the sink, she threw up. The retching continued for a good ten minutes. Miserable, she wiped her mouth and then drank a glass of water.

"You know I have the perfect solution to morning and afternoon sickness."

She looked up to see her twin standing in the doorway.

"I thought you were out riding with Aiden, fixing the fence posts."

"Cowboy's job. I came here to check on you. I'm worried, honey. You don't look so good."

"I don't feel so well, either," she admitted. "This pregnancy business is hell on my body."

"I have just the thing. An old wives recipe. From an old wife." Nia rummaged through the refrigerator and withdrew a shiny red apple.

Niki looked dubiously at the fruit. "An apple a day keeps the OB-GYN away?"

"Lupines don't require much fruit, but this is loaded with vitamins and it will quell your nausea."

Taking the apple, Niki examined it. It was shiny and pretty, but her sharpened wolf senses, even more honed since her visit to Tir Na-nog, warned her that something was odd about this fruit.

"Oh, go on, eat it! It won't kill you. And then I'll cook you a hamburger. You need the meat."

Nia seemed very put out at her hesitation, so Niki bit into the apple. She sat at the table, chewing, as Nia removed a frying pan from the cabinet and set it on the eight-burner stove.

But the taste of the apple seemed tinged with something nasty. Niki set it down on the table.

"What's wrong?" Nia demanded. "I'm trying to help you, Niki."

"You're not the wicked queen trying to poison Sleeping Beauty, are you? It tastes funny."

The joke fell flat as Niki looked at the apple again. Several white worms began to crawl out of it. Suddenly her stomach muscles tightened and her heart began racing.

Too fast.

"It's a bad apple," she whispered.

"Like you are," Nia agreed cheerfully.

She wondered why her twin looked so mirthful. And then her stomach clenched hard again and a bout of dizziness seized her.

Nia's face became a blur as her twin released a malevolent laugh.

"What did you do to me, Nia?" she whispered.

And then weakness overtook her as she struggled to stand. Niki tumbled to the floor, unable to move.

He had a score to settle with Gideon's sister.

Tristan materialized inside the enormous living room of Gideon's Irish castle.

On Earth, the Crimson Wizard had created a castle as a home, but it held no warmth. Gideon lived in the past more so than any other of the Brehon.

Until Tristan knew Mara had been dealt with, he could not rest easy. The Fae could destroy Niki, and the babe inside her.

The heavy door opened and Gideon walked inside, his lovely sister on his arm. Tristan whirled, his temper rising.

"You could have knocked," Gideon said mildly.

Tristan ignored him and looked directly at the Fae who had caused so much grief, the woman whom he now suspected of killing Nikita in her former life. Not that he had proof.

"Mara. I asked Gideon to bring you here. You sent those wraiths after her in the Shadow Lands."

The Fae's blue eyes widened. "Tristan, darling, I have no power there."

"Do not lie," he warned. "You sent the worm after her before she entered the Shadow Lands and you sent your wraiths to harm her once she was there."

Gideon narrowed his eyes. "Only an evil Fae, one who's sold his soul, can command such power from beyond. And such a Fae would carry a mark on his hands, a pointed star on his palm. Mara, show him your palms."

She did, opening her hands. No mark. It could be Fae glamour, but still...

"It is not my glamour," Mara said, sighing. "I shall drop all my glamour so you can see."

Suddenly her face began to change and then the full ripe, red mouth became thin and tight. Pink scar tissue marred one perfect cheek. Mara opened her palms.

They remained unmarked.

Tristan stared as Mara assumed her glamour once more. "I am hundreds of years old, wizard, and I have seen much. I choose not to share my scars with the world."

He could almost feel pity for Mara, but for one daunting fact.

"That does not excuse the evil you did to my Nikita. It was you who hurt her. I saw this in my visions...you brought her the potion that killed her in her past life. You are the one who found the dragon eggs and when I refused you in my bed, you sought your vengeance and betrayed me to Emer!"

Gideon stiffened. "Are you accusing my sister of Nikita's murder?"

Tristan looked at Mara's velvet-clad feet. "If the pointed shoe fits..."

A snarl came from Gideon, but Mara shook her head. "Brother, please. Hold your temper."

"You wanted to seduce me. And after all these years, you expect me to trust you are my ally, and bear no ill will toward me? You are Fae, Mara. Your people hated mine," Tristan said.

"Wait a minute," Gideon began.

But Mara held up a hand, silencing her brother.

Mara looked at him, and for the first time, Tristan noticed how sad she appeared. "I had no ill will for you or your mate, or even for your people, wizard. My brother asked a favor of me, and I agreed, for not all Fae bore shifters the same ill will as Emer. I did not give you the dragon eggs because I wanted you in my bed."

Arms folded, he waited.

"Oh I teased you, because you were so serious." A twinkle lit her gaze, reminding him of her impish streak. "You still are. But I had enough lovers. I helped you because you needed an edge in the war, an edge to win over Emer's forces. Many of us had tired of Emer's dictates, and saw shifters as friends, not slaves. Gideon could not aid you directly."

The Crimson Wizard rested a hand upon his sister's shoulder. "But I chose not to heed the call of Emer as well, when he cried out for justice to me while fighting your forces."

A shadow crossed his friend's face. "As their judge and guardian, I could do nothing but ignore the cry of my people because I knew their fate. They had brought this upon themselves. I, the guardian and judge of Fae, was helpless to prevent their own downfall. All I could do was issue warnings, warnings Emer chose to ignore."

And then Tristan knew that his friend had been a

true guardian of justice, and how deeply he had hurt during the Drakon War, listening to the constant screams of the Fae as the shifters defeated them, and doing nothing. Because Gideon knew it was for the best, even though he felt grieved and anguished. Gideon had suffered, much as his sister had suffered.

"I am sorry, Mara," he said stiffly. "Will you forgive my accusations?"

Mara looked sly. "The mighty Tristan, at my power. Oh, I don't know what to do."

"Mara," Gideon warned. "Play nice."

She rolled her eyes. "Fine. Maybe if you make it up to me with a chocolate ice cream cone. I do adore chocolate. More than I like sex."

I don't care if you like eating cockroaches as long as you stay away from me and mine. He waved a hand and two chocolate ice cream cones appeared in her hands.

Mara blinked at him. "Two cones?"

"Enough to keep you busy for a while." He gave her a stern look. "And a warning—stay away from Nikita."

She waved a hand, chocolate dripping over her fingers. "I have no intention of getting near her. Wolves bore me. You're forgiven, Tristan. Enjoy your bride. Ta! I'm off now."

Then Gideon's sister gave him a critical look. "Tristan, you must know that all Fae are not your enemy. But watch out for those who are. Looks can be deceiving."

Then the Fae vanished, leaving Gideon and Tristan alone. He looked at his friend, deeply troubled. "If Mara did not poison Nikita, and neither did Drust, who did?"

"I know not." Gideon paced the room. "It means

whoever hurt your Nikita in the past, and tried to hurt her in this life, is still out there."

Tristan searched his memories. As usual, they were clouded with images of Nikita. He concentrated, and the images cleared. The Fae were powerful and clever.

Looks can be deceiving.

Horror pulsed through him. "Gideon, all Fae have the ability to employ glamour...and can disguise themselves."

At once his friend looked stunned. "Someone imitated Mara, to implicate her in poisoning Nikita. Another Fae. But who would have cause to injure Nikita? Even King Emer saw her as no threat."

But who? He wanted to rush down to the Mitchell Ranch and check on Nikita. Tristan went to the mirror hanging on the wall and waved his hand, conjuring a window to Nikita's present.

As always with anyone he loved, the vision was watery and indistinct. But he could see through the opaque veil enough to know Nikita was in the kitchen with her twin, Nia.

He waved his hand again and conjured the past. Again, it was fogged. Yet one face did come more sharply into focus.

And then it was as if the cloud cleared entirely from his mind and he could see miles down a foggy road, into the past and into his former life.

Fae. Fae could glamour, and imitate anyone.

Even a beloved twin.

Nikita was in real trouble.

Tristan turned on his heel. "I know who it is. And she's with Nikita now."

"Wait," Gideon cried out. "Tristan, you cannot interfere in Nikita's fate!"

Tristan ignored him. He dematerialized into time and space, knowing his mate faced her killer from the past.

He prayed he was not too late to save her.

CHAPTER 21

She was dying, killed by someone looking like her beloved twin.

Nia's body suddenly rippled like water, or a mirage. Her twin no longer stood over her, laughing.

Instead, a stranger with ash brown hair, a long nose and a thin mouth regarded her with a cold smile. "The apple tastes good, does it not?"

Her throat constricted. "Who...where is Nia?"

"I have no fucking clue, you bitch wolf. But I know where you are headed. Straight to hell, where you belong. Where you should have gone the *first* time I killed you."

And then a long black gown appeared on the woman's body, and her hair was twisted up in a silver snood.

"*Camilla?* Drust's wife?" She struggled to breathe. "You were my friend."

"Friend? I pretended to be your friend so I could get close to you. I have been waiting for this moment ever since I discovered you would finally be freed from that silver bastard's protective grip."

"Why?" Niki gasped. "I did nothing to you."

"You did nine hundred years ago! I would have been the rightful would-be queen of the shifters, if not for your damned mate leading the shifter army. He made Drust second-in-command when Drust should have been the leader! All the riches and glory and power would have been mine! I vowed Tristan would never be the ruler of the shifters. It was I who told Emer of the dragon eggs and betrayed Tristan. But he had to die without issue, so his son would never seize power. You had to die as well."

"It was Mara..." Oh gods, ... Air, she needed air.

"It was me, glamoured to look like Mara. I am Fae. I mated with Drust to watch over his children. I agreed to aid him in the war, and in exchange he kept my secret and told everyone I was dragon. It was easy enough to cloak myself as a dragon, even easier to mask myself as Gideon's sister and make you think I gave you the potion that took your life. Drust won the war and then he settled for peace with my people. But then he found out I was sleeping with my former lover, and banished me. I was left with nothing!"

"Tristan," Nikita moaned. "Help me..."

Camilla kicked her in the side and Niki screamed with pain. "Your powerful wizard can't help you now, just as he could not back then. Nor could he aid you in the Shadow Lands. I had my spies in Drust's cavern—blowflies—to alert me so I could summon the Shadow Eaters to the Dark Gate." She snorted. "Alas, I failed to consider Tristan's damned nobility. He just had to sacrifice himself for you."

With all her might, Nikita began crawling across the kitchen floor, forcing her weakened limbs to move. Niki drew upon the flickering life inside her, willing herself to the counter where the butcher knives were kept. A sudden burst of strength filled her, and she pulled herself upward and grabbed a knife.

Turning, she flung it at Camilla. Camilla looked down as it landed in her stomach. Then the Fae laughed and pulled out the knife. No blood coated the blade.

Camilla turned over her palms. On the left one was a black pointed star. "No one can kill me. Not even your wizard. I gave my soul to the Dark One, and in becoming his servant, I am now indestructible."

"Please," Niki moaned, sliding back to the floor, her limbs growing paralyzed once more. *I can't die again, not like this...not when I have so much to live for...all this time I've longed to be free and experience life. Have great adventures. Climbing mountains, waltzing at a formal ball. Tristan gave me all that.*

He gave me the freedom to be myself.

And the greatest adventure of all was falling in love with Tristan all over again, and recapturing the passion we once shared.

A flash of brilliant silver smoke filled the air. Tristan stepped out of the haze.

He tossed a ball of energy at Camilla. But she dodged it and laughed. The energy globe hit the wall and destroyed part of it.

"You can't destroy me, wizard. Your mate will die in agony, just as she did all those centuries ago. And with her death, the second time I killed her and this time a sacrifice to the Dark Lord, I will have power second to none, even you, Tristan! No one can control me ever again!"

Tristan threw another energy ball. This time it hit

Camilla in the neck. She screeched and writhed, and changed, no longer an attractive young woman.

Gasping for air, her windpipe constricting, she struggled to remain conscious. The back kitchen door opened and Aiden and Nia rushed inside. Aiden took one look at Camilla, her hair now turned to a mass of writhing snakes, her eyes dark pits, and ugly gouges on her face.

"Son of a bitch! What the hell is THAT?" the alpha yelled.

"Stay back, Mitchell," Tristan warned, lobbing another energy ball. It smashed into Camilla's chest, making her stagger backward.

Nia rushed to her side. "Honey, don't leave us, please." Her twin held her tight and began breathing slowly. "Don't panic. Listen to my voice, Niki. Conserve your air. Remember how we once swam in the pond and you taught me to hold my breath. Slow. Easy."

Nia's calming voice and her touch grounded Niki. She struggled to keep at bay the panic now consuming her oxygen, making an effort to draw in short breaths.

Her sister's mate looked at her and his expression grew infuriated. Then Aiden looked at Camilla.

"No one messes with my family, bitch!"

Aiden, dear feckless Aiden, ignored the wizard's warning. He shifted into wolf and the alpha rushed the demon, but she flicked a bolt of black energy at him. Aiden the wolf yelped as he crashed into the table.

"Aiden," Nia screamed.

The wolf bounded to his feet and shook his mighty head. Tristan raised his hands skyward. "Caedryn, Gideon, Xavier, to me NOW!"

Xavier and Gideon, and another man she did not recognize appeared in the kitchen. Camilla threw a stream of black energy at Xavier. It slammed into his arm. He looked down at his burnt shirt sleeve in amazement.

Snarling, he flung out a hand and a crystalline net, spiked with shards of quartz, encased Camilla. She froze in time.

"That will hold her, but only for a little while," said the wizard she did not recognize, the one with long hair the color of gold, the tips dipped in gray.

As Xavier went to fling an energy ball at the demon, Tristan stayed his hand.

"No! Use all your powers to maintain the netting, Xavier." He turned to the wizard she did not recognize. "Cadeyrn, you're the strongest and the eldest. Destroy her, and Gideon and I will aid you. Now!"

All three of them conjured glowing balls of energy. Silver for Tristan, red for Gideon, gray for Cadeyrn. The wizards chanted and the deep notes of their ancient spell lifted some of the terrible pressure off Niki's chest. It was like listening to an ancient choir, she thought in a daze.

The magick net around Camilla began to crack and she struggled to escape, poking one arm through. Xavier growled and more crystals appeared on the net, but the demon cackled and poked another arm through. Strain showed on Xavier's face.

"Hurry," Xavier urged. "She is freeing herself and I can't hold her much longer!"

"Now," Tristan roared. "Aim for the heart!"

Tristan, Gideon and Cadeyrn threw scores of energy balls at Camilla, hitting her square in the chest. As the good, powerful magick of the wizards consumed her, she writhed and screamed. And then she exploded into a shower of black ash.

Tristan, breathing heavily, leaned over and braced his hands on his knees.

"That was one tough demon to kill," Xavier said solemnly. "You have always been able to kill them on your own, Tristan."

"A very bad omen," Cadeyrn said. "We have never had to fight such evil."

"We may have to do so again," Gideon warned.

"Forget about that," Nia screamed. "Save my sister."

The four wizards became a hazy blur as Niki struggled against the ensuing grayness pushing at the edges of her vision. Gasping, she tried to draw in precious air. Tristan, her beloved wizard, dropped to the floor beside her.

"Niki." Panic flared in Tristan's dark eyes as he gathered her close. "No, goddess, no, you can't leave me. Not again."

She could not speak, for her throat closed up and the grayness pushed at the edges of her vision. With all her might she touched his face one last time. "I…sorry."

And then she closed her eyes and the darkness rushed up to greet her at last.

CHAPTER 22

Nikita was dying, just as she had nine hundred years ago. And he, the immortal, powerful Silver Wizard, could not stop it.

Do not interfere with her fate, Tristan.

The goddess Danu's warning rang in his mind, but he ignored it, staring at Nikita's pale face and her mouth, opening and closing like that of a fish, as she tried to suck in air.

His three fellow wizards crouched down beside him.

"I am sorry, Tristan," Gideon said gently. "I am so sorry, my friend."

"No." He rocked her back and forth in his arms, placing a palm on her belly, and with his powers, felt the tiny flutter of life inside her struggling to remain alive.

Xavier squeezed his shoulder. "I am so sorry, Tristan."

The trio stood, but not before Caderyn, the oldest of them and the most powerful, flashed a warning with his gray gaze turning to pure white. "Do not interfere in her destiny and do not give her your powers."

With a wave of their hands, they vanished.

Kneeling beside him, her cheeks wet with tears, Nia sobbed. "Niki, not again, please, I can't lose you again."

Then she pointed a shaking finger at him. "You bastard wizard, the prophecy was right! You killed her! You found her, made her your lover and your bride and you killed her!"

He could not meet her gaze, for she was right. He spoke to Aiden. "Mitchell, get out of here and take your mate with you. I need a moment alone."

Aiden shifted back from wolf and went to his mate. "Come, my love. Give Tristan time to say his good-byes."

The Mitchell alpha tugged his mate out of the ruined kitchen.

Tristan held Nikita close as he rocked her in his arms, singing softly to her as he brushed back her hair. He put a hand on the slight swell of her belly, the tiny life inside slowly perishing.

His song turned into a moan as he clutched her. So many regrets. Should never have released her. Why had he let her go? He could not foresee her future, for it was too intrinsic to his own. Too interwoven with his.

Tristan lay Nikita down and wiped his eyes.

Call upon me in your greatest hour of need. The words Drust spoke to him echoed in his mind.

He started to, and hesitated. Drust was a new wizard by now, but he could not save Nikita. Only he, Tristan, had that power.

Do not interfere in Nikita's fate, Danu had warned. Those were the rules, the absolute truth that governed his power.

Fuck the rules.

Nikita came first. He promised to protect her with his body and his magick. His chest tightened. *One last kiss, my love. One last kiss before I lose you forever and I turn to shadow.*

He knew what he must do. Bending over, he gave her one last, sweet kiss.

I love you. I shall love you through all eternity. You will live forever in my cold, dead heart, my dearest love, though I shall never see you again.

Summoning all his magick, he closed his eyes and made a fist with his right hand. Power hummed and sang in the air like an electrical line. Tristan flicked a finger and the knife Nikita had used to stab Camilla sailed into his left hand. With his magick, he purified the blade. No demon blood must touch it in the face of what he was about to do.

Tristan looked skyward. "I, Tristan Kearny, the Silver Wizard, guardian and judge of all shifter OtherWorlders, do this of my own free will, as wizard of the Brehon."

He stabbed Nikita in the heart.

Tristan did not hesitate, for Niki's light was fading quickly. He summoned all his powers, his aura pulsing in a silver-white glow. Blinding white light filled the room.

Tristan forced his powers into his right hand, and then placed his palm over the bleeding wound in Nikita's chest. A brilliant, luminescent, silvery-white glow encased her body. Her chest began to rise and fall once more, and the wound sealed shut.

Dropping his hand, he sat back on his haunches.

It is done.

His aura faded. A terrible pain seized his chest and he gasped.

The back door opened and Aiden and Nia rushed into the kitchen. Nia ran to her twin. By now the glow surrounding Nikita's body was fading.

"Niki! Niki!" Her blue eyes wild with grief and hope, she looked at Tristan. "She's alive, isn't she?"

Beyond weary, he nodded. "She lives. She will take a moment…or five or fifteen, to awaken."

Ah, at least he still had a sense of humor. Perhaps it would sustain him in the shadowy world he was now cursed to live in for eternity.

I wonder if they have cable in the Shadow Lands?

He smiled, but even that gesture proved too taxing, and he let his mouth go lax.

Aiden crouched down next to him. "Tristan, you're looking bad. What the hell did you do?"

He gave a little laugh. Typical Mitchell. Always direct. One reason he liked the fierce alpha Lupine.

"I gave Nikita my powers. My immortality. She can never die now, and the babe she carries in her womb will never die, either. My love, and my legacy, will live on."

He started to stand and then collapsed.

He knew it was the end for him. But Nikita would live.

She would live.

He himself would be banished to a living hell—as a ghost damned to walk the Shadow Lands forever.

It was so quiet, peaceful and lovely in this transition place. Niki blinked and looked around, seeing nothing but grayish fog. Yet she had no fear. Someone whispered to her, words of such deep love she felt immediately secure.

And then she began walking toward a brilliant yellow-white light that her spirit recognized from her time with Tristan.

Tristan! Where was he?

Barely had she time to contemplate that question when suddenly the light in front of her winked out and she felt herself lying on a soft surface.

Niki opened her eyes.

She was on a wide bed, several of the ranch Lupines surrounding her. She recognized Darius, Kyle and Dale, and their mates. Aiden stood by the bed, looking grief-stricken. Nia sat beside her, holding her hand. Her twin gasped and hugged her tight.

"It worked! You're alive!"

Confused, she blinked. "What happened? It felt as if I died and was entering Tir Na-nog."

Immediately she placed a palm on her belly, fearing the worst. But the very faint heartbeat she'd felt before still pulsed with life. Her baby lived!

But Aiden and the others shuffled their feet and would not answer. Aiden's jaw tensed as he jammed his hands into his jeans pockets.

"Tristan saved you," Aiden finally said. "He saved you and then we brought you in here to the guest room so you could recover...and he could...he could...be with you."

Sitting up, she realized the wizard was on the bed next to her. But Tristan was pale and he seemed to be fading...turning insubstantial as mist.

"Tristan!" She went to clasp his hand, but her hand went through his as if he were spirit, not flesh.

"Nikita," he rasped. "I love you. Always remember this…"

Her twin began to weep, and Darius, Kyle and the others looked stricken.

"What happened?" she demanded.

Aiden shook his head. "You were dying. He gave you his powers to save you."

"All of them," Darius added, with none of his usual joviality. "He sacrificed his immortality to save you."

No! She gathered Tristan in her arms, feeling his life force ebb. Nikita looked around wildly. "You have to save him! Someone!"

"We can't," Kyle said brokenly. "We don't have the power. Gods, if I could, I would, because he's saved me so many times before."

Sorrow pierced her, making her chest hollow. She glared at them. "Get out. All of you, get out except Nia and Aiden. Now!"

The Lupines scurried away.

She screamed and looked skyward. "Gideon! Xavier! Caedyrn! Tristan is dying! Please, damnit, listen to me and come here NOW!!"

The three wizards appeared in the bedroom, standing near the bed.

"Help him, please," she begged. "He's fading from me. He gave me his powers."

Gideon paled. "All of them?"

She nodded.

"Damn," Xavier muttered.

"He was warned against this. He was warned to not fall in love with you again," Caderyn said in a deep, ominous voice.

"He's not dying, for he cannot die. He is immortal,

like us," Gideon said solemnly. "He's turning into a spirit, damned to the Shadow Lands forever."

Oh gods. The Shadow Lands, the worst fate for Tristan. To become a ghost, forever wandering that place that caused him so much grief.

"It will be hell for him if this happens. So many bad memories will haunt him for eternity. This can't happen!" She looked at the kind Xavier, who seemed the most approachable. "Please, please, do something! I beg you, or I'll die with him. He is my heart and my soul. I have his powers, surely I can help him."

"You are far too weak and it will do no good," Xavier said gently. He looked at the others. "Call Danu. We must ask permission to share our powers. It is the only way."

All three vanished. In a few moments, they returned. By now Tristan's lower limbs were nothing but shadows on the bed.

"Well?" she demanded.

"The goddess cannot be reached and it takes a full day to request a formal petition of her," Caderyn finally said.

Niki began to sob. "Please, save him. Please."

Xavier made an impatient sound and climbed onto the bed.

"No, X!" Caderyn tried to pull him back, but the Crystal Wizard shrugged him off. Xavier sliced his wrist and dripped white blood into Tristan's gasping mouth. Tristan became slightly more substantial.

"It's not enough." The Crystal Wizard looked at the two others.

"We are forbidden to share our powers with each other. We had to gain special permission from Danu to make the potion that saved your life. This goes beyond a mere droplet of our blood," Gideon said solemnly.

"The consequences can be dreadful." Caderyn looked deeply troubled.

"And if you lose him, it will be worse! All of you need him! You saw what happened with that demon! You need him as a wizard, need his strength and his courage. Save him!" she screamed.

The walls trembled and the pictures on the nightstand beside her rattled with the force of her voice. Nia and Aiden stepped back, their faces filled with awe.

Rage consumed her, a terrible rage she'd never before felt. She was losing the one male who truly cared about her, whose tremendous sacrifice was done in love, not duty. And he'd be damned forever for it.

He deserved to live.

She flung out her hands and tiny silver energy balls cascaded from her palms, slamming into the walls and denting them. One nearly hit Aiden and he yelped.

"Save him, now!" she roared. "Or I'll use my powers and destroy everything in sight."

Tristan offered a smile, his mouth barely visible now. "My warrior Nikita," he whispered. "Do not be so angry. It was…worth it to save you and our babe."

"We must do this and damn the consequences," Xavier finally said. "We can't afford to lose him. I will not allow that to happen. I need your help, now! Are we in agreement to aid our friend?"

Finally, they nodded. Xavier waved a hand and a table filled with vials and jars appeared beneath the window.

They made a potion of their blood and forced Tristan to drink it. His color returned and his body became corporeal.

He opened his eyes and then closed them again. Niki cried out and hugged him, only to find him solid, but seemingly dead. His chest did not rise and fall and his face remained pale, oh so pale.

"What's wrong with him?" she cried out. "Is he dead?"

"He is deep in *Anamsha*," Xavier told her. "All of us went through this after we were anointed as wizards by Danu. *Anamsha* lasts but a day for us after we become wizards, but for him, under these circumstances, I know not how long."

"The sleep of the immortals," Caedryn said. "We use it on occasion when we are weary of the world and need to recharge from dispensing with evil. It is a cleansing rest. He will be like that for twenty-four hours, perhaps less, while his body adjusts to becoming immortal again. It is natural."

"But he will be quite vulnerable at this time." Gideon sighed. "Now is the time when his enemies can easily destroy him. He will need constant protection."

"And we cannot do it." Xavier examined his hand with a rueful look. "We have weakened ourselves to save him, and our magick has waned. It will be restored with the next sun, but until then we must conserve our strength."

"That is why it is forbidden to do what we have done. We lack sufficient magick to administer to all our charges." Caderyn growled.

Aiden straightened. "He won't be alone, and neither will Niki."

He went to the door and called Darius, Kyle and Dale.

When the Lupines entered the room, Aiden pointed at Darius. "Gather the entire pack. Everyone. Assign chores, and as for those who aren't assigned chores, they're sleeping here tonight. Men, women, children. No exceptions. Post guards around the lodge. No one but pack gets in or out."

He gestured to the slumbering Tristan. "This is your wizard, your guardian, and he's faithfully protected us. Now it's our turn to watch over him. Got it?"

"I'll set guards around the perimeter," Darius assured Aiden.

The three wizards nodded. "Tristan is fortunate to have such loyal subjects," Cadeyrn mused. He glanced at Xavier. "Remain here, and teach the mate of Tristan how to deal with the power she has been given. And her...emotions. They are quite raw and she could accidently hurt someone. Watch over her. Gideon and I shall deal with Danu and what we have done."

Throat tight with emotion, she could only whisper her thanks to the wizards. With a nod, Cadeyrn and Gideon vanished.

She turned her attention to Xavier. In his black T-shirt, faded jeans and boots, he looked like a cowhand, but for his black beard and curly hair with crystals on each tip. "Come, Nikita. Let Tristan sleep. I must show you how to control this new power of yours. We need to go outside to practice, far from anything you might injure."

"I don't want to leave him," she said, her throat tight. "He might wake up and need me."

"And if you do not accompany me now, you could

hurt him with your powers. Do you wish that?" Xavier asked.

Aiden pulled up a chair and her twin sat on his lap. "We'll watch over him, Niki. Go," Aiden said gently. "Nothing's going to get past us."

Taking Xavier's hand, she closed her eyes. When she opened them, they were standing outside, on the bank of the river cutting the Mitchell Ranch into half.

"Lupines are loyal and fierce, but you have more power to protect your mate." Xavier gave her a level look, and she shuddered.

Such power. How could she possess such power? She didn't even know the extent of it. Or how to use it.

"We're still on Mitchell territory, so you're safe here and so am I. But here you can practice using your new power. And then when he awakens, you both will be a formidable force." The Crystal Wizard gave a rueful smile. "The two of you shall be even stronger than the rest of us."

Then he took her hands into his. She gazed at him, trusting this wizard who had sacrificed much to save his friend and her love.

"Teach me how to use my powers."

"It will take many days for Tristan to teach you. But I can teach you how to control your emotions so you do not destroy those who anger you. It is the first lesson of the Brehon. Close your eyes."

She did.

"Breathe deeply and slowly, and imagine the happiest scene from your life. Engage all your senses and place yourself there in your mind."

She thought of how she and Tristan made love, how tender and passion-filled his gaze had been.

"Good," Xavier's deep voice droned.

She felt a sharp pinch on her arm and yelped. The vision shattered. She opened her eyes and saw him holding a small crystal dagger, the point indenting her forearm. He removed it.

"Close your eyes and focus," he scolded. "If you do not have control, you will be dangerous!"

And then she realized the tight control Tristan had held over his emotions, and why he'd been so remote at times.

She did as he asked, and let herself go. This time another sharp pinch of dagger's tip did not phase her.

"Good. We will practice more later, but for now, I must teach you to dematerialize, taking him with you in case you are endangered and need to make an emergency exit. Just be warned that these things I will teach you, they are sacred to us and it is forbidden for you to share them with mortals."

He clasped her hand. "Close your eyes, think of the person whose hand you hold, and wish a place where you want to be. Not someplace far for your first try."

She found herself on the other side of the creek, without Xavier.

"Not bad," he called out. "Now bring yourself back to me."

She did so.

Xavier raised a dark eyebrow. "Are you certain you've never done this?"

"Never."

"Odd," he mused. "It's almost as if you had these powers all along. Perhaps your bloodline is more pure than I realized. Then again, you are a Lupine twin, and they are special."

Only one place she wanted to be more than any other. She closed her eyes and imagined herself back in the guest bedroom where Tristan slumbered.

Niki materialized on the bed... Tristan still slumbered. Aiden sat in the wing chair by the window, Nia in his lap.

"Niki, are you okay?" her twin asked. "I've never seen you so...upset."

"I'll be fine." She looked down at Tristan. "As long as he is fine."

Xavier materialized on the bed opposite Tristan and sighed. "True love. Who am I to try to keep you from your mate? I must leave you anyway. I have my duties, and besides, if he awakens now and finds me in bed with him, he will be most displeased."

"Will he know me?" she asked.

"Not at first. It is like awakening from a deep coma. He will be temporarily confused." The wizard's face darkened. "It is one reason I seldom use this sleep to recover. I fear losing my memories and to lose one's memories can make you quite insane."

"Thank you, Xavier," Niki told him, liking this wizard more than the other two. "You are a true friend."

He gave her a brief smile, then waved a hand and vanished. Still Tristan slept, as if dead. But his chest rose and fell with reassuring regularity.

In his black tunic and black leather pants, he looked as regal as when she'd known him nine hundred years ago. Tristan was handsome and noble. She wondered what he would look like in a kilt. Niki closed her eyes. When she opened them, Tristan was bare-chested, bare-legged, wearing a red and black kilt.

"Wow." Nia whistled. "Did you do that?"

"I guess so." Niki stared at her mate.

"Oh my," Nia said softly. "So rugged. I wonder what Aiden would look like in one of those?"

"Oh no." The Lupine held out his hands. "Niki, don't you dare…"

Grinning, she flicked a finger and the big alpha found himself in the same attire. Nia whistled. "Thanks, sis! Nice legs, Mitchell. You look sex-y. Yum!"

Aiden looked down at the kilt, rubbing the blue and green checked material. "Feels odd. Nothing underneath."

"I bet it's very convenient for sex. Hey Mitchell, this is your official new uniform. Don't you dare remove it."

"Nia, I'm a rancher, not a Scot!"

"Learn to ride a horse in it."

As he started to mutter something about chafing, she pressed a finger against his lips. "Just for a little while. I want to admire your manly, handsome body."

Niki smiled softly at Aiden's resigned expression as he bent his head and kissed her. She caressed Tristan's hair. The door opened and Darius strode inside.

"Hey Aiden, I have the guys assembled to patrol. Where do you want…" Darius stared at his alpha.

"Don't laugh," the alpha growled.

Darius doubled over, chuckling. "Look at those hairy knees!" He ran to the door. "Kyle, bring the guys. Aiden's wearing a skirt!"

"It's a kilt," Nia countered.

Darius, Kyle, Jackson and five other male Lupines rushed into the room. They hooted with laughter. Then they looked at Tristan.

"How is he?" Darius asked.

"He's sleeping. I hope." Her voice trembled.

Darius shook his head, his gaze kind. "Tell us what we can do to help. Tristan brought Sam and me together. Anything I can do to protect him, say the word."

"Me too," Kyle echoed. "He saved my Arianna."

"He's a good wizard," Jackson chimed in. "Tell us what you need, my lady, and we'll get it."

The other males gathered around, looking respectful. "He's our guardian. We pledge our loyalty and protection to him, and to you, as we do to our alpha and leader and his mate."

Emotion clogged her throat as the big, rugged cowboy Lupines fell to one knee and bowed their heads.

Then they filed out of the bedroom and a sense of peace stole over her.

For the first time, she believed everything would be okay, no matter what.

He felt as if he were emerging from a deep pit to new life.

Tristan slowly awoke to find a dark-haired man opposite him, in a rocking chair. He blinked in total confusion. Where was he and *who* was he?

Memory proved elusive. He inhaled, and smelled wolf. Lupine, he remembered.

Seeing him struggle to sit up, the dark-haired man came over to the bed. "Thank the goddess you're awake, Tristan. About damn time."

Confused and his mind sluggish, he tried to orient himself. "Are you a great laird?"

The Lupine stared.

"You're wearing a kilt."

"I'm not Scottish," the man said. "I'm wolf."

He sat up and rubbed his nape. He breathed slowly and deeply, and inhaled a masculine scent into his lungs. Lupine. He knew this scent.

"Alpha," he muttered. "Mitchell."

The man nodded. "Aiden. And you're Tristan, the Silver Wizard."

He was beginning to recall some of his memories. He flipped through them in his mind like playing cards. Odd. The names sounded familiar, yet upon searching his memory, he had no recollection of them. "Why am I here?"

"You used your immortal powers to save Niki." Aiden took a deep breath. "Your true love, and your mate."

He frowned and rubbed his nape again, hating this sluggish feeling. "Why would I mate with a male?"

"Nikita." Aiden spoke slowly. "My mate's twin sister."

"Nikita." He tested the name on his tongue. It felt like a good name. "She sounds quite lovely."

Aiden smiled. "She is. Just like her sister."

Suddenly a blonde woman of ethereal beauty appeared in the bedroom. Dressed in a blue shirt and jeans, she saw him and her gaze softened. "Oh thank the goddess you're awake!"

Tristan climbed out of bed and caught the woman in his arms, kissing her deeply. And then he remembered everything, and fell into her like water, still kissing her.

"How..." he pulled away, searching her face. "Did I come back?"

Niki looked up at him, her expression filled with wonder. "Your friends, the other wizards. They combined their powers and gave you their immortality. A portion of it, anyway."

He stilled the hand caressing her hair. "It is forbidden. They broke the law."

"I made them do it, Tristan. It was the only way to save you."

For now, he had his Nikita back in his arms. His love. His forever mate.

He kissed her again and heard Aiden mutter, "I'll leave you two alone, and tell the others you're awake, and very occupied."

The door closed behind him. He barely noticed. Nikita's lips were sweeter than the most fragrant honey and her hair...he tore his mouth away and buried his head in her satin locks. Her hair smelled like apples and flowers.

"I love you," he whispered, nuzzling his cheek against hers. "My greatest fear as I lay there fading into shadow was leaving you behind, and never seeing you again. Just as I feared I would never see you again when they killed me all those years ago."

"I'm here now, love." She took his palm and placed it on her belly. "And so is our babe. He's fine."

"Our babe?" Tristan searched with his powers and felt a tiny life pulse there. Joy filled him. "I will be a father, at last. And we will be a family."

But her smile looked troubled. "I have your powers now, Tristan. And I'm pregnant, so does that mean our baby will as well? What will that do to him, or her?"

"I do not know." He kissed her brow. "But our son will grow and be strong."

She rolled her eyes. "And if it's a girl?"

"He is a boy. I can tell." He nodded with satisfaction as he used his powers to feel the baby, no larger than a walnut, stir beneath his hand.

"Right. My mate, the wizard sonogram."

A tingle rushed down his spine, a rush of tremendous power. He knew what this meant—Danu was calling him back to Tir Na-nog.

Alarm filled him. He looked at Nikita, his mouth tight. "The goddess calls us both to join her in Tir Na-nog."

CHAPTER 23

He knew this time was coming, and dreaded it.

Nikita gripped his hand. "Tristan, what will happen? I'm scared. You broke the rules and so did I."

He kissed her brow again. "I do not know, but Danu is not capricious. She is firm, but fair. Are you ready?"

She looked at him with a question in her eyes. "Where are we going?"

"Tir Na-nog. Now that you are as immortal as I am, you do not have to go through the Shadow Lands."

Holding tight to Nikita's hand, he let the power consume him, closing his eyes, feeling the dizzying rush. When he opened his eyes, he and Nikita were standing on a bed of the softest emerald green grass in a field. Purple and blue mountains dotted the horizon.

With a soft pop of air, Xavier, Caedryn and Gideon appeared next to them. Tristan felt his concern rise. "What is this?"

"Reckoning day," Caedyrn said grimly. "The goddess called us here."

A violent trembling shook Nikita's hand. Tristan

murmured soothing words, but even he was apprehensive.

And then a brilliant flash of light illuminated the air, and the wizards dropped to their knees. Tristan did as well, but Nikita remained standing.

"Nikita," he urged, "kneel before Danu, the mother goddess who created us all. Please, do it now!"

But as he dared to glance up, he saw his beloved stare at the goddess, a look of wonder on her lovely face. Nikita looked as radiant as the goddess herself.

"It's you! I remember you!" she cried out, and ran to the goddess.

Shock filled Tristan as Nikita embraced Danu, who laughed and embraced her back.

Slowly the wizards stood, looking at each other in pure bewilderment.

"You were the one who greeted me when I died. You told me everything would be all right and I would find happiness again. And my baby would be reincarnated to someone very special who needed him." Nikita's eyes were shining now as she stepped back. "I forgot all that when I left this world the first time. When I was here before, you helped me create a world here where I could forget all my past sorrow, and be fully wolf and free again."

She took in a deep breath. "I was here for a long while, and then you sent me back to Earth."

Danu gently touched Nikita's cheek. "As wolf, to live in the wild as a pure, untamed creature of nature. You ran free and wild until it was time for you to be reborn, and fulfill your destiny as Tristan's mate. That is why your wolf needed to run at night, my child. She remembered well your time on Earth as wolf that heeded the call of her pack, and her spirit."

"Being wolf helped me overcome my sorrow. Thank you, Danu." Nikita bowed her head.

"My beautiful child, you have turned out to be a lovely woman with a good heart, just as I had wished," Danu whispered in her pure, musical voice.

The goddess smiled at Nikita as his mate rested her head against Danu's shoulder. But her look turned severe. She gently disentangled herself from Nikita's grip and flicked a finger. A pack of wolves appeared.

The lead wolf was pure white and her tail beat the air as she saw Niki. Niki inhaled the air.

"You're granting one of my dearest wishes. It's my Mom," she breathed.

The goddess nodded. "After she died birthing you and your sister, your mother chose to remain here, running as wolf. You may join her. Go, my child. Go run with her and the pack. I have business to discuss with my wizards."

Nikita cast a worried look in his direction. "I broke your rules. Don't blame them. I made them do it."

Danu looked amused. "My dear child, they cannot be forced into doing anything they do not wish. I know, for I made them immortal, and I know their hearts, and their stubbornness." She gave Nikita a gentle push. "Go, run with your brethren wolves who watched over you when you were here before. I shall call you back when I am ready."

With a last worried look at him, Nikita waved a hand and shifted into a beautiful white wolf. Howling, she raced toward her mother, who nuzzled her with great affection. Then the pack tore off, running through the meadow.

The goddess watched them a moment with a soft smile. When she turned back, her smile had turned into a severe look.

"Uh oh," Xavier said softly. "We're going to get it now."

"You broke an ancient law I warned you to never break, my wizards. You, Tristan, gave Nikita all your powers as the immortal wizard." She turned to him and he felt the tingle of her power rush toward him. He looked her in the eye.

"I did it for love, my lady. I would do it again in a heartbeat, to save her."

"Love is not enough. You interfered in her fate, her destiny." Danu took a deep breath. "She was not destined to die. She would have been saved by another, had you not interfered. Drust would have saved her."

Jaw dropping, he could only stare. Drust? His old friend, the Coldfire Wizard. "I am most sorry, my lady. But how was I to know?"

"Your apology cannot erase what you have done, Tristan. Had you trusted in fate as you have done for all your charges over the centuries, and called upon Drust for help, he would have appeared to you. You promised him that you would call upon him in your hour of need. But your pride prevented you from doing this.

"I taught him to control the coldfire specifically to revive the dying. He would have shocked Nikita's heart back to life and in doing so, eased the guilt he still feels at being mated to the one who caused her death all those years ago. The balance would have been even. And you removed Nikita's choice of choosing immortality with you or mortality with her family, albeit for the right reasons."

Her gaze was kind. "I have no choice, my son. For this transgression, I am removing part of your magick and giving it to Drust."

To lose his powers, after regaining them was too ironic. Tristan felt panic surge. "Which part?"

"The magick inside you that allows you to control any dragon shifter. It will require you to work with Drust, as his mentor, to guide the dragons until Drust is experienced enough to do it on his own. Should you ever require magick to exterminate a dragon, you shall have to call upon Drust."

Grief and alarm filled him. Losing his magick was like losing his left arm. Even a small part of his powers made him feel helpless all over again. He tried to tamp down his fears with a joke. "I suppose that is better than losing my balls all over again."

Danu gave a slight smile.

He hated giving up an ounce of his magick, for it reminded him of how helpless he'd been when he'd died long ago. Surrendering it for love was one thing. But surrendering it as punishment...

But as always, the goddess was right. He had failed to trust his instinct, and let his blinding panic and grief cast aside all the level-headedness he always had used in dealing with a crisis. And he had failed to let Drust even the balance and erase his own guilt.

With a heavy sigh, he bowed his head. "I understand, and accept your judgement, my lady."

She came forward, bearing a silver sword. He braced himself and the other wizards winced.

Danu sank it into his heart. White-hot pain exploded

in his chest. Tristan gasped for breath, trying to steady himself. Power flickered along the sword, tendrils of pure silver magick.

It stung like a hot needle, and felt worse than the ritual that he'd undergone to become the Silver Wizard. But he bravely endured, though tears came to his eyes. Finally, Danu pulled the sword out.

It was over.

She waved a hand and the sword vanished. She looked at the others. "The rest of you also will suffer the consequences of your actions. Though you did it for noble reasons, you were forbidden from draining your magick without permission, leaving yourselves vulnerable as when you were mortal." Her gaze turned emerald hard. "Vulnerable at a time when you are most needed and I had not the sentinels in place to cover for your weakness."

She turned to Xavier. "You were the first to do so, Xavier."

"My lady," Xavier began.

"All of you must suffer the consequences." She smiled gently. "This is not to be cruel, but bring you to a greater lesson, and to what your heart desires the most, which will make you whole and even stronger for the times to come."

The three looked at each other.

She lifted her hand. "Xavier, my Crystal Wizard, you shall lose what is dearest to you. Your memory. You will walk the earth as a wizard, but with no recollection of your true identity."

Xavier paled. "No…"

With a flick of her hand, he vanished from sight.

Gideon swallowed hard and Caderyn looked deeply

worried. The goddess gave them a severe look. "Times of darkness are approaching. You will all serve your punishment before they arrive. In the meantime, go, return to your duties and do not break the law again."

They vanished from the meadow. Danu called out Nikita's name. The white wolf instantly appeared, tail wagging.

With a pat to her head, Danu turned Nikita back into a woman again, draped in a fine silver gown.

Nikita looked at him, gnawing on her lip.

"Ask your question, my dear," Danu said gently.

"Are you ok?" she asked him.

Tristan nodded. "I am fine, my sweet."

Nikita turned back to Danu. "What happens to me now? I had the choice of taking the potion of the Blood Moonflower and staying here, or remaining mortal and being on Earth. Must I still choose? Will I lose all my new powers?"

Her voice broke. "Will I ever see my twin again?"

Danu gave a gentle smile. "The choice was taken away from you by Camilla's evil and Tristan's sacrifice to save you. Such a sacrifice made for love is the greatest of all and Tristan has paid the price. You will maintain your powers and your immortality if you drink the potion again, which you must in order to guard the child inside you. And you may see your twin again, but you will never again walk the earth as you once did."

Nikita looked at him, her gaze steady. "I thought long about that as I ran with my mom and her pack as wolf, Tristan. If I had the chance to choose, I would have chosen you."

Overcome with joy, he went to her, but did not touch her, mindful of respecting the goddess. "I love you,

Nikita. You are my heart, and my life, and always will be."

"I love you, Tristan. All these years you waited for me, and my heart knew I would return to you some day."

Danu held out her hand. "Tristan, my Silver Wizard. Approach me and take my hand."

Kneeling, he took her hand. "My lady."

Danu gently placed his hand into Nikita's. Standing, Tristan felt a surge of joy, for this indicated the goddess formally approved of their union.

"Take your beloved Nikita as your forever mate. Make her happy. Love her, as she deserves to be loved. As you work together, you will be nearly invincible, and she will help you find balance, so much balance that you will not miss ruling over those troublesome dragons."

Nikita bit her lip. "What of our baby? Will he or she be all right?"

A slight smile curled Danu's mouth. "It is a he, as Tristan predicted. And rest assured, he will be fine, though both of you will have your hands full in dealing with an immortal child who has powerful magick. Having a child who is immortal will be your greatest adventure, my dear."

He looked at her and grinned. "I shall let you change the diapers, my sweet."

Nikita rolled her eyes.

Danu turned to Nikita and kissed her cheek. "Go my sweet child, and be happy. Be his mate and live the life you were denied all those years ago."

With a flick of her hand, she vanished.

"Danu," Nikita whispered. She wiped her eyes. "I'm

so happy I met her, and remembered. And I got to see my mom, finally! I can't believe how happy I am."

"I can make you even happier. Let us return to Earth and have sex. Lots of very hot sex."

"Tristan!" Laughing, she ran to him and punched him lightly in the chest.

He grinned and kissed her. "I have permission to make you very happy. I know what makes you happy."

Nikita looked at the spaces where the wizards had stood. "I stood at the edge of the meadow and saw what happened. Are you okay?"

He nodded. "The goddess's punishment was just. I worry, however, for Xavier."

"That was very scary. What will happen to him?"

He did not know. But deep inside, he had a sense that their punishment was benevolent, and intended for a reason. "Danu does nothing without a greater purpose. Let us return to the Mitchell Ranch. I know you are anxious to spend more time with your twin"

"Not as anxious as I am to spend more time with you." She rubbed her cheek against his jaw.

They materialized inside the guest bedroom where he had nearly gasped his last breath. Tristan pulled Nikita into his arms, his heart no longer heavy. He kissed her again, and tumbled backwards onto the bed. Niki laughed as he rolled her over and straddled her soft body, eager for love.

"Are you sure you're up for this? You just came back to life."

"Very much so," he murmured. "I was dying and I want to celebrate life with you. Our lives, Nikita, and the life growing within you."

She caught a brief flicker of lonely vulnerability

shadowing his expression. "You're scared that something bad could happen to me again, Tristan. It won't. I told you before, I'm stronger now. I'm not the Nikita from the past."

"You were my life once, Nikita. And you are my life again, and my heart. I would have died over and over again, to protect you and keep you and our babe safe. Being separated from you caused more agony than the executioner's blade. Not knowing if I'd ever see you again, hold you in my arms, hear your laughter and see your smile. That uncertainty became the knife slicing my heart over and over again."

This was more than she'd dared hope for—a wolf who admitted how deeply he cared for her, and didn't regard her as someone merely to carry his child and fulfill a promised legacy. He surrendered all his powers to save her, choosing love over his duties as Silver Wizard.

This was the Tristan from her dreams, the partner she'd always wanted who wasn't afraid to share himself. And living with him and raising their child would prove to be as freeing, and as adventurous, as her dearest hopes and dreams.

She pressed a hand against her belly. "This time, we're with you to stay, Tristan. We'll never be parted again."

As he began to kiss her, she glanced with anxiousness at the closed door. "Are you certain we have time for this?"

"More than enough," he murmured, his heart filled with joy and peace. He smiled down at her. "We have eternity."

EPILOGUE

This was going to be one hell of a reunion.

Drust took a deep breath and dematerialized, appearing in the courtyard of Skylar and Sebastian's castle. Damn, the process still made him dizzy. But what the hell, he'd been immortal only a few days.

Or so it seemed.

And his target was all wrong. He'd wanted to end up in their living room.

"At least I didn't materialize in the bathroom," he muttered to no one in particular.

His great-grandsons, Sebastian and Alexander, were meeting within the castle. He had a little surprise for them. Actually, a big one.

Drust opted against doing the whole dematerializing gig again. Dragons were accustomed to flight. Being immortal and a wizard would take a little time, as Tristan advised.

Before leaving Tir Na-nog, Drust had drunk the goblet of Blood Moonflower, the secret and sacred fairy drink that all the wizards of the Brehon imbibed every six months to maintain their powers. As a new wizard, he had to drink once a week.

It had filled him not so much with power as purpose.

The goddess Danu had granted him immortality for a reason, and the reason started here, with family. Tristan had given him a parchment signed with his silver blood.

It was a start.

He walked into the castle through the open oak double doors. Hearing his kin's voices, he followed them to the living room.

Skylar and Sebastian sat on the sofa, talking with Alexander, who paced before the great stone fireplace. Alexander glanced up, saw him and halted.

"Holy shit," Alexander burst out. "Are you a ghost?"

"Mind your tongue before the lady." Drust strode over to Skylar, and nodded. "My lady."

Skylar's mouth hung open. "I've seen your painting in the history books. You're Drust!"

Alexander growled deep and Sebastian looked anguished. Drust held up a hand. "Before you go all dragon on me, I did not betray Tristan."

The crown prince to the throne of Clan Drakon looked clearly irritated. "That's not what Tristan said. Or what you admitted."

"Control that temper of yours, Alexander. It will prove troublesome to you in the future if you are not careful," Drust warned. He sighed. "Tristan told me you would not believe me any more than he had. So he wrote this to give to you."

After he handed over the scroll and the three sat, reading it, he gazed at the ugly painting over the fireplace mantel. Another dragon. *That should be me. I am their blood, not some paint-by-the-numbers dragon.*

Alexander looked up, stricken. "It's a blood oath stating you didn't kill Tristan, and you didn't have

356

anything to do with Nikita's death. But Pops, you said it was your fault."

A shard of guilt pierced him. "It was my fault, Alexander. I failed my friend. As you go through life, you will find that family is most important and you will defend them to the death, but some bonds of friendship can be equally strong and important and deserve the same."

Skylar rose, her lovely eyes wet. "I'm so glad you are innocent, Drust. Welcome to our home. I am most honored you are here."

She glanced at the painting hanging over the mantel, and then at him. "We can finally replace your portrait. I really hate that dragon. He looks so…fake."

Pleased, he smiled at her.

"But how are you here?" Sebastian looked totally flummoxed.

He drew himself up. "I am the new Coldfire Wizard, guardian to all dragons."

"Hot *damn*," Sebastian crowed, while Alexander paled.

"You?!" Alexander burst out.

He pointed to the chair. "Sit, Alexander."

Alexander sat, looking even more upset. "Why are you here, Pops? Because I am a Shadow Jumper and I did something wrong?"

He gentled his voice. "You did nothing wrong, Alexander. But I am removing that power from you until I can teach you how to control it."

Before Alexander could react, Drust went to him and placed a hand on his forehead, yanking the ability from his great-grandson. Alexander yelped and Sebastian winced.

Alexander rubbed his forehead as Drust resumed his seat. "That hurt. And that's the only reason you're here?"

He sat and looked at them. "No. I am a young wizard, and there will be a transition time until I fully take charge of all dragons. Until then, Tristan and I are working together as guardians and judges of dragons. I need your help."

The trio exchanged glances.

"The coming days will be difficult for our kind, and the dragons must unite in all the clans. All three of you must initiate this." He turned to Alexander. "You must set aside your grievances with Clan Tyrith. There is a special dragon there, Michael, who can teach you much. You may require his assistance in the future."

He waited, watching Alexander grow red-faced as the prince struggled with his temper.

His formidable temper.

Alexander pointed at the fireplace and a flame shot out of his finger. Logs ignited. "No one from that clan can teach me anything. The dragons that attacked Em are from that clan."

"Leave them to me, Alexander."

"No."

"Take heed, Alexander," Drust warned, drawing on his newfound power. He fisted a hand. When he opened it, blue fire glowed there.

"Tristan and I will deal with justice for Emma. Is that understood?"

Alexander scowled, but nodded. "If you fry their asses, I'll agree."

"Frying their asses is not the first item on my agenda," Drust said dryly. "But all of you are. You are my legacy, and you must survive. Things happened for a reason."

He turned to Sebastian and Skylar.

"Skylar, thank you for sacrificing your diamond scale. It served a dual purpose and helped to grant me access through the Dark Gate so I could pass through to Tir Na-nog. Sebastian, you went into servitude to Tristan for your impulsive behavior, but your sacrifice of your dragon's heart gave Tristan the potion that saved Nikita from the parvolupus disease and enabled her to enter Tir Na-nog. Because of Nikita reuniting with Tristan, he finally returned to the Shadow Lands and convinced me to move on to Tir Na-nog."

"What does all this mean?" Sebastian asked.

"The true reason why I agreed to become the Coldfire Wizard is to unite the clans, and—to protect all of you during the days and nights the other Brehon and the goddess Danu know are coming."

Skylar clasped Sebastian's hands. "What exactly is coming, Drust?"

He closed his fist, seeing the blue coldfire pulse brightly. "You need not worry about that, Skylar. It is far away. But you must all learn to work together, and you must begin now, for the sake of future generations."

He gave her a gentle smile. "Including your own children. Congratulations, my dear."

Skylar blushed.

Sebastian's eyes rounded. "We just found out," he said.

Alexander slapped his cousin on the back and kissed Skylar's cheek. Drust watched them with satisfaction, his immortal heart beating hard. He was glad of the diversion, and that they no longer questioned him about the future.

He could not tell them the full truth.

He knew what was coming, and it filled him with dread.

What is coming? Only the night when wraiths are released from the Dark Lands, and possess the dead, forcing them to arise from their graves. The night of the dark soul when zombies walk among us, driven by the madness to eat the flesh of every living OtherWorlder that breathes, including the flesh of dragons.

AUTHOR'S NOTE

Thank you for reading The Mating Season. I hope you enjoyed it!

Would you like to know when my next book is available? You can sign up for my newsletter at www.bonnievanak.com, follow me on twitter at http://twitter.com/bonnievanak, or like my Facebook page at http://facebook.com/bonnievanakauthor. Reviews help other readers find books. I appreciate all reviews, whether positive or negative.

You've just read The Mating Season, Book 6 in my Werewolves of Montana series. Alex's book, The Mating Destiny, can be ordered *by visiting http://www.bonnievanak.com/maitingdestiny.html.*

Turn the page for an excerpt from

THE
MATING DESTINY

Book 7 in the Werewolves of Montana series

BONNIE VANAK

THE MATING DESTINY

She was dragon, and had fought every step of the way for what little she had. No parents to assist her, few friends within her own clan.

Only Sabrina, bless her, who understood her thirst for knowledge and desire to improve her status through reading.

But the damnable caste system in Clan Ciamoth could not be changed.

Still, Alex was here, with her now. In a brothel, and he had purchased her body. Taking a break from the bracelet, for her wrist was chafed and hurt, she stared at Alex. Emma licked her lips, studying his very nice buttocks as he knelt on the seat cushion to wrap his hand and test the bars again.

Khaki material stretched over the twin globes, cupping them tight. She wondered what it would feel like to cup his ass, to squeeze and knead that smooth skin as he lay atop her, and joined his muscled body to hers…

Alex, nude in bed with her. Arousal filled her, the wicked thoughts that haunted her long, lonely nights. He was strictly off limits, especially now after the warning from her attackers, but a girl could still dream.

"Is it true what they say about male dragons?" Em tried to avoid looking at Alex's rather large, elegant hands and his long fingers.

He turned from the iron bars. "What?"

"That if a dragon's middle claw, er, finger, is longer than his ring finger, it means he is, ah, endowed. At least an inch longer."

Alex stared.

"You know." Em pointed to her crotch.

He burst into laughter. "Em, that's a myth."

"Oh." Heat suffused her chest and neck. She felt silly for bringing it up, but one of the girls in the basement had said it was true.

Alex held up his right hand. The middle finger was considerably longer than his ring finger. "It's two inches, not one."

"Oh. Ohhhh." Now the blush spread like wildfire across her face.

A wicked grin touched his full, handsome face. "Would you like to see the evidence?"

"Um, that's okay." She rose off the bed and went to the table that held fruit and a pitcher of ice water to pour herself a glass. She drank deeply and set the glass down. It was getting hot in here. Too hot.

He took his polo shirt and studied the black marks magick had left behind on the knit fabric. Powerful magick indeed. The darkest kind. He put the shirt back on.

"I'd offer to launder that for you, but I'm afraid I don't know where the washing machines are."

"Em." Alex twisted the gold signet ring on his left pinkie. He always did that when thinking. Maybe the ring was hard-wired to his gray matter. "This is serious."

"Don't I know it? I'm trapped here in a brothel, you bought me for the night and I don't even know if they have my favorite pasta here or cable. I'm kinda out of luck. Plus I lost my phone. I hate it when I lose my phone. How am I supposed to tweet now? I was so looking forward to posting on Instagram and Facebook that I'd been dragon-napped and I was at a brothel, forced to wear a harem outfit and learn to like grapes and cheap wine."

Crossing the room, he enfolded her into his arms. "You're shaking."

Like a leaf in the wind, but no need to tell him that. Even if she could disguise her fear with jokes, he could detect her scent. Dragons were excellent at sniffing out fear.

It made prey all the easier to track down, and kill.

She lifted her head and saw him staring down at her. "I'm not going to hurt you, Em," he said quietly.

"Or eat me?"

The question was a hoarse whisper, though she'd intended it to be light and teasing. Alex's mouth quirked in a slight smile.

"Not for dinner."

But she caught his racing pulse, his dilated eyes and heard the heavy beat of his heart. "Maybe for...dessert. With whipped cream and a cherry on top."

"No need for a cherry. You did buy a virgin, you know."

His beautiful blue-green eyes widened to dinner plates. "Em…"

She cut in, not wanting to pursue that particular thread. "Alex, remember last year when you and I snuck into the Trolling & Strolling strip club because you left your wallet there after that bachelor party, and you saw the python in the stripper's dressing room and you realized how hungry you were…because the strip club offered only cheese and crackers and hard liquor…and you ate him?"

"Em…"

"And I had to grab your wallet and the manager saw us and shifted into a grizzly bear and threatened to bite your balls off? Remember how scared I was?"

"Em…"

"This is worse." She swallowed hard. "Much worse. I'm trying hard to pretend this is all a nightmare or a dream, because you are here and it's a dream to be with you, but I'm so scared I feel like my heart's jumping out of my chest."

He smoothed back a tendril of hair from her cheek. "Em, I'm here. I will not let anything happen to you."

Look for **The Mating Destiny**, Alex's book, coming soon!

Learn more at
www.Bonnievanak.com

The Werewolves Of Montana

About the Author

Bonnie Vanak is a *New York Times* bestselling author of paranormal werewolf romances. A former newspaper reporter who became a writer for a major international charity, she travels to destitute countries to write about issues affecting the poor. Her books take readers from the mysterious, dark alleys of New Orleans to the sweeping plains of Montana. Visit her Web site at www.bonnievanak.com or email her at bonnievanak@aol.com.

Stay updated with previews of more Werewolves of Montana books by visiting my website, http://www.bonnievanak.com and signing up for my newsletter. Or visit my Facebook page at www.facebook.com/bonnievanakauthor